TWIST OF
TRUTH
~ AND ~
TOMORROW

BOOK TWO OF THE SOULSHIFTER SERIES

ALSO BY HILARY THOMPSON

THE STARBRIGHT SERIES

Justice Buried
Stian's Mistake
Balance Broken
Lexan's Pledge
Destiny Risen
Atian's Revenge

TWIST OF TRUTH
～ AND ～
TOMORROW

HILARY THOMPSON

Star Shadow Books
United States

Published in 2017 by
Star Shadow Books
United States

This is a work of fiction. The names, characters, incidents, and places are products of the author's imagination or used fictitiously. Any resemblance to actual events, locales, or persons, living or dead, is entirely coincidental.

Summary: Corentine and her friends must find and kill the Restless King before his secrets destroy the kingdom.

August 2017 First Edition

Cover design by Deranged Doctor Design
Edited by New Writers Interface
Book design by Eight Little Pages
Ebook design by Monica Corwin

This is my dream, but you are dreaming it.
This is my wish, but you are making it.
This is my magic, but you are creating it.

What you find here, all of it, is for you.
You know who you are.

PRUSTIAN SEA
WESTEN SANDS
MATINS HOLD
MOONSHADE CASTLE
SUNMELT LAKE
STARSHELM PALACE
WHISPERING MTS
LISTENING FOREST
CONQUEROR'S CHANNEL
SULIT
NEWMOON FALLS
RUROK
MAGI SEA
SHEDRECK RIVER
HUNGRY RIVER

I

The EvenFall market was as busy as Resh had ever seen it, as though all the city's people had poured from their dark, hot houses to soak in the sunshine and sniff at the mysterious changes in the fresh air. Surely he wasn't the only one who felt the dynamic possibilities swirling around them.

Sy and Coren were going to kill the Restless King. They'd be at StarsHelm within two weeks, and Riata's throne would soon be free.

Change was like a storm cloud on the horizon, and Resh vibrated with its energy.

Weaving past a group of vendors selling bolts of summer-weight fabrics, he thought of how he loved watching such storms roll in over Weshen Isle. Thick and monstrous clouds rushing like upside-down waves over the gray-green sky. Lightning streaking in a deadly current through the waves. Wind like the goading push of racing someone side by side down the sands.

The power of a storm was like a siren song to him, and sometimes he thought he could follow such strength anywhere.

If only he wasn't stuck babysitting these Wesh and playing messenger boy between Sy and Father General. Resh knew he needed to work fast if he wanted a shot at the action in the palace.

"Are you up for the mountain passage?" he asked, barely glancing at the slim boy walking next to him.

Nik shrugged. "I'm sure I've been through worse."

Resh paused to examine a cheap blade in a vendor's stall, allowing himself the chance to compose his next question. The vendor didn't even give him a second's peace, though, and Resh slammed the blade on the table and stalked away. He felt Nik close at his back, weaving effortlessly through the knots of people, and he glared.

There was something about this kid's ease he didn't quite trust.

Of course, *kid* wasn't accurate. They were the same age, and somehow Nik had twisted Sy into showing an interest he'd never allowed for a single Weshen girl. Resh's brain was still struggling to comprehend the development. Sy's interest in anyone was rare enough - Resh was his brother's only friend, too. Perhaps it shouldn't have been a surprise, though. Sy never liked the hunts.

It was just for a different reason than Resh always assumed.

At any rate, he knew their Father General would hate it, and that made Resh happy.

The crowds thinned a bit around the entrance to a dim alley, and Resh stepped in a few feet. "Look, Nik," he began.

"Yeah, so I can tell you don't trust me, and you aren't too keen on the idea of me kissing your brother. But we have a lot of junk to get done, so let's just agree to have each other's backs for now, and maybe later we'll get around to being friends. Or whatever you can manage on that level." Nik's words spilled over like a torrent, and Resh blinked at his steady, pale blue eyes, trying to process.

"You *kissed* Sy?" he said, flushing that this was what popped out. Of all the things. Resh cursed under his breath.

"He kissed me back." Nik's shoulders tightened in defense.

Resh swore again, trying to resist the laughter bubbling into his throat. He failed and choked instead.

"By the Magi, Sy," he muttered. His eyes flicked back to Nik, who resembled an animal forced into a corner. "You should be proud of yourself," he finally said. Nik's eyes widened, and Resh gave in to the laughter.

"Why is this funny?" Nik asked, his eyes flashing.

Resh held up a hand in apology. "It's very rare that people surprise me. Before this summer, I thought I knew everything about my brother. And then he falls under Coren's spell, and yours, evidently."

"It's not witchcraft." Nik backed down a bit, but his shoulders remained tense and ready beneath his thin shirt.

"Relax. I understand that hag down there has completely different magic than you." Resh gestured to

3

the booth at the end of the alley. "But it *will* take me some time to wrap my mind around something I can't do. I don't like to listen and look. I like to touch."

"Yeah, you do," a voice agreed, and Resh swiveled to find a cloaked figure less than two feet behind him.

Another curse of surprise fell from his lips. He'd spent years sharpening his edge on the world, yet this summer found him dulled. Then again, Shanta was more silent than a spirit, her fingers faster than thought. He didn't mind being bested by her. Too much.

"Really, Resh," she chided. "Use your adult words more sparingly, or they'll lose effect. And stay on better guard. That witch down there could have you by the ba-"

"Got it," Resh cut her off. "So, what's going on with the Wesh? Are they ready to go?"

She sighed and shook her hood back a few inches. "Malnourished and exhausted. Scared. I don't see how they'd make it through the passage if it's as bad as Sy claims. The wounded ones can barely walk as it is. If the goal is to get to your General quickly, you two need to go on ahead."

Resh considered her words, resting his gaze on Nik.

"It's close, right?" Nik asked. "I mean, it won't take us long to show off a bit for the people and convince your father to accept the magic's return. Then we can come back for them."

Resh nodded. "I could be through the passage and in the city by nightfall. The men are probably still on the island, though, so that's a day on the water."

Nik grinned. "Never been in a boat."

"It's horrible," Shanta grimaced. "You probably love it," she added, rolling her silver-blue eyes at Resh.

4

He grinned. "I love the rocking motion. Perfect for-"

"Save it for someone who doesn't know better. I'm keeping the kids. Go see the General and check back with me in a week." She tugged her hood over her eyes again and slipped sideways into the crowd before either of the boys could manage a word.

"Bossy, isn't she," Nik said, watching the people bustle past them. There wasn't even a ripple in the crowd where she had vanished.

"She's used to being in charge. It's a common problem among my friends, actually," Resh admitted, a smile of pride capturing his lips. Between himself, Shanta, Coren, and Sy, they could rule the three kingdoms and more.

"Not me," Nik said, lowering his lashes and his voice. "I fly low, so nobody notices me. Or I tried to, but the slavers always found my power."

"How much power do you actually have? I mean, you know some spells, too, right? Have you ever shifted into a MagiCreature like Coren?" Resh stepped back into the rush of people, heading for one of his favorite food vendors.

Nik stayed close on Resh's heels in the crowd. They passed a stall hawking roasting, seasoned meat. He breathed deeply and groaned. Kid was always hungry. Resh nearly laughed, but he remembered Nik's stories of forced starvation by the slavers. Another method to find deeper shifter power.

"Coren is the only one I've ever seen shift like that," Nik answered. "Although they say it used to be common. Hard to achieve, but if you had talent and worked hard, it was attainable. Before the Shift, the Restless King had dozens of them in his army. Commanders, mostly."

Resh spread this information out in his mind as they wove between the stalls and clustered bargainers. He hastened to mesh it with what he'd learned as a child. He'd always dismissed so much of this as fairy tale and rumor, or at the very least, something he'd never see return in his lifetime.

"Here," he said, joining a line. "We'll buy some food for the road and head out. If we're not bringing anyone else with us, I'd like to move fast."

They ended up buying twice as much as Resh expected because Nik kept sampling everything before adding it to the packs.

"Okay, I'm out of coin," Resh said, shouldering his bag. "Let's move."

He led them through several back alleys, doubling over their tracks in a couple of places just in case. An hour later, they entered the open meadow outside of EvenFall, and Resh hurried them toward the shelter of the forest.

"Who would be following us?" Nik asked when they were hidden beneath the dense canopy.

Resh shrugged. "You said the slavers always seem drawn to your power. Maybe witches are, too. And we'll have to be on watch for MagiCreatures, too."

Nik's eyes widened. "I've heard that! Powerful magic draws powerful MagiCreatures."

Resh noted the discrepancy in his words. "Then you haven't experienced it?"

Nik shook his head. "The slavers kept me pretty sequestered. It was sheer luck that Coren came across me in that stream. Usually I was kept underground, out of sight. Bound so I couldn't escape."

"Why the change?" Perhaps the slavers had noticed the uptick in Weshen magic as well.

"They were trying to force my magic. Make it stronger so they could use me to get more slaves. But I'd sooner die."

Resh slid his eyes to Nik, noting the dark tone his voice had taken. "Or kill them?"

Nik's jaw tightened. "I'm no soldier. No combat training. But I'd drop a slaver in a minute."

"Good." Resh was glad he wouldn't have to convince Nik that sometimes death was best. Sy had always been reticent to take a life, preferring to believe in redemption.

Resh believed that if people deserved a second chance, it was up to the Mirror Magi to give it to them. He didn't have the patience for anyone's rehabilitation.

The forest was dark and too quiet for Resh's liking, and he hurried them through. His neck prickled with the absurd sensation that even the trees themselves wanted to listen in on their conversation.

Soon enough, though, the passage beneath the NeverCross Mountains opened before them, a slim cave set in a sunlit clearing.

Resh scanned the sky and the cliffs above.

"This is where Shadow attacked Coren. And the Vespa."

Nik followed his movements, but nothing stirred around them besides the breeze and the bright wildflowers mixed with the tall grasses.

"Coren got really sick in the passage, right?" Nik said, his voice tight with nerves he was trying hard to hide.

"It's spelled to keep out any blood except Weshen. If you're not full-blooded, you'll have trouble. If you don't have any Weshen blood, it'll kill you." Resh explained.

Nik chewed a corner of his lip. "Might as well," he said, stepping in front of Resh and slipping into the narrow tunnel.

It had been less than a day, and Corentine was already regretting traveling to StarsHelm with Kashar.

Finding out the father who abandoned her was also the King's Prodigal Knight had formed a fissure in her mind. She knew she needed to cross it to keep moving forward, but learning he was a traitor as well as a deserter meant she had no idea how to begin trusting him.

Not to mention that with each plodding step through the stonetree forest, the entire goal of killing the Restless King seemed to stretch farther from reach and reason. Each casual glance over her shoulder, expecting to see Vespa wings, seeing only the bulk of her brown pack instead, echoed in her mind the impossibility of the task.

And with each quiet breath, she ached to hold her family again instead of her weapons. Her fingers curled into themselves, remembering how it felt to cup Penna's cheek and Kosh's shoulders. Her imagination refused to allow them safety, instead creating a thousand ways for them to find harm.

As they packed up camp after breakfast, she fastened her bag and immediately sat down, crossing her legs before her. She stared up at Kashar, beginning with the easiest issue to address. "I'm not going another step with you until you tell us why we've been traveling east when StarsHelm is north."

She pointed accusingly at the rising sun, directly before them. She and Sy had noticed the shift in direction last night, but Sy whispered a warning to let Kashar lead. He wanted the Knight's secrets as much as she did, but he was content to riddle them out himself, like a hunter following his prey straight to the den.

Coren was no longer content to listen to either man.

She had no patience for stalking prey that should be blood-bound to speak to her.

Kashar rolled his shoulders beneath his pack, aggravation plain on his unshaven face. "It takes at least ten days of hard travel to move between EvenFall and StarsHelm on foot. I can't rent a coach, or I'll risk the King's suspicion. I only summon coaches when I have wounded Wesh, and I've already delivered the Wesh to the palace. This is a different option," he gestured vaguely in the direction of the rising sun.

"*This* is still not new information," Coren hissed. Sy flicked his gaze between the two of them, just watching. Coren turned her aggravation and impatience on him. This whole Magi-cursed adventure had been his suggestion in the beginning. "And you...just along for the walk? Do you even care about reaching StarsHelm anymore?"

Sy blinked at her, disbelief spreading up his brow. "Of course I do. I haven't forgotten our mission in one day."

She knew it was true, but it was easier to pick at an argument than face the tasks before them.

"Maybe that kiss addled your brain," Coren mumbled, her heel scratching a rut in the dirt.

Sy was on her in an instant, crouching low to look her in the eyes. She glared, but she was glad to have provoked him into some reaction, at least. Something besides following Kashar docilely.

"*You* have no room to talk about kisses. You were *terrified* of my brother on the island. Outraged that he might hunt you the way we'd been taught. And then you kissed him back?"

"I did not," Coren huffed, but she knew it wasn't the truth. Not really. She hadn't *meant* to kiss Resh back. It had been a momentary lapse of feeling instead of thinking. Of giving in instead of denying she'd ever wanted. Denying she was capable of wanting such a thing.

She rose to her feet, and he followed in one smooth motion. "And I was never terrified of him. You know what I can do to a man with my whip."

Sy's face flickered with guilt, and her fingers twitched, curling into fists. She still wasn't proud of killing that man in Weshen City, but Sy didn't get to claim responsibility for her actions. She'd also hated that slaver for what he'd done to Nik, and given the chance she knew she would kill him again.

But she hated the darkness inside her that celebrated the spilled blood just as much. She knew those deaths would be the least of her sins before this journey ended.

As dread entered her heart, she realized this was her real problem with the mission - she didn't want to kill Zorander Graeme.

Deserved or not, she didn't want another person's blood on her hands ever again.

But saying so would only make Sy feel guiltier. Stepping closer again, she made her voice into a dagger of iron and stone and delivered each word like a small, precise blow. "Sy, you do not get to feel responsible for the things I've done. Those are mine to own. Mine to pay for."

He backed up, the blood rushing to his cheeks. "I just want to keep you safe."

"And innocent?" she challenged. "There's no such thing as safe and innocent in war. We travel to StarsHelm to start a war, Sy. You're not my personal guard."

"No, but I thought I was your friend!" Sy growled back, and a flash of remorse stirred in her chest.

Kashar shoved between them, and Coren blinked down at the hand held up to stop her.

"Listen to me," he said, grinding the words out before she could choose more of her own. "These woods are spelled, and it's obviously affecting both of you. We need to be through the trees as fast as possible, or we'll lose our minds and tear each other apart."

"What do you mean, spelled?" Sy asked. "By Sulit?"

"By Graeme, using Sulit witches for the work. Only the knights know about it, and we take precautions. Counter-spells. Speed. Traveling alone if necessary. If you're with a group, staying too long in the forest turns you against one another. Now, I have a plan, but you have to follow me."

"I won't follow you blindly!" Coren argued. She turned away from the hand Kashar still held before her. "I don't trust you. At all."

Kashar sighed, and the slump of his shoulders spoke of a sorrow he'd carried there for many years. But Coren didn't care. She knew she was acting unreasonable, but she'd done so much on her own, for so long. And she'd managed.

The first time she depended on Sy, she'd been banished from her home. She'd lost her family and had her body torn apart and rebuilt as a Vespa. Then, as a final insult, she'd lost all that beautiful, magnificent power.

She turned enough to glare at Sy.

"I wish I'd never run the hunts this summer. I was happy enough taking care of the twins on my own. We were doing. Just. Fine." The words dropped into the silence between them like pebbles plopping into a still lake. Then the ripples of reaction began.

Kashar made a noise like a wounded animal and turned away, his head in his hands.

Sy punched a nearby tree, roaring incoherently.

And Coren shouldered her bag and stalked alone into the trees, changing her direction to north instead of east. She didn't care if the Sulit magic was dismembering her mind or not - she had to be better off away from these two.

2

StarSeer had been studying Maren covertly for days now as they moved up the golden brown Shedreck River and deeper into western Sulit. As far as she could tell, the Weshen woman knew nothing of the twin prophecy the witches clung to, or its failings to be fulfilled in the last two generations.

She remembered seeing the twins in her dreams of the future, but so far, the details of the visions remained locked away, trapped beneath the skin of her mind. If this boy and girl were what she hoped, they would all need as much protection as possible.

The children never strayed more than a dozen feet from their caretaker, and for that, StarSeer was grateful.

Maren had very little magic to use, though. Her shifter strength was even less than the spell ability of young witches. But her strong presence and intent purpose naturally helped to block the twins' pure energy.

StarSeer could feel it vibrating through the gold-streaked sand as she paced the riverside campsite, spelling its border for safety.

Hopefully, her darker Brujok sisters would not feel the same vibrations.

"We should think of leaving soon," she said to Maren as she finished. "The Brujok will find us eventually if we stay."

"Where will we go?" the little girl asked.

Penna, StarSeer knew, though none had spoken her name aloud since landing on the shores of the Shedreck. It was too dangerous; Brujok spies were everywhere. In the birds, and the snakkas, and even in the leaves of some of the trees.

For the Sulit, knowing someone's full name was the key to controlling their spirit.

"We can travel the Shedreck deeper into the Listening Forest, but we must be careful what we speak aloud," she reminded the girl.

"Because the forest is always listening," the boy agreed. His face was serious as always, and StarSeer wondered idly what sort of man he would make. A boy who never smiles could become a man who never forgets, just like the dark abomination on the throne of Rurok now. The Lord of Witches.

"You have not told me enough of these Brujok," Maren chided as they watched the twins hunting bright pebbles from the riverbanks. "How they came to power, and what they seek."

StarSeer shrugged. "They seek what most people in power seek. More power. I don't know exactly how it happened. I was young, and uncaring, and uninvolved. Until they took my partner."

She bent to grasp a rare clear pebble from the black and gold sand that swirled into the shallow water. She hid it in one of the many pockets sewn between the layers of her skirts, immediately feeling how its air magic increased her stamina.

"According to my mother, the Brujok are the same Sulit we have all always been. You know we have no need for men except to occasionally father our children. More than ever though, some use other ways..."

"I thought that was a myth," Maren laughed.

"Every myth has a kernel of truth, old woman," StarSeer said, then flushed at the harshness of her tone. "I am sorry. Disbelief in myths and doubt in the dark abilities of those who want power are what have ruined my people. Sulit used to believe that our power was only viable when we rose together, not one above another. The Brujok compete with one another to be the best. It is not the Sulit way. And a man on the throne of Rurok is heresy against the Mother!" Again, her cheeks heated in embarrassment.

Maren rested a leathery hand on the young witch's arm. "These are strange times. Don't be afraid to offend, even if it's not in your nature to be cruel. If the truth is painful, then it is bleeding poison from a wound."

StarSeer nodded, taking a steadying breath. She wished her mother were still with her, or her aunt, or any of the southern Sulit she had depended on her whole life. She desperately missed her partner and searched for her face beyond every tree.

But they were gone, all of them. Until Maren had washed onto the shores of Sulit, StarSeer had been utterly alone.

"The Brujok seek to go beyond the traditional power of the witches. This one on the throne - this Lord of Witches - he uses darker magics to help them get what they want. Blood magic."

"And what do they want? Besides power."

"They want destruction," StarSeer whispered. "Sulit have *never* wanted that before."

Maren was silent, and StarSeer sensed her shock. The Sulit Mother allowed destruction only for healing growth, like lightning taking an old tree to gain sunlight for a young sapling. But none of the southern Sulit believed the Brujok were like a young sapling.

"We will help your people, as you will help ours," the boy said, approaching with silent feet. The girl was farther away, but she looked back and nodded.

Maren made a strangled noise, and StarSeer knew the woman would have trouble letting the children do anything other than hide. But no matter the hiding spot, Sulit was not safe for children or shifters.

"I would be honored to have your help," she said, bending to grasp the boy's outstretched hand. A spark of energy passed between their palms, and StarSeer's eyes rolled back. Her muscles seized, locking her in place. Her fingers clutched Kosh's hand like he kept her in the world.

And the new vision lit up her mind like a burst of midnight lightning, chasing the shadows away and illuminating the dark shapes.

When her eyes returned to the riverbank, StarSeer was staring up into the trees, the black sand at her back.

"Are you okay?" Maren asked, her calm voice edged with worry. They were all kneeling next to her, peering down with wide eyes.

"A vision," StarSeer whispered. "My gift from the Mother." She took a deep breath, closing and opening her eyes slowly. "These *are* indeed the children we have waited for. The Mother always protects those who protect her. She will show them how to help us defeat the enemies within." She didn't dare say more.

Rurok was poised to begin a war that could tear Sulit in two, or spread it across the land. The vision had shown her witch fighting witch, and witch fighting Riatan. None of that was part of protecting the Mother, but she knew Maren would rip the children from her and take her chances alone if she thought them in danger.

"Enemies within?" the girl asked, her voice small against the tumbling water.

"Those who seek to make Sulit into something new. And those who use us against ourselves. We must hurry," she added, stumbling to her feet. Perhaps it had already begun. Her visions were sometimes in the future, and sometimes immediate. But they were always true.

Glancing back to make sure they were following her, StarSeer hurried away from the river and deeper into the dense growth of the Listening Forest. It was time to stop hiding.

She was terribly afraid for all of them. They had lost so much, but there was always more for the darkness to swallow. So many of the witches had backed meekly away from their history and their future, fear of the

17

Brujok paralyzing them. And a civil war would destroy many more lives than the scattered rebellions had.

But if the southern witches could reclaim their history and power stolen by the Brujok, then they could grasp the future, and Sulit would begin to grow again.

Destruction would be worth it if the Mother could heal the Sulit land.

Sy had no intention of letting the Prodigal Knight lead them anywhere he didn't want to go. But by the Magi, he wished Coren weren't so stubborn!

He ignored her steps crashing away into the trees: He could track her down in an instant. Instead, he turned his rage on Kashar.

"This is on you!" He pointed. "You've barely said a word to her about why you left all those years ago. She's had to carry the burden of those twins, and her mother's death, and her brother's banishment, all alone. Even the other women on the island left her alone. She's had nothing since you left!"

Kashar still hadn't looked up from his hands, which covered his eyes. His palms began to scrub at his face, and a blur of emotions cycled through Sy as he realized the Prodigal Knight was crying. He settled finally on curiosity, so he waited.

"I regret so much," the man whispered. "But it had to be done." He turned to Sy, his eyes red around the edges.

"You would do anything to protect your family, wouldn't you?"

"Of course." Sy might disagree with Resh and even Ashemon, but if they were in trouble, he knew he would drop everything and give everything, even down to his life. As they would for him.

"I see it in your eyes. But those sacrifices were not what was asked of me." Kashar sighed deeply. "The Magi asked something far heavier. I turned on my family, made them believe the worst of me, so that I could protect them from afar. I abandoned their present to protect their future."

Sy eyed the man. His statements were too vague. "What exactly do you do in StarsHelm to protect Coren?"

Kashar grimaced, glancing above them at the trees. He shook his head. "I can't. I've already said too much here."

"The trees?" Sy asked, his voice laced with impatience. But Kashar only nodded. Sy knew of Sulit magic that gave the trees ears, of course. There was even a whole section on his father's map of Sulit labeled *Listening Forest*. He'd just never considered that such spells might be active in Riatan territory.

"We need to find Corentine," Kashar pleaded. "Before someone else does."

This idea pushed Sy's suspicions to the background, and he nodded, grabbing his pack and heading into the trees. They caught up to her within an hour of tracking.

She didn't even look at the two of them.

"Coren," Sy began.

"No. I'm not changing direction without a reason."

19

"It's the trees," he tried. "They're filled with Sulit spells, and we have to wait until a safer spot."

Coren huffed. "Some story."

"You know, you sound more like Resh every minute," he said, switching tactics.

It got her attention, and she stopped walking to turn and glare at him. "What?"

"He doesn't believe in anything he can't touch. You sound just like him. But you know better."

Kashar stepped forward, just a bit. "I'm so sorry, Corentine," he whispered. Sy could see her examining her father. Her eyes widened a bit when she noticed the signs of tears still streaking his cheeks. "I promise I'll explain as soon as I can. But not here," he added, glancing up at the light-dappled canopy. The sun was about a quarter of the way across the sky - mid-morning.

"Corentine, can you give me two more hours?" Kashar asked. "If you follow me that much more, I promise you'll get your answers."

She narrowed her eyes at him, considering.

Sy rested his hand gently on her shoulder. "I'm sorry for what I said about Resh. I shouldn't have thrown that kiss in your face. My brother is complicated. It's no wonder he would make everything else that way."

Coren glanced between Sy and Kashar, and Sy saw the moment she made her decision. He breathed a sigh of relief.

"Two hours," she warned.

"Thank you," Kashar said, a hesitant smile on his face. Coren didn't answer the smile, but she did turn and follow him east.

The sun rose higher in the sky as they trekked the forest in silence, and Sy watched Coren as she watched the sun. He regretted so much, but he knew they wouldn't be successful in StarsHelm without her power. Even without her Vespa form, she had incredible shifter magic.

Just as the sun reached its apex above them in the canopy, the trees parted to reveal a narrow clearing. In the center sat a roughly-made cabin, dwarfed by an enormous barn behind it.

"This is my friend's home," Kashar said. "It's safe to speak here."

"Then speak," Coren said, her voice flat.

But Kashar kept walking, intent on the cabin. Coren glared at Sy, and he shrugged. He wouldn't blame her if she took off now, but he prayed to the Magi that she wouldn't.

"We'll meet the friend," she said grudgingly.

Sy bit back a grin. Strangely, he *was* feeling better, as though a pressing weight had been lifted once he was free of the forest. They hurried to catch up to Kashar.

There was no answer to his knocks at the door, so he led them around the back of the cabin to the barn.

"Lana?" he called.

Sy heard rustling and a squawk from the building. A door flew open, and a woman tumbled out, catching herself on the handle and slamming the door shut.

"Kashar!" she cried, her face lighting up. She hurried her steps and practically fell into his arms, a look of bliss closing her eyes and smoothing her beautiful face.

Sy glanced warily to Coren, and he could tell she saw it, too. This woman seemed a bit more than a friend to Kashar.

They broke apart, and Kashar turned to Coren. "Lana, this is my oldest child. Corentine."

Coren stiffly allowed the woman to embrace her before stepping slightly behind Sy. Sy reached his hand out. "I'm Syashin, the First Son of General Ashemon of Weshen City," he said, and the woman giggled at his formality.

"Lana," Coren repeated, almost to herself. "Not Weshen, then. Or did you change your name?"

Sy understood her confusion. The woman looked somewhat Weshen, with her earth-colored hair and tan skin. She blended well with the elements, like the Weshen people. But her name had none of the feminine *en* that all Weshen women's names contained.

"I'm half Weshen, half Sulit. And half EstenSands," she added with another giggle.

Kashar smiled down on her, but neither Coren nor Sy showed amusement.

"Who are you?" Coren continued, challenge in her voice.

"Corentine, Lana is a good friend of mine. I've known her many, many years. She can be trusted. She controls the clearing, keeping the King's spells away, and we can talk freely here."

"If we can talk freely, perhaps you should explain why your hand is still on her waist," Coren said, turning on her heel and marching back toward the cabin. Sy debated following her, but he really wanted to know what was in

22

that barn. That level of rustling was definitely not from stormcloud chickens.

"You might try to be a little more sensitive," he said to Kashar. "She isn't going to be very impressed that you love someone other than her mother."

Lana's face flushed, and she stepped away from Kashar. "You didn't tell her," she said, no giggle in her voice.

"How could I?" Kashar murmured, bending to grasp her hands. He led her several feet away, speaking in a low voice.

Sy huffed and stepped toward the barn. His hand grasped the handle just as Lana shrieked "No! Don't open-"

But it was too late. Sy had already cracked the door. Whatever was inside had evidently been waiting for such an opportunity, and the door burst open all the way, knocking Sy to the ground.

A rush of wind blew across his face, forcing his eyes closed, and by the time he blinked them open, there was nothing but a blur of brown in the sky above the clearing.

Lana sighed, pushing a wavy piece of hair behind her ear. "It took me all morning yesterday to chase that one down. And ten pounds of meat."

"What is it?" Sy asked, squinting against the sky. He'd seen a lot of creatures and MagiCreatures, but this one didn't look familiar.

"I call it a cheetair," Lana answered, pride leaking through her soft words.

"Lana's a breeder. She actually *created* a new species," Kashar said, his hand brushing the hair from Lana's neck.

"Non-magical, of course. Or the King would be able to find them," Lana clarified. "It's a sort of animal alchemy I've invented."

Sy watched the animal still circling above him. He didn't know exactly what she meant. Lana unstrung a wooden flute from her belt and played a few notes. The creature dipped and sailed past them, just out of reach.

"Stubborn thing. That one's named Stonewall because that's what his mind is like when it's made up." Lana walked to a stout metal container next to the barn and opened it, using a hooked stake to withdraw a fist-sized hunk of bloodied meat. The animal circled a little lower. She used one hand to play a longer tune on the flute and the other to toss the meat in the air.

Stonewall caught it mid-flight, gulping it down. It was close enough now that Sy could see its size. Large enough to carry a fully-grown man, with broad, strong wings.

"Is this how we're going to avoid the forest?" he asked. Kashar grinned.

"Yes. Now if only Corentine would come see them."

"Give her time," Lana murmured.

Stonewall spiraled down again and landed, nosing against the container for another snack.

"He'll be wanting to check you out," Lana said as the animal tilted its head at Sy. It padded closer to him, and he saw the resemblance to the Cheetana he and Coren had fought off in the mountain passage. Sleek, strong build. Glistening black and midnight blue fur, with tufts of bright teal at the paws and ringing the eyes.

The wings were puzzling. "What animals did you breed together?"

Lana grinned. "Proprietary secret. Cheeten, of course. That's the non-magical cousin to the Cheetana."

"I'm a Weshen Paladin. I know my creatures," Sy said, annoyance creeping into his voice, despite his manners.

"The wings are from a very rare animal," she continued, excitement spilling her secrets anyways. "One that used to have a magical counterpart. Have you heard of a mountain drakka?"

Sy raised his brows. He'd thought those were extinct, just like the mythological Draken, one of the only MagiCreatures more fearsome than a Vespa. "Those look like winged snakka, right?"

Lana nodded. "They have the slim bodies of a snakka, and the scales and deadly fangs. But their wings are incredibly large and strong for their size. Overly strong, almost like a tribute to their Draken ancestors."

Sy shook his head, and the animal nuzzled up to his palm. Then it nipped at his fingers.

He snatched his hand away, squeezing bright drops of blood from the wound. Lana giggled. "Don't worry. No poisonous fangs on these. They're pretty harmless, unless they throw you off their back at a thousand feet!"

With that, she grasped the shiny fur at the animal's neck and hopped between its notched, leathery wings. Giving a whoop and a brisk kick to Stonewall's side, she laughed joyfully as the animal leaped into the air and beat its way into the orange and purple-streaked clouds. Sy could hear her glee spilling down from the darkening sky as she circled the clearing.

He glanced at Kashar, who was watching the woman with the sort of awe that was almost embarrassing to witness.

"Okay, I can see why we're here. But a little advice, Prodigal Knight? Go talk to Coren now, before she disappears into the forest again."

Kashar whipped his head around just in time to see Coren striding toward the edge of the clearing, her pack bobbing at her back. He threw an exasperated look at Sy, who just shrugged.

"She did say two hours," he called after Kashar as the man sprinted to catch up with his daughter. Sy bent his head back to watch the circling cheetair. This was going to be an interesting journey.

He only hoped Nik and Resh were faring better. There was bound to be suspicion between them as well, and Nik had to undergo the added test of the passage beneath the NeverCross Mountains.

Sy said a silent prayer asking the Mirror Magi to keep them safe, and to grant them favor with the General when they arrived in Weshen City.

Nik took a deep breath of the dank tunnel air. His pulse surged at the dizzying energy he felt. The sacrificial magic that veined through the slick rock walls of this tunnel.

It tugged at the shifter magic in his veins, separating the sources in his very blood. Smothering the life from any blood that wasn't Weshen.

He reached a hand back. Resh placed a torch in it, and Nik started to jog.

Maybe if he got through this place fast, the magic wouldn't have time to seep all the way into his blood.

Yeah, right.

The first ten minutes was only dangerous because of the dark. The chill of the rock was tolerable, but his feet felt heavier with each dragging step, and his lungs had to work so much harder than normal to bring the air into his body.

Slowing and slouching against the wall, he handed the torch to Resh and held up a hand.

"Just need a minute," he grunted out. It was more than a minute when he managed to peel himself from the damp stone and grasp the torch again. His pace was even slower this time, and his stomach churned as though it hadn't been filled in weeks.

Nik pulled at his magic and tried to shift some of the dense air away, seeking thinner, cleaner stuff to fill his lungs.

But that drained him even faster, and he stumbled to his knees, the torch bouncing onto the sandy path.

"Come on, kid," Resh said, tugging at his pack.

His voice sounded far away, as though Nik were listening from beneath the water. His lungs struggled to pull the air in, but he grew confused, worried he might be breathing in liquid. He closed his throat against the sensation and staggered to his feet, holding his breath.

27

Grasping the torch again, Nik made it a dozen more steps before his body forced him to breathe, and he choked on the sensation of water rushing into his lungs.

"It's an illusion! Push through!"

The voice was even smaller now, nearly lost in the rush of the river in his ears. His wrists burned from the ropes binding them to the stakes. His arm muscles screamed from being twisted in opposite directions.

No.

He wouldn't let the slavers win. He wouldn't shift. He wouldn't break or be ripped apart. He would rather die than give them what they want.

But someone was pulling at his arms, gentler than the slavers had ever been. Yanking him to his feet again.

Maybe it was that bird girl, come to save him again.

A growl in his ear told him it was no girl.

Nik gurgled a pitiful semblance of a laugh. It was *that* brother. Not the one he wanted.

"Breathe!" the voice yelled, and Nik could feel the frustration in the word shoving at his ear. It hung there, a command, an idea, and suddenly a desire.

He opened his mouth and sucked in the air and water and horrible, wonderful magic until his brain dimmed from the pressure and he sunk below the surface, deeper and deeper until he bounced onto the black bottom of the riverbed.

3

Resh had no idea how he had managed to drag Nik all this way.

The kid was heavier than he looked, and they both needed a break.

They had just made the circular room in the passage's mid-point, and Resh set the two packs down, then dumped Nik's lifeless body on top of them.

Well, not lifeless. Nik was breathing, despite his earlier determination not to.

Resh had finally knocked him out with a blow to the temple. Once his mind was asleep and immune to the magic's illusions, his body knew how to stay alive. Resh filed this information away for when he would bring the other Wesh through. Maybe Shanta could help him find a good sleeping potion from a reputable witch.

Resh snorted.

No such thing as a reputable witch.

He pulled a water skin from his pack and dribbled some into Nik's mouth. The kid coughed and swallowed, but his eyes didn't open.

Resh downed the skin and ate his way through an entire sandwich before Nik stirred again.

"Welcome back," he said as the kid's pale blue eyes cracked open.

"There?" Nik croaked, and Resh handed him another water skin.

"Only halfway." A smile edged across his face as he saw the despair creep into Nik's eyes. "Relax, kid. I'll make sure you get to Weshen City alive. You're my proof, after all."

Not to mention Sy would beat him senseless if anything happened to Nik. Resh still didn't trust that connection - the speed and level of Sy's interest. If Nik betrayed him, Sy would never see it coming.

So it fell to Resh to remain suspicious. Really, they knew nothing about Nik other than he was likely more powerful than Sy or Coren.

"Thank you," Nik whispered. Resh could tell it was hard for him to say, and he appreciated the kid more for it.

"You know, it's funny. I've tried for years to get Father General to rescue more of the Wesh. I can understand now why he always resisted. It's dangerous. For both parties involved. We can't afford to lose any Weshen at all." He looked directly into Nik's eyes, noting the resentment there. "But I still intend to push him. More than ever, we need to rescue every last person with Weshen blood. I hope you can convince my father of something Sy couldn't."

"What's that?" Nik asked.

Resh stood, offering him a hand. Nik took it and rose shakily, then leaned against the cave wall. "I need you to convince him that the magic is back for real. Not just in Coren and Sy. Not just a fluke. But all over Riata, in the diluted blood of those we've ignored for far too long."

Nik grinned, his chest still rising and falling too quickly, like the air just wasn't enough to feed his lungs. "Well, I convinced you. Your old man shouldn't be too hard."

Resh was surprised into laughter. There was truth in Nik's statement. He'd seen Coren's magic and thought she was using Sulit spells. He'd seen his own brother's shifting and assumed Coren had him under a spell. It had taken Nik, and Shanta, and Shadow, and all of the events in EvenFall, to finally convince him that the Weshen shifters had indeed returned.

"And then I need you to find my magic, so we can show him that's possible, too," Resh continued.

A dark look flashed across Nik's features, and he stared at the ground, avoiding Resh's eyes. "I hope it's all that simple," he finally said, when Resh made no sound or move to leave.

Resh shrugged. He hoped for simple, but he was up for complicated too. "Well, let's go find out." He slung his pack over his shoulder, then Nik's as well. Handing Nik a torch, he gestured for the kid to go ahead in the passage.

Their pace was almost unbearably slow, but Nik did manage on his own feet.

Resh talked as they went, gauging Nik's presence of mind by his occasional grunts of agreement.

"I think that pool is a sort of oasis for those traveling the passage. It's a good point to stop and rest or eat if you need. The water there is fresh and drinkable. Sy and I looked for the opening above so many times. It's probably in the outlying pastures that are set into the mountainside, but we were never able to find it."

Nik paused to rest against the wall again, but he kept his grip on the torch this time. Only a few minutes passed before he pushed off the rock and plodded forward. Resh smiled. He was strong.

"The passage does its best to kill the non-Weshen blood. That's what you're feeling, you know. Your blood dying."

"Not helping," Nik growled, and Resh laughed.

"Once I found a half-eaten Riatan soldier near that pool. There aren't many animals down here, but enough that they keep the passage clean for us."

"Ugh."

"Cycle of life, kid. Imagine how awful it would be to have to come down here and dig out dead bodies. The Mirror Magi did us a great service by creating this way in and out of Riata." Resh clutched the prayer beads at his throat and said a brief prayer of thanks.

The will of the gods was the only thing in Resh's life he had never questioned, though he wasn't certain why. Everything else in his life was about what he could see, what he could touch. But never his faith in the silent, invisible Magi.

Perhaps his mother had instilled this faith, but Resh remembered nothing of her, thanks to the borrowed Sulit spell that charmed the minds of every Weshen child.

"How much more?" Nik asked, stopping again to catch his breath. His torch cast odd shadows around them, and Resh felt a creeping shiver across his shoulders. Thank the Magi that things like Umbren creatures were kept out of here, too.

"Let me go first. I think I see a bit of light up there, so we might be really close." Resh strode ahead, turning a curve in the passage. He heard Nik begin to haul himself along, and sure enough, soon they could see a growing pinprick of light.

"Stay back. Best that the guards see me first." They approached the thick metal gate that served as a last defense of the mountain passage. "Guards!" he called, alerting them as he neared the bars. "Open the gate for your Second Son!"

Resh smoothed his shirt as best he could and summoned his favorite haughty expression, ensuring the guards knew he held more power than they did.

A brief silence passed, and he called out again. Nik sidled up behind him just as a figure became visible, lumbering through the trees.

"Why was there no guard posted?" Resh demanded.

"I'm sorry, sir," the guard answered. "I was here a moment ago, but there was a noise."

"And where is your partner?" The gate guards always worked in pairs, and often in threes and fours if a threat was imminent.

"Sick," the guard shrugged. "I've asked for another, but summer is slow. With the General still on the island," he added.

Resh sighed. He'd hoped his father would have the intelligence to return to his city early.

33

"And we've just replaced Melshen." The guard carefully avoided looking at Resh.

"Ah," Resh nodded. He'd nearly forgotten about killing the summer commander in his rage. That was when he still thought Coren truly was a witch, controlling his brother and likely any man she could. Resh had reasoned that he was protecting his city from a possible threat, but he was also protecting Sy from any repercussions of the man's death.

He grinned, remembering the criss-cross of whip marks on the man Coren had killed. Even before the Vespa shift, she'd been powerful.

"Sir?" the guard prompted, and Resh blinked back at the open gate before him.

"Thank you. This is Nikesh, a Weshen I have helped rescue. I have no evidence that anyone followed us through the passage, but be certain to guard it with your worthless life. If there is another noise in the forest, ignore it," Resh warned the guard, who nodded swiftly and hurriedly turned to lock the gate behind them.

"I'm starting to feel better," Nik said as they walked through the slender stretch of trees that separated the city from the passage.

"Good. We'll eat and rest, and I evidently need to brief the new commander on proper gate patrol. We can leave for the island in the morning."

Nik didn't respond, and Resh saw his gaze riveted on the city that spread open before them, glimpses of faded grandeur between the stones in the high, crumbling wall and the iron gate.

"I never thought I'd see Weshen City," he said, his voice barely a whisper. "I've dreamed of it. We all did.

But to *be* here…" His words trailed away, and Resh felt a mix of pity for this boy's mangled life, and pride that he could help Nik find a better one.

"I'll make certain you're treated well here," he said.

Nik nodded, one corner of his mouth lifted in a smile. "Thank you."

They traveled in near silence through the rings of Weshen City. Resh named the spaces for Nik and let him look. The packed-earth outer ring where the guards patrolled, then the wide, grassy fields for animals. The market circle, which was a poor imitation of EvenFall now. It had once been just as bustling, according to the oldest men. The commoners' houses, which were still nicer than many Resh had seen on his travels. Run-down and empty now, but better built.

All remnants of a once-powerful country.

"And this is the government ring," he finished, allowing Nik a moment to rest. They had been climbing a steep path as they moved through each section, and the government circle was the highest. "We can see the entire city and half the mountains from here," Resh added, throwing an arm wide. Weshen City wasn't what it was two generations ago, but he was proud of it.

Prouder still of what his people were about to accomplish.

"Where do we sleep?" Nik asked, fatigue threading his voice.

"Here," Resh said, pointing to the impressive building before them. "This is the main government building, but it's also my home. The General's home."

Resh led them past a pair of guards who bowed before him, and once inside, he called for a servant.

"Prepare dinner at once. Ready my room and one near it." He dropped the dusty packs on the floor of the grand hall.

The servant bobbed, already shuffling backward.

"Bring the food to us when it's ready. We'll be in the meeting room," Resh added.

He threw open the doors of his father's cavernous office and collapsed into the wide leather chair. It was the closest Weshen had to a throne, and Resh sat there each chance he found.

"Anywhere," he said to Nik, who stretched out full length on a long couch and sighed in a satisfaction that sounded bone-deep.

"You must have had a nice boyhood," Nik murmured, his eyes closed.

Resh laughed, though the memories weren't funny. "We always had plenty to eat and soft beds to cradle our heads. Beyond that, we raised ourselves and mostly survived our training. There's more than one way to harden a child for the world."

Nik opened an eye, evaluating Resh's statement, but he said nothing.

Resh rummaged in a drawer and produced a bottle of liquor and two glasses. He offered one to Nik, who groaned and shook his head, so Resh downed them both.

He had just kicked off his dusty boots when a cart of steaming dishes wheeled into the room. It was stacked so high that the servant steering it could barely be seen.

Nik nearly tripped over his long legs trying to get to the food, and the boys feasted, not even speaking until their bellies were nearly bursting.

"I could get used to this," Nik mumbled, stretching back onto the couch. He was snoring softly within minutes, and when the servant came to announce that the rooms were ready, Resh waved him away.

"Send someone to watch him. He shouldn't be left alone." Resh climbed the stairs slowly, glancing at the home he had taken for granted his entire life.

What had Coren thought of all of this? He knew Sy had brought her here. He knew she'd even been in his room, for whatever reason. She'd looked through his clothes and weapons, taking what she wanted from him. She'd been so angry with him then, though he knew it was for a good reason.

His bag was waiting on the wide-planked floor, but he ignored it, turning his attention instead to the curtainless window. The moon hung low in the sky, nearly level with his gaze.

Resh flopped back on the wide bed, imagining Coren in his room, rummaging through drawers and closets.

What made her so powerful, he wondered. Shanta's research and the bits of information Kashar let go of both pointed toward family. Her brother had been banished, and it was apparent now that he had possessed true Weshen magic, not Sulit spells.

But it was so long ago. Why would there have been such a gap? Such a scattered return of the magic?

Resh knew Ashemon didn't have any magic. His only hope for a piece of the shifter power was a mother he'd never be able to find. Or Nik, who claimed to have methods. Torture methods.

Resh set his jaw in the dark.

He had once thrust himself wholly into the idea of becoming a Paladin, and he'd been successful. Perhaps not so much as Sy, but he'd learned to overcome any fear of pain. Then he'd thrown his efforts into the hunts, achieving even greater success there. He'd learned to master the lure of pleasure, and despite what he led others to believe, Resh had taught himself to balance his life with equal and alternating measure of both.

If the shifter magic had returned, he wanted it. The Magi dealt heavily in balance and equal opposing forces. Pain or pleasure or both, he would master their gifts as well.

Weshen would rise again, just as the Restless King was falling. Resh planned to be there, waiting to pick up the pieces of Riata and puzzle them together under his own hand.

Nik woke in the darkness, his mind clear and purposeful after food and rest. The leather of the couch beneath him was cool against the summer heat and molded to his body in greater comfort than he had felt in many years.

Still, he got up.

Moving about the room, he let his senses tell him where to go. Eyes closed, Nik focused his SourceShifting power until he could feel the distinct energy each source contained. Wooden objects vibrated differently than metal, and water was easily distinguished from earth.

It was one of the many horrible, yet useful, exercises he'd endured with the slavers. They would lock him in a pitch-black room filled with dangerous items and force him to puzzle his way out.

His mind skipped effortlessly over the rough, warm grain of wood before him: the spacious desk where Resh had sat, which surely belonged to the General. He felt the cold strength of the smooth, inlaid stone tiles at his feet. He numbered the volumes and slowly decaying pages of the many books on their wooden shelves. Their smell was particularly interesting, as he'd rarely been around books. They didn't smell like the trees which had been harvested to make them, but instead like the river water mixed into the pulp, and the glue and leather of their bindings.

He almost paused to take one apart to isolate and learn the many sources, but there were other things he needed to do.

Nik breathed deeply and stretched his senses beyond the meeting room, feeling for other sources, but the building was nearly all the same wood and stone.

He could tell there were very few people in the house now, and that suited him well.

Nik paused before opening the door and concentrated his power in a different way, forming an image in his mind of their servant. The tingle and gentle sting of SelfShifting magic filtered through his limbs, shortening his legs and plumping his stomach, lightening his hair and softening his features. He pushed the door open, and dim electric lights shone down onto the gnarled hand that was too wrinkled and scarred to be his.

The sweeping entry hall was silent and still, and Nik paused before a wall-sized mirror.

He grinned. The likeness was perfect. The expression was wrong, though. He formed his new features into a mask of deference and slight fear.

His masters would have been proud if they weren't dead, he thought, a gleeful and grim satisfaction resting in his newly fat belly.

Mimicking the shuffling step of the servant, Nik headed up the stairs he'd listened to Resh climb earlier.

There were two options at the top of the stairs. One hall felt empty and cold to his creeping senses. The other held the distinct scents of the brothers, both Resh and Sy, and another he guessed could be the General himself.

It was incredible to Nik that he could still recognize Sy's scent, as it must have been weeks since he'd been here with Coren. Nik's energy had renewed substantially during his stay in EvenFall, but his magic had limits, of course. Part of the power of this scent was Sy himself, and the intentions Nik had for the First Son.

There was only one other in Nik's memory whose scent had such staying power, but it was for all the wrong, most horrible reasons.

Nik's mood darkened, and he felt his disguise slipping.

He pushed into a nearby room and breathed deeply several times to calm and cleanse himself, systematically erasing the dark power of that memory. He allowed himself to slip back into his own form as he relaxed and reminded himself he would never see that cruel boy again.

As Nik let the SelfShifting go, his other senses sharpened again. It took great energy to sustain multiple types of magic at once, and he needed to work back up to that sort of stamina.

He groaned a little as he realized he'd chosen Sy's room after all. He sank face-first into Sy's bed, pressing his nose into the crisply-made bedding. It had been cleaned since Sy had been here, he sensed. But Sy's scent overpowered the soap and wrapped around him, just as powerful as the other memory, but bringing comfort and pricks of intrigue instead of fear and pain.

Never again, Nik thought, closing his eyes and working hard to exile the hollow-eyed face that still haunted him.

He would never again be someone's puppet or plaything.

Several minutes passed until Nik was breathing steadily again. He pushed off the bed and wandered the room. His eyes lighted on a trio of potted plants on the balcony - the only living thing he'd seen in the building since waking.

Nik grinned, relief tingling across his chest, smoothing all the stress away.

He could use this time to send a message. It had been nearly a year since he'd been strong enough, or alone for the necessary time. He only hoped MistCall was still alive. Of course, she'd threatened to haunt him after death enough times that he was fairly confident she still ruled the back alleys of Rurok.

Gathering a handful of petals from the potted rosewhip vines that climbed the balcony railing, Nik spread them on the stone balcony. He sat and crossed his

41

legs before him, turning his face to the moonlight. The words of the spell came easily, but the magic was much harder to capture.

Non-witches could perform certain Sulit spells, even men, though the results were never as strong. Nik had been taught by a spellmaster, though, and the magic had been harshly bound to his fingers and lips many times. He pushed those memories away once more, hard, and focused on the incantation.

Slowly, the petals began to flutter into shapes, then words. The light, blush-colored outer petals arranged themselves above a carpet of darker pink heart petals, spelling the message.

Once the words were visible, Nik changed the spell slightly, sticking the petals to each other and infusing them with a choice memory: Corentine aloft in the air, her great gray wings spread, and his own child form clutched in her arms. Her face wasn't visible, and he didn't look like that any longer.

This way, even if someone managed to intercept the message, they could not trace the memory directly to him.

Except for MistCall, no one alive had seen him at that age. Before leaving Rurok, Nik had made certain of that.

Fatigue began to slow his chanting as dawn edged onto the horizon. It had taken him much longer than it used to, and he was grateful to have completed his task without interruption. Despite the flashes of strength earlier in the night, Nik knew he was still too weak.

He hovered his fingertips over the petals, testing the strength of the message. It would hold. He scooped his hand beneath the petals, and they stayed together, stuck in their pattern of letters like a woven quilt.

One last bit and he could sleep again.

Nik stood, holding the petals over the edge of the balcony, and used his shifter magic to pull at the particles of the wind - the invisible solid pieces that made up the sources of everything. He flexed his power, grinning that though his Sulit spells were weak, his shifter magic had certainly rebounded well.

He shifted the petals back into a large, fluffy flower, like an overgrown rosewhip. Then he nestled it into the breeze he'd created and combined the two magics to float the spelled petals from Sy's balcony in Weshen City, across the MagiSea and NewMoon Falls, all the way to the towers and streets of Rurok.

4

Coren sat across the narrow table from Kashar, Sy at her right and Lana at his. Lana had prepared a delicious-smelling meal, and Coren was hungry, but she hadn't eaten a single bite.

She was too busy asking questions, afraid Kashar might stop answering them.

"Sorenta grew up in StarsHelm, just like me. But we never met until the night I helped her escape. Odd, considering we were both at the palace quite a bit. I think I would have noticed her," he smiled, his gaze slipping over Coren's features. She knew she looked very much like her mother now.

"But you're full-blooded Weshen?" she asked.

He nodded. "My father, Rashar, was a runaway from Weshen. He never told me the whole story, I don't think. But I know he and his twin sister were in the slavers' hands. Back then, the slavers worked with the witches instead of Riata. Twins brought the highest coin.

But Rashar's sister never made it to the witches, and when he had the chance, he ran. Zorander Graeme saved him."

Coren tilted her head, disbelieving. "Saved him to take his magic?"

Kashar shrugged. "Rashar was loyal to Graeme until the day he died. I don't think Graeme ever mistreated him. He was mostly raised by the Weshen soldiers in the barracks, and he became a great Commander. I followed his path, as expected by pretty much everyone."

"Until you met Sorenta," Sy said, his voice displaying a similar distrust. Coren slipped him a smile. She was glad he was finally demonstrating judgment against the Prodigal Knight. It made her feel less guilty about the ill will she bore toward the man who still claimed to want to be her father, despite so many contradictory actions.

"She was so beautiful. Much younger than me. Innocent. And she never displayed any power that night. It was only later, on Weshen Isle, that I learned she was a shifter."

"What happened that night?" Coren asked.

Kashar hesitated. "I don't know everything. She told me she and her mother were trying to escape. For some reason, they had waited longer than pretty much all the Weshen to leave the city - too long - and it was dangerous. The Sacrifice had already happened, and passage to Weshen City was proving deadly to so many of mixed blood. She and her mother were caught just beyond the palace, in these same woods, and I was part of it." He swallowed hard. "I was assigned to the patrols that week, and we'd seen nothing for days. Then there they were, running like mad with nothing even in their hands. Her mother pushed her in one direction and ran the other way, splitting up to try and lose us. She was throwing Sulit spells and shifting the earth at us and everything. But Sorenta sort of just disappeared."

"Disappeared?" Coren repeated. "Did she SelfShift into someone else?"

Kashar glanced up, and she saw tears hung at the rims of his eyes. He looked so like Kosh then, and her heart gave a painful thump. "I don't know. Possibly. There were lots of soldiers there, and it was dark. We lost her, though. By the time I returned to the main group, they had captured Lorental. Graeme was there, and several of his personal guards. The...the executioner drew two curved blades across her throat, and that was it. Graeme didn't even wait to see her body hit the ground."

"Why would he wait?" Sy asked, and his question directed Coren to the strange detail, relieving her momentarily from the odd grief she felt swelling for this woman. A grandmother she'd never known.

"Graeme was friends with Sorenta's mother. Before the Shift. But he completely turned on her, and in that moment, I saw what he could do to my family as well. I was afraid, and even though I'd never been trained to use my shifter magic, I'd seen what the King's Alchemists had begun with Weshen prisoners. I faded into the forest, abandoning the rest of my friends, and I looked for that girl until I found her. I promised I'd protect her with my life, and deliver her to her people. *Our* people."

"Sorenta never told me any of this," Coren whispered. "She spoke so little of her mother. I guess this is why."

"And then he brought her to the safety of Weshen City," Lana broke in, smiling proudly. "They fell in love, and had you and your brother and sister."

"And my twin," Coren added sharply, still unwilling to let Kashar forget what he had lost.

He sighed rubbing both temples with one hand. "Jyesh's power was so unexpected. None of us even realized he had magic until that day."

"When he SourceShifted a man?" Sy asked, grimacing. Kashar nodded.

"Sorenta was never emotionally strong. But that day broke her in two. I tried for so long to help her find her way again."

"A year was not long enough," Coren snapped, finally giving in to the food before her. She'd reached the point in the story she didn't want to talk about.

"So why did you go back to StarsHelm, after all those years?" Sy asked, giving her the reprieve she needed.

Silence fell over the room, so complete that Coren could hear the cheetair creatures rustling in the barn. Kashar stood and took his plate to the sink, his back rigid.

It seemed as though they had all stopped breathing. Coren felt like even the sources around them had paused, ready to hear what possible excuse he might give. Every part of her hoped he had an excuse. *Needed* one. When too many minutes passed, and he'd given her nothing, her patience shattered like a dead, winter-iced branch.

"Traitor," Coren hissed, and the kitchen erupted into chaos.

"I am no traitor!" Kashar roared, swerving around to face her and banging his fists on the table so hard a glass knocked onto the floor, splashing water and shattering. Lana jumped up, her actions torn between trying to calm Kashar and clean the mess. Sy reached to grasp for Coren, who had stood and was staring her father in the eyes, every muscle tensed to fight.

"You left your people - your family! We needed you! You went to work for the *Restless King*!" she screamed. A lifetime of rage and grief was surging through her like relentless waves of a summer storm, and suddenly Kashar began to scream as well, but without words.

His toes left the floor, and his fingers scrabbled for purchase on the table, but to no avail. He was hovering several feet in the air, and his skin was beginning to dissolve.

Coren felt her rage turning to pure power, and although something deep in her heart was begging her to stop, she had lost that ability several minutes ago. Her mind seethed with dark desires that drowned out everyone's cries. Her hands raised gently as she flicked her fingers, and a mist of bright blood burst into the air.

Kashar's blood.

Lana began to wail, and Coren turned on her, shadows crowding her vision. In less than a second, the woman had joined Kashar at the ceiling, her mouth frozen open in a soundless scream.

"Traitor," Coren whispered again, but it was an accusation to herself as much as her father.

She should have never left her family. She wanted Kashar to be in as much pain as she was in, and this seemed to be the only way to make him feel what she felt.

She closed her eyes against his pleas just as something collided with her temple. Physical pain spilled into her conscious, overpowering her broken heart. She felt her hands drop, releasing Kashar and Lana just before her knees buckled, and everything went black.

By the time one of the servants found Nik, curled asleep on Sy's balcony, it was mid-morning and Resh was ready to slit the kid's throat. He settled for ordering the incompetent house servant to be reassigned to the boys' laundry.

"What's for breakfast?" Nik said, the words distorted by a massive yawn.

"You're lucky I had the kitchen pack you anything. I wanted to be halfway to the island by now," Resh snapped. He'd been bathed and ready since dawn. "What were you doing in Sy's room? And why were you sleeping on the balcony?"

Nik shrugged, rubbing at his eyes. "Just looking for a bed to stretch out in. Must have fallen asleep looking at the moon."

Resh eyed him. That didn't make sense, but he had neither time nor patience right this minute. "Bathroom's down there. Don't take long, or I'll leave you here."

"Which would be amazing, actually," Nik grinned. He sauntered down the hall, leaving Resh wishing he really could leave without the kid. It would be pointless, of course. He needed Nik to show Ashemon the shifter magic.

They traveled the long stone staircase down to the General's private dock quickly enough, though, and Resh threw their bags into the bottom of the narrow boat.

He tossed Nik an oar, and Nik looked at it doubtfully. "Get in. I'll show you what to do. Step in the middle and sit down on the center of the seat so you don't tip us."

He watched Nik climb in, a little clumsy but better than expected. Resh seated himself in the back, untied the boat and used his oar to push away.

"You said it would take a day to reach the island?" Nik asked, twisting his head back to watch Resh steer the boat into the sparkling water.

Resh nodded. He demonstrated to Nik how to use the oar, dipping the broad end deeply but not wetting the handle or losing his grip. Satisfied, Resh added his strength and steering, and soon they were cutting through the smooth water at a brisk pace. The MagiSea was quiet, with little wind for the sail Resh had rolled away.

A few dawngulls wheeled above them, crying plaintively to one another as they swirled beneath round puffs of clouds.

The sun crept across the sky, seeming to stall directly above them. Resh peeled off his sweat-soaked shirt and dunked it in the sea, wringing the water down his face. The salt dried too fast, leaving his skin encrusted with grit.

"Let's take a break and eat," he said, chucking his oar to the bottom of the boat.

"Thank the Magi," Nik wheezed. He gingerly swiveled in his seat to face Resh. Eying Resh's naked torso, Nik copied him, groaning as he pressed the wet fabric to his face and pushed his dark curls back.

Resh tossed him a sandwich and a skin of fresh water.

"So how are you doing with the fact that I kissed your brother?" Nik said just as Resh took a huge bite. He choked on the mouthful, and Nik smirked.

Several seconds later, Resh had cleared his throat enough to glare at the kid. "In theory, I'm okay with the fact that you kissed him. But realistically, I'm not okay with what it means for Sy."

Nik cocked his head in challenge. "What does it mean?"

"Our people - here in the city and on the island - have been focused on building our numbers. For two generations, that's all we've done. That's the whole reason for the hunts. Keep love out of it, and keep the babies coming."

"You've been building an army the old-fashioned way," Nik said, going back to his sandwich. His expression was hooded, and he kept his eyes down.

"Exactly. Your involvement with my brother isn't going to go over well with the General. Sy is the next General, expected to keep the traditions up and protect the people."

"And he can't do that with me."

"Not exactly," Resh agreed. "But maybe it's time some of our traditions change," he added, and Nik glanced up. "I mean, they've only been traditions for two generations."

A slow smile began to spread across Nik's face, and he straightened.

"The magic changes everything," Resh admitted.

Nik nodded. "I like that answer." He crammed the remaining bite of sandwich in his mouth and dipped his hands in the water.

It took Resh a few seconds to realize they were moving, and that it was all because of Nik.

"What are you doing with the water?" he asked, leaning over to get a better look.

"Shifting it around the boat. The movement of the water pushes against us, and we go."

He closed his eyes in concentration, and they were suddenly jetting across the water, faster than Resh had ever traveled even with a full sail.

"This might work for proof for Father General," he grinned. "Just don't wear yourself out."

Nik laughed. "This is easy. Wait until you see what I can do with the ground."

"Coren!" Sy called again as her eyelids fluttered. He'd hit her pretty hard, and she'd been out an hour.

But she'd nearly killed her father.

They were all still reeling from that realization, and he knew that Coren would feel a crippling guilt when she woke. At least, he hoped she would.

Lana retreated to the barn in angry tears, seeking the comfort of her creatures. Sy mended Kashar's skin as best he could. He knew how to knit sources together, but he was no healer. Kashar's skin looked more like storm-ridged sand than a smooth layer.

"I wish I had never left them," Kashar murmured bleakly. "It's done so much good for our people, but it's done so much harm to the most important people. My family."

"She's capable of great forgiveness. Just be honest with her," Sy cautioned, thinking of how she'd changed her mind on Resh.

Coren groaned then, her fingers tapping at her temple. Her lips frowned, and finally her eyes opened.

"Kashar?" she asked, sitting too quickly and shutting her eyes again, slumping against the chair back.

"I'm here," Kashar said, scooting closer.

"Shouldn't have... I'm sorry," she whispered, and Sy's heart sighed in relief. "Horrible..."

"It's okay, Coren," Sy said. "I healed his arm. He's fine. He's ready to tell you some things now."

She cracked a tired smile. "I should hope so."

Kashar tried to smile, but it came across more like a grimace. "Corentine, I'm so very sorry. For all of what happened. I wish I had proof, as I fear you'll never believe me. But it was your mother who asked me to go back to StarsHelm. Sorenta begged me to help our people in StarsHelm. To be a King's knight and a spy for the Weshen. And she was right. I've helped so many Weshen trapped in Riata, bound in slaver rings and the King's prisons, play things for the Alchemists. I can keep them from horrible pain and death."

"You were right. I don't believe you. She flung herself from a cliff after you left."

Kashar sighed, rubbing the back of his neck. "When could I have been there for her? Would the summers have been enough? You know the men aren't allowed to love, but I loved Sorenta. I loved you and Jyesh and the babies."

Sy noticed the past tense in Kashar's words, and he knew by the set of her jaw that Coren heard it, too.

"But I love Weshen more."

Coren nodded slowly, her eyes tracking the stars beyond the window. "That I do believe."

Kashar ran his fingers lightly over the newly-pocked skin of his forearm and took a deep breath. "What I need to tell you, what you need to hear, must remain a secret. When we return to StarsHelm, you will see me as the Prodigal Knight. Returned again. Conquering again. It's vital that this facade remain true. I capture the Wesh, but not to hurt them. I teach them, Coren. I show them how to improve their magic, but only up to a certain level."

"Why not the extent of their abilities?" she asked sharply.

"Because the King and Queen can sense the strongest of them. The few who move beyond my instruction, from SourceShifting into SelfShifting, always disappear into the King's private rooms. None ever return."

"The rumors are that he scrapes the magic from their bones," Sy said, hating that he needed to ask about such an impossible atrocity.

"The rumors have validity," Kashar said, his eyes dropping to the table. "Graeme hunts the SoulShifter. There hasn't been anyone with that ability for generations, but still he searches."

55

Sy felt his face pale as his heart clutched tightly to the blood in his chest. Damren had said Coren might be strong enough to become the SoulShifter. That Coren's family - her blood - had held that power last.

Kashar was watching him with narrowed eyes, and Sy felt as though the man could read his thoughts.

"I hope Jyesh was the SoulShifter, and the power is gone again for generations," Coren bit out. "At least then his death would have some meaning for our people. A sacrifice instead of a waste."

Familiar needles of guilt crept up Sy's spine as he thought of how his family had treated hers.

He placed an arm around her shoulders, and she startled a little at the touch, then slumped into him.

"What's your plan for us, then? Certainly, our magic will be strong enough for Graeme to find," Coren said. "What's to stop him from capturing us and scraping the magic from *our* bones?"

Sy rolled his neck and shoulders. He could manage plans and action. As long as Coren wasn't trying to kill her father, he could handle just about anything.

"I have a friend in the palace who does a Sulit cloaking spell. It doesn't last long, but I want you two in and out and on the way home to Weshen within a few days. Like assassins."

"Riata dies this moon," Coren murmured, staring out the window.

"I'll take you to my friend and show you the way to Graeme's chambers. But I cannot be seen with you more than that."

"Why haven't *you* tried to kill Graeme?" Sy asked Kashar, wondering at the misalignment between the man's words and actions.

"The King and Queen are well-warded against any damage I could do. I would be dead before I drew my weapon. But it's not about my life. I have responsibilities to our people. Currently, nearly five hundred Weshen live in the palace."

Coren's eyes went wide with shock. Sy's stomach churned at the thought of all the people his father could have saved. And many more had died at the hands of slavers and Graeme's men. If they could be rescued...

"Our army has been waiting for us in StarsHelm all this time," he said. "Not being birthed by the women for a battle twenty years in the future."

No one spoke for several minutes before Kashar cleared his throat. "So how exactly do you plan to overpower the King? I can get you in and hide your magic, but you'll need to do the hard part."

"I can tear him apart with a thought," Coren said, her voice dark and flat.

Kashar shook his head. "He's well-warded against Weshen shifting. Queen Mara is quite the spellmaster, and she's often near him. As is Lord Aram."

"Who is that?" Sy asked, the name vaguely familiar.

"Mara's twin. I have not once seen one without the other. He doesn't use spells because he's mute, but he's lethal with many weapons."

Sy was beginning to feel the edges of exhaustion. "We need to kill three people. Not just the King."

Kashar nodded. "If Graeme dies, Mara takes the throne. But they have no blood heirs. Many have desired to kill Graeme. Fewer have tried, and none have succeeded."

"Well, Sy believes our power was given to us for this very purpose," Coren said, standing to stretch.

Sy nodded absently, though his confidence was shaken. He wondered if it had been his own wishful thinking for Weshen freedom that brought the ambition, not a true message from the Mirror Magi.

And could Kashar be trusted? The man should be leading his newly-found daughter *away* from this sort of danger, not into the middle of it. He sighed, thinking of how he had always thought Ashemon a coward for failing to act. But he was beginning to understand his father's fear. If they succeeded, yes, the world would change.

But it would certainly be simpler and safer to stay in Weshen and await the Mirror Magi's explicit instructions.

Sy rose, stretching like Coren. Kashar looked up at them, a curious expression on his worry-lined face. "It is a pity neither of you can shift to your MagiCreature. I've always thought Graeme might be vulnerable to that sort of attack. It's one reason I've waited so long. That magic is stronger than any Sulit spell I've seen and totally unexpected."

"But Shadow stole that power," Coren said, glaring out the window.

"Temporarily," Kashar said, and she whirled to him. "It isn't gone forever. I knew as soon as I saw you that the transformation was incomplete. That's why Shadow could affect it in the first place. You must find the MagiCreature itself. You must merge with it."

"Incomplete?" Coren repeated.

Sy's brain pulsed with excitement. If she could shift into a Vespa again, they would have no problem fighting three people. It would even be worth delaying their mission a few days for her to regain the power.

"When SelfShifting with a MagiCreature is complete, the person disappears completely, their mind and sources held inside the body of the animal. It's a fluid, painless, and complete shift," Kashar explained.

"Have you seen it?" Sy asked, his words running together in excitement.

Kashar shook his head. "No. But there are still knights alive who have. The Silver Sovereign once had an army of Weshen fighters, and his Commanders were always powerful shifters."

"So, I need to find another Vespa to merge with?" Coren asked.

"Not just any Vespa. The one you've already partially merged with," Kashar answered. "A MagiCreature only ever bonds with a single shifter, and a shifter can only bond with a single creature."

Sy's shoulders sagged with fatigue and the impossibility of such a task. He glanced at Coren, and her face was as sour as a lemondrine.

"I'll never fly again, then," she muttered, and turned on her heel, heading into the night.

5

Pale moonlight spread itself through the night-black towers of Rurok as the Lord of Witches paced his black and gray and cold marble floors, enjoying the click of his heeled boots. His rooms were the only ones like this, and he hated the feel of wood and - even worse - moss beneath his fine shoes.

But he needed to focus. Lord had been awoken by magic, and he couldn't find its source. It was pricking away at the calm he held so tenuously.

"I'm the only shifter here," he called to the darkness, as though it might simply answer. "Where are you?"

But there was no answer.

No sound.

No movement.

Still, he sensed the traces of shifter magic, somewhere in the castle. Somewhere close. He felt it like whispers of heat at his back.

He crossed the open, empty space of the throne room and picked up the black iron bell to call a servant.

"Bring me Strike," he commanded when she entered. The young witch trembled, and for good reason. Strike enjoyed her sleep and would not take kindly to being awoken in the dead of night.

But Lord didn't care. Not about the young one's misfortune, and not about the old witch's sleep habits.

He'd been here as long as any of the hideous Brujok, and he was their Lord and master.

They whispered, yes. An abomination to have a man on the throne of witches. But they had placed him here to threaten the southern Sulit, and here he stayed. Brujok witches were the most powerful, and Lord was drawn to their strength.

They had ruled Rurok for many years now, first in secret covens of cruelty, and now in open courts of pain. Rebellions were common, of course, but each was stamped out as soon as it started, like embers smothered beneath thick sand.

A begrudging growl surfaced behind him. "My Lord."

"Strike," he acknowledged. "I heard a noise. I felt a shifter presence."

The witch sighed, her gnarled fingers twitching against the magic pooling in their tips. "My Lord, our guards would sense any shifter within a thousand steps of the palace. There is no shifter here but you."

"I felt it," he insisted. "I want a complete search."

Her fingers rubbed idly together, and lavender sparks jumped from one to the other like tiny shards of lightning. The boy narrowed his eyes. She had never hit him with her spells, but other witches had tried. The after effects were not pleasant, for either party involved.

Many witches had died at his hands, but never yet a Brujok.

Still, Lord kept up his own research and training during these late night hours. If they thought to replace him, they would have to use more than Sulit spells.

"A complete search," he prompted, realizing she still stood there.

"Yes, My Lord." Strike shuffled away, banging the tall iron door after her.

Lord glided to the massive window, pulling his dark velvet cloak tight against the chill air. The castle of Rurok was built as a great cylinder, its outside wall consisting of rows of spiraling towers. It resembled a staircase that climbed and spiraled into the clouds. In its center, far beneath him, were a handful of shops and hovels where lesser witches lived. Rurok was less a city than a fortress.

The gray stone was nearly silver in the ever-present mist from the falls, though, and Lord ached at its serene beauty.

It was nothing like the beauty he had known as a child, though - sparkling, white sand and blue sky. Opposite. He hated that openness. That vulnerability to sun and sea.

None of that mattered now, though. He needed to find the source of the shifter magic.

If it wasn't a person here in his castle, perhaps someone had sent a message using shifter magic. His guards had intercepted such before, and he was sensitive enough to detect it, even if the Brujok weren't.

Firelight began to spread through the tiered windows across from his, and noises echoed from the staircases. He stepped over the window's low frame and onto the balcony of his throne room, watching as the torchlight spread and spiraled around the insides of the towers.

It was soon lit like the rib cage of an animal, its heart glowing red and warm as Strike set her guards into action.

He rang the bell again, and the young witch appeared. He noticed a new scratch across her cheek. It made her less beautiful, he decided. "Bring me Strike."

"Y-Yes, my Lord," the girl stammered. She hurried away, and Lord turned back to the window.

Several minutes passed before a witch entered. It wasn't Strike, but Chaser instead.

"My Lord, Strike is occupied with the search you ordered. How can I assist you?"

"We have a prisoner. She received a message once from an old friend we share, one who is both shifter and spellmaster. Bring her to me."

"What is her name?"

"I don't know! There is only one such witch in our prisons! Find her and bring her to me!" Lord's impatience pushed his voice to a screech, and Chaser turned and swirled from the room, trailing darkness after her. Lord cursed her impudence. These Brujok had raised him to be exactly what they wanted.

He had formed himself into a tyrant for them, and now they expected special treatment. He refused such hypocrisy.

Lord picked up the bell again. The girl must have been waiting, for she was beside him almost instantly. "Bring me something entertaining while I wait."

She bobbed a curtsy and disappeared. Lord loved giving his servants such challenges. Once, one had even brought him a real pet. The same pet whose indiscretions had resulted in imprisonment for the very witch he sought now.

He closed his eyes and smiled, remembering the boy's eyes. They could flash between emotions faster than anything Lord had ever seen. Open and clear as a sky crystal, tinted an impossibly light shade of blue.

"Is this the prisoner you seek?" Chaser asked from mere inches behind him. He turned and glared at them both, examining the woman. He had no idea if this were the right one. All the witches in the prison looked the same - filthy.

"Did you receive a message today? Do not lie," he commanded, already beginning to whisper an incantation to bind her to the truth.

The witch's face was so dirty that when she opened her mouth, Lord realized he'd been staring at the wrong place. "Yes," she rasped, struggling to keep the word from her lips.

"Where is it?"

Chaser dropped the witch on the floor of the throne room and wove her hands over the woman's robes. A surprisingly clean and lush pink flower pushed its way from between the folds, hovering in the air.

Lord snatched at it, the fragrance bringing memories he'd long repressed. "Rosewhip," he whispered. "Weshen."

"Reveal it!" he ordered the witch. Of course, he or Chaser could just as easily do the same, but he enjoyed making the prisoner show her secrets. It was so much more fun to do things against people's will. Especially the small things.

She struggled against the truth spell, but she was sick and starved. Within a minute, she had spread the flower into a palm-sized message. Lord and Chaser stared at the words for many silent seconds.

"Lord?" Chaser finally questioned, and he clenched his fists and jaw to keep from slicing her head away with a spell or shift. She must know what those words would mean to him, and still she questioned his intentions.

He should lock her in the dungeon with the prisoner, but she'd only escape.

"Weshen rises," he repeated instead, letting go of her stupidity and whirling away from the two witches. He focused on a nuance of the petals that may have evaded the old witch. There was an image embedded in the flower, separate from the words themselves. It could only be felt, not truly seen. And the image was confusing.

Lord was intrigued. He did love puzzles.

The boy in the image was so young. Unfamiliar. But still, there was something in the arms, akimbo yet limp in the other person's grasp. If only the eyes had been visible…. The wings flapped rhythmically as the boy was carried across the treetops, somehow held by human arms.

Who in all the land had learned to fly? The face above the boy was too hazy to see as well, as though the boy had been drifting in and out of consciousness. What did the message mean?

Whoever had sent this message was powerful. And knew the prisoner. And had access to both Weshen shifting and Sulit spells.

Lord steadied himself against a column. The boy he'd tried to love yet only succeeded in losing - could he still be alive? Lord had been certain he'd died many years ago, attempting to escape Rurok.

The boy's betrayal was worse than anything the Brujok had ever done. It had been the final break in Lord's heart. After that night, Lord had used the last of his light to heal himself.

His face hardened even more, and he crushed the petals to pulp in his palm. Now, he was too strong to break.

The boat crunched onto the shore of Weshen Isle as the sun slipped into the western horizon.

Nik had traded his shifting for the oar in mid-afternoon and slept the rest of the way, despite his bragging. Resh rowed them to the edge of the men's camp, and he knew by the bonfires that the beach would be empty save for a guard or two.

It looked to be a feast night, celebrating yet another hunt.

He allowed himself a brief longing for the simplicity of the summer hunts, where he could catch a girl in the sand, drink too much, and take her to bed for as long as they both wanted.

Even as he smiled at those memories, Resh acknowledged that for him, that Weshen was already gone.

Gone in a flash of shifted water on the beach, and a brush of silken wings against his fingertips, and a dreamy glimpse of an empty throne.

For years, Resh had wished idly to become General. But he would never go against Sy. And it seemed his loyalty and patience was being rewarded, as this larger goal opened to his eyes. More than anything now - more than magic, more than Corentine - he craved the throne of Riata.

He had no right to it. He knew this.

But neither had Zorander Graeme, once.

"Reshra." The voice was low and too near. Resh stood and jumped out of the boat into the damp sand. He bent to shake Nik awake, then straightened to formally greet the broad shoulders now blocking his way to camp.

"Father. I have returned. Sy is safe beyond the mountains." Resh almost added that Coren was, too, but he wasn't certain this would be good news for the General.

Nik stumbled from the boat, swaying on the sand as he struggled to move his legs properly again.

"And you have brought a stranger into our home," Ashemon said, looking over his gaunt frame. Disapproval set his jaw, and Resh stepped instinctively between the two.

Nik's fingers curled reflexively at his sides.

Resh bowed his head in the most deference he'd shown his father in many years. "Nikesh is only one of many Wesh we have rescued. The others are healing and strengthening for the journey home."

"This is not their home," Ashemon answered, and Resh felt a dagger of betrayal poking at his ribs. "This island belongs to the women, and the city to the Weshen. This boy fits nowhere."

"They are our people," Resh began, clamping down on his anger at Ashemon's nearsightedness.

"They cannot be trusted. Do you think I am proud of these deeds you did behind my back? Against my permission? You are too young to have seen the horrors I have seen, and you speak of bringing them into our oasis of safety."

Nik stepped forward, his shoulder squaring with Resh's. Ashemon turned his head, slow and deliberate, but Nik didn't waver. "I've seen plenty of horrors. I only hope they aren't the same horrors, General. Have you seen children whipped until their bones shine white in the sun, just to see if they can heal themselves? Girls impregnated again and again to see how much magic can be leached from their blood? Boys bound to stakes and drowned, then revived, only to be drowned again, until they find enough magic to shift the water from their lungs? Have you, General? Have you seen such horrors? Because I have not just seen them. They are my horrors, and I live them every time I close my eyes, no matter where my body sleeps."

He was shaking now, and Resh laid a warning hand on his arm. Nik flinched away, his fingers clenching into full fists. Resh's instincts kicked in just in time to avoid the punch of sand that came at his gut like a giant fist.

Ashemon sucked in a breath, and Resh knew that, seconds after landing, they were losing the argument. Nik's lack of control was only making it worse. Behind them, the water churned and rose, slinking from its sea bed.

"Think of Sy," he hissed to Nik. "He wouldn't want this. Calm yourself for him."

Nik jerked his face to him, and Resh repeated the instruction, noting how pale Nik had grown, how hollow his eyes were. Haunted. To their left, the boat began to dissolve silently into splinters, board by board.

"Think of Sy," he repeated, hoping his voice was too low for Ashemon, but knowing it wasn't. Behind Ashemon, the sand had begun to drift higher and higher, blocking their view to the tents and shutting out the light of the bonfire.

"Hold your anger," Resh whispered one last time.

"Sy," Nik whispered, awareness blinking back into his pale eyes. He flicked his chin and spread his fingers wide, reining in the chaos that had swept the beach. Thick walls of water dropped back into the ocean, and the sand rolled down from its huge dunes, smoothing the beach again. The wood of the boat knitted itself back together from the jagged scraps floating in the air.

"What is the meaning of this?" Ashemon asked when the world was whole again. His voice was darker than the midnight sky above him, and Resh felt his stomach churn and then tighten, his lungs holding their breath.

He let it out slowly, choosing his words. "The boy and Sy have become good friends. Sy is his mentor."

Nik snorted. "More like I'm *his* mentor." He slid a sly smile to Resh.

Resh widened his eyes, willing the kid to be quiet. "Perhaps we can discuss this in more detail in the morning, Father? We are very tired."

Ashemon grunted and stalked away, and Resh slumped in relief. At least his father hadn't packed Nik right back in the boat. After such a blatant demonstration of magic, Resh knew this was a victory, however temporary.

"Come on," he said to Nik, willing himself calm again.

The kid followed him silently up the beach to the tents, and Resh slipped inside the one he and Sy had shared for a few weeks. That seemed so long ago, like another life.

"You can sleep in Sy's cot. I'm right on the other side of the curtain. Nobody will bother us here."

Nik nodded and sank onto the soft blankets. They were still mussed from the last time Sy had slept there. And Coren, Resh remembered. He didn't even feel like the same person who had threatened her to offer Sy an heir.

It seemed like a lifetime ago that he had been the arrogant Second Son, so certain magic could never return that he had followed her on the beach and revealed her secrets to the entire island.

His fingers went to his temples, regret searing through his brain. He needed sleep. Pushing aside the curtain, he turned to Nik once more. "That could have gone better, but tomorrow we'll talk to some of the ones who like Sy and me more."

"Are there others who are impatient to fight?" Nik asked, pulling off his boots and stretching flat on the bed.

"Many."

Coren realized her mistake as soon as she stepped out of the house.

Lana had just exited the barn, leading three of the cheetairs. "Get out of my house tonight! Take my animals if you want, as a favor to Kashar. But I don't want to be anywhere near you," Lana bit out. She yelled for Kashar, and he burst through the door, obviously worried.

"I'd say you're welcome to stay, but if I send them, I know you'll go, too." She turned on her heel and retreated to the barn, banging the door behind her.

Kashar let out a deep sigh. "Let's get our bags." He slouched back into the house.

Sy rubbed at his eyes and offered Coren a half-smile. "Well, here's your chance to fly again."

Coren cursed at him, and his smile grew. They trudged inside as well, collecting their bags from the unused beds.

"I was really looking forward to a restful sleep," Kashar muttered as he passed them in the hall.

Coren didn't answer him, although she could have used the same. They were all tired, and their night was about to be much longer. She knew it was her fault, but the guilt wasn't stronger than the resentment toward Kashar. She doubted it would ever disappear.

All these years, he had been free to roam Riata, choosing his own path and loving another woman. All the same years that she had been a child struggling to raise the twins and hunting the plains of Weshen Isle for rockrabbit. Claiming the sacks of food that grew smaller and smaller each summer. Trading her pride for extra rations in the hunts.

No, she wouldn't feel guilty for depriving Kashar of a night's sleep with his new woman.

But for hurting him, yes. She felt a seething guilt for that, and it had turned into a sharp, defensive bite, like an animal backed into a cage. She hated that her instincts had been reduced to that defense, and she suspected it would only worsen if she entered the palace with intent to kill another man.

"Have you ridden one of these?" Sy asked Kashar, breaking into her thoughts. The animals were surprisingly docile. Coren reached a tentative hand to one, and it nuzzled its nose against her palm.

Kashar nodded. "They're trained to fly to the outer forests of StarsHelm and return. Lana's done fantastic work with them. I wouldn't recommend dozing off, but it will be a comfortable ride."

He swung a leg over the back of the nearest cheetair, strapping his bag around his chest. Sy mounted his cheetair quickly, but Coren hesitated. She'd never ridden any sort of animal before. The women's island had nothing large enough.

"They're safe," Kashar called, kicking at his creature's side. It broke into a run and leaped in the air, circling above the clearing. "Just don't fall off!"

Sy shrugged and copied Kashar's movements, and Coren steeled herself. She double-hopped awkwardly onto the animal, clutching the thick fur. It barely gave her time to get well-seated before jumping in the air after the others.

Balancing on the animal's back took nearly all her concentration for far too long, and she missed much of their flight over the treetops. This was nothing like flying, she grumbled to herself.

Sy and Kashar flew slightly ahead of her, and she could hear their voices but not their words. Her eyes were sliding shut every few seconds by the time dawn stole over the land, lighting not just the trees, but something glistening in the distance.

"StarsHelm!" Kashar called, as his mount began to circle toward a clearing in the trees below.

The landing was a jolt of muscle against bone, and Coren slipped sideways off the cheetair in relief. Her legs and arms ached from gripping the animal for so long, and all she wanted was to close her eyes. The cheetairs were fine, though. Free of riders, they jumped into the air again, their wings flapping hard to gain altitude.

"Will they fly straight back to Lana's?" Sy asked. "Don't they need a break?"

Kashar shook his head. "Bred for long flights. They'll be back at her barn by mid-afternoon, eating their weight in meat and hay."

"How near are we?" Coren asked, keeping her tone light.

Kashar flicked his eyes at her. "A few hours on foot. I think we should climb these trees and rest, then enter the city at night. It's a little safer that way, though there is always danger in StarsHelm."

"In all of Riata," Sy added. Kashar nodded, and they each found a stonetree they could climb, hauling their bags in after them,

Coren fell asleep almost immediately, and her dreams were filled with the sensation of flying.

She woke to the hot stickiness of mid-afternoon.

Kashar was still draped across his branch, but his eyes were open, watching her. Sy's tree was empty, but he must not be in trouble, or Kashar would have gone after him.

It was this knowledge which lodged in her head, mixing with the guilt that surged forward as his dark eyes studied her. He seemed lost in thought.

"Do I look like Sorenta?" she asked, her voice soft against the still afternoon.

Kashar nodded, and she saw enough sadness in his face that she began to forgive him.

"I'm sorry I used my magic against you. I have no idea what happened." She hadn't even meant to, was the thing. A little like what had happened with her whip and the man in Weshen City.

"Shadow," Kashar grunted.

"What?"

"Once blood magic - Shadow - has a taste of you, it never leaves. You'll always be darker than before. You'll always have to work harder to find the light."

Coren swallowed hard, all her unspoken fears lumping together in her throat.

"Can you teach me to control it?" she whispered.

Kashar stared into the distance. Finally, he glanced back to her. "I don't know."

6

Resh bolted upright in his bed, disoriented. Blinking around him, he realized he was in the tent on Weshen Isle, and it was that odd, still moment between night and day, when nothing stirred and anything was possible.

He would not have been surprised in that moment to have pushed aside the curtain and find Coren secure in Sy's bed, all of them pretending she was there because of Sy's prowess in the hunts.

But when he slipped into the tent's other chamber, he found the cot empty and a strange, slimmer indent in the blankets. Nik was gone, though his boots sat next to the bed, and a dirty shirt that would never fit Sy's broad shoulders lay discarded across the chair.

Resh ducked out the tent flap and scanned the camp. Everything was quiet and empty. Torches doused and ashy, the bonfire still smoking. A few older men were slumped in chairs around the logs, sleeping off their wine.

He turned toward the beach, his eye snagging on a figure farther down, slim and pale.

Resh tugged a shirt over his head but left his boots in the tent. He crept down the beach, interested to see what Nik did when he thought he was alone.

As he neared enough to see, his eyes widened, and a smile tugged at the corners of his mouth. The kid was practicing his shifting, and it was beautiful.

The ocean leaped and danced beneath his long fingers, dividing into tendrils and vines of crystal water, weaving patterns of foam and dark blue between. Against the sleepy light of dawn, the water looked like a tapestry held to the sky with nothing but Nik's mind.

He let the blue go, and it sank with a splash. Turning to the sand, Nik pulled at the grains, tugging them into craggy towers and arches, forming a castle of pure golden grains as he cast aside the odd colored bits of sand and flecks of palmpress grass. Resh realized Nik wasn't just moving the particles; he was sorting them. The castle grew until it was nearly as tall as Nik, and the kid was grinning like he might crawl inside and live there.

As Resh watched Nik flex his strength, a fierce longing flared up. He wanted power like this. He could do so much for his people - for all of Riata - with power like this.

Nik must be convinced to teach him, pain or not.

Resh had always welcomed the pain of training because it spoke of growth. Besides, he could counter it with a little pleasure on the side. Measures of each, doled out in ready when one became too much or too little.

"Nik," he called. The sand castle crumbled before his eyes as Nik turned to him, shifting back to its natural ridges and planes. "Teach me."

Nik grinned. "We've been over this. I'll have to torture it out of you if it hasn't already awoken. It might work, it might not. But it *will* hurt."

Resh nodded. "Do it."

Nik studied him, and Resh held his gaze. He knew Nik didn't want to go back to this place in his mind, and Resh realized he was asking too much.

But he wasn't backing down. He wanted this. Weshen needed it.

Finally, Nik shrugged, a gesture of nonchalance that Resh didn't believe for a second. "Well, then find something to bite. I'm going in."

"What?" Resh balked. "Going in where?"

"Your blood. I'm going to take it apart and find the magic. Wake it up."

"Are you joking?"

Nik turned to face the open sea, his bare shoulders slumped, and Resh knew it was not a joke. The sun was higher now, and he could see a bit of smoke from camp. The men were stirring, and he wanted to begin before Ashemon found them and stopped them.

"Fine." He pulled his belt from its loops and sat, clamping the leather between his teeth. "Go."

Nik turned back, and his eyes were nearly colorless against the ferocity of the sun on the water. "I'm sorry," he whispered. He placed a gentle hand on Resh's arm, and Resh was instantly lost in a universe of pure pain. His eyes squeezed closed against the tears that his body was spilling as fast as the blood running out through his pores.

He was afraid to open them again. He feared seeing his skin flayed open, his bones exposed to the sun like a bleached skeleton, his blood soaking the sand.

At some point, the bright, hot pain turned black and drained his conscious, and Resh slipped into a dreamless void.

"I will not put a single one of my men through that," Ashemon declared to Tag. "It is unproven and may cause lasting damage."

The two men watched Resh and Nik from the cover of their tent. After seeing his younger son - one of the fiercest Paladins he had - faint from pain, Ashemon was even more determined that the magic must be allowed to return on its own time.

This forcing was brutal and unnatural. It could anger the Mirror Magi.

"If it works, though," Tag said, awe in his voice. He was watching Nik build a palmpress grass toy boat with just the tools of his mind, the grass floating in mid-air as it shaped itself. "His hands aren't even touching that grass."

Ashemon snorted. "Unnatural. I recognize a few Sulit spells, and that boy uses them, mixing them with his Weshen shifting. See how he changed the color of the grass? Spelled."

"Why do you fear the magic so much?" Tag asked, and Ashemon bit back some harsh words. This was his oldest friend, and he still didn't understand Ashemon's fears. How could he expect the people to?

"I *don't* fear the magic. The magic is blessed, but only when it comes from the Magi. I do fear this forced magic, done without our gods' consent. I fear what will follow, and its potential to destroy our country and our people completely. If we regain magic now, the King will come for it. He will kill us all searching for it, and imprison any who have it. The magic was not enough to beat him when our people were at full strength. How could it possibly be enough now, when only a few have it?"

Ashemon watched his son, still sprawled unmoving in the sand. He assumed Reshra was not injured, or the Wesh boy would have certainly notified someone. Or run, if he knew enough.

He turned back to Tag. "That boy could be a spy for Rurok for all we know. That's why I never bring Wesh here. We don't know where their loyalties lie."

"I think Reshra's loyalty lies with his people. Surely he trusts this boy, or he would never bring him through the passage."

Ashemon glanced over, noting how the sand was discolored with blood. His own family's blood. Ashemon gritted his teeth. He'd had a man beaten for less once. The only people who drew blood from his family and escaped retribution were those training the boys.

And even then, there were limits.

"Reshra has always wanted our people to be free, certainly. But I believe he wants much more. He would

81

take the First Son position gladly. I can see it in his carriage, the way he sits and stands and surveys the men. He believes them his already."

"But aren't they? With Sy banished…" Tag allowed his thought to trail away.

"Do not speak to me of Sy's banishment," Ashemon growled. "You know I wish it could have happened differently, but I had no choice. The people must be protected."

He didn't want to watch this futile training exercise any longer or have this discussion again. He rose and stalked away before Tagsha dared remind him that he alone had the authority to create different choices or lead the people in a new direction.

Ashemon had made his decision publicly, and he hated its consequences, but he would never reverse it and allow Syashin to return as First Son. Such an action would speak of weakness.

He heard Tag's steps behind him. "What if some of the men volunteered?"

"Volunteered? Who would do such a thing? Who would welcome such pain?"

Tag smiled. "Your son, for one. There are others who desire the power. They may be willing to try, at least."

Ashemon considered his friend. Tag had always been overly pushy, but only when he was confident in the rightness of his beliefs.

"The magic is back, Ashemon. There is no more denying it. We've all seen Sy, and Coren, and now this boy. There have been rumors for years of Wesh all over Riata, using some remnants of shifter power. It isn't all mixed with Sulit. There's no way Coren's magic could have been so influenced - she'd never even been off the island!"

Ashemon sighed. This had swiftly become a tired argument. "Fine. Ask the men to watch the boy tear apart Reshra's arm. If any express interest after that, it is their own decision. It does not exempt them from other duties, however."

Tag's grin was contagious, and Ashemon, for once, allowed himself a sliver of hope that he might see the fall of the Restless King in his lifetime after all.

As long as the consequences to his people were not so costly as they had once been, he could manage to find joy in such news.

"Wake up. It's over." Nik's voice was near but still muffled, as though Resh were hearing it through a thin wall.

Resh groaned and tried to move his head, but his neck felt fused to the ground. His legs were crumpled beneath him, as though he still lay where he'd fallen.

"You passed out. It was probably for the better."

Resh peeled one eye open. It was still mid-afternoon. The sun was still in the same place. "Time?" he croaked.

Nik shrugged. "It was only a few minutes. That's all anyone can bear at first."

Resh's head swam. At first? He'd have to do that again?

Nik sighed. "I know. And yeah, that's something that usually gets done every day for months. Some people find their magic faster. But that's what we're up against. So keep praying to your Magi, Second Son. Ask them to bring the magic back the easy way."

"But did you find any?" Resh asked, his voice slight against the ocean breeze.

Nik shook his head, then rose and scuffed away, leaving Resh cursing to himself and trying to figure out how he would ever convince another Weshen to take part in such madness.

Resh closed his eyes against the bright sunlight and retreated to a mental examination of his body, a task he'd completed a thousand times after training with Ashemon and Sy and the others. He turned over each bone, slipped his mind along each muscle, feeling for injury and willing the pain to subside.

Pain was a natural reflex, he knew. Messages from the body to the brain, calling out to stop whatever was happening. Warnings that survival was being threatened.

But Resh also knew that he could convince his body to calm. This internal examination allowed him to find the pain, and reassure his body that the message had been received. That it was no longer needed, and the repetition was wasting energy better left for healing.

It was so with this pain, and soon enough, Resh found that his arm had ceased its screaming, and he could stand without much dizziness. He glanced at the sand. There was indeed a reddish stain, but nothing drastic. A few drops, not even as much as a bloodied nose.

He felt along the skin of his forearm. The skin was slightly rougher than usual, but there was no scar. Nik had taken apart living sources, separating the very essences of his body.

And then brought them back together.

Resh thrilled to such a thought, and he knew that he could endure this new sort of training with such an ability as the prize.

He moved slowly down the beach, eventually catching up with Nik as he walked the smooth sand of the hunting beach.

"I have lots of good memories here," he said conversationally. "You wouldn't like it, though. On Weshen Isle, men only hunt women."

Nik grunted, clearly not interested in joking. "Where would I fit in, then? I'm no Paladin. I can handle myself with magic, but I know little of weaponry. I'd never hunt a woman, or father a child. I don't belong in this Weshen."

His voice was dark, and Resh saw the shadows under his eyes. Resh didn't want to admit that if Nik had found his own way to Weshen City before this summer, he likely would have been turned away. He didn't want to acknowledge the impossibilities of Nik among the Weshen people. People who should have a place for him, but did not.

"Well, this Weshen has only been around for two generations. And we're about to stand it on its head, anyway. You fit where you want to fit." He wanted to reassure the kid, knowing even as he did so that there would be much prejudice against Nik's power.

Even knowing that a month ago, he would have been among the first to cast the boy aside. But if he could change - if he could be convinced - so could others.

"With Sy," Nik mumbled. "I fit with Sy."

Resh shrugged, not ready to agree, but not convinced he disagreed, either. Then he thought of Coren.

"How do you know?" he asked Nik.

"Know what?"

"That you fit with someone?"

Nik tilted his head at Resh, hesitation in the set of his jaw. "Weshen don't ever partner anymore, do they."

Resh shook his head. "Not since the Separation. Women here, men in the city. Love discourages the hunts, and the hunts increase our numbers quickly."

"Seems like a punishment, not a protection," Nik murmured.

At the beginning of the summer, Resh would have argued or laughed at such a statement. But now...he wasn't certain his people had made the correct interpretation of the Magi's instructions. This alone was enough to frighten him. He clutched at the prayer beads around his neck, fingering the smooth surface of each bead, tracing the links of silver that connected them.

"You know by the tightening here," Nik said, his voice soft as he laid his hand over Resh's. Resh glanced down, seeing Nik's slim fingers pale over his own, pressing against not just the prayer beads, but his heart.

"When you fit with someone, your heart knows. It grows tight, full to bursting with a swirl of happiness and fear."

"Fear?"

"Of rejection, or loss. Of acceptance. Of forever. Or never." His fingers slipped away, and Resh found himself a little breathless, like a fog had lifted and he was looking down, only to realize his toes hung from the edge of a cliff.

Barring any label of man or woman, desire or friendship, shifter or witch, he could suddenly see why Sy had pledged to come home for Nik. His brother, who held his impossible ideals so tightly they became inseparable from his actions.

Not like Resh, who could easily separate his ideals from his actions when needed. Who could easily rationalize and justify that his conflicting deeds were all part of a grand plan. That his mistakes were usually a prelude to a serendipitous opportunity.

And where he'd thought Nik weak and innocent before, he realized with a flush of shame just how wrong he'd been. This kid was stronger inside than any of the Paladins he'd trained with. All his life, he'd been given nothing but power and people who abused it.

"Do you feel that with Coren?" Nik asked, jolting Resh back to the moment.

"Coren?" he repeated, uncertain how to answer. He'd felt things for Coren, of course. His emotions about that girl were as complicated as it got. Distrust of her odd power over his brother, over himself. A confusing lust for her silken wings and the magic they represented, and a familiar desire for the quirk of her full lips and challenging spark in her eyes as well. Approval of her dedication to her family. Amusement at the way she bested him time and again. Respect for how she had saved him. But happiness? Fear?

Resh shook his head. "Coren is complicated."

Nik laughed. "Love *is* complicated. I'm not insinuating you love her, of course. But matching your goals and hopes and fears to another person's and trusting them not to take advantage of that vulnerability? Yeah. Complicated."

"Her Vespa form..." Resh began, but stopped, guilt flushing his neck. He twisted the beads again, and they formed a sort of noose. He deserved to burn for the things those wings made him imagine.

Nik cursed in agreement. "I get it. There's something mind-blowing about that level of magic and power. If Sy ever shows up like that...."

Resh grinned, imagining all of them with wings, rushing the palace in StarsHelm. What fear would that strike into the heart of a King?

"But if all you lust after is her power, you'd better stop."

Nik's voice was like an iron wall between them, abrupt and inflexible.

"Excuse me?" Resh said, offense rising. Who was Nik to tell him-

"I've been on the receiving end of that. That lust for power. When someone lusts after power so much that they consume a person's trust to get closer to the power, things get ugly. Fast."

And with that, Nik turned and stalked down the beach, his back ramrod straight and muscles tensed. Resh could tell if he tried to follow, there would be a fight he wouldn't walk away from.

He let Nik go, wondering who in the world had destroyed such trust in Nik.

He wondered if he only wanted Coren for her power. If he was capable of consuming her like that, without a change taking place in his chest.

He didn't think so.

Resh might have taken a lot of girls to bed, but he'd never analyzed it. Not before and not after.

The very fact that Coren made him think of these consequences set her apart in his mind.

There wasn't any tightening in his chest just yet. But there was possibility, he thought.

7

Coren had just decided to slide down from her tree and wash in the nearby stream when Kashar sat up straighter. He held a hand to his lips and whistled. Bird-like but piercing, meant to catch someone's attention more subtly than a shout could have. Coren peered at him more carefully through the leaves, following his pointing arm down to the forest floor.

Her breath caught in her throat and she began to slip from her branch.

"No!" Kashar whispered fiercely. He was still high in his tree, scrambling to get purchase enough to fire his bow sword. "Corentine, stay where you are!"

Coren paid him no attention, crawling silently down the trunk of her tree. Her hand grasped the handle of her whip as soon as her toes touched the sparse grass.

Sy was stretching his muscles by the stream, completely unaware of the threat looming down on him from thirty feet above. For a bare second, Coren wondered why he hadn't sensed the MagiCreature.

She could feel its energy pulsing lightly, like a tug at her veins.

Then he put his fingers to his temples and knelt by the water, pain crossing his handsome face. Her attitude softened. He was likely exhausted and worried about their task in StarsHelm. In that quiet moment by the stream, when Sy thought no one was watching, he looked as though a million things were weighing him down.

A twig snapped above them, and Sy's face swiveled toward it. Coren looked in the same direction, and her heart sank. The creature had spotted Sy. It was enormous, one of the most threatening MagiCreatures she had ever seen.

Beautiful, surely. But undeniably deadly.

Sunlight glinted off its golden and rich brown fur. Even from her place hidden in the shadow of the forest, Coren could see the luster of its claws as it rose from four legs to a standing position. Its belly gathered to black, and the muscles bulked even beneath the thick coat. It must be twice as tall as a man.

She recalled seeing drawings of this creature in her father's journal, but the name escaped her memory.

Sy rose from the stream, incredibly slow and smooth. Continuing the same movement, he reached around his back for the bow sword strapped there.

Then the animal roared in indignation or righteous challenge, and Coren sank to her knees in the brush, weakened by the fear that sound thrust into her limbs. Not fear for herself, but for Sy.

She couldn't lose him.

"Grizzlin!" Kashar yelled then, and panic clawed at her lungs as the creature's fearsome reputation clawed through her brain. Sy ignored the knight's warning, instead positioning his weapon at the ready.

Coren had heard of the Grizzlin's power. How its jaws could crush a man's skull with a single bite.

"Sy, get back!" Coren called, sick with the need to have her Vespa wings back. "It's too close!" If only she could fly above the creature and threaten it from above like it was doing to Sy.

The Grizzlin roared again, and she could see its palm-sized golden eyes, watching Sy from the cliff ledge. It could hurl its massive body straight down and be on him in an instant.

Sy merely held two fingers up to them, signaling to wait, and Coren had to bite her lips to keep from shouting at him. The Grizzlin was scanning the woods and the tree line now too, likely looking for the origin of both of their voices.

Her whip might snap the necks of rockrabbits and slit the flesh of cowardly men, but the weapon would be nothing against the mass and power of such a creature. Even her shifting was doubtful - what good would a wall of water or a fissure in the earth be against such raw power?

Kashar had stopped rustling above her, and she risked a glance up just in time to see him release an arrow. The Grizzlin seemed to sense the air splitting before it, though, and lowered itself to the ground as the arrow whiffed over its back. It roared again and backed up a step or two.

Coren let out her breath in hopes it was retreating.

But it sprang forward with a growl, leaping out into space. Coren screamed as it broke several rocks from the edge of the cliff, and she sprinted toward Sy without a thought.

The Grizzlin landed directly on top of Sy, its gigantic body completely covering and crushing him. Coren collided head first with the creature's side. Its paw rose and batted her away, sending her sprawling onto her back. Her whip bounced into the grass, and the animal growled, its throat rumbling.

She stumbled to her feet and snatched up her whip, intent on snaking it around the beast's head, but the Grizzlin twisted and rolled into the stream. Sy was caught in its clutching paws, rolling with it. He was alive and still fighting though, and her heart skipped with hope.

"Coren, back!" he called just before the pair splashed into the water, which was much deeper than she'd realized.

They sunk beneath the surface before bobbing and splashing up again, several feet downstream.

Kashar trotted up to her and knelt on the bank, trying to aim his bow sword. "They're moving too much. I'm as likely to hit Sy as the Grizzlin," he cried, shaking his head.

Coren ran along the edge of the bank as they struggled and splashed in the water. She pushed her fear for Sy down into a deep place and focused instead on shifting the water from the wrestling figures. She could keep him from drowning, at least.

The Grizzlin roared again, the sound echoing in her ears and up the sides of the cliff at her back. It clawed at

94

the opposite bank, dragging itself onto the far side. Sy was dragged with it, clinging to the fur on its back now. His knees gripped the beast's back, and he held a longknife in each fist. He was struggling to find purchase on the creature's thick hide.

They tumbled into the dense brush, and Coren lost sight of them in the trees. "Come on!" she yelled at Kashar, who was simply standing on the bank. He had already fastened away his bow sword, and her rage spiked in his direction. "You're ridiculous! All this talk of being a knight and a soldier and so powerful, but you'll just let that Grizzlin tear him apart?"

Kashar ignored her tirade and put a finger to his lips, asking her to be quiet. He pointed to the trees.

Coren made a strangled noise of disgust and leaped into the water, barely glancing at the trees Kashar was watching. There was indeed a rustling there, but she wasn't going to wait around and see if the creature emerged gorging itself on Sy's innards. She struggled across the stream, reaching the other side in a pant.

The Grizzlin burst through the trees just as she rose from the water, dripping and muddy. She flicked her whip at it and gathered her magic to shift the ground from beneath its feet.

Sy was nowhere in sight, and her stomach heaved with the impossible thought of him on the forest floor, bleeding. Dying.

The Grizzlin staggered and slumped down before her, front legs flat on the ground and head bowed. A rumble came from its chest, but it seemed almost a moan, rather than a growl.

Kashar let out a bark of laughter, and Coren spared him a wary glance. Was he losing his mind over this creature? She stepped forward again, her whip snaking along the grass.

"*Stop!*" Kashar bellowed. The creature lifted its head then, and its plate-sized eyes stared right into Coren's. She noticed with a start they were no longer golden, but a dark, stormy blue. The Grizzlin sat back on its haunches, moving slowly as though it didn't want to startle *her*.

She heard Kashar splashing across the water, but she couldn't take her eyes from the creature before her, which was still staring intently at her. She could almost swear it was trying to *communicate* with her.

"Sy?" Kashar called, and the Grizzlin swiveled its massive head to the man, breaking the connection with Coren. Kashar laughed again, the sound more triumphant, and she snapped.

"What is your problem?"

"Sy?" Kashar asked again, stepping closer to the animal. It didn't move, its eyes fixed on the Knight. Kashar stopped only a few feet from it. Close enough for the Grizzlin to grab a clawful of his belly if it wanted.

Kashar reached out a hand and rested it on the golden fur, and the Grizzlin ducked its snout a bit, permitting the touch. Coren's breath grew shallow.

"What are you saying?" she whispered, an impossible idea forming.

"This is Sy," Kashar answered, turning to her with a grin. But as soon as his back was turned, the Grizzlin let out a ground-rumbling roar and dashed into the trees, its hind legs knocking Kashar to the ground.

"Let him go!" Kashar called as she started forward. "He'll come back. He *shifted*, Corentine! He shifted into a Grizzlin!"

She shook her head, mute and disbelieving. That was nothing like what had happened with her and the Vespa.

She needed to get in that forest and see for herself if it hid the mangled body of her friend.

Sy crashed through the forest, uncertain if the Grizzlin was chasing him, or he was chasing it. He felt the creature and its magic all around him.

The ground pounded up to greet him as he ran faster than he'd ever run, and still he couldn't escape the sensation of the Grizzlin.

Just before the creature had leaped from the cliff, Sy felt a presence in his mind, pushing at him to do something. There hadn't been words, just emotion, but Sy was left with a sort of mandate to remain calm and open.

He didn't know what that meant, but he certainly wasn't going to stay put if a Grizzlin was chasing him, and even if he died today, at least Coren would have a chance to escape if he drew the beast deep into the forest.

He stumbled and fell to his knees, but his tumble was cushioned, and he barely felt the bite of the roots and sticks beneath him. It felt like he wore his heaviest winter cloak, though he wasn't hot. Just *thick*.

Lumbering to his feet, he fell back to all fours. Crawling should have been awkward, but for some reason, the movement felt natural. His head cocked up at an unnatural angle, and his hips and spine seemed more fluid than they should have been. One of his hands splashed into a stream, and Sy felt his tongue slip out of his mouth to lick at the drops splashing across his face.

The scent of Grizzlin was everywhere, but he couldn't see it. Crouching down, he listened.

Footsteps pounded the ground, but he could tell they were still far away. A brief shout.

Coren, he decided. But if he knew she was so far, how could he hear her movements so well?

And her scent, he realized. A sweet salt and freshness clung in the air, brought to his nostrils on a slender breeze.

She didn't seem to be in any danger. She was looking for him. The Grizzlin must have gone.

"Sy?" her voice called, nearer. He sniffed the air and judged her direction and distance, then startled at such a thought.

Even with the training of a Paladin, his senses had never been this good. What had happened to him? Had the Grizzlin given him some of its magic, somehow?

As much as he'd love the idea of merging with a Grizzlin, he knew he hadn't shifted. He could see his feet, still laced into their boots, and his hands, scratched raw from branches as he'd run through the brush.

"Syashin!" Coren was closer now, her voice more desperate. Sy rose and turned in her direction.

"Here!" he called, but just as the word left his throat, a growl rocked the trees around him. He dropped down, scanning the area for the Grizzlin. He had to find it before it found Coren.

But then she was there, her face streaked with tears.

"Sy?" she asked, one hand held toward him. Her fingers were shaking.

He tried to reassure her he was fine, to ask her what was wrong and where had Kashar gone, but another growl overpowered his words.

"It's really you!" she cried, wiping at her cheeks. "Can you understand me?"

Sy shook his head in confusion. Why wasn't she reacting to the growls? Was his hearing that much better than hers?

"Can you shift back?" she asked, and he startled.

"Shift back?" he repeated, and the growl sounded again.

Frustrated, Sy swung in a circle, searching the trees. No Grizzlin. He smelled it, heard it, but there was nothing to be seen.

He heard and smelled Kashar, though, before the Knight crept up beside Coren.

"He doesn't realize," the man whispered to Coren. Her brows shot up.

"How could he not?" she asked, glancing back to Sy.

"Sy, you've shifted into a Grizzlin," Kashar said, looking Sy straight in the eyes.

Sy looked down at his body and shook his head. One of them had lost his mind. But he trusted Coren, and she didn't deny Kashar's words.

"Why can't I see it?" he asked. Again, only growling sounded in his ears. He roared and shoved at a nearby tree. Coren and Kashar jumped back as the tree toppled over, its roots now in the air. He stared at the destruction in disbelief.

"Sy, listen to me," Coren began. "We're going to figure this out. Can you understand me? Raise your hand if you do. Your paw, I mean."

Sy shook his head and raised what he saw as a hand. Not a paw.

"Good!" She smiled, and he grumbled to himself. He was not some pet to try and train.

"Let's keep walking and figure this out as we go. I need to be at the palace," Kashar spoke up.

Eventually, they came upon a small lake, and when they paused to rest and drink, Sy strayed around the banks to a quiet spot. He stared at himself in the water. His own face looked back, as normal as ever.

No, not exactly.

He could see it now - a faint outline of fur around his head and shoulders. As though the creature stood just behind him. Reflexively, Sy glanced over his shoulder, but he was alone. He could still see Coren and Kashar sitting on some flat rocks on the other side of the lake.

Sy closed his eyes and tried to quiet his mind, looking for that same presence that had probed him just before the Grizzlin jumped.

Are you there? In my head? he thought, feeling foolish.

But then something answered him.

We are both here. Your mind, my body. My mind, your body. I will be with you always now, Weshen. It is up to you whether you use my strength or my magic. But it will never leave you. We are merged.

100

Merged, Sy repeated in wonder. It was just as Kashar had said, but it was nothing like what had happened with Coren and the Vespa.

He focused on the presence of the Grizzlin, tuning into it with every sense. And when he opened his eyes, glistening golden and bronze fur shone before him, covering every bit of his body. He looked down at his chest and belly, where the fur swirled and darkened. He held up a hand, and saw it as a paw, with curved claws on each finger.

Looking down into the water, he saw his own eyes, set deep into a wide, furry face. A snout and rows of sharp teeth.

Grizzlin, he marveled.

Yes. Now, look for yourself again. Look deep inside, to where your voice still waits. It is not gone. Consider this shift another weapon you may master. I offered myself to you because together, we are stronger. We animals feel the imbalance of power in the world as well. Let us work together to heal it.

Sy closed his eyes again and searched his body with his mind, like he had when first learned to call on the shifter magic. He found the consciousness of his own body, his skin and muscle, the feel of his bare feet on grass, and how it felt to touch another person. And when he peered into the water again, he saw his own body.

"Coren?" he called, and he heard his own voice. She looked up from the opposite bank and waved, jumping to run toward him.

"You did it!" she exclaimed, jogging to where he sat. "Can you go back and forth?"

Sy shook his head, dizziness slowing the movement. "I feel like I'm about to pass out."

Kashar arrived next to them. "It takes tremendous power, but soon you'll be able to shift at will. Lemondrine would help, and you need to practice and build strength, like any other shift. But now you have the weapon you needed to wield against Graeme!"

Sy grinned, but he caught the shadow of disappointment cross Coren's face as she turned away. He wished she could have her power back, too.

But how would they ever find the wounded Vespa?

8

Nik held his bare shoulders rigid until he was certain Resh hadn't followed him, then he slumped in defeat, breaking into a desperate run. The beach soon gave way to rock, and he climbed and slipped, blinking away hot tears of rage.

He would not give in to the dark pull of any of those memories. Not of the slavers' torture, and certainly not the boy who had twisted his innocence and left him open and raw.

He had sworn long ago that none of it would have power over him ever again, but by the Magi, Resh had drawn it from its depths in his soul.

Perhaps it had been the act of opening Resh's veins. Seeing the trust Resh put in him, even if it wasn't exactly child-like, brought back too much. Too many innocent, young eyes, including his own, growing jaded and hopeless as their bodies were inundated with pain more often than their bellies were filled.

Seeing Resh's skin peeled open, the bones visible through the meat of his arm. Pulling apart the sources, taking measure of the blood and finding it lacking, always lacking. Hearing the dull swoosh and thud of skull against sand as pain overpowered consciousness.

Nik gritted his teeth against the crawling sensations on his bare skin. Throwing his arms wide, he yelled wordlessly into the open air. A nearby boulder blasted into dust, and he sank to his knees. He'd grown so much stronger since Coren rescued him from the slavers.

An amazing irony, that.

Nik tried to push his lips into an appreciative smile, but the shadows were still too strong at his back, although he knelt in an empty field in the mid-morning sun.

"You shouldn't be here. These are the women's plains."

The voice behind him shot through him like lightning across water, whipping him to his feet. A wavy-haired girl stood several feet away, carrying a woven-grass trap with a limp rockrabbit inside. She eyed his bare chest, and Nik suddenly wished he'd brought his shirt.

"I'm sorry, I didn't know," Nik said, curiosity rising. "Why are there separate areas for the women?"

The girl blinked at him, and he realized this must be a stupid question.

"I'm sorry," he repeated. "This is my first time on the island. I arrived yesterday, from Riata. With Resh," he added, lest she think him a spy and try to report him to Ashemon. If he were trespassing, that likely wouldn't improve their chances.

"Reshra," the girl repeated, narrowing her eyes. Something in her look was a warning to Nik, and a dark curiosity tugged a question from his lips.

"Do you know him?"

"Of course. Everyone knows the General's sons."

Her voice was tight, and Nik wondered what history the two had. "But you know more of him than you like," he guessed.

Her face flushed, but she kept her expression neutral.

"And what of Sy?" he asked, suddenly wondering if perhaps there was more to these brothers than he'd found so far.

"Syashin. First Son." She nodded, and her eyes softened a fraction. Nik grew hopeful. So this girl approved more of Sy than Resh. This was also his instinct. "When have you seen him?" she asked, hesitation halting her words.

"A few days ago," Nik answered before thinking. When her eyes widened in question, he remembered Sy and Coren had been banished. They were supposed to be dead. "He and Coren are alive and well in Riata," he offered, and she smiled, relief washing her face.

"I'm so glad," she whispered. "My name is Lorenya, by the way. I'm no one of consequence to the General, but Corentine is a good person. And Syashin is noble."

Nik's chest tightened at her words. *Noble.* Yes, that was a word he would use, too. "I'm Nikesh. Nik. Do you know them well?"

Lorenya shook her head. "I have been caught by both brothers, but only once each."

"Caught?"

"In the hunts," she said simply. Nik's stomach flipped as he realized this girl and Sy had been together. It twisted as he remembered the purpose for the hunts.

"Do you...did you and he have a child?" he stammered, hating the jealous heat he felt creeping up his neck.

Lorenya blushed as well, lowering her lashes as she shook her head. "I have four children, but none by the General's sons."

Nik didn't know what to say next. He wanted to ask her so many things, but all would have been intrusive. He opened his mouth, then shut it, then opened it again, but before a word had slipped out, a cry came from the sky above.

They both saw the gigantic creature at the same time, and Lorenya shrieked in terror, ducking to the ground. Nik instinctively bent to cover her, readying his shifting. Scorching summer air was forced down on them by the beat of the creature's wings as it dipped and circled the plains. It wasn't very close, but still so huge that Nik knew it must be a MagiCreature.

It swerved away into the far cliffs, and Lorenya whispered, "What was that?"

"I'm not sure. MagiCreature, by the size. But I've never seen one like it." It wasn't a Vespa; he knew that much from his time with Coren. Despite his training, Nik had seen very few MagiCreatures with his own eyes.

"MagiCreatures don't come to the women's island," Lorenya said, her voice a tremble of fear.

Nik had heard rumors of this protection, but he also knew everything changed. "The magic is returning to the Weshen. Perhaps the creatures will return as well."

She gaped at him. "So Coren? And Sy? It's true?"

Nik smiled, nodding. "And there are many others in Riata."

"Wesh," she supplied, standing.

"That's what I am."

"You have magic? But the General will surely banish you!"

Nik laughed. "I wouldn't be surprised. But Resh brought me here to help the others. To help Weshen find its magic again."

"Reshra brought you? But he hates magic! He's the one who found Corentine's magic and showed it to the General!"

Nik had known this, but hearing it again from someone who had been there brought up old suspicions of Resh. How had he changed his views so much? And why?

"Can you show me?" she whispered, watching his hands as they brushed grass from his shirt.

Nik smiled. There was something honest and simple in this girl: she was open, though she was wary enough to guard her trust. He liked her. He plucked a few blades of grass and held them in his palms. Separating their sources was easy, and he swirled the green mist until the water was pulled from the grass, leaving a pile of dry dust in one hand, and a sphere of light green liquid in the other. She reached to touch it, then drew back.

"It's okay. Here." Nik dropped the sphere in her hand, keeping its shape controlled as she rolled it and tried to squash it.

"Why doesn't it burst?" she marveled.

"Because I'm shaping its sources as you move it." He let go of the water, and it splashed over her hands.

"But how is this a weapon?" she asked, and he grinned. Coren had made the island women seem like shallow gossips who cared for nothing but boys. But Lorenya was different.

"I can make more than a tiny sphere of water. I can make a wall to keep a ship from passing. Or a funnel to drown a person. Or a path through the water for someone to walk into the ocean bed. Of course, my strength has limits," he added as the shine in her eyes grew.

She opened her mouth to ask another question, but a flicker of shadow passed between the sun and the plains.

Nik sensed the creature's magic this time, and he shouted as he shoved her to the ground beneath him. The force of the creature's wings flattened them to the earth for a few seconds.

The creature's scream was guttural and both high and low, like a bird's cry mixed with thunder. Nik twisted his face to see it, but it was only a blur of leathery wings and a long, sinuous body ending in a wickedly-spiked tail.

It swirled around them once more, rose in the air, and plummeted toward them again. Nik threw his hands in the air to block it with a rush of wind, but instead the earth they were lying on exploded around them, flinging rocks and clods of dirt up at the creature, and settling on top of their crouched bodies as though they were in a cave.

The sudden darkness disoriented Nik, and he clawed at the earth above him, punching through the thin layer of dirt.

Blue sky peeked through, and he sensed no more magic. He peered through the slight opening but saw nothing of the animal.

How had he lifted the earth when he meant to move the air?

Nik realized then that Lorenya had been silent since the earth had covered them. He pushed away more dirt, keeping them sheltered but allowing more light.

He cursed as her face came into view. Blood ran bright from her nose, and her eyes were closed. She breathed, though. Perhaps a stray rock had hit her face. He lifted a corner of her shirt and wiped the blood from her face. Something in it sparked to his touch.

Blinking, Nik held his fingers to the light. Where her blood flecked his hand, his blood seemed to rise to the surface. A slight golden sheen sparkled in the red smears.

"Shifter," he whispered, staring down at the girl. Then he looked again at the earth mound covering them. His magic hadn't gotten confused. *Hers* had created this shelter.

Nik scrambled to his feet, anxious to find Resh. They had none of the lemondrine tonic he knew Sy and Coren depended on. He didn't even know how to make it - he had been trained to revive his magic with time and meditation instead.

But Lorenya should have woken by now, even if she'd never used her shifting before.

"Lorenya," he whispered, shaking her shoulder gently. She didn't respond.

Nik quickly shifted the dirt away, smoothing the ground. He still saw nothing of the MagiCreature in the sky. Perhaps it had determined they weren't easy prey and moved on.

But as he scanned the horizon one last time, he spotted movement among the rocks.

Too small to be the creature. The figure came into better view, approaching steadily, and Nik breathed easier.

"Resh!" he called, waving his arm. "Hurry!"

Resh broke into a jog and was on them in seconds.

"What did you do?" he asked Nik.

"A creature attacked us. Something in the sky. I've never seen one before."

"Not a Vespa?"

Nik shook his head. "But just as large. Maybe more. Enormous wings."

"Did it hurt her?" Resh asked, peering at the bloodied piece of cloth and the few dark smears still on her cheek.

"No, listen. Resh...I think she shifted the earth."

Resh's eyes snapped to Nik's. "She has magic?"

Lorenya began to stir and groaned, shielding her eyes from the sun. Nik placed a hand behind her shoulder and helped her sit.

"What did you do?" Resh asked her, his voice sharp.

"Reshra!" she choked, and instinct seemed to send her scrambling to her feet. She swayed a bit, and Nik caught her, drawing her close.

"It's okay," he murmured in her ear. "The creature's gone. Resh won't hurt you. It's okay."

Her body was trembling against his, and her fingers grasped his wrist so tightly he thought the blood might cease flowing.

"Lorenya, have you ever shifted before?" Resh asked.

Her face paled, and she shook her head violently. "How could I even begin to know that magic?"

Resh narrowed his eyes at her.

Nik held up a hand. "Resh, relax. You're making her nervous. Lorenya, nothing is going to happen to you. Resh isn't going to have you sent away."

"Banishment?" she whispered, nearly crumpling in his arms. He tightened his grip, and she sank into his chest. "I can't...my children. No, please."

"I won't tell the General any of this," Resh snapped. "But do you have magic?"

She shrugged helplessly, her eyes round.

"Maybe the attack triggered it," Nik suggested. "Extreme emotions, like fear, can bring the magic to the surface just like the other methods."

Resh cocked his head, still studying the girl. A twist of a smile pulled at the corner of his lips. "Of all the girls on the island, I would not have suspected you," he said, turning his face to the sky. "But this is good. This means the others can wake their magic."

He turned back to Lorenya, who had begun to stand taller, though she still clutched Nik's arm.

"I've been thinking of a plan to present to Ashemon," Resh began. "I want to ask the men for volunteers to learn to shift. Nik, you can show them the process on me, and even though we'll lose some interest with that method, I think many of my men will agree to try."

"You want me to wake all of their magic?" Nik asked, and it was his turn to feel weak. He didn't think his mind could stand that. Inflicting just the few moments of pain on Resh this morning had brought so many horrible things to the surface.

"What about the women?" Lorenya spoke up. "What if some of them want to learn?" Her voice was strong again, and Nik smiled as she pushed away from him. "We're not all weak and stupid. We have skills beyond the bed and fire stove," she said, advancing a step toward Resh.

Resh grinned. "I do enjoy those skills, though. But yes, if any of the women want to learn magic, I think that would be wise. Though Ashemon probably won't let you off the island," he added, annoyance lacing his words.

"But if I have this magic, then I can protect my children. My home." She glanced at the sky. "If MagiCreatures can come here, then anything can. If the men begin fighting again in Riata, the women will be alone and vulnerable."

"You would train, then?" Resh asked.

Lorenya glanced to Nik. "I would train with you," she said to him. Nik smiled, and he couldn't help the push of pride that she'd chosen him, approved of him. There was some sour history between her and Resh, but at least she was willing to look beyond and into her future.

"We need to get back to camp. Ashemon will be looking for us," Resh said, already striding away.

Lorenya snickered. "He doesn't have magic, does he?" she whispered.

Nik shook his head. "No, but he wants it. What did he do to you?" he asked suddenly, wanting to know.

She glared at Resh's retreating back. "Nothing he wasn't taught to do. But not all girls are willing to be hunted, and not by all the boys. Syashin caught me, but I liked him. I allowed it. Reshra caught me out of competition. He was not honorable."

She gathered the trap with the rock rabbit and began to stalk away.

"If you don't want to be near him, I can train you alone," Nik called. She turned and smiled.

"Thank you. But if he doesn't have magic, and I do, I'll enjoy the opportunity to show him just what women are useful for."

Nik choked out a laugh. Yes, this girl would make a good student, and maybe even a powerful shifter one day.

He hoped there were hundreds more with magic snaking through their veins, just waiting to be woken.

Even more, he hoped he wouldn't have to use the slavers' methods to wake it.

Once Sy recovered his energy, they moved quickly. The cheetairs had indeed dropped them within a day's journey of the palace, even accounting for the detour of Sy's Grizzlin shifting.

Rounding a bend in the trail, Sy saw the palace come into view, and he had the sensation that he had been virtually nowhere in his life. Kashar had described StarsHelm Palace, and there were drawings in Ashemon's journals, but none of it could begin to chip away at the dwarfing effect of standing before such a massive structure.

It rose above the city like a hulking shadow, glistening walls of black marble and ebony turrets reaching into the clouds. White stone streaked and spiraled up at the corners, marking the many wings and added structures. From this distance, the pattern of white and black appeared prominent and planned.

"The King has added much to the palace in his reign," Kashar muttered. "It wasn't always this size."

The blackish-green of Riata's infamous maze tangled around the castle grounds, massive and threatening. It draped the gentle slopes like a thick cloak, protecting the palace from its own city's supplicants as much as from outside threat. To the west, the city crowded its walls and crimson-tiled roofs against the maze from all angles, like disorganized beggars at the feet of the King himself.

Sy couldn't take his eyes away from the maze. Its edges were shrouded in an odd mist that seemed to seep from the very leaves and branches of the woven vines. He shivered, though the evening was still warm. He would hate to be in there, lost and disoriented.

"It's spelled," Kashar said, and they both turned to him. He gestured. "The maze. It's spelled so it's never the same. You might find your way out once and never again, or the maze might decide to point you in the direction it wants you to go. Many have disappeared forever in those twisted corridors."

Coren's eyes were as round as the moon above them, and Sy was glad he wasn't the only one intimidated by StarsHelm palace.

"I'll show you the easiest way in and out, but if you choose to sneak away, I cannot help you. You must rely on me," he warned.

Evidently Coren and her father had come to a sort of understanding, because she nodded without protest.

"Who are we to take on this task?" he murmured as they watched the torches of the city flare to life.

Kashar turned midnight eyes on them, intense and pleading. "You are the only Weshen SelfShifters we know of. Syashin, you're the First Son of General Havenash, and heir to Weshen City. And you," he nodded to Coren, "have the blood of the most powerful Weshen family that ever existed in your veins. You may have seen only its dregs in your mother, but she sacrificed more than her life for you children. Once we find that Vespa - and we will - you two will be the greatest force Riata has dealt with in two generations."

"But Shadow was sleeping during that time, wasn't it," Coren said.

Kashar considered. "We have little knowledge of Shadow and Umbren. Little of blood magic. But I think you're right. Only the witches have kept their spells, but they struggle against each other more than against the outside world."

He adjusted the strap of his bag and began to walk. Sy glanced at Coren, and he saw her take a deep breath, as though to fortify herself for the coming tasks. He felt the same. He'd fought MagiCreatures and slavers, but he'd never been in a true battle. Never hidden in wait, making plans of assassination.

They crossed the last bit of wooded area quickly, slipping into the city without issue. There was no wall around it to protect the citizens, and Sy wondered at the design.

"Where do the people go if attacked?" he asked.

"Attack from an army has never come to StarsHelm," Kashar answered, shrugging. "And so they have never built city walls, in an ostentatious display of power. But the city is warded in many ways besides stone."

"Sulit spells," Coren guessed, and Kashar nodded.

"The King and his guards know everyone who enters and exits the city by their magical detection. They will know I have returned because special alarms are set up for me. That's why it's vital that you stay near. It's expected that I'll be traveling with Wesh prisoners who have shifter magic. If you're alone, your magic would be detected and flagged as a spy, or an attack, or even just a boon for the slavers."

"Do the Sulit work *with* Graeme?" Sy asked, surprised. Surely this many spells were not the work of enslaved witches. It would not be wise for the King to put so much trust in his servants.

"Many do. I'm never surprised by what money and luxury can convince someone to do, and there are several spoiled Brujok in Queen Mara's employ. But most of the witches under Graeme's control are like the Wesh he possesses."

"Slaves," Coren supplied. "What will happen to all of this?" she wondered.

"What do you mean?" Kashar asked. Sy thought he knew what she meant, though.

"If we kill Graeme - *when* we do - what will happen to the city? To its people? They're not evil just because they're Riatan."

"Chaos," Sy said. "It would become a civil war like in Sulit."

Kashar nodded. "Graeme has no heirs. Only a few advisers. They would fight each other, and the winner might take the throne."

"Or you?" Coren asked.

Kashar laughed, drawing the attention of a beggar woman in a nearby doorway. She rattled her cup at him, and he added a few coins to it. "I'm not the one for that."

"Perhaps someone neutral, then. A peacekeeper who could sort out the countries and tribes Graeme has conquered and send them home. Someone who could dissolve the Riata we know and allow people to be free."

Coren's suggestion sounded naive to Sy. The fall of an empire would not be met with peace.

"No," Kashar said. "Many of those under Riata's control no longer have a home to return to. They must stay here. A strong leader must be in place because if one mighty kingdom stumbles, another will rise in its place. Perhaps one even worse."

They walked the emptying streets in silence for several minutes. The stalls and shops had shuttered and closed as the sun sunk lower, giving the city an abandoned feel. Not like EvenFall, where taverns and hotels blazed to life at dusk, and a whole new crowd of spenders emerged from the houses.

"Is night a threat here?" Sy asked.

"Yes. It's very dangerous to be on the streets after dark," Kashar confirmed. "But we're nearly there."

They rounded a corner and ducked into an alley that appeared to end in a brick wall covered in vines. Kashar glanced behind them, watching for a few seconds before pushing aside the curtain of vines. He motioned them forward. As Sy stepped into the dark opening, he realized he was inside the palace maze.

"This is a secret, spelled entrance. Its spell counters the maze's main spell and allows us to slip into the palace quickly. Most of the time," Kashar added. "Magic is unpredictable, especially Sulit spells, which rely on the Sulit Mother - the power of the natural world."

They hurried through the green-black vines whose flowers were just on the cusp of closing for the night. A tendril reached out to Coren as she passed, delicately stroking along her neck, and Sy saw her jump away. Another vine flicked at his cheek, and he recoiled.

"It's okay. The vines are tasting your magic. It's part of the spells," Kashar said.

"That's not reassuring," Coren said, dodging another looping vine.

"Just stay with me," he replied.

The palace loomed above them, framed by thousands of stars, and Sy again felt a sense of insignificance as they wove through the narrow halls of the maze.

Insignificance broke into helplessness as they turned a corner, and the vines grew between Coren and him in an instant, like a curtain dropping.

"Coren!" he called, unable to reach or see her through the dense vines whipping at his face, pushing him back like arms.

"I'm here!" Her voice was muffled, as though very far away.

Kashar roared at the maze, drawing his dagger and hacking at the vines. They only snaked around his wrist, relieving him of his weapon and secreting it away within the hedge. The ground seemed to roll beneath them, the rosewhip roots rising and urging them along, closer to the palace and farther from Coren.

"I'll find you, Corentine!" Kashar yelled. "Keep the palace in your sights! I'll find you!"

9

As soon as the intruders had entered the maze, the silent alarms had begun.

Magic, magic, magic, they hummed into the ground.

The words pulsed like a second heartbeat in the ears of the witches hidden in the palace's corners. The palace Brujok were fierce guards, and they had kept Zorander Graeme's grounds safe from magical attack for dozens of years.

They had also located some of the strongest witches and shifters trying to enter the palace in secret.

But none had ever been so strong as the presence detected tonight.

Grand breathed deeply, imagining she could even catch the scent of MagiCreature. If these intruders could shift…. She cast a spell into the wind, doubling her running speed as she tore through the convoluted passageways to the Queen's chambers.

The second heartbeat of warning changed to a triple beat as it invaded her skull as well.

She knew her guards wouldn't wait much longer for her instructions. They all loved a good chase.

Aram was the first one she saw.

He nodded as though he knew why Grand was here, opening the door only enough to make her squeeze through.

Grand sneered at him. He was always testing the guards, seeing how far they could be pushed in their struggle between loyalty and dignity. She had no time for those games tonight.

"My Queen, there are intruders," she began.

"I have sensed it, too," Mara answered softly, her back to Grand as she stood before an open section of the wall-width window. The black corridors and twists of the maze were spread far below her, but they were too high to see anyone who might be running it. "I don't think it means to attack us now. The magic is moving away. Lost in the desires of the maze."

Grand saw her own reflection in the window glass. Her smile grew sharp and lethal, a slit of inside-out blade as her red lips parted over her silvered teeth. She loved it when they got lost.

Mara turned, and in the opposing glows of silver moonlight and golden candlelight, Grand was struck at how little the Queen had aged over the decades.

Sulit spells could only help so much, and Grand had no idea what else Mara used.

Mara stalked forward, her lavender skirts swishing with each step. She studied Grand as the witch examined her. Grand noticed that though her skin was still smooth and her body lithe and firm, her eyes had begun to crack and sink away, like those of a fresh corpse losing its water.

Mara raised a brow, as though she could hear Grand's thoughts.

"I want these intruders for myself. Do not allow your guard to report this to Zorander," she instructed. "And Grand, be certain to mark the signature. If they escape tonight, I think they will return."

"My Queen?" The question slipped out, and Grand stepped backward slightly, regret tightening her muscles.

But Mara was already turning away, disinterested in punishment tonight. "I've felt this level and type of magic before. It's been gone long enough that its appearance tonight is no accident, nor has it escaped my notice that our Prodigal Weshen Knight is in the maze as well. Mark it, Grand."

Grand bowed to the Queen's back and hurried out of the room, ignoring Aram's dark gaze as she slipped past him.

Magical signatures were always unique, but certain patterns could be found. Grand sped through the halls and down the spiral stairs to the section of the maze where the intruders had been sensed.

She wondered if the Queen detected a pattern of family or teacher. Either would be interesting enough to examine the intruders a little herself before handing them over to Mara.

After all, Queen Mara's interests weren't the only ones she served.

She crept into the maze, arms stretched wide, her fingertips ruffling through the tangle of vines at both sides. They guided her, tugging her one way and the other, until the alarms beat like war drums, nearly unbearable in her skull and ribcage.

Turning a last corner, Grand saw her. She was moving away down the corridor, her steps slow and her back rigid beneath her pack. Grand thrilled to the power seething from the girl.

Shifter, she whispered to the wind, knowing the vines would carry the word to her sister guards.

Mine, she added, drawing nearer. The alarms subsided, allowing Grand the presence of mind to ready a spell. She drew a dagger as well, just in case.

The girl's pace slowed even more, and Grand knew by the tilt of her head that she was listening. She'd noticed the witch following her, and she was paying attention. She wasn't panicking and waving a weapon at an invisible threat. She was waiting. Gathering information. A hunter, then.

Grand raised a thin eyebrow. This *was* interesting - she'd never met a female Weshen hunter.

Just as the girl neared the corner of the living hallway, the vines moved and twined together, blocking her exit. It seemed the maze also wanted to see a demonstration of the girl's power. Grand swelled with the anticipation of winning a fight and bringing her Queen a prize.

Or maybe keeping the prize herself, if it were the right kind.

The girl turned fluidly, dropping the weight of her bag and drawing a dagger in the same movement. Then another weapon appeared in her opposite hand, like a snakka descending from beneath her tunic.

A whip.

Grand hadn't seen one like it before, but she smelled the tang of iron lacing its braid. *Blood magic.* Not yet strong, but this, too, was something rarely seen at StarsHelm. Grand wanted to clap and dance like a child.

Queen Mara would be *very* interested indeed to meet this strong young shifter who dabbled in darkness.

"What do you want?" the girl said, her voice low. There was no quiver of fear in her gaze, though Grand thought she could scent it.

"I'm here to invite you to tea with Her Majesty," Grand said, the offer sounding as false as it was true. Mara's odd habit of dining with intruders was infamous. A last meal of sorts, before she shredded them and scraped the magic from their bones, soaking her half-moon blades in their blood.

"Another time, perhaps." The whip snapped at the air between them, like a snakka's tongue tasting the wind. "I have something more pressing just now."

"And what could be more important than meeting your Queen?" Grand was stalling, pulling at the words for a truth spell. She began to whisper them beneath her breath.

"She is not my Queen," the girl spat. "I would slice her throat if given the chance."

Her expression when the words slipped out against her will drew a cackle from Grand. It had been a long while since her spells had been this easy to wield. The girl's power was honing her own, drawing it out to play. And the young thing was weak, untrained in resistance.

Oh, this would be so much fun.

Grand opened her mouth to ask another question, but the girl shifted the earth and opened a chasm in the

125

ground between them. Grand stumbled forward, sliding into the earth nearly her body's height. She scrabbled with the vines, wrapping them around her wrists and commanding them to draw her back up.

Wind whipped through the passage, the force of it knocking one arm loose from the vines. Grand shrieked a spell to the maze, to wrap around the girl and stall her waving hands.

But even with her arms spread and bound to the wall of rosewhip thorns, the girl managed to shift the ground beneath them. It rolled like ocean waves, unearthing the roots of the plants and toppling the walls of the maze.

Grand was breathing hard, struggling to stay on her feet, too disoriented to cast another spell. How could she capture this shifter without killing her?

The vines began to slip from around the girl's wrists, and Grand decided brute force was better than magic just now. She snatched her dagger from her belt and hurled it, end over end. The blunt bone handle of it struck the girl's temple, barely splitting the skin, and her eyes rolled back. The ground settled, crumbs of earth rolling into new ruts.

The vines slowly knitted themselves together like an animal licking its wounds. The roots inserted themselves back into the fresh-turned soil, righting the walls of the maze. Grand stepped closer to the girl, watching her carefully to make certain she wasn't pretending.

Her breathing was steady, though, and her eyes didn't move behind their lids. Grand nodded, satisfied, just as the alarms began again.

The other intruder. Grand closed her eyes to better focus on the signature the alarms were beating into her chest. Another shifter! And just as strong! Her eyes and lips flew open as she began to chant the spell that would bring her sister guards to her.

It was time for pride to take a step back.

She wasn't going to lose either of these Weshen tonight.

The last word left her lips just as the girl behind her began to breathe differently. The notice was not enough for Grand, though. The vines slipped from the shifter's arms, dissolving into a haze of green.

The girl's amber eyes flashed golden as the green mist sucked itself together, forming not a tangle of narrow vines, but a single, thick rope. It hit Grand in the mouth with enough force to knock her backward, crushing her lips to her teeth with a slick of blood and binding the spells in her throat. The rope twisted down and around her chest and waist, wrapping her arms to her sides.

"Tell the Queen I'll take her offer if she can wait for my return," the girl said, bending low to whisper in Grand's ear. Grand struggled and fought against the vines, but it seemed their magical alliance had changed with their form.

Shame in being bested subsided as her heart beat in excitement. The shifter girl had changed not just the outward source, but the inner source as well! Grand would have thought it impossible.

Oh, the power in this one…. Her sisters in Rurok must be told.

She closed her eyes and breathed as deeply as she could, filling her body with the girl's scent and signature. When this girl returned, she and her sisters would be ready.

Grand watched her shoulder the bag and disappear around the corner. She was strong, but not enough to beat a dozen Brujok. Her sisters were coming, and they would hunt this girl.

War was beginning in Sulit, and this shifter was exactly what the Brujok needed to win against their southern sisters, then advance into Riata. Mara had always been good to the witches, but it had been too many years of waiting. The Brujok chafed under the control of StarsHelm.

The power walking away from her now could be their key to unlocking Zorander Graeme's hold on the world.

"Sy! This way!" Kashar yelled as they ran through the maze. They were frantic to find Coren before the palace guards. "Stop trying to shift the vines, or more alarms will sound, and we'll have a dozen Brujok to fight!"

Sy pulled the magic back to him, hating that he had no other way to help Coren. He'd only taken a minute to grab his bow sword from his bag before trying to shift the maze and find her, but she'd disappeared immediately. Shouts followed them already through the maze. He focused on staying close to Kashar, who seemed to know where he was going, at least.

Sy cursed the Sulit magic as he ran, sympathizing with how Resh had always distrusted witches.

Suddenly, Kashar shoved him sideways through a tiny gap in the vines, one he hadn't even noticed. They stumbled out of the maze walls and onto a dusty stone walkway leading to a mass of carved columns set in rows six deep.

"The training arena," Kashar said, pulling Sy along. "I need to get you cloaked before we go any further."

"But Coren-"

"Can handle herself against the guards, I think. I promise I will find her. But your Grizzlin shift *must* be hidden!"

"I won't leave her in there!" Sy protested, skidding to a stop.

Kashar swerved back to him. "You're no good to any of us dead, which is what you'll be if the King gets his hands on your magic. *You're* the weapon now, not her. We have to keep you safe!"

Everything in Sy rejected this, but Kashar yanked at his arm. "This won't take long, and it will keep you safe. You know nothing of the maze. Leave that to me. Use your brain, boy."

Sy wanted to fight the man, but his words rang true. Their mission would be even more compromised if he were caught. And Kashar would die himself before he let Coren suffer at the hands of the guards, that much he knew. He hated the decision, but he knew Coren would want him to make it.

They wove through the columns, finally reaching a back wall and a series of doors. Kashar pushed through one of them and banged on a second, interior door.

"It's me! I need your spell now!" he called.

The door cracked, then opened just enough to let them inside. A rotund man peered up at them in the semi-darkness of the room. He was dressed in a nightshirt, and his legs were comically thin against the bulk of his body. His head barely reached Sy's chest.

"I was sleeping," he said, annoyance in his reedy voice.

"And I apologize. I had every intention of seeing you properly tomorrow, but-"

"But you always seem to have urgent issues. I know," the man waved him away, his mouth splitting wide in a yawn. He lit a candle and held it to Sy's face. "My," he murmured, traveling the light down Sy's body.

Sy stepped backward, beginning to feel very uncomfortable.

"It will be a *pleasure* to cloak you." The man smiled, and Sy glanced at Kashar, who seemed to be biting back a smile.

Kashar stepped toward the door. "Stay here. I promise I'll find Corentine. I know the maze."

And with that, he was gone, leaving Sy alone in the room with the strange little man.

"Shall we?" the man said, setting down the candle and rubbing his plump palms together. "I am Giddon, by the way. Please remove all of your clothing."

"What?" Sy said, stepping back again and cursing Kashar in his head.

"I can't cloak you *through* the fabric, boy. Skin," Giddon said, his smile growing coy.

"What are you? Not Sulit." Sy said, stalling. He truly did not want to undress before Giddon. He should be helping find Coren.

"Of course I'm not Sulit," Giddon laughed. "I'm a man. But my family is from the WestenSands. I visited Sulit often, and I've become quite the spellmaster in my life. Graeme keeps me here to test his soldiers and keep an eye on the Brujok guards."

Sy shook his head again. Brujok were the fiercest kind of witch. And Coren was alone in the maze with them. "I need to-"

"Relax, my young man. The Knight will find your friend. He knows the maze better than most. Now, off with it. The cloaking doesn't hurt a bit, and I promise not to touch you," he sighed.

Sy ground his teeth but told himself Kashar wouldn't have gone alone if he couldn't handle it. The faster he got this done, the sooner he could help Coren. So, trying his best to ignore the small man's greedy eyes, he stripped his shirt and pants and underclothes.

Giddon paced in slow, repetitive circles around Sy, tossing a fine-grained sand at him as he muttered indecipherable words. The sand was sticky-smooth, and it coated Sy's skin with a subtle sheen of blue, as though Sy were looking at himself under the water.

"There," Giddon said finally, stepping back to admire Sy. Sy glared at him, but Giddon just shrugged. "I just enjoy my work," he grinned. "The spell will last until you bathe and wash away the powder. It won't rub off without water."

Sy scrubbed at a spot on his arm, finding the blue did indeed only seem to intensify, rather than brush away.

"Can I dress now?" he asked.

"If you must."

Sy hastened into his pants and was just reaching for his shirt when another knock sounded at the door. Kashar's voice rang out, and Giddon scrambled to open the door, drawing his fingernails in a complex pattern on the wood before the knob turned on its own.

Coren stumbled in, Kashar at her back. Sy crushed her within his arms, relief flooding into his veins.

"I thought you were lost," he whispered against her hair.

I'm okay, Sy," she murmured against his collar bone, returning his embrace. Then she pulled back and studied his bare chest. "Why are you blue?"

"Hello, I'm Giddon," the man said, pushing his hand between them. "If you would, please undress."

"What?" Coren cried, slapping Giddon's hand away. Sy snatched at her wrist, which had already begun to flick her whip down from its coils on her arm.

"It's okay, Coren. He's going to cloak your magic." He rubbed at his stomach, and her eyes fastened on his skin, still a pale, shimmering blue. "But he needs to put the powder on your skin."

"No," she shook her head at Giddon. "You're not touching me."

Giddon sighed and held his hands out in surrender. "Kashar, you owe me double for tonight. Even with the pleasure. Next time, give your friends a little more information."

Coren snorted. "That seems to be a common request for the Prodigal Knight." She glanced at her father. "Corner. Both of you."

Kashar nodded, and the two turned their backs. Sy heard the swish and drop of her clothing, then the soft murmur of incantation and the brush of powder on skin.

"It's done," Giddon said several minutes later.

132

"How does this help us hide if we're blue?" Coren asked.

"The color will fade soon, remaining just barely visible. That's why I skipped the exposed skin of your faces and hands. So, you *will* register as possessing magic, but only a fraction of the power you truly have. As long as you remain dressed and don't bathe, you will be safe from the guards."

Coren groaned, cursing lightly under her breath.

Sy checked himself in the round mirror on Giddon's wall, noticing that where he had smudged the powder before, the blue had already faded from his fingertips. Kashar produced a handful of thick Riatan coins, each stamped with the crest of the Graeme family.

"We can stay in the palace safely?" Sy asked. He wasn't sure he trusted the strange spells. The maze had also used Sulit spells, and it hadn't protected them. The witches' powers from nature didn't seem to follow rules and laws like shifter magic did.

"Safe from the alarms," Giddon said. "There are plenty of other dangers in the palace."

"Thank you, Giddon, as always." Kashar bowed and exited, motioning for them to follow him.

Just as Sy was almost to the door, Giddon grabbed his arm and pulled his ear close.

"I don't know why you're here, young man, but your power...it could save us all. Please remember us. We Riatans may look content. We might not show our scars. But we have them. I hide behind humor and my work. Kashar hides behind his good deeds. But the Restless King has come for all of us at one time or another, and he will come again, and *again*, until he has everything. His greed is insatiable."

Sy stood and stared down at the man, whose face was so desperately earnest. So frightened and laid bare of all the teasing humor of before.

"Sy?" Coren called from the hallway.

"Coming!" He bent low to the man. "We are here to help, but please be patient."

Giddon smiled, then sadness pulled the edges of his mouth into a grimace. "Patience is all most of us have left."

He shuffled to the corner and picked up a broom. He began to sweep the remainder of the powdery blue sand into a tidy pile, eyes downcast, never again looking at Sy.

10

Resh stood before his father in the semi-darkness of the General's tent. He had finished the story of finding Sy, of Coren's shift into a Vespa form, of rescuing the Wesh, of his injury at the claws of Shadow.

And he was waiting for a single word of response.

"How many wait for you in EvenFall?" Ashemon asked finally, barely looking up from his journal.

"Two wounded adults and four children. They stay with a Wesh healer named Shanta and her friends."

Ashemon snorted. "Wounded. Children. These are the additions you propose to our army? You are now First Son by default, but you'll never match your brother's ability to lead."

The words hit Resh like a blow, and he reeled back a step. Nik's firm hand between his shoulder blades steadied him, though, reminding him what they were here to do.

"The magic is back, Father. I was wrong about Corentine using Sulit spells. She is a powerful shifter."

Ashemon finally looked up, studying his son. "You covet her power. You have no magic of your own."

It wasn't a question, and Resh didn't answer it. His father had determined the truth regardless.

"I ask permission to train any of our men who are willing."

"Train them in what? How can you train them with a weapon you do not possess?" Ashemon sneered.

Resh struggled to overcome his temper. Words like this were like a lullaby from Father General.

"I possess it," Nik said, stepping in front of Resh. "I spoke to you last night of the horrors I have witnessed. I wish that pain on no one. But the slavers know what they're doing, and the Restless King owns hundreds of shifters. He grows always stronger, never weaker. Shadow, too, grows stronger, never weaker. Even Sulit is in uproar, witch against witch against all of Riata. General Ashemon, even if you don't approve of Weshen rising to meet Riata, you must understand that by not accessing the magic as it does return, you're allowing Riata to rise even further. You're making your people more vulnerable. Once the King learns the shifting is back, Weshen will be in incredible danger."

Ashemon rose, staring down at Nik. Resh knew the look on his face. The General was fighting his anger. Resh reached reflexively to pull Nik out of striking distance, but Ashemon only turned abruptly away.

"Volunteers only. And I will not have a crowd gather to watch."

"What?" Resh asked, stupid with surprise.

Ashemon turned back and caught his younger son in a harsh glare. "The boy may be right, but if even one of

136

my men is injured by this experiment, then we have gained nothing. I place the responsibility on you, Reshra."

He sat again, dismissing the boys with a flick of his fingers as he returned to his book.

Outside, Nik breathed a laugh. "He's like a hollow rock, your father. Intimidating, until you find where to strike."

Resh smiled, but it was he who felt hollow. His father doubted his ability completely. But Resh would prove him wrong. Here in Weshen, then one day in Riata.

The return of shifter magic meant so much more than renewed Weshen power.

It meant that the world itself was shifting. Countries would fall and new ones rise.

They spent the morning talking to the men, and Nik demonstrated his power again and again, until he pleaded for rest and food.

Perhaps a third of the active Paladins agreed to return that day for the training, and even a few of the older men who no longer left the city for missions.

After lunch, they gathered in a secluded section of the beach. Tagsha was the last to arrive, a sheepish curiosity widening his eyes. Resh smiled at the guard, thankful that he, too, was challenging Ashemon's stubborn beliefs.

Just as Resh was about to begin, a group of four women arrived, led by Lorenya.

She said nothing, only raising an eyebrow to Resh in challenge. Resh saw Nik bite back a smile.

"I've spoken to most of you today," Resh said, glancing to the women, "but just to be clear. Nik has learned many methods of waking magic in dormant shifters. Some are painful. We'll start with the easy ones, but if something becomes too much for you to bear, please step aside and allow another to take your place. A threat from Riata rises against us, but Weshen trains to be ready!"

Several of the men cheered at the familiar training mantra, and one stood. "I'll go first."

Resh nodded at him. "Thank you for your faith in us. First, though, we'll be doing some exercises to stretch our awareness of the magic."

A snicker sounded from the men, but Resh ignored it. He also ignored whispered comments about baby steps being for babies and instructed everyone to close their eyes and listen to Nik.

"The magic rests in your veins," Nik began. "It sleeps. It's dormant. You must find it and wake it, but this isn't easy until you accept that it's been there all along. I believe the Magi allows the magic to awaken in anyone who is ready to wield its power fairly and for a just cause."

He paused to let the words sink in, and Resh couldn't help but wonder if Nik meant the last bit for him. True, he wanted the power to help Weshen rise. But he wanted it for so much more.

"Shifter magic has many levels, many abilities within these levels," Nik continued. "All shifters can SourceShift, and that will be your first skill. Sources make up everything in our world. Your skin is made of sources. The sand on the beach is a mix of sources. Even the wind carries sources within its movement. Once you learn to feel the sources, you can learn to move the earth and water without touching it, and control the breeze and embers of a fire. Open your awareness to what is around you. Feel the movement of the blood within your veins. Your magic is there."

Nik was quiet for several long moments, waiting for everyone to perform the exercise.

Resh struggled to focus. His eyes kept blinking open, watching the men to gauge their interest and commitment. Most were quiet and serious, attempting Nik's instructions with as much intensity as they normally used when practicing with a bow sword or longknife.

"Now, feel the sand and rocks beneath you. There's an energy to the sources, and each is different. This allows us to sort or separate the sources, the way a child sorts rocks into piles by color and shape."

Resh felt nothing, and he was growing restless. But he pushed against his impatience, willing the magic to make itself known.

Nearly an hour later, Nik allowed everyone to rest and stretch. One man strode away, claiming all he'd found was the desire for a nap. Resh looked to Nik. "Is it time for another method? I don't want to lose anyone else."

Nik's eyes flashed in objection, but he nodded.

Resh called everyone back together. "Sometimes the magic can be woken with strong emotion. Fear, grief, or extreme happiness can call forth the magic."

"When you experience these emotions, take time to search for the sources," Nik added. "Don't try to distract yourself from feeling, but instead examine your reactions. Magic is often felt here." He clutched his hand to his stomach and then his chest.

With no warning, rocks from the cliffs above began to tumble and hurtle down toward the group. Resh had known Nik would shift the stone, but he still felt a surge of fear for his people as dozens of boulders slid and bounced down the cliff, large enough to smash any of them.

Many of the people were shouting and scrambling backward into the ocean for safety, but a few were stunned into stillness, watching the rocks hurtling toward them. Just as the rocks were mere feet above their heads, they burst into a shower of dust and pebbles. Everyone gasped in relief, but Nik wasn't done yet. At their backs, a tidal wave rose, taller than two men. It crashed down on them with enough force to knock them under in the shallow water.

Resh struggled with his fear that an accident might injure one of them. Ashemon would stop their work before it began.

"Nik!" he cried, just as another wave rose to challenge the few still standing.

The waves parted with a crash, exposing the sea bed and the spluttering people. One figure stood upright in the wet sand, arms stretched wide.

Lorenya, Resh realized. She yelled at the others to get to safety just as her strength gave way, and the water splashed together, swallowing her. She bobbed to the surface within seconds, though, and Nik applauded her.

Everyone straggled back to their places on the beach, coated in dust and soaked with saltwater.

"I can't replicate happiness, and I don't ever want to make you grieve," Nik said to the crowd. "But I know fear. Were any of you afraid?"

They all nodded, whispering to each other as they gazed up at Nik. Resh saw the moment a few of his men realized this slim boy could kill all of them with a twist of his fingers.

"Good. Did anyone feel the sources?"

Lorenya grinned. "I felt the water." Several of them laughed.

"What did it feel like?" one of the women asked her.

She flushed under their gazes. "It felt...like a rush of sweet wind inside me, warming every part of me. My fingers were tingling like I'd touched a warm stove. Not hot enough to burn, but a twinge."

Nik grinned at her description. "Magic can be very sensual. That rush of power is a pleasure to use, especially if you're doing something you want, like saving your friends." He nodded to her, once and deeply, and she reddened even more.

Resh thought idly that Nik was quite the charmer, and he was glad the boy was handling the people so well.

"But what if we still felt nothing?" a man called from the back of the group.

Nik glanced at Resh. "There are other ways, but all of them are painful. And they don't always work right away. And some people simply don't seem to have magic."

"This was true generations ago," Resh reminded them. "There were always some Weshen who possessed no real shifting magic. And just like with physical strength or talent with a weapon, there will be those who have more natural ability."

"Would you like to try what we did yesterday?" Nik asked Resh in a low voice.

"Yes," Resh agreed, although he was wary of showing such a great weakness before his men. "They should see before they commit."

Nik nodded and began to explain his process. Resh lay back, slipping his belt from his waist again.

Moments later, his eyes screwed shut in pain as Nik opened his flesh and stirred the blood from his veins, separating the sources in the hopes of finding magic. Resh bit and ground into the leather of the belt, resisting a scream as long as he could. Resisting the blackness of unconsciousness as many minutes as possible.

But both overpowered his will, and it was some time later when Nik was shaking him gently awake, holding a cold strip of fabric to his temple.

"They've all gone. I sent them away to decide," Nik said.

"They'll come back," a female voice said from nearby. Resh blinked his eyes open slowly to see Lorenya sitting nearby, an unreadable expression on her face.

"How do you feel?" Nik asked.

"Normal. That is, not magical," Resh grunted, sitting. Disappointment flooded through him.

"Why do you want it so?" Lorenya asked, studying him. "You have so many other privileges."

Resh slid his eyes to her. He remembered catching her. He knew he'd done it roughly, with anger at his brother. He'd used her to try to figure out Sy's mysteries.

"I'm sorry," he murmured, dropping his gaze. "I'm not the same boy who hunted you because of Sy."

She stiffened, and he saw Nik's interest fasten on their conversation, no doubt at the mention of Sy's name.

"I don't know if it matters, but I'd like to think I've changed. Grown. Learned. My horizon is larger."

She looked away, toward the ocean. "Mine is not." She rose and gathered her damp skirt in her hands. "But I accept your apology."

Kashar showed Sy and Coren to a vacant room deep in the knights' quarters and left to fetch their dinner.

"Get some sleep," he advised when he delivered the plates of food. "Don't leave this room until I come for you in the morning. There's a bathroom beyond that door, but careful of the powder."

Coren nodded and locked the door after him. She ran her fingers over the lock. It seemed flimsy, and an idea flashed into her mind. She shifted the wood of the door into that of the wall, weaving the sources together until no door existed at all.

She grinned at Sy, and he raised a brow. "How will he get back in?"

"We'll let him in," she said with a shrug. "But now no-one but another shifter could enter."

Sy pursed his lips. "I'm sure there's other magic here that could breach it, but it's clever."

"I hope he brings good news in the morning. If only we had a quick, easy plan, and we could be done with Riata this moon. Then I could go to Sulit."

Sy sank onto one of the beds. "I know you're worried about your family, but I promise we'll find them. First,

143

we need to finish what we came here for. Weshen may not have a chance like this again."

"I know." She stretched her limbs on the bed, slipping under the thin blanket. She looked up and over at him and remembered how she once had to force herself to trust him. Now it was natural. But she couldn't trust his judgment with this because he didn't know everything. She had to tell him.

"I'm afraid, Sy," she admitted in a whisper.

"Of getting caught? That worries me, but with my Grizzlin shift-"

She shook her head. "Of success. Of what will happen to me if I continue to kill. I didn't need to kill that man in Weshen City. And I didn't have to kill that slaver to rescue Nik. But I did, and I was proud of myself for it. I shouldn't be proud of murder."

"I would have done the same," Sy broke in fiercely. "Coren, when people misuse the lives of others - when they cause more harm than good - they lose their rights. I'd prefer imprisonment over death, but sometimes the only way to protect the good is to remove the evil."

She didn't ask her next question, but it hung in the air between them. What if she lost control again like she'd done with Kashar? What if she *became* the evil that needed removing? She was no-one to decide the tipping point between harm and good.

Sy leaned back on the bed, stretching his arms up behind his head. Even in such a relaxed pose, she'd never seen him stronger. He could handle this burden himself, and she wished she were strong enough to ask him to do it.

Weshen needed freedom, but she didn't want such a cornerstone role in its liberation anymore.

She rolled to her stomach and pressed her face into the pillow. "I just want to save my family and live a quiet life." She remembered standing on a plain on Weshen Isle, wishing just the opposite.

But this was nothing like what she'd yearned for.

"Coren, you may not have been raised as a leader, like me. But the Magi didn't give you this power to hide. That anonymous *somewhere* doesn't exist for us. Our magic will always be tracked. You can be hunted for a pawn, or you can fight as a force of your own will. You told me once that nothing is small when it's against your will. But your will isn't the only one being imposed on."

Coren remembered what Resh had insisted on the rooftops of EvenFall: her family wasn't more important than anyone else.

She still chafed against the stark truth in his words.

Sy reached over to grasp her fingers. "Together, we can do more. Once we have Resh and Nik back, we can do it all. We just need to trust each other."

Coren felt her chest grow warm with affection. He was right - together they had so much more power. "I spent so many years shutting out everyone who could hurt my family or me. Thank you for not giving up on me."

Sy smiled, and they drifted into sleep, his fingers tight around hers across the open space between their beds.

Coren slept restlessly, though, her dreams filled with seven hazy figures, golden and shadowed at the same time. They advanced on her, then retreated, over and over. She never saw their faces, but her ears rang with the echoes of their cruel laughter as she was jolted awake by an impatient banging at the sealed door.

"Let me in!" Kashar yelled. "We have a problem!"

They scrambled to their feet, and Coren instinctively began pulling on her boots as Sy shifted the solid wall into a movable door again.

"Two problems, actually," Kashar amended as he clicked the bolt behind himself. "First, Graeme isn't even here. He left for MoonShade and the EstenSands right after I delivered the Wesh."

"We could follow him. Track him," Coren suggested. "He may be more vulnerable outside of his palace."

"Perhaps, but the second problem is that I'm being sent to Sulit," Kashar said, slamming his fist into the wooden door. "Now. Today."

Coren's heart leaped with hope. She could find Penna and Kosh!

"No." Kashar shook his head firmly at her. "You're not coming. I'll be tracked the whole way there and back. Brujok witches. You met one of them in the maze earlier," Kashar added.

"Can we follow behind?" she suggested. "Stay hidden? We could wait here a few days first."

Kashar looked between them, conflicted.

"We won't be able to do much without Graeme here, and we do have the cloaking," Sy said, his quick agreement giving her pause.

"Why exactly does Mara want you in Rurok?" Coren asked, her excitement falling away to reveal another hard kernel of distrust. She'd assumed Kashar was the King's man, not the Queen's. What more secrets might he be keeping?

"I'm to bring an offer of peaceful acceptance, showing Riatan interest in the Sulit plight," Kashar said, as though reciting.

"So, surrender and we'll help control your country?" Sy asked.

Kashar cracked a grin. "Yes. Sulit is on the verge of civil war. Eventually that war will bleed into a bid for power in Riata. The witches have huge numbers hidden away in the forests and mountains. If they ever unite as one force, they could easily attack StarsHelm."

"Witches don't naturally unite, though, do they?" Coren asked.

Kashar shook his head. "They prefer small, independent covens. Having a single leader in Rurok at all is odd. And the fact that it's a male...I'm very interested to meet this Lord of Witches."

Coren's eyes narrowed. It certainly was suspicious. A land of independent, powerful women, allowing themselves to be led by a man they called Lord.

She quickly hashed out her options. She couldn't travel *with* Kashar, but following a few days later would work. That would also allow Sy and her to formulate a plan for overtaking the throne once they returned.

"But why *you*, specifically?" Sy asked, glancing to Coren. She nodded. Surely Kashar's place was in the palace training the Wesh, not traveling as an ambassador to a hostile country.

Kashar shrugged. "Mara's requests are often odd. Graeme has others he might send for such a task, but without him here, it's up to Mara. I do have good history with the Brujok. When they first came to the palace years ago, I did many of the guard placements."

"Would she want you gone from the palace for some reason?" Sy pushed. "Something about the Wesh, perhaps?"

Kashar considered. "It's possible. I'll alert my men. And you'll be here to watch over them while you wait for Graeme."

Coren shook her head, unwilling to let the opportunity pass. "The King might be away for weeks. I'll follow you."

Kashar sighed. "I have no power to force you to stay, but please reconsider. I have connections to the southern Sulit. I promise to enlist their help in finding the twins."

"Trying to find them may put them in more danger," Sy pointed out. Her jaw tightened at the thought.

But how could she sit back and do nothing?

"Stay here. Strengthen yourself. Devise a plan. Those things *are* helping your siblings," Kashar instructed, reading her frustration. "We need your power here, Corentine. Maren will protect the twins with her life. They're in good hands."

Coren nodded, but she hadn't made her decision.

Kashar's relief was immediate and evident, and it irritated her. "One of my men will guard you and show you the palace, and I'll leave you a map and coin to hire a boat across SunMelt Lake if you must follow. But think of all you could accomplish with waiting. Hone your strength. Search for the Vespa. Learn to merge completely into your shifted form. Giddon might know a spell for tracking, if you can convince him to help."

Coren stared down at her shoes, refusing to commit.

"Thank you for your help," Sy said, filling the silence.

Kashar bowed. "Just ask my guard, and he will take you where you need to go. I'm sorry to leave, but Mara cannot be ignored. And if you go against everything I advise, at least wait five nights to follow me."

Coren nodded, avoiding looking him in the eyes. She wanted to give him something for Kosh and Penna and Maren, to write a note, but she didn't know what words could possibly take her place. What words could she scribble that would offer encouragement and apology all in one?

There was nothing, so she let Kashar slip out the door without another word.

He'd been gone only long enough for Sy to seal the door again before Coren allowed herself to collapse on the bed, her shoulders shaking in a burst of silent sobbing.

She felt Sy lift the blanket and curl behind her, his strong, warm body offering her a safe place to grieve, just as she had once offered when he lost Damren. His arm crossed her waist and tightened, hugging her close to him, and as the tears flowed, Coren drifted back into a dreamless sleep.

StarSeer rose before the others, working quickly to complete her protection spell. They had traveled deeper and deeper into the Listening Forest each day, until she was certain the sun and moon could no longer guide them.

This made their travels more difficult, their need for protection much greater. But it also meant that Maren could not see how their direction had shifted north, rather than west.

StarSeer was guiding them, a few steps at a time, toward the very thing they had fled to Sulit to escape.

Certainly, the old woman believed she'd brought the twins to safety in Sulit, escaping persecution by their own people. She'd been angry at their leader and taken the twins from his use as a preemptive strike.

But the real persecution was here in Sulit. It had always been here.

For generations now, Sulit had searched for the Weshen twins that might fulfill their Mother's prophecy. The Mother had given StarSeer the gift of sight beyond time, and now she believed Kosh and Penna were the ones they'd waited for.

The Sulit Mother asked for balance from all people, not only the ones who worshiped her or used her power. This prophecy extended beyond any boundary of skin color or blood allegiance or names for the lands they traveled.

One final time, StarSeer paced carefully from the center of their camp, where the fire smoldered: north, then south, then east, then west. Creating a compass with the heart of fire. This was balance, and it soothed her.

North was Riata. South was Umbren. East was Weshen. West was Sulit.

Balanced, as it should be, with the heart of the MagiSea.

Kneeling beside the fire, she chanted the last prayer, then bent to begin breakfast.

"What are you doing?" The girl's eyes were so steady that StarSeer knew she'd been awake for several minutes.

"Cooking your meal."

The girl shook her head. "What else are you doing? Do you still mean to protect us?"

StarSeer met her gaze. "Always. I will always protect you."

"Even when it no longer suits your purpose?"

StarSeer startled at the question. The girl was too young for such insight. Yet, her life had made her old inside. This much the witch could recognize.

"Will you protect us when it is your lifeblood to spill or ours?" The boy moved, leaning his head on his sister's bent knees, as though they joined in the middle. One body, two faces questioning her.

"Always," she repeated. And she meant it, though she knew her limits.

"We go to Rurok, don't we." The girl didn't speak it as a question. "I heard it from the trees."

"The trees...you can hear the trees?" StarSeer struggled to draw breath. Her chest tightened and withered with the effort.

"Of course I can."

"I can't," said the boy, vague disappointment in his sloping shoulders. "I hear the creatures, though. They call to me on the breeze, asking me when I will return. They want to know which of them I will choose."

"Choose for what?" StarSeer whispered, barely able to move her lips around the word.

"For the SelfShifting. When the power is mine. They want to know which MagiCreature I will choose."

Maren rustled her blanket, stretching and lifting her face to the fire. The children silenced.

"Will we travel today?" Maren asked, tightening the braid of gray hair at her back.

StarSeer nodded. "We are close. We must not stop now."

II

Nik wanted to sleep. He craved the bed even more than his dinner, which was saying a lot.

But still, Resh was relentless. He wanted to find his magic so badly that he would do nearly anything. Nik felt as though he were being pushed step by step toward a cliff, and soon enough he would tumble backward into an abyss of paralyzing memory.

But Nik hadn't said a word. He didn't want to appear weak, or Magi forbid, useless. His sole purpose for coming to Weshen Isle was to help the Weshen find their magic. If he were unable to do this, he knew Ashemon would order him away.

He had nowhere to go.

And so he did as Resh asked, each time getting just a little closer to the crackling black fire in the back of his mind.

"How do you feel?" he asked Resh, who had just gained consciousness again. Another fruitless search through the Second Son's blood.

Nik was beginning to fear Resh just didn't have any magic in his blood.

"Fine," Resh grunted. "Let's eat and go again before bed."

"Are you sure? This method is really only productive the first few times. After that…"

"Don't even say it. I *have* to have shifter magic. It's there. You just need to help me find it."

Nik sighed, knowing Resh wouldn't give up on something he felt was his birthright. The Magi knew he'd sunk his teeth into plenty of desires that weren't his by right, either. Like having Sy.

Nik hoped he would dream of Sy tonight. It comforted him to wrap up in Sy's blankets, to run his fingers over the same tent canvas Sy had slept in.

But after a fast meal and another failed invasion of Resh's arm, Nik was in a dark mood.

When he dreamed, it was not of Sy, but of another pair of smoldering eyes and another sly smile.

The boy who had been his world, in the way only a prison of dark desire can be. As the stars twinkled unseen above Nik's head, images flew through his sleeping mind, twisting his face into a grimace and his fingers into the sheets.

He woke with a shout, and as he blinked into the darkness, he heard another shout.

"Nik!" The voice called his name, but he was too disoriented to find it. "Control it!"

He sensed the turmoil around him before his eyes could understand it. Sources were out of place everywhere. Spots in the tent walls had dissolved, letting the moonlight shine through in ragged patches. Sand

154

floated in the air, and water pooled on the ceiling. Bits of leather and cloth had swirled together to create odd, soft daggers, and even the wood of the chair had twisted into the semblance of a throne.

Nik leaned too far over the edge of the cot and fell to his knees, heaving his dinner onto the rug. One by one the sources began to drift to the ground around him, and he heard swearing from behind the torn divider.

"Resh?" he called, his voice scraping along his throat as though he'd been screaming.

"Hold on."

Nik staggered to his feet, pushing himself up with the cot. The tent was chaos.

"What did I do?" he asked softly as Resh stumbled past the divider.

"I guess you were dreaming. Look." Resh gestured to the bare skin of his chest. Grains of sand were embedded into his skin in a wide arc, as though the sand had been hurled at him so harshly that their sources blended. His skin sparkled a bit in the moonlight.

"By the Magi, I'm so sorry," Nik whispered. This loss of control hadn't happened in a long time.

"Have you ever done this before? Shifted while dreaming?"

Nik shook his head, turning his face away in hopes Resh wouldn't see the lie. It had been years, but he *had* been dreaming of the one who used to cause it. Even before the slavers added to his nightmares, Nik hadn't been safe from demons that stalked him at night.

Resh ran his hands over the newly spiked chair. "This is crazy."

"I'm sorry," Nik mumbled again. He began to pull at the misplaced sources around him, quickly mending the holes and replacing the sand and water. He spun away his sick from the rug, sending the smell out of the tent with a breeze. "Taking that sand out of your skin will probably hurt."

"Let's just do it tomorrow when you go in after the magic," Resh said, wincing.

Nik hung his head and sunk onto the cot, cursing softly.

"It's okay. I've been through worse. Try to get a few more hours of sleep. Just don't dream." Resh grinned, rubbing at the stubble on his cheeks. Nik nodded and lay back, knowing sleep wouldn't come.

He was right, and morning found him overheated and suffering from a pulsing headache.

But he drank several cups of strong tea, wishing for some of Sy's lemondrine tonic as he followed Resh to the secluded beach for training. This was his only job on the island, and he wasn't going to let his past interfere with it.

"I'm glad to see many of you back," he said to the gathered crowd. And indeed, nearly everyone had returned. "Today Resh wants me to look for magic in each of your blood. This means me opening the sources of your skin, pulling apart the sources of your blood, and looking for the source of the shifter magic. It's painful, but it doesn't take long. Unfortunately, many people need this done a few times to be successful."

A large, burly man stepped forward, and Nik saw Resh nod, grinning.

"Going first, Tag?" he asked the man.

"If Sy has magic, I want it too," the man grumbled, but his eyes twinkled. He sat against a rock, and Resh handed him a stick to bite. He waved it away. "Been through a lot worse."

Nik shrugged. He could see many scars lining the man's arms and face. Still, this was a new sort of pain, one none of them had ever experienced. He began, and Tag made it about two minutes before his eyes rolled back in his head, and he slumped against the rocks.

The same was true for nearly everyone, men and women alike. Nik was pleased to see the women handling themselves just as well as the men, too, although he knew they had no formal training or experience with the pain of combat.

He'd nearly begun to allow himself to think of these as his people, and he was growing proud of them.

But as morning progressed into afternoon, and Nik caused scream after scream to rip from the throats of these people he was learning to like and respect, his mind began to disintegrate at its edges.

"Should we take a break?" he asked Resh, hoping it didn't sound like begging.

Resh considered the people strewn about the narrow strip of sand. They looked exhausted.

"Everyone, let's rest for a few minutes, then we'll do one last session!" Resh called. Nik began to breathe a little easier, although he dreaded beginning the blood work again. Then Resh leaned in close. "Now, when they're off guard, do the rocks and ocean attack you did yesterday."

Nik startled. "But rest-"

"Will come when we have more magic!" Resh snapped, still managing to keep his voice at a whisper. "Go."

Nik glanced around. None of the Weshen were watching him. They were chatting and laughing quietly, relieved for a break. He sighed and flicked his hands at the rocks. A rumble shook the cliffs above them, and one of the women cried out. Nik pulled rock after rock, this time allowing them to clatter to the ground. He worked furiously to keep the largest ones away from the people, but smaller pieces he allowed to connect.

Fist-sized rocks struck arms and legs, temples and backs as people scrambled over each other for cover.

The shouts turned desperate, and Nik turned to the ocean, calling huge waves to splash onto the shore. The first few only splashed around their ankles, but the waves soon grew taller than a man. Still he called them, losing himself in the motion of pulling sources and weaving them into chaos.

The screams gave him a grim, constant reminder of his job, and though they still tugged at the compassion in his heart, Nik shoved that deep enough to drown.

This was his job. His purpose. Just as bearing it himself had been.

And helping the slavers with the younger and newer Wesh slaves had been his job.

And living through the cruelest pulling and pushing of sources of all, when he was barely a young man.

The memories and images from his dream began to seep into his fingers, curling them harsher, and the pain soaked into his movements, edging them stronger. He heard the change in the people, felt it.

It wasn't the fear of pain anymore.

It was the fear of extinction.

But he had reached a point of helplessness, where his own will had been replaced by the chaos of the sources around him. Nothing was in its place. How could he possibly put it all back now?

"Nik! Nik, stop!" Resh shoved at him, then yanked at his arms until they were bent backward, but Nik didn't have to move his fingers to move the sources. "Stop it now, or I'll stop you!"

Nik couldn't remember how to stop. He wasn't just pulling the sources. He *was* the sources, and his pain and anger and the cruelty he had been taught burst through and onto the beach, hurling itself at the people in every drop of water, every crumb of sand, every sliver of rock.

Then the beach went black as something struck his head.

Thankfully, the blackness was velvet and midnight and silence, not the silken whispers of his dreams.

Nik drifted, everything important in him shutting down until blissfully, there was nothing left of pain or pleasure.

Resh stared blankly at the scene before him, unable to process exactly what had happened. People lay everywhere in contorted positions, moaning. Crying. Cursing as they tried to right their broken bodies.

Blood mixed with sand, swirled into ocean water, splashed by rock.

And Nik, prone and unmoving on the sand before him. Resh clutched the chunk of bloodied rock in his hands still. He hadn't wanted to hurt Nik, but Nik nearly killed them all.

He had lost control.

Both of them had lost control.

Lorenya was the first to stand, and she turned to Resh with horror written on her face. Slowly, she helped brush away the sand from another woman's face. A sliver of hope grew in Resh as he watched her push at a rock with her magic, trying to move it from crushing someone's leg, but the rock only rolled a few feet before Lorenya gave up, exhaustion plain in her slump.

A few others began to stir, looks of shock on their faces, and accusation in the glances they flicked to Resh and Nik.

"That wasn't training, sir," one of the younger men grunted out, wiping blood from a deep gash on his arm. "That was chaos."

"Tagsha!" One of the men cried, and Resh snapped his attention to them.

His heart fell. An enormous boulder blocked the guard's face. Resh hurried to them, his gait hobbled by a twisted ankle.

"No," he whispered, sinking to his knees in the sand.

Blood spilled bright from Tagsha's mouth, and his eyes stared blankly at the sky. Unseeing. His spirit had already gone.

Resh choked on the realization that Nik had killed him.

No - *he* had killed Tagsha. His father would see it no other way. Tagsha was Ashemon's oldest friend, and Nik was Resh's responsibility.

Panic tugged relentlessly at Resh, like a tide rushing in from the ocean, threatening to yank him beneath the water.

"This was madness," one of the men said.

Resh pushed himself to standing. He had to salvage the situation. "I'm sorry. I'm so sorry," he began. Several of them turned away, shaking their heads at each other.

"Wait! The magic is there! We can all find it. We have to trust each other."

"Well, I won't be trusting that Wesh any longer," a woman said. "I have children to go home to. I can't put myself in this kind of danger again." She rose and set off slowly down the beach, limping a little. Two men stood and followed her without a word.

"Please!" Resh cried, hating how desperate he sounded. "Weshen needs this magic!"

"How quickly your mind has changed," a deep voice boomed from above them on the cliff.

Resh felt his heart scuttle into the deepest parts of his chest as he looked up and saw his father silhouetted against the sky, his shape dark against the bright sun.

"Father, I-"

"You have proved your inability to lead. Again."

Ashemon stepped slowly down the rocky path to the beach, each step taking hours in Resh's mind. He glanced furtively at the unmoving form of Tagsha.

"You will take this Wesh from our island," Ashemon said when he stood before Resh. He scanned the beach,

161

looking at everything but his friend's body. "You have killed a man. Take the boy and leave. Now."

With that, Ashemon turned away from Resh and began helping the wounded men and women stand.

Resh's heart surged back to life as he watched his father ignore him utterly. He felt it would beat his ribcage to pieces with the rage that pulsed through it.

"You will not ignore me longer!" He had meant to say the words with iron force, but they released as a cry of desperate fury.

Ashemon did not even look at him.

"I've already made too many mistakes in my young life, but the largest one of all was trusting a coward to be my leader," he yelled, and every head on the beach swiveled to him.

Every one except Ashemon's. Resh noticed his shoulders had tensed though, so he continued. He was playing the game like he'd never played before. For once, he didn't care what he lost.

"Yes, I was wrong about the magic. I regret everything I did regarding Corentine's banishment. I was wrong! Yes! Reshra was wrong!" He paused to catch his breath. Ashemon had stopped moving, his form hunched as still as a Cheetana before it pounced. "But you! General Ashemon Havenash…revered *leader* of Weshen City. You are wrong, too! Yet you refuse to admit it!"

Nik stirred to life in the sand, blinking up at the sun. Resh threw him a warning look, willing him to stay silent.

"You may rule these people however you want, but you no longer rule me." Resh held a hand to Nik and

162

helped the boy stand. Nik looked dazedly around him, guilt washing his face as he took in what had happened.

Finally, Ashemon turned to look at his son, who was now standing shoulder to shoulder with Nik.

"Get off this island. Be gone from my city before I arrive. Never come back," he said, his face a mask of false calm.

"I accept your terms," Resh said curtly. He spread his gaze over the remaining people. "Anyone who wants to continue their training is welcome to come with me. I promise to take measures to make it safe, but it will never be easy. You may choose, however. An easy, quiet life wasting here on an island, or the dangerous thrill of helping your people escape the chains Riata has placed us in." He gestured to the cliffs above. "Weshen is no longer a country lying in wait, as your General wishes you to believe. It is a prison cell, and we are all slowly expiring, despite everything he tries to convince you of. The future of our people awaits us beyond the NeverCross Mountains. I leave today to meet it head to head. Join me at the dock if you care to save your people from extinction."

Ashemon straightened and surveyed his people, whose frightened faces were swiveling between father and son. "My good Weshen," Ashemon began, lowering the scrape of his voice to kindness, "please consider your lives at stake in this decision. Those who follow Reshra Havenash may not also follow me. Weshen has always listened to the Magi. Reshra was once one of the Mirror Magi's most devout followers. Yet today he asks you to put your will before the gods'. The magic will be

163

returned to us when it is needed and when we are ready. To force the issue is to blaspheme all we hold dear."

A few began to murmur, and Resh felt his chest crack in two. He was *not* a blasphemer. He loved the Magi and trusted them.

Surely, they would not remain silent much longer. Surely it wasn't sacrilegious to thrust himself before the gods and claim readiness to help lead their people from darkness.

He wanted to sink to his knees and scream to the empty sky that he was here. He was ready. *Use him.*

"Resh, it's okay," Nik whispered. "We don't need him."

"No, we don't," Resh muttered, bitter as uncured chokecherries. He turned to Ashemon. "I guess we'll have to wait and see who is right in this argument. May the Magi choose our next leader wisely."

Without a glance back at any of the people on the beach, Resh grabbed Nik's arm and hastened from the beach. As he slogged through the sand and up the rocky slope to the boats, he systematically blocked every memory of his father from his mind, save the image of him condemning his Second Son to banishment as well.

Ashemon was no General to him any longer, nor was he a father.

Reshra Havenash was on his own, as he cared nothing for such cowardice.

Resh ignored every word Nik spoke to apologize. "You lost control, but I knew you were tired. I pushed for too much. Now help me ready the boat." He regretted Tagsha's death, but he was strangely glad to be free of his father's expectations and disappointment.

He should have struck out on his own years ago.

When they arrived at the docks, Ashemon was nowhere to be seen. There were, however, dozens of Weshen gathered, curious to see if anyone would leave with the Second Son.

Lorenya stepped forward first. "I regret that I can't go with you, but I promise to continue my practice here. The island may soon need protection. Thank you for all you've done for us," she added, embracing Nik quickly. He looked dazed at her praise, and Resh nodded to her in gratitude.

Two young Paladins turned to face the crowd. Brothers, Resh remembered.

"What happened to Tagsha saddens all of us," one of them said to the gathered people.

"But you should know that though the training was dangerous, it worked," the other finished. Both held up their hands, pulling drifts of sand to their knees. Whispers swept through the watching crowd, and Resh felt his chest swell. Magic lived in his people.

They had awoken it.

Nik had awoken it.

The brothers turned to Resh. "I'm sorry, but we cannot leave our people," the older one said. "They'll need us here in the days to come."

Resh's hopes began to crumble.

"We'll remain with the men, but we pledge to practice the shifting," the younger brother continued.

It was the same with each of them. Willing to practice or seek their shifter magic, but unwilling to follow a shamed Second Son. Unwilling to leave their homes for the unknown, even as he did the same. Resh was hollow, betrayal coursing through every vein of his body - every vein where the cursed shifter magic refused to awake.

As the last one stepped back into the crowd, he vowed to try harder. He would seek a teacher more strenuous than Nik if necessary. Shanta may know one. This was not the end.

Lorenya helped Resh shove his boat into the water, and before letting go of the bark, she placed a hand on his arm.

"Thank you for what you've done for us," she repeated. "It may seem hopeless now, but Weshen will follow you one day soon. Ashemon's fear can't hold them forever, especially now."

Resh nodded, holding her eyes a second longer. "Take care of them," he said, flicking his gaze to the people on the beach.

"Take care of *him*," she answered, nodding at Nik, who had hunched low in the boat, his eyes on the water. "He's so broken inside. I can feel it now. He needs to heal from something vast and terrible."

"I'll watch him," Resh answered, uneasy with her warning. The boat drifted alone into the open water.

"What will we do when we reach the city?" Nik asked, his voice dull.

"Gather supplies. Head back through the passage. Find Shanta. Continue training."

"I don't think I can do the training anymore," Nik said, gazing at the island fading into the horizon.

"I need to be ready," Resh pushed. "We'll lead many of those Weshen one day. Ashemon won't live forever."

Nik shook his head. "Maybe you will, but I'm no leader. I just killed one of them."

"No, you're wrong," Resh said, his voice harsh enough to gain Nik's attention. The boy responded well to anger, he'd noticed. "All your life you've been told what to do. Often with cruel consequences, right?"

Nik's pale blue eyes hardened around the edges, but he didn't answer.

"This will be your chance to mold these people. Not cruelly, like you've been shaped. When they come find us - and they will - show them the beauty and the strength of what the Magi have given us. Show them that Weshen is no longer a country bent beneath fear of the Restless King. We will rise, Nik."

Nik slipped Resh a half-smile. "You should have said that on the beach."

Resh rolled his eyes to the sky, examining the puffs of clouds. "I have little experience leading," he admitted, his voice barely reaching beyond his throat.

"But you have the instincts of a leader. You shape people, too. You see what they need, to become what you want them to be. I'm not sure I have that vision. I've been broken too many times. Healed up all wrong," he added, drawing a stream of water into his palm and shifting it into a broad-petaled flower.

He plucked the water petals and discarded them one by one, letting them float on the surface of the sea like sparkling gems.

Resh watched him play for a few seconds. "Once I pinned Coren against her will. I hurt her. But when she got her wings, she realized her power gave her dominance. And she pinned me. She could have killed me, but she didn't. She had the power to hurt, but also to refrain. You have that, too."

Nik dropped his hold on the floating petals and watched them vanish back into the water. "Great power always draws greater power. Coren hasn't met her match yet. I'm not sure I can bestow that on someone who isn't ready for it."

"Were you ready? For any of it?" Resh asked.

Nik's face paled, and he seemed to choke on his words. "Never," he whispered.

"Then help us grow ready," Resh hissed, leaning close. "Give us the chance you never had, then claim your dominance."

Nik's fingers trembled against his sides, and he pressed them into his thighs. He took a deep breath and nodded slightly. Resh closed his eyes, a silent prayer to the Magi flitting across his mind. He would push Nik the way he had always pushed Sy, and had begun pushing Coren, and would push the Weshen when they joined him later.

But he must also remember to push himself.

If Sy returned, he could have Weshen. Ashemon would give him the First Son rights again, Resh was certain. As for himself, he wanted Riata. The Magi had taught him many things in his lifetime of bent-kneed prayer, but the greatest was the importance of balance.

Riata was imbalanced, and Resh was an equalizer, skilled in tipping the scales a little at a time.

168

12

Kashar's knight was as helpful as promised, though he barely spoke. He merely followed their requests, identified each room, and punctuated their questions with nods and shakes of his head. Any question that could not be answered in this way earned a shrug, including his name.

Sy dutifully toured the palace, making hundreds of mental notes that he later transcribed in a leather-bound book, not unlike the ones Ashemon carried. He learned the main halls and secret halls, the grand staircases and hidden staircases. He got as close as Queen Mara's doors before the knight yanked him into a side stair.

He went to watch the Wesh slaves, though he did not say a word of their mission or the reason for his presence. He fumed at their isolation and hopelessness, though he had to admit they seemed well-cared for.

He watched the King's Alchemists try to bind magic once, but the process made him ill. The ingredients on their tables were plain:

MagiCreature talismans, powdered Weshen bone, and sheets of Sulit spells.

He knew he was biding time, and he hated the slowness of it, but Sy would wait here for years if it meant a chance to kill the King.

Coren was not so content.

Every time he looked for her to join him, she was absent. She rose before dawn and sneaked into the arena. He often found her with Giddon, who despite being very kind and jovial, continued to refuse to help her search for her injured Vespa. By dinner time, she had always returned, and they ate together. She stayed customarily silent while he recounted the new knowledge or experiences each day had brought.

"I can't take this another day," she said to him on the third night, when he had paused to take a bite. "Surely it's been long enough, and I can follow Kashar."

"He said five nights," he reminded her. "Everything depends on us killing Graeme. We can't fail." He only earned a glare for his comment. They were both growing restless with waiting. They were both interested in opposing tasks, and they were both irritated with the others' failure.

Coren hated his stealthy learning of the palace secrets. Sy hated her reckless visits to Giddon and the arena.

The single room always seemed too crowded for two people.

The single knight Kashar had provided could never take them both on the same day.

The single mission Sy waited for seemed farther away each morning, as though he might be trapped in an endless loop of days.

"Why don't you come with me tomorrow?" he asked, feeling like he'd asked it a thousand times.

"Because I want nothing to do with this palace. I don't want to learn its secrets or befriend its inhabitants. I'm not going to stay here, Sy."

"But you'll be back, right? Once you find the twins?"

She shrugged. "By then, you'll probably have found and killed Graeme. You're suited to it. You have the weapons training and the Grizzlin shift. Which you should be practicing."

He sighed. "And just where am I supposed to practice a magic that will alert every Brujok in the palace to my whereabouts?"

"Giddon's," she answered, as though it were simple enough.

"If he's that trustworthy, why hasn't he helped you find the Vespa?"

Coren shook her head. "He's still too scared. But I'm working on it. I trust him."

"What does he have to fear?" Sy asked, though he knew it was an endless answer.

"He says calling for the Vespa is like screaming in an open field. Anything with ears can hear it. Witches, Shadow, other MagiCreatures. He still believes *you're* the one," she said, a sly smile creeping onto her face. Sy opened his mouth to protest Giddon's preferences, but she held up a hand. "You are, Sy. You're the one who can do this. It was never me. Can't you see that? I just got thrown into the mix. But you were the first. The Magi chose you first."

They'd had this conversation before. "Are you still having the nightmares?" he asked, changing the subject. They had begun the first night in the palace.

"Every night, Shadow comes in seven." She looked down at her plate, pushing the food around without eating any.

"Seven?"

"Always the same seven figures. Always cast in darkness and a strange golden glow."

"Always seven?" Sy repeated, uneasy with the number. It was only one short of their sacred number, eight.

"I think I'm the eighth," she whispered, and her fingers shook enough that the plate slid from her knees and onto the floor.

"What does that mean?" Sy asked, bending to help her clean the mess.

"I don't know, but it's all the dream ever speaks. I can't even see their mouths, but they taunt me. Their laughter. Somehow it speaks to me. Seven dead, one to go."

"It's just a dream, Coren," he tried.

"It's *not*. Dreams are memories and bits of the day put together in odd ways. This is a message. I'm not supposed to be in this palace."

"What does Giddon think of it?"

"I haven't told him," she answered. "He worries too much already."

"Perhaps Kashar will know what to make of it."

"I'm not waiting for Kashar to return. I'll ask the Sulit witches. The Brujok if I have to. Or Maren, when I find

172

her. I'll stay the next two nights, but then I'm leaving for Sulit."

She pulled back the covers and slid deep under them, turning her face to the wall.

Sy knew she would not change her mind, and part of him understood. It did make the most sense for him to go after Graeme. He did have the most training. The Grizzlin shift. She may even be right about the Magi choosing him for the task, although Damren had never been certain.

But the opposing argument was the same it had been since the day they were banished from Weshen Isle. Sy didn't want Coren to travel to Rurok. He feared that land with a ferocity that seemed unnatural, but as a Paladin, Sy knew when to trust his instincts.

King or not, if he couldn't keep Coren here, he would have to go with her.

Nik lay flat on his back in Sy's bed in Weshen City, paralyzed with fear of the decision he needed to make.

He could no longer live with putting the people he cared about in such danger. He himself was a danger, and he knew others followed him. Brujok witches sought him. Riatan soldiers sought him. Weshen slavers sought him. Even Umbren darkness sought him. He'd seen them all in his dreams, both waking and asleep.

Resh. Coren. Sy.

All their faces rotated in his mind. These were his friends. Sy, maybe more. He'd had lovers before, but never love, and he feared its vulnerability. Nik knew he couldn't be ruthless if his friends' fates rested in his fingers.

He couldn't expose them to what he had suffered.

He couldn't heal if he were too focused on not hurting them.

And, despite what Resh believed, Nik was not as powerful as Coren. He wasn't a natural, compassionate leader like Sy. He was horrible at reading people's intentions. The opposite of Resh.

Other than the magic he'd been given and taught, Nik had nothing to offer them but danger.

When weighing the two against each other, Nik knew the decision had already been made.

His friends could learn magic from many, but they should never earn danger at his hands again.

He forced himself from the bed, grabbing an empty pack from a hook on the wall. Sy's room was meticulously organized, and Nik seemed to know where everything was. It was all so logical and intuitive, just like Sy. He stepped into the closet and breathed in the scent of leather, fur, metal. And Sy's heady scent.

Like crisp mountain air and the flash of iron, but cut with a pure sweetness, like a lemondrine flower just before it burst into fruit.

Nik sank into the hanging clothing, burying his face in the scents, willing them to fill him with the strength he needed to leave this future behind.

He pulled several garments from their hangers, choosing the warmest cloaks and thickest tunics, well-oiled leather boots and double-layered pants.

Nik stripped himself naked in Sy's closet, slipping into the new clothes with a guttural sigh. He could do this. He could leave. It was necessary to protect them.

Nik repeated these thoughts like a mantra until they soothed the ache in his chest enough to step away from the closet and over to Sy's desk. He needed to leave a note, to explain some of what he felt.

What words could he find to possibly explain what he felt? There were none.

So instead Nik drew a flower. He'd always made flowers - shifted petals and stems from water and wood and fire. Made his messages into things of beauty, however ugly the words might be.

And as he finished drawing the last petal, the words formed themselves beneath.

MY YOUTH WAS NEVER
MINE BUT WITH YOU I COULD
BE YOUNG AGAIN

He wanted to promise he'd return. He wanted to offer his future to the strength of Sy's arms and the kindness of his eyes, but he knew the world didn't work that way.

Nik left the few words as they were, and turned back to the room. He gathered a few weapons from the cupboard on the wall, slung the pack over his shoulder, and stepped silently out of Sy's door and down the hall.

He glanced back at the mansion, silhouetted against the inky sky, and whispered a prayer begging the Magi to keep his friends safe.

But because he didn't have much experience with answered prayers, Nik slipped through the silent circles of Weshen City and climbed a narrow path into the chill of the NeverCross Mountains. His friends would never be safe with him nearby, but perhaps the things that followed him would continue to do so, leaving everyone else in peace.

Resh awoke too late. His mouth felt stuffed with cotton, and his eyes seemed swollen shut.

He tried to remember how much he'd drunk last night, but their arrival at Weshen City was nothing more than a blur now. He recalled downing a drink Nik had poured him, and then nothing afterward. Staggering to his feet, Resh ruffled his hair and scrubbed at his jaw.

By the Magi, he felt awful.

Perhaps he *had* kept drinking, drowning out the previous day's loss with a mockery of celebration.

Resh gathered fresh clothes and padded into the adjoining bathroom. He turned the water cool and stood under it longer than necessary, using the time to collect his thoughts.

They could travel to EvenFall, find Shanta, check on the Wesh. Send a message to Sy.

Or he could just deliver the message himself, Resh realized. Now that he wasn't tied to teaching magic in Weshen, he could join Coren and Sy at StarsHelm.

Shaking the icy droplets from his dark hair, Resh rolled his shoulders and twisted the muscles of his torso. Yes, that was exactly what he would do. He finished toweling his body and buttoned up a dark green shirt, then slipped his tall black boots over dark, fitted pants. His string of prayer beads rested with a familiar weight at his throat. He felt powerful in his own way - the way that always made people look up at him when he strode by.

Resh rang the bell for a servant and requested breakfast be brought to his room and Nik's, and then he began to pack.

Eschewing personal items and all but his favorite clothing, Resh instead filled his bag with jewels and gold-plated weaponry. More than anything, he would need coin. He could take what little Ashemon kept in his office, but he would need more if they were to gain information from Shanta and travel safely to StarsHelm.

He was wondering just how much it would be to rent a coach when the servant opened the door.

"Your breakfast, sir. But I have not been able to locate your guest."

Resh paused his packing, narrowing his eyes at the man. "Where have you looked?"

The servant cowered. "No one has seen him this morning. He isn't in Syashin's room or any of the others on this floor, and the bathrooms are empty. The doors are still bolted from the inside."

Resh cursed, pushing past the servant to Sy's room.

Of course, Nik could easily shift through a bolted door. But why would he leave?

Half of the answer waited for him on Sy's bed, where a single handwritten note waited to be found by the bed's owner.

Resh roared a curse, punching at the bed post. Nik was gone.

He crushed the note into his pocket, calling to the servant to pack his breakfast and lunch in a sack. Gathering his things, Resh strode out of his father's mansion in Weshen City.

He made it to EvenFall just before dusk. Along the way, he'd pushed aside all thoughts of what had happened on the island, instead dangling the promise of StarsHelm before himself like a treat for an animal. But as he slipped into the abandoned building that once housed Shanta's crew, he knew he might as well get the story straight. He'd be explaining it many times over.

"Shanta?" he called, but there was no answer. Resh knocked on the hidden door, but there was nothing. He wondered if Shanta had moved, or if some odd circumstance had pulled her entire crew away from home. Such an idea made him nervous.

He fished an old, broken key from his bag, grinning at the memories of their first meeting when she had stolen his hotel room key and refused to give it back. He'd been hunting a mythical half-moon blade, and she'd offered to help him if he helped her.

Resh strung the key on a thin chain and left it on the door. If she returned to this building, she would know he'd been through, at least. The key was just a teasing reminder of what she'd claimed from him as payment.

He headed from the empty building straight into the crowded market, where he began the aggravatingly slow and careful process of trading weapons and jewels for coin. If he bartered too much at one stall, suspicions would be raised. If he bartered with too many different stalls, people would notice his movements.

EvenFall had no organized set of soldiers, but it had a merciless ring of pickpockets and worse.

After a particularly sour deal, Resh ducked into an alley to avoid further eyes finding the bulge of the sack he carried. His impatience had made him reckless, and he needed to wait until the vendor was distracted before slipping past to another aisle of the market.

"Well, well. Second Son," a raspy voice called. The voice was barely above a whisper, but it snaked up the dead alley and directly into his ears. Resh spun, drawing his longknife. Who would know him here?

Then he saw the stall, alone at the end of the alley. A single figure hunched there, hidden beneath a deep hood.

"You!" he hissed. "Call on your Mother, witch, because I'm about to end your life."

She cackled and leaned against the brick wall of the alley, unconcerned. "You won't. If you do, you'll never find out what I know of the blades you seek."

"You are a liar."

"I am a witch," she said, shrugging.

"They are one and the same," Resh sneered. "I've always known this."

"I tell the truth when it suits me, and the bits of it that stir my fancy. Just like everyone else. Or do you think your people immune to lies?"

"What do you want?" Resh remembered how she had taunted him before, speaking in riddles.

"Perhaps one of those jewels you carry. You mean to trade them, yes?"

"For Riatan coin."

"I have none of that. My currency is much more valuable. Secrets," she whispered, taunting him with a half-smile.

Resh considered her. Yes, she had led him into a trap before. But she had also known the location of the half-moon blade. Impulsively, he unlaced a pocket of his pack and pulled out a seastone. Blue and pearl and hints of jade glowed in the darkness of the alley, like looking up at the sky through deep water. The stone was wider than his palm, and he knew it would be worth a lot to a witch without direct access to the sea.

"Yes," she breathed, shuffling closer. Her fingers stroked the surface of the stone, and its lights moved with them, following the warmth of her touch. "This is not so valuable a payment as what you've given me these last weeks, but it will do. Yes, Second Son, it will do."

Resh snatched the stone away into his pocket. "The blade?" he asked, refusing to fall into her trap. He wasn't about to ask for an explanation of her riddle.

The witch blinked at him, her eyes still swirls of desire for the stone. He had chosen well. "The blade you seek is in StarsHelm. Or in Rurok."

Resh bit down on his aggravation. "No seastone if you can't even narrow it down to a single city."

"There is no single city, for there is no single blade."

"The blade exists. I saw it myself, strapped to the back of the most disgusting MagiCreature that has ever lived."

She cackled, rolling her eyes back in her skull with glee. "What a wonderful night that was!"

Resh took a few steps back, heading out of the alley. This was pointless.

"Wait, you foolish boy. I'm allowed a little fun. I'm a witch," she said again, as though that explained her pleasure at his near-death. "There is no single blade. But there is a *double* blade. What you seek is not one, but two. One in StarsHelm. One in Rurok."

"Twin blades?" Resh said, his voice hushed with the implication. Not only were there two to wield, but such double magic was more than he had ever dared dream.

With one of those blades, he could conquer life.

With both, he could conquer death.

The clues had been before him all along, in the teachings of the Mirror Magi. *Everything* came in pairs; everything must have an equal and opposite to create balance.

The witch cleared her throat delicately, twirling a lock of tangled hair around her blue-painted nail. "The stone?" she prompted. As though in a trance, Resh slipped it from his pocket and into her waiting palm.

The half-moon Kitsuun blade had plagued his dreams for years, and he was powerless before his desire for it.

If a second blade waited somewhere in the world ....

By the time he brought his focus back to the alley, the witch was gone from her stall. There was no trace of her in the crowd beyond, but he did glimpse Shanta, standing just behind the post of a nearby stall. Their eyes connected through the mass of people, and she shook her head, her lips curling in mockery.

She was beside him in seconds. "Still listening to lying witches, I see." She looked beyond his shoulder at the empty alley and raised her brows.

"Nik is gone," Resh said, answering the question she hadn't asked. "But the witch just told me there's a second blade, so there's that."

She laughed. "Count me out. We nearly died trying to find one. *And* I compromised my pricing structure," she added.

Resh grinned at her. "But working for kisses is so much more fun than coin."

"Not if you want to eat. So, what happened with Nik? Did he run away to find Sy?"

Resh sighed and leaned against the alley wall. "I think he cracked. He disappeared last night. I think he even slipped something in my drink."

Shanta snickered. "Well, he hasn't been through EvenFall that I've heard."

"It's a big city, Shanta," Resh said.

"Not for my crew. I knew you were here, didn't I?"

He shrugged. "Nik tried to awaken the magic in me. And some of the other Weshen."

"I guess it didn't go so well," she judged.

Resh shook his head, staring at his boots. "Ashemon banished me," he mumbled.

Shanta whistled and swore under her breath. "That man is fast asleep to the reality of the world," she murmured. "The day he wakes may very well be the day he sleeps forever."

Resh nodded. "I used to think he was such a great leader. Everyone respected him. Did what he asked without question. But really, he's made them all lose hope. He's a rock around their feet in deep water."

"You'll do better. Sy, too."

Resh glanced up at Shanta. It was rare for her to offer anything besides overly honest advice and derision. But now, her face was open and earnest. Her fingertips brushed his arm briefly.

"Look, Resh. You have a lot of issues."

Resh cracked a grin. There she was, the Shanta he knew.

She gripped his arm tighter. "But you have the trust of some of the most powerful people I know. The Restless King and Queen Mara and all the Sulit witches and Shadow...all of them are nothing against Corentine and Sy and Nik."

"I'm just the tagalong," Resh muttered.

"No. You're the master. You think no one notices what you do, and you're right. Except for me. I notice because I do the same thing with my crew. I see their talents and their fears and their desires, and I use them. I love them, but I use them. That's why I know you'll do remarkable things for Weshen."

"And Riata," he added, slipping her a sideways grin as he admitted something he'd never said aloud.

"And Riata," she agreed, barely even blinking. Likely she had guessed that in him as well. "How about we finish selling your weapons and stones and find you a coach. Then you can get to StarsHelm and set to work creating a king killer."

Resh debated whether to thank her, but a sharpness in her eyes warned him away. Also like himself, Shanta rarely let people get close. She loved her crew, but she used them. Resh nodded to himself. He'd been part of her crew for less than a few nights, and he hadn't minded either one.

Instead, he gave her a generous cut of the coin he'd traded.

"I always did like you," she grinned, pressing her full lips to the corner of his smile.

"It might take longer than we planned for me to come for the Wesh," he warned.

She shrugged. "I'm not worried. I charge by the day." She handed him a scrap of paper with a name on it. "Give this to the driver when you arrive, and he'll take you to my contact. Pay him double what he asks."

Resh swung up into the coach and settled his bag at his feet, knowing it would do no good to ask her for more details. Propping his freshly-shined leather boots onto the plush cushions, he saluted Shanta and watched through the squat window as EvenFall faded into the afternoon sun.

13

"**G**iddon, please," Coren said as soon as she stepped through his door. "I'm leaving tomorrow morning, no matter what. I need my wings."

"They aren't *your* wings," Giddon chuckled. "The MagiCreature who chooses to merge with you never disappears. It joins forces with you. It could almost be described as a twin power."

Coren snorted. She and Jyesh had never had a chance to develop such a connection. Sure, their childhood had seen them finishing each other's sentences and equally matched in running and mock battles, just the way Penna and Kosh were now.

But they had been torn apart before anything stronger could develop. Jyesh's power had been lost to the MagiSea forever, and she would always feel incomplete.

"I've had no luck locating your family with spells, I'm afraid."

Coren sighed. She hadn't expected that plan to work, anyways. Giddon didn't have a single piece of information to go on.

"Why can't we just kill Queen Mara now, and Sy can wait on the throne for Graeme to return?" she asked, not for the first time. She smirked at the image of her friend lounging on the throne when Graeme walked in. Even better, Sy as a Grizzlin, pacing the floor of the throne room, Zorander Graeme's black-diamond crown perched on his furry head. "Wouldn't it be easier to manage them one at a time?"

"Perhaps, but Mara is the most protected person in all the country. Between Mara, Aram, and her guards, you'd be fighting the greatest spellmasters of Riata with nothing more than that whip."

Coren stretched onto Giddon's bed since he occupied the only chair. His room was so small that it afforded no walls, and the entire room was bedroom, library, and kitchen in one. Only a tiny bathroom existed in privacy, tucked behind a thick, paneled curtain.

"I've killed with this whip before."

"Not a witch, you haven't. It has no more power than an old rope. I'd be able to scent the blood magic on it."

"A shifter."

Giddon shook his head.

"A Weshen, then," she amended. It was unlikely that the fat Weshen guard had any magic in his blood, and it had been her Vespa talons, not the whip, that ended the slaver's life.

Giddon shrugged, unimpressed. "Cutting down one regular Weshen is like cutting grass, and blood magic is only powerful if the blood is powerful. Queen Mara would snap your neck with a flick of her fingers."

"I bested one of her Brujok guards in the maze," Coren returned.

Giddon rolled his eyes. "The maze isn't spelled against shifting. Going against the Queen is a ridiculous idea. Spend your time searching the skies for your Vespa. Graeme will return one day, and you and Sy can have a go at him first. At least he isn't a spellmaster."

Coren pushed off the bed in irritation, pacing the brief length of the room, then back again. She knew Giddon could help her find the Vespa. She just needed the right incentive.

"What will you do once you have your family again?" Giddon asked after several seconds of watching her pace. "Will you return here and use your power to help Riata?"

Coren glanced at him in disbelief. Was her possible desertion the reason he refused to help? She could make that promise easily. "I swear, once my family is safe, I will return and help Riata in any way I can. Whatever power I have will go to restoring my country and yours."

Giddon chewed at his lip, and Coren fought to keep a grin off her face. "Will you bind yourself to that promise?"

She hesitated a bare second, then forced a nod. As long as her family was safe, nothing else mattered.

"Calling the Vespa will draw lots of other powerful magic here as well," he warned. "Like Shadow."

Coren stopped walking and stared at him in confusion. "Shadow is buried in the forests beyond EvenFall."

Giddon shook his head, the movement excruciatingly slow. "Shadow is a multitude. A *legion*. Not a single entity you can stuff under the earth for all time."

Coren clenched her muscles, resisting a shiver itching across her shoulder blades. This was not what she had been expecting. "So why hasn't it been following us? Why haven't I seen it since Sy stuffed it deep in the earth?"

Giddon narrowed his eyes. "It may be possible to delay it for a time. But defeat? No. Shadow is eternal."

"If it's eternal and insurmountable, then what's the point in delaying? The Vespa defeated Shadow once, saving me. Cast the spell, and I'll be able to do the same," Coren reasoned, forcing a bravery she didn't feel.

"The Brujok will also sense my spell. And not only the ones here in the palace, but those as far as Rurok. They have their own collection of Weshen shifters, I've heard. They're especially fond of twins."

Coren gritted her teeth. That was precisely why she had to find Kosh and Penna. "Lucky for me, my twin died long ago."

"Hmmm…" Giddon nodded, watching her fume.

"I want it back. I don't care who I have to fight afterward."

"No guarantees."

"Begin!" she cried, frustrated with his stalling. This was the break she had been waiting for.

Giddon held out his palm, and she resisted hugging him and clapping. She dug in her pockets for Kashar's coins. "I need enough for passage to Rurok."

"Oh? Won't you be flying across SunMelt Lake on your recovered wings?"

Coren pocketed a handful of the coins. "Passage for Sy, then."

He clucked at her, but he stashed the coins at his belt and turned to the wall of jars and covered vats. Murmuring to himself, Giddon gathered enough ingredients to fill the rickety table. Trying to tame her excitement, she went back to pacing as he measured and whispered over the iridescent rainbow powders and slow-bubbling liquids and dried bits of skin and bone.

"Where did the Vespa leave its poison?" he asked, after enough of the afternoon had passed to pull the sun sideways toward dusk.

She lifted the hem of her tunic, revealing the faint scar across her navel.

Giddon flashed a knife across her stomach faster than she could react, and the blood beaded across her skin. He smeared it in eight tiny circles with his fingers, then scraped the residue into the pot before him.

"Don't touch," he warned as she moved to rub at the thin cut. He tipped the pot's contents into a large mug, and Coren grimaced.

"I'm to drink that?"

"Of course. The magic inside of you calls to the Vespa already, or it would not have known to snag its claw in your belly. The spell amplifies this call, like shouting from a cliff into a valley. But it must amplify from within, of course."

"Of course," Coren repeated, staring at the brown mass in the mug. It could hardly be called drinkable. She may even need a spoon.

"Do you want your wings or not?" Giddon asked, his tone goading her.

She glared at him, pinched her nose shut with finger and thumb, and upturned the mug, allowing the goo to slide unhindered down her throat.

It tried to stick in her gullet, but she gagged it down, gratefully accepting a fresh mug of water.

As soon as the mess hit her stomach, it began to burn inside of her, sloshing her innards like it might claw its way back out. Her stomach began to churn and pulse.

"The call," Giddon said, nodding at the quiver in her lips. She pressed them tightly together, feeling as though she might scream and vomit all at once. Surely, he didn't mean an actual call that she would utter to the wind.

Giddon propelled her from the room, yanking her through the grid of columns until they reached the open air of the arena.

Coren could control her mouth no longer, and her lips burst open, a great and inhuman shriek tearing from her tongue. Again and again, the Vespa cry shrieked from her throat, until the skin was raw inside.

The spell waned as the sun slipped into view along the gray horizon, and Coren slumped against a column, fearing she might never be able to speak again. Her stomach had finally calmed enough for her to realize it had been hours since she'd eaten.

"And now you wait. It could be an hour, or a week, or forever," Giddon said, glib and grinning. "Oh, and I bound your promise to you as well." He gestured to the sore spot on her belly where he had sliced her skin. "Be sure you keep it."

Coren raised her heavy eyes to his plump form, agreeing with herself that she might smack him if she weren't quite so drained.

Silent, she trudged back to her room, where Sy watched her pack her things. Neither of them said a word.

They had broken every possibility into pieces that no longer fit together, and both were set on the path they had chosen.

But as she pulled the covers to her nose, trying not to swallow and disturb her throat, Coren felt Sy reach for her fingers. They slept their last night in StarsHelm together with hands linked, seeking comfort to keep away the knowledge that this could be the last night they'd ever spend together.

"Grand, I believe it's time," Mara said as the witch entered her Queen's chambers.

"The message?" Grand asked, unable to keep the glee from her voice. She'd been anticipating this moment for a long time. All their years of work and waiting was finally going to bear fruit.

Mara nodded and looked to Aram, whose smile stretched across his face.

Grand had always thought of the silent man as a reflection of Mara's emotions - without composure or rumination. He showed his pleasure and displeasure equally, like a child, and he played tricks and tested others like a spoiled child as well.

"Zorander has been long enough at the EstenSands. He may very well be voyaging home. Tell him of the

191

shifters. Show him the girl you found in the maze. Be certain he understands - the time of the SoulShifter is upon us."

"And what direction would you have me give him?" Grand asked, knowing how Mara loved to tell her husband each part of the plan in sequence, so he didn't get too far ahead.

"Take his army to Weshen City," she said, a smile of satisfaction beaming from her beautiful face. Watching her Queen, Grand imagined a sleek catten playing with an insect in the breeze, batting it to and fro.

Some days, Zorander was the insect, or Grand herself.

But today, the world was Mara's plaything.

Grand strode to the balcony, surveying the potted collection of Mara's favorite bitebuds. She watched a plant carefully, and when it turned its buds away from her, she snipped one off at the stem. The other buds reared back, their serrated petals ready to slice, but she stepped easily backward into safety.

Separated from its roots, the bud drooped and spread its petals in a mild display of repentance. Grand focused her gaze on the horizon, searching the whispers of the trees for the King's location. She nodded.

"He is indeed returning. He will be here by midday tomorrow."

"Aram, send word for the army to be readied. And the ones we've been preparing just for this day," Mara said, lowering her lashes coyly at her twin. He nodded and left the room. Grand thrilled at being alone with Mara, even for the few moments it would be. She had earned the Queen's utmost trust.

Grand scratched the message into the petals' flesh with a sharp fingernail, digging the letters carefully so Graeme could not mistake the words, one sentence on each wide petal.

When she was finished, she handed it to Mara to read.

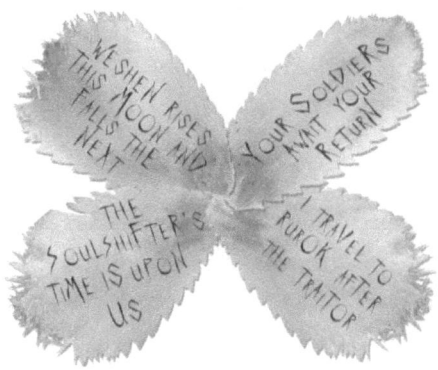

Grand watched as Mara read the final sentence and arched her brow at the witch's assumptions.

"Yes, you are correct," the Queen agreed. "It is time for that as well. Aram," she said as the door opened again, "ready the boat. It is time for us to remind the world that though Zorander and Mara's Riata began as restless, young, and ruined, we are now the noose about their neck. Let's make some countries squirm."

Grand knew that if Aram possessed a voice, he would be laughing. The ghost of a sound that would never be seemed to echo throughout the room, pushing her nervously onto the balcony. She hurried to send Mara's message so she could be free to retreat to her room.

After all, Grand had her own words of warning to send.

Kashar docked his single boat in the seemingly empty Sulit harbor. SunMelt Lake had been equally calm for the length of his journey from StarsHelm, and it was easy to forget the bustle he had left behind.

He knew the barren atmosphere was a trick. A test. He hoped he would pass. Rurok was home to the Brujok, after all, and they saw everything. He knew he had been tracked, and he knew his trackers had used their spells to telegraph his arrival. And of course, the same sensors employed around the palace were in place here.

At some point, someone would meet him.

For now, all there was to do was walk the black sand beach, keeping a safer middle ground between the gently sucking edges of SunMelt Lake and the dark-barked trees of the Listening Forest. An hour of steady travel put him on the descent around NewMoon Falls, at the bottom which rested the famed towers of Rurok.

The spiraling points invoked both admiration and apprehension. They grew from the ground like thorns and stretched down from the clouds like great bolts of black lightning, connecting the Sulit Mother to both earth and sky.

As an ambassador from Mara, he didn't fear for his life, but neither did he expect a warm welcome. The towers loomed nearer, and Kashar could no longer see the tops. He was peering straight up their twisted stone sides when a door slid open in the nearest tower.

A witch stood in the open space, watching his approach.

She was young and still beautiful, with raven hair and piercing silver eyes. Many of the Brujok had lived too long, sacrificing their beauty for a hard sort of power and an alluring strength. But this girl was round instead of sharp, her cheeks flushed instead of gray.

"Lady Mara sends her greetings," Kashar said when it became evident that the witch was not going to speak first.

She narrowed her eyes at him. Nodding, she turned and vanished into the darkness beyond the door. It stayed open like an invitation, though, so Kashar followed her, feeling his way through the narrow space until his boots bumped a stair.

As he made his way up the dozens of spiraling stairs, he began to come across a candle here and there that lit the various corridors branching into the tower. Kashar began to feel as though he were climbing the interior of a tree, with halls like branches connecting the massive structures to each other. The witch remained just far enough ahead to keep out of sight, but he knew he was being led. If he strayed, it would be his final misstep.

He'd lost count of the stairs and nearly begun to wheeze when the last stair appeared before him, opening only in one direction. The young witch waited at the top, murmuring something to another witch in the corner. Kashar thought she was vaguely familiar, but many of the older Brujok looked alike to him. They tended to dress in dark robes and wear their iron-streaked hair in the same style of braid.

Kashar took a minute to examine his surroundings, and the two witches seemed content to wait. The throne room was nearly black with shadows. Curtains lined the curved walls, hinting that the darkness was a purposeful act. Kashar's boots echoed neatly on the polished marble floor. The witch leading him had halted too far from the throne for Kashar to see anything except the outline of a male form, and he was unwilling to proceed closer than her.

"The Lord of Witches," the young witch announced, flourishing her hand toward the center of the room. A round, iron candelabra began to descend from the ceiling, directly above and circling a raised dais. As the hundreds of lit candles lowered enough to illuminate the throne, the figure seated there turned to Kashar.

One hand stroked up and back down the twisted carvings of the black throne, and the stones in his crown sparkled. The face was young and the hair dark, but it was too dim to see anything else.

"Why have you come?" The voice was dull. Higher than Kashar had expected. Bored, as though the Lord of Witches cared nothing for the question or its answer. As though he, too, were playing a part in a game. This thought struck Kashar, and he found he couldn't rid himself of the image that they were all simply players in a long, complex game.

The only problem was he wasn't certain who controlled the board, ultimately.

"I'm here pledge Riatan interest in the Sulit plight," he began, reciting the lines Mara had given him.

196

"And what is the Sulit plight?"

Kashar cleared his throat. "Witch fighting witch."

"And why do they fight?"

Kashar clenched his jaw. He had not been sent here to be quizzed by a shadow king, surely. "This is your kingdom. Do you not know why your people fight?"

A tiny intake of breath sounded from the young witch, but the Lord of Witches made no move. He simply tilted his head, the crown catching another glimmer of light and sparking it toward Kashar.

Several minutes passed in silence.

"A Weshen man…without shifter magic," the Lord said, almost to himself.

"I have lived apart from Weshen for many years. I know few with any sort of shifter magic."

"Yet your King has quite the collection, I hear. Perhaps you didn't know?"

Kashar clasped his hands behind his back. Something in the Lord's voice told him that his occupation at StarsHelm was well-known in this room. "I come to bring an offer of peaceful acceptance. King Graeme is willing to aid Sulit in calming its internal strife." He recited the ridiculous lines Mara had given him.

The Lord of Witches chuckled. "Certainly. But I believe I will wait for Mara's visit to officially accept. She did promise me a visit at the end of the summer. Surely the killing can wait a few more days."

He stood without warning, and Kashar felt the floor tilt and the air tug at him as the young man passed. His black robes swished unnaturally as he moved, billowing and floating just above the floor.

"Lock this man in Tower Four until Mara arrives."

197

Before the Lord of Witches made it the dozen steps to the window, the older witch had darted forward and bound Kashar. His hands, feet, and even lips were sealed by their spells.

The Lord of Witches flung the curtains back with a flick of his wrist, never touching the fabric. Daylight flooded in, revealing his tall, slim form in silhouette against the cloudless sky beyond. Tower after tower stretched beyond the glassless window, and Kashar stared in rage at the Lord's back until he was dragged away.

The next morning, Coren and Sy followed Kashar's knight to the edge of the palace maze together. She was still fighting the guilt of leaving, but her heart told her not to delay a second longer.

"I'm sorry," she whispered finally, embracing him. "I have to-"

"I know. Just come back." His eyes were so open and earnest that she nearly broke down and changed her mind, but then she imagined a similar look on Kosh and Penna's faces. "I know you think I can do this alone, Coren. But I can't. I can't," he ended on a choke, his words barely audible. "Please come back."

She grasped both his hands and squeezed. "And here I thought you just didn't want *me* to be alone," she said, trying to smile. His look wiped the smile away, though. "You think I'm going to my death," she said, finally speaking the fear she had sensed in him since Kashar had left.

Sy looked up into the sky, blinking away his frustration. "Something horrible is coming. I can feel it."

"I feel it, too. But my family…"

"I know." His voice was rough, and Coren wondered for the first time if there wasn't a bit of jealousy mixed with his fear.

He walked with her a few more streets into the hot, dense crowds of the StarsHelm marketplace. Neither of them had returned to the city since sneaking through it on their way to the palace, and Coren was struck by how different it seemed in daylight.

"These people seem happy enough," she said, surveying the bustling crowds. They weren't so different from EvenFall. Perhaps they were wrong, and the Restless King was at rest in old age.

"No, Coren." Sy's voice was a firm warning to her waver. "The Restless King has toppled dozens of cities like this, killed thousands who refused to be ruled by him. Made our people into slaves. Remember *those* things. He's come for our people, and he'll come for us again. No one is safe from Graeme."

"Or Queen Mara," she added reluctantly. "She has too many secrets. For rulers who haven't even built walls around their city, they keep too many guards. Watch yourself in the palace. Don't do anything before Kashar comes, at least."

Sy narrowed his eyes at her. She knew he was thinking he'd rather wait for her, and she was grateful he didn't voice the words.

She stretched her arms around him once more, burying her face in his shirt and breathing in the comfort of his strength.

She opened her mouth to tell him he was her family, too, but he suddenly pushed her away.

"Sy?" she swiveled after him as he stepped into the crowds.

"Resh!" he cried, clapping a black-shirted figure on the shoulder. As the young man turned, Coren felt her stomach flip.

By the Magi, she'd nearly forgotten how handsome he was.

Resh broke into a grin. He embraced his brother warmly, but his dark eyes watched her over Sy's shoulder the whole time. She could barely breathe for the look he gave her.

And then he was before her, his arms loose around her shoulders in a light, questioning hug.

She answered without thinking, curling her fingers into his waist. Her body pressed flush against his, and his hand came to rest at her hip.

"Yeah, I've missed you, too," he whispered into her hair, his lips at her temple. Coren balked at the intensity of her body's reaction, and she forced herself to step away, adjusting her pack so it rested between them like a barrier.

"Where's Nik?" Sy asked, scanning the people nearby.

Resh's grin slipped, and Coren felt her heart stop, afraid to hear the answer. In the fraction of time that passed, she begged the Magi *please* and *no* a hundred times.

"Nik's gone," Resh said, looking at his boots. Coren saw the words hit Sy like a kick to the stomach, and she clutched his arm. "He left Weshen City in the middle of the night." Resh pulled a crumpled paper from an inner pocket in his coat and pressed it to Sy's chest.

Sy seemed to cave in on himself as he read the few words, and he stumbled back into the wall behind them, seeming instantly smaller and broken. "He left? But why?"

Resh only shook his head. "That's all he left behind. I think he wanted to protect you. All of us."

"*Protect* us?" Sy repeated, disbelief pulling his jaw tight.

"From his darkness," Coren whispered, and Resh snapped his eyes to her.

"How do you know?" he asked.

She met his gaze steadily, but she could tell he caught the shake of her fingers as she pushed them into her pockets. "Because that's why I would leave. Nik has darkness in him. He hurt someone, didn't he." She glanced at Sy, thinking of Kashar and Lana. How she feared that same darkness taking her mind again.

Resh scrutinized her, wonder in his eyes, and she knew she'd guessed right.

"I nearly killed my father," she said, answering his unspoken question. "The rage took over, and the lust for blood was too much. It was like the magic owned me, and I couldn't control it. There's no balance in my shifting. If I kill again..." She didn't even want to finish the thought.

There was another beat of silence as Resh looked between them. Sy stared down at the paper, clenching it too tightly for her to see the words.

"Who?" Coren asked Resh gently.

"Tagsha," Resh whispered, and Sy made a strangled noise.

"What happened?"

Resh choked out the basics of the story, and Sy's expression grew tighter with each word. He turned and punched the building behind him, but as soon as the wood splintered, he shifted the sources back. Coren stepped in front of him, scanning the crowd, but no one was paying them any attention.

She slipped an arm around Sy's shoulder and leaned in close to him. But before she could suggest that at least now he had Resh to help him in the palace, he turned his face to hers. His storm-dark eyes searched hers.

"Take him with you," Sy whispered, barely moving his lips. "Please."

Coren raised her eyebrows. "Why? Isn't Sulit too dangerous for a man?"

"Please," he repeated, pressing his lips to her temple to hide the words. "I don't want you to be alone."

And as soon as he said it, though he'd said it a thousand times, she realized she'd never wanted it, either. She knew Sy wouldn't leave the palace before his mission was complete, so she hadn't asked him to leave.

But Resh.... She turned and gave Resh an appraising look.

"I've heard the witches can awaken Weshen magic." She hadn't, but she knew that was what he wanted.

Resh narrowed his eyes. "I'll never trust a witch."

She gazed at him, holding his challenge. "I'm going to Rurok. Right now. Come with me."

The last words were barely audible, and her chest fluttered in anticipation. If she stopped lying to herself, Coren knew she wanted Resh with her.

"Of course," Resh said, his eyes wide with curiosity. She felt her cheeks flush under the intensity of his gaze.

"Good. Keep each other safe. Come back for me," Sy broke in, his voice rough. "I'm not leaving until Zorander Graeme is dead."

14

Resh glanced back one last time, nodding a final goodbye to his brother. Coren had already slipped beyond the gates of StarsHelm and was waiting for him in the light tree canopy that bordered the Conqueror's Channel.

"I thought I'd walk the channel. Save coin," she said, her voice nearly shy. She looked down at her fingers, not up or anywhere near where she might meet his eyes.

"I have coin if you want-"

"No. I want to walk," she said, rushing the words. "I want to watch the skies," she added.

Resh nodded, reluctant to push her. He'd come to StarsHelm to help slay the Restless King, and he'd never even made it into the palace.

All because this beautiful girl had asked him to come along on likely the most dangerous journey of his life. Like a fool, he'd said yes without even a pause.

"You know, the last time I went somewhere on the advice of a witch, I nearly died because of her trickery," he said as they traveled the edge of the channel.

"Anyone of any race can be treacherous. And anyone can be genuine."

He shrugged. He'd yet to meet a witch that wanted to help him without some steep payment. "Tell me about the palace," he suggested.

"The King has been gone since we arrived. I never saw Queen Mara, but I fought one of her Brujok guards." She grinned at the memory, and Resh vowed to get the details. "There are many good people there. They seem so earnest that we help them, but I never saw the mistreatment everyone feared. I can't help but wonder…"

"Wonder what?" he asked when she didn't continue for a long moment.

"I just wonder if maybe we'd be better off backing away and letting Riata take care of its own problems."

Resh's feet dragged to a stop.

Perhaps he had greatly misjudged her. "Sy told me once that you believed nothing is small when it's against your will. And I laughed when he told me. I thought it was horribly naive."

Her eyes flashed. "Because you likely never had to bend your will to others' wishes, Second Son."

He was surprised into a bitter laugh. "Second Son? The title ensures that my will has rarely been my own. Do you think drink and women are all I'd ever want? That fine clothing and jeweled weaponry would be enough? You know nothing of the ways my will has been twisted by the General, by Sy, by all those who seek to use my position for their gain."

"At least you had enough to drink and eat. You had fine clothing. You didn't have to sacrifice your dignity or your safety just to feed your family!"

"At least you had a beach to run and plains to hunt. At least you had your family and your own home and your own free will, however limited it may have been! Don't you see, Coren? Free will is relative. None of us truly have it. I have more than you, but you have more than the Wesh in the palace. And Zorander Graeme has the most of all."

She strode ahead, her spine straight and her shoulders proud. But he knew he was right. Resh hurried his steps to catch her. "I think you're feeling sorry for yourself," he taunted.

She whirled on him, her palm pressed hard against his chest, and he stumbled back a bit at the force. "I am not."

"You had family, and it was taken. You tasted power, and it was taken. You had a father, and a friend in Sy, and a kiss from me, and it's all been taken. Now, you feel like it would have been better if none of this had happened. How right am I?"

She refused to answer, but he grasped her arms, keeping her from turning away. His fingers loosened as their eyes connected, though, and he saw the tears pooling in the corners.

"Would it have been better for Nik if none of this had happened? He's hurting. He's on his own. But for the first time in his life, he's free from physical chains. And what about your brother and sister? Would it have been better to just let him be taken from the island as usual, and her to run the hunts?"

At some point, his words had pulled the fight from her, and she slumped as though her pack were too heavy to bear. Resh gently slid the straps from her shoulders, reaching around her to drop the bag on the ground. His arms stayed, pulling her close to his chest.

"Is this against your will?" he whispered, his lips brushing her ear. "Or this?" he pushed her a little more, dropping a kiss at the edge of her jaw. "Or this?" He bent his mouth to the base of her throat, where the blood pulsed strongest.

As his lips pressed into her skin, he could have sworn he felt the spark of that blood. Its magic tugged him closer.

Her body was limp in his. She didn't push him away, but she wasn't participating, either. So Resh pulled back to look in her eyes. They were still edged in unspilled tears and blank with an uncaring surrender he dreaded seeing in anyone.

"Don't lose your fight before you've begun fighting," he said, slipping a finger beneath her chin. Her eyes tracked up his face. "We'll find your family. But when we do, and you hold those children tight to your chest, think of all the children who will never see their mother or father or siblings again, because they're slaves. Because someone ripped apart their family, murdered one of the people they loved most for the greed of magic."

Resh stopped there because he saw the light begin to flicker again behind the black veil that seemed to shroud her gaze. But his words had also hit a little too close to his own comfort. He'd been greedy as well, and he knew his desire for the magic's return had driven Nik away.

"We should keep going," Coren murmured, stepping away from his grasp and pulling on her pack.

Resh sighed, falling into step next to her.

The morning grew hot as they walked in silence. Coren scanned the sky as much as the ground before her.

Ever since Giddon had called the Vespa for her, she had kept a constant loop of prayer open, asking the Magi to restore her wings. To return her power, so she could save her family and return to help Sy.

But after Resh's challenge, the prayer felt a little false.

Even she couldn't ignore the signs that the Magi pointed her toward. Getting to EvenFall had been easy. StarsHelm easier still.

But she'd had to fight every step to even begin the journey to Sulit. She wasn't giving up her personal mission to find Kosh, Penna, and Maren, but an insistent voice in her head told her it was selfish.

As they made their way west toward SunMelt Lake, Coren resolved that yes, she would do what she could to rescue her family.

But she would also think of the other families ripped apart by the King and Queen of Riata. She would take what power she had, and she would fight in Sulit and in Riata and in Weshen. She would fight wherever she was needed, and she would never back down until all the world's people were free from the bondage and persecution her people had faced.

And if that fight stole her life, then at least it would be a life she'd been proud to live.

Her steps quickened with each word marching across her mind, and energy surged in her veins.

As they crossed a brief clearing, a shadow wheeled above them. Coren felt her knees weaken, buckling beneath her as her strength evaporated. Her stomach began to churn and heave, and a hopeful cry choked its way out of her throat.

A scream from above met her weak voice, and as she fell to her hands and knees on the path, she managed a grin.

Lolling her head back, she had just enough time to hear Resh shout in panic as a dark, winged shape barreled into her. The pain was instant and overpowering as it flattened her against the earth, smothering her beneath the metallic scent of its body. Her lungs had no room to expand, and she grew dizzy without air. Another scream echoed so deep in her brain that it became the rush of blood in her ears, the sound as eternal and natural as the sound of her own wordless thoughts.

She felt her body begin to separate into its diverse sources: skin dissolved and blood floated and bones shattered.

The pain had become so much that she was numb, and at some point, even it separated from her consciousness.

A voice boomed in her head, echoing in whispers as it bounced behind her eyelids.

I am yours and you are mine and now we fly and now we fly and now we fly...

The weight on her chest slipped through her body, sinking like mud through water, and came to rest at her back. A mass of weight on her spine, familiar and blessed.

And now we fly and now we fly and now we fly...

The weight formed wings and the wings pushed up and off the ground. Her sources collected around her as her body propelled upward, gathering form as the trees whipped past and the blue sky rushed up at her.

And now we fly...

As the bones snapped into their new places, muscle wrapped and twisted around them, new patterns of movement arising as naturally as running once had been. Four wings flapped and thrust her into the great blue nothing above.

Her belly grew warm as the sources that were once skin shifted into feathers, coating her body from the chill above the clouds.

Coren somersaulted - wings to the sky - and glided in the still summer air.

Her eyes darted around her, too fast to focus at first. She wanted to smile, but her lips no longer existed. Instead, she cracked apart two hard bones of beak and released a scream of triumph.

The Magi had answered her prayers. She didn't think Vespa could cry, and for this, she was also thankful. She wanted all her emotion to sink into the power she possessed. The magic she could do again. The help she could provide for her family and her country.

It was this last thought which sobered her glee and clipped her wild wings to drift back to the clearing.

The Magi had answered her prayers, and she had a promise to fulfill.

Her golden claws sunk into the earth next to her abandoned pack, and Coren tucked her wings back. She shook the mist of cloud from her feathered body and swiveled her eyes around the clearing.

Focusing her vision, she realized she stared straight into the deadly point of Resh's arrow.

"Show me Corentine, or you die now, Vespa." His voice was as strong as his aim, and the barely-contained ferocity thrilled Coren's senses. His rage sang to her new form, and his righteous claim on her warmed the feathers along the edges of her wings like a lover's caress.

Thinking of her panic when Sy had shifted into the Grizzlin, she ducked her head low in a semblance of a bow, spreading her wings in surrender. Resh likely knew nothing of SelfShifting's complete form, and he may be assuming her dead.

His fingers shook on the weapon, and Coren knew she had only seconds to collect her thoughts.

Closing her eyes to the light, she searched within for her own sources. They must be tucked inside. Sy described it like a double-sided sack - one side leather and the other fur. You could reverse the sack, and you could reverse the sources.

She just had to find them before Resh shot her.

Now we walk, she spoke in her mind, reversing the Vespa's call to fly. *I am still yours, but now you are mine, and now we walk.*

She felt the feathers begin to dissolve around her, and her claws shrunk, the gold seeping back into her body.

212

Now we walk, she chanted in her mind, and within seconds, she had fallen again to the ground, naked on her hands and knees in the dirt.

She raised her face to see Resh staring at her like his world had just flipped inside out along with her body.

She grinned, shifting the sources of her clothing around her body, and stood straight before him. The wings were still a weight, but they rode in her chest now, compacted into the knowledge of waiting power.

"How about that?" she said, laughter spilling from her lips.

Resh had dropped his bow sword to the ground, fingers loose, but he still stood transfixed. Finally, he began to shake his head. The corners of his mouth pulled up, one side at a time. "That...that will be one of my favorite memories. Forever," he added, his eyes scanning her body in awe.

Grand clutched the railing of the boat, the metal bar being the only thing grounding her to reality. Her mind swam in magic, awash in its heady waves.

SelfShifting, she whispered to herself, wishing she were still close enough to StarsHelm for her sisters to hear the word.

Somewhere nearby, a Weshen had just merged with a MagiCreature, and Grand felt like a young witch again. Her magic thrilled in the presence of the shifter, alive in every way as an abundance of magic-bright sources swirled in the air.

She knew she needed to get a message to all her Brujok sisters - those behind her in StarsHelm, as well as those waiting for her arrival in Rurok. What she didn't know was when she'd have the chance.

Even as she thought this, footsteps approached from behind.

"Are you well?" Mara asked, joining her at the railing. Her eyes scrutinized Grand, seeking the reason for her youthful grin and glow.

"I'm greatly enjoying the breeze," Grand answered, hoping it would be enough. She saw Aram sidle up to the railing, several feet away. "It's been a long time since I could feel the ocean this close."

Mara nodded, but Grand felt the Queen's eyes rest on her a few moments too long. She must be very careful. Grand did not want to be the one to ruin so many years' worth of planning and hiding and deferring to a King and Queen that was hers in name only, never in spirit.

Just because Mara was a great spellmaster and had lived in Sulit as a girl didn't make her an equal with the witches.

Even more, it would never make her their true Queen. Their collective power would always be greater than hers, if her Brujok sisters could convince those silly southern witches to unite. The battle they were heading into today would help change their minds, she hoped.

Once the rebellion was effectively crushed by Mara's plan, Grand hoped the southern Sulit would see Riata for the threat it truly was. Mara was playing right into the Brujok's hands. Grand could barely believe their luck. By feeding a battle between the witches, Mara was unwittingly laying the path for a united Sulit.

Once Sulit was united again, the Brujok could stop biding their time as spies in Mara's employ and prepare for a full takeover of StarsHelm.

And once they found the right twins to fulfill the Mother's shifter prophecy, they could overpower Umbren.

Grand slid a glance to the Queen standing beside her, then another to the brother on her opposite side. Both looked too young for the years they'd spent. Neither their bodies nor their powers had shown significant sign of age.

Although...Grand did wonder why the Queen hadn't yet felt the shifter power floating nearby on the breeze. Perhaps Mara *was* slipping a bit.

They were nearing the docks, and they would be in open water within half an hour.

"Zorander's bridge. A fool bridge for a fool man," Mara remarked, pointing at the pylons sunk deep in the water at the edge of the NewMoon Falls. Only a few of them had been joined with a platform, and the unfinished bridge stretched across barely more water than the boat floated on. Each time the King made progress, the Sulit simply gathered forces and called on their Mother to wash away enough to set him back. A forever game of over and under, to and fro.

"It would be nice to travel directly across the lake," Grand countered, wavering between pride and the desire for ease. She loved the boat voyage, but the trek from the docks and south to Rurok would slow them. She was impatient for the battle. And there was always the problem of moving the people in their cargo hold.

"I should check on the prisoners," she said, and Mara nodded. Grand crossed the polished deck at a quick pace, hoping neither of them would follow her. She really needed to send a message to her sisters about the shifter power.

But a shadow fell before her, bringing a mild curse to her full lips. Aram followed, his huge boots clomping the wood a few steps behind. Grand was used to being followed, but she also knew this meant her Queen didn't fully trust her, and this was very dangerous for the Brujok.

The message would simply have to wait until she arrived.

15

Zorander Graeme stepped into the empty, silent throne room. Mara's message had reached him only a few hours' journey from the palace.

His troops had already left, though, and so had his Queen. He grinned at the thought of her sailing to conquer Sulit while he did the same with Weshen. Their plans had been slower to fruit than they'd expected, but each year Riata's holdings grew. He felt the years in his bones, but his muscles remained lithe and ready for the upcoming battle.

Before him, the twisted silver throne shone in the light cast by a wall of torches. Hundreds of fist-sized fires welcomed him and warmed the throne for his return. The chair itself had been melted down from his father's throne, once the Silver Sovereign was dead.

Zorander had ordered the back hammered to look like the silhouette of StarsHelm. Black diamonds sparkled in its miniature turrets, and he gazed on the scene in satisfaction.

StarsHelm Palace.

He'd been born here, in a room in the East Wing. That room had been shut away for many years, though, as the only memories he had of it were tied to a mother he'd hated, Queen Jessamal.

She'd caused him pain in life, both by her actions and her inactions, and he wasn't about to allow her the same power in death.

Zorander wished the same could be said of his seven brothers. Dead longer than he'd been King of Riata, they still haunted his movements about the palace because he was the one who had wished their deaths. The debt was his curse, and though he had paid some, much of it could only be bartered with his blood.

So, over the many years, Zorander had become quite accustomed to the fact that though he had wished his brothers dead, he hadn't exactly wished them gone. He must now live with this mistake.

Their footsteps pattered forever behind his. Their whispered plottings kept him awake in the stillness of every midnight hour. Their warm breaths of laughter caressed his bare ankles when he rose each morning to piss and bathe. Their fingers pulled the very food and drink from his mouth sometimes, lending him the reputation of carelessness.

If only these playful inconveniences had been the extent of his curse, Zorander would have borne the spirits gladly.

After all, at the end of the story, their crown rested on his head.

But playful was not the spirits' true and constant nature. His brothers had been cruel in life, and that magnified itself in spirit. He knew the SoulShifter could break the curse, but that power had long been out of reach. Until today.

Most assumed the King of Riata traveled so extensively and conquered cities wherever he went because he desired more power or land or riches. This was the pattern of kings through history.

Instead, it was the search for a cure which made Zorander Graeme into the Restless King.

Zorander stepped unhurriedly up the shallow steps and settled his body into the throne's clutches, sinking back as the silver warmed his body. He should be an old man by now, but his appearance and athleticism refused to comply with the passing years. Sulit magic kept him young and handsome and limber enough to fight with his Queen each day, and bed her each night.

He had done all he wanted for Riata, and more, as the decades passed. It was now the greatest nation in all the land. Many small towns and hamlets prostrated themselves before his throne each year, begging to slip inside the noose of Riata's holdings. Those who didn't beg paid, and those who didn't pay, the Restless King forced.

It was an agreeable life, and he didn't have any intentions of letting it go.

He searched the darkness of the hall before him.

"I know you're here." His voice barely carried beyond the marble dais, but it didn't need to. His brothers, wherever they were, would hear. They would come.

As he waited, he remembered the first time he'd seen Braddon's spirit. He'd been such a child then, frightened of everything. Willing to do nearly anything to save himself from the threats and ugly deeds his brothers handed out like favors.

But as the years passed, and the curse seemed no closer to being reversed, his debt no closer to being repaid, Zorander Graeme had simply learned to live with death.

If he could find the SoulShifter, now awakened in Weshen blood after all these years according to Mara, all this could change.

The SoulShifter was a myth to most, but a promise to Graeme and his Queen, whose souls desperately needed tending to.

It was a weapon against the seven spirits that slipped into the throne room just now, whisps of smoke and sunlight where none should be. Golden shadows, cast like candlelight around the room.

"Welcome, brothers," Zorander murmured. "Do you like my new ring?"

He held the massive gem aloft in the darkness, examining the intricate carving in the silver band. "A present from a tribe in the EstenSands. I increase Riata's holdings yet again, while you whither on these grounds."

His laughter would have sounded cruel to someone who hadn't known the brothers in life. Whatever cruelty Zorander paid them, they had given him the inspiration first.

A flash like heat lightning snapped at his left. "Lumien," Zorander sighed. The silver arm of his throne was suddenly burning beneath his fingers, yet he took his time removing them, bearing the pain because Lumien would only find worse.

Always worse.

Ready to join us yet, old man?

The voice was a blade against his ear, tucking away a lock of silver hair.

"I've never been one of you. And by the time death claims me, my debts will have been forgotten."

Zorander knew this last bit was a lie, but he was bold enough tonight to speak it. Tomorrow he would ride for Weshen, and when he returned with the SoulShifter, his brothers would be the ones finally claimed by death.

If the legends were true, and Zorander fervently believed each one, the SoulShifter could put spirits to rest, and call others to play. But the greatest talent of all, the one only whispered about in prayer and curse, was the talent to separate the source of a soul from its body and shift it into a new body.

Immortality.

Necromancy.

Unlimited power with unlimited life.

Zorander Graeme smiled, leaning back in his throne, relaxing his muscles for the onslaught of pain. Whatever horrors Lumien, Braddon, Brys, Owin, Anyon, Saith, and Derec had prepared while he was away were nothing compared to what he would find for them in Weshen City, in the blood of a young Weshen shifter.

"You will not *carry* me across that lake." Resh crossed his arms and turned to her, refusing to walk another step.

"But I think I can fly faster than the boat," Coren reasoned. She wasn't completely certain she was strong enough, but once the idea took hold in her mind, it refused not to be voiced. She had the wings; she might as well use them. And they could save the coin for bribery and sundries in Sulit, rather than renting something they didn't need.

"No. Go on ahead if you must move faster. But I'm taking a boat."

Coren sighed. She wouldn't split them up, and he knew it. "At least let me show you-"

"No."

Coren watched him a few seconds longer, gauging his stance. There was a stubborn set to his shoulders that she'd never seen before. Or not in Resh, at least. "Are you afraid?" she asked, her voice tentative enough to let him know she hated asking.

He glared at the ground. "Heights," he mumbled. "Can't do heights."

She nodded, pressing back a smile. Everyone had fears, she knew. She wasn't one to tease. But she had never suspected Resh's fears might be so physically based.

"Don't they train Paladins for all sorts of terrain?" She began walking again, and he followed, rolling his shoulders to release an obvious tension.

"They train us for everything. That doesn't make us good at everything."

Coren didn't ask him any more questions, and she could tell he was grateful for it. As they walked, she split her lunch with him. She was about to ask him what he knew of Sulit when a horn sounded through the trees, from the direction of the channel.

"A boat!" He beckoned to her, and they slipped through the trees, careful to keep hidden.

The Conqueror's Channel flowed through the countryside before them, straight as a sword. It was a masterpiece of cut stone, with water deep enough for large boats to travel between the palace and SunMelt Lake.

"This channel has allowed the King to conquer so much of the vast WestenSands," Resh told her as they approached its edge. "Riata builds the boats in StarsHelm's dry ports, then slips them up the channel and north across the lake. Graeme's soldiers were upon the Sands before the native people had even an inkling of attack. And if the Riatan troops became overwhelmed, they could always retreat to MoonShade Castle."

"I thought MoonShade was neutral?" Coren asked.

"That's where Mara is from. MoonShade isn't an official Riatan city, but Graeme includes it in his holdings, and its citizens both benefit from and pay for the association."

A sleek white and black boat churned up the channel toward them, eating up the distance between StarsHelm and the lake more quickly than Coren could have imagined possible. As it drew closer, she saw the thick masses of river plants rising up beneath the boat in green waves, pushing and pulling it along.

"Sulit spells," Resh said, disgust twisting his mouth. Women lined the front edge of the deck, arms spread to the water below them. "Witches."

"And shifters, I think," Coren added, pointing to where the water separated just before the hull of the boat, creating a narrow space for the craft to surge ahead. It was like what she'd done with Sy, only on a much larger scale. She didn't see anyone who looked Weshen, but perhaps they were chained up somewhere in the bowels of the boat. Coren felt her anger growing as she watched this Riatan craft, powered by Sulit and Weshen labor.

"This is the royal boat." Resh gestured to the hammered silver crest set into the painted wood along the boat's length. The pattern repeated in a flash of reflected sunlight as the boat passed them.

"Where is it going?" Coren asked. "The King is supposedly in the EstenSands, so this must be Queen Mara."

Resh raised an eyebrow as the boat swished away from them. "Go check it out, then, Vespa-girl."

Coren grinned. Of course.

Maybe they could hitch a ride, solving both Resh's objections and hers. She dropped her pack and called to the voice within her.

Now we fly!

The voice was quick to respond, its fierce joy coursing through her blood as the magic shifted her form. This time there was no pain, and Coren shot from between the trees, spiraling up and up into the blue sky. She would have laughed, but her voice was now a screech, and so she screeched with pleasure.

Higher and higher she flew, flexing the muscles of her wings, as tight as if they'd been waiting for her all these weeks, resting instead of searching for her. Oh, how she wished she could share this feeling with Resh. Something in her yearned to put such a smile on his face, even as she knew he would be too terrified to enjoy it.

She leveled out, and her claws trailed lazily beneath her, stripping upper leaves from the treetops. The channel was to her left, a stark slice through the earth. StarsHelm Palace shimmered behind her, and the mist and thunder of NewMoon Falls gathered at the southern edge of the sparkling lake.

Her upper wings and lower wings beat in a rotating spiral of rhythm, around and around and up, until everything - even the mighty StarsHelm Palace - was nothing but ink blots on a map spread beneath her.

Above the clouds, the breeze pushed at her back, and a sheer nip of ice crusted her outer feathers. She gave them a powerful shake, and all the ice crackled away.

Coren rolled to her back, tucking her wings close to her body and free-falling. She plummeted like an arrow through the clouds, banking and coming up far behind the boat.

She peered at herself as she flew slow and close to the water.

Beady bird eyes stared back at her - different yet still somehow recognizable. Just like Sy's Grizzlin form, she saw how the Vespa form retained something of her personality. But Coren was slightly taken aback to realize the parts that remained. She didn't see anything of the love she felt for her family or her friendship with Sy. None of this emotion was evident in the majestic slant of her beak or the round flatness of her eyes.

But the ferocity of necessity and survival were there. The plain statement of self-preservation at all costs and the determination to do her own will was evident in the curl of her claws and the beat of her four wings. She thought of what Resh had said to her once, on an EvenFall rooftop, in the rain.

Four wings, two arms, and two legs. Eight ways to help her people.

She felt the renewed pull of his challenge. Yes, she would help her people. She would answer their cries with a battle.

She felt the Vespa then, too. Somewhere deep in her mind, smiling and pulsing like a second heartbeat.

Approaching the back of the royal boat, she saw that it was paused at the edge of the docks, awaiting whatever checks a royal boat might need to go through. Coren knew she needed to hurry if she and Resh planned to board. Skimming to the right and above the treetops, she spotted Resh on the ground, still making his way to the docks. He was near enough, she thought.

He glanced up, and his eyes tracked her form as she swerved lower, directly behind the boat. Her claws scrabbled at the sleek surface of the boat's side, and she considered shifting back to board silently.

But a shout reached her ears, and her stomach flipped.

They'd seen her already. It was hard to hide a huge MagiCreature, and she'd been too excited to fly to think of a good plan. She cursed at her stupidity. Throwing her wings wide, she pushed away from the deck and into the air.

The men looked tiny as they gathered on the deck far below, but now they were shouting, pointing excitedly. At her.

Their yells were easy for her Vespa hearing to make out, and she rose again. Not only had they spotted her, but they knew what she was.

But they were afraid, she noticed, as a tang of sweat drifted up to meet her nostrils. And rightly so. Weshen Paladins alone were trained enough to survive MagiCreature attacks, and even then, many died at the claws and talons and poisons of these powerful animals.

It was why the Weshen had become so valuable to Riata in the first place, long ago.

Coren swooped closer to the trees, meaning to drop out of sight in the canopy, but a glint of metal caught her eye. She realized too late that one of the men had produced a bow sword. He aimed it up to her body and fired, the arrow vibrating in the air toward her.

His aim was shaky, though, and she easily swerved, the arrow missing her by a hand's breadth. She swore at them, but it came out like a shriek. The men below gathered closer together, others pulling short-range weapons.

Another arrow flew to her left, and she dropped into the trees, out of their sight. But her beady eyes could magnify and see what should have been too far away. Coren's heart beat double, then double again, as she saw and scented what could only be Queen Mara of Riata.

Tall and beautiful and surprisingly young, she stepped to the center of the deck, surveying the trees where Coren hid.

A witch stood near her, and a man, equally tall and statuesque. Aram, Coren guessed. She stared at the witch and realized it was the same Brujok guard she had fought in the maze.

She should shift back into her Weshen body, sneak away to find Resh, and rent a rowboat as they had planned.

It would be the smartest thing.

But the Queen was here, before her. Aram was here.

She could kill them both right now before they even left Riata.

Coren climbed claw over claw up the tree she was perched in, stretching her neck for a better glimpse of the woman. Raven-dark hair and a crown of rich silver and glittering black diamonds. A dress of pure silver, trailing behind her, molten in the sun. Impractical for a voyage, surely, but stunning.

The thunk of another arrow firing reached her ears and processed in her brain too late, and she cried out as its shaft pierced the joint of her upper right wing. It was no ordinary arrow, either. As soon as it lodged between her feathers, it began to spread and grow, like a branch sprouting leaves and vines.

Coren found herself tumbling from the tree, immobile, as the arrow transformed into a box made of coarse, stiff chains.

A cage.

She was trapped inside a magical cage.

Coren shrieked and beat her wings against the flimsy-looking weave of her prison walls, but nothing helped. The magic was stronger than her Vespa body. No longer able to stretch her wings enough to lift herself into the air, she began to fall, tumbling against the flexible edges.

She hit the ground in a moan of bruising, and the box began to move, dragged through the brush toward the channel.

Brambles and rocks tore at her feathers and scraped the paper-thin skin of her legs.

Desperation shot her into panic, and she shifted out of her Vespa form just as the cage burst onto the bank of the channel.

The crowd of men and witches gasped as they saw her female body, a shrunken and plain prisoner compared to their catch.

But the Brujok gave a shriek of recognition, and Coren felt a spark of magic light her skin on fire as the witch cackled. Coren reached for the sources of the chains, wrenching them from the witch's hold and shoving her body through a brief opening. She misjudged her momentum, though, and tumbled down into the channel, her head dizzy as she sank beneath the green water.

She could sense the turmoil in the sources around her, water and plant and stone and earth. The witch was pulling at the natural elements in a way Coren had never experienced, and it confused her shifting abilities.

The plants tickled her arms and legs as Coren tried to kick away from them. She fought her lungs, convincing them not to breathe in the deadly water. Tendrils wrapped around her ankles and wrists, pulling her deeper and deeper, until she felt the hard stone bottom of the channel beneath her sodden boots. Her chest pushed against itself, muscles screaming to expand her lungs.

She had to get away from the plants. They were like the maze of the palace - spelled by the witches to trap her.

Coren bent her knees and pushed against the bottom as hard as she could, shooting up toward the surface of the water. Her outstretched palms collided with the belly of the boat, then the rest of her body bounced hard against the wood.

She was going to drown here, sucked under by the plants and trapped by the boat's mass. Reflexively, her fingers scratched at the wood, and she used her last bit of inspiration to dissolve the wood before her, hoping it would lead her to air.

The force of the water immediately pushed her through the new opening, and she rolled, coughing and gagging, onto the floor of the ship's inside.

Coren swiftly sealed the hole she'd made in the ship, preventing the water from filling the room. She crouched on her knees, heaving up lungfuls of river water, blinking into the blackness.

Would they know where she was? Surely the witch could find her on the boat.

She needed to get out. She could breathe now, but she was just as trapped here. Maybe more. The witch and the Queen knew *what* she was, and that was bad. Once they figured out *where* she was, her life would be forfeit.

Coren recovered enough to realize that she was not alone in the black belly of the ship. As her eyes adjusted to the darkness, she could see that squat iron cages lined the hull of the boat. Inside each was a person watching her silently with round eyes. Coren stumbled to her feet, peering back at them.

"You're here to save us," one said, and Coren turned to the voice.

It was a Weshen girl, no older than Penna, dark-haired and short enough to stand in her cage.

"You're going to set us free," she said again, and Coren found herself nodding.

Yes, that was exactly why the Magi had tangled her in this mess.

"But you need to leave the way you came in," another voice said. "Before the Queen finds you here. Or you'll be bound in their spells just like us."

Coren stepped forward and saw a young boy. Looking more carefully around the room, she saw the prisoners were nearly all children.

"Weshen?" she whispered.

"Wesh," one agreed, and she winced at the shortened slur.

"Do you have shifter magic?" she asked. There were murmurs of consent. "Then you may call yourselves Weshen. My name is Coren, and I used to live on Weshen Isle."

"Why did you leave?" the girl asked.

Coren looked directly into the large, dark eyes studying her. "To find the Restless King and kill him, so you may be free."

"Forget about the King," said one of the few men in the crowd. He was slumped in a corner of his cage. "It's the Queen who rules everything."

Coren opened her mouth to question him further, but light shot down into the hold as a door opened from the deck above.

"Go!" whispered the girl, and Coren did not hesitate. She shifted a hole in the side of the boat, tumbling out and slipping into the water within seconds. The hole was quickly mended, and Coren stroked silently toward the bank, her heart heavy with a new task to complete.

Just like the night she found Nikesh bound in the river, she knew she would not be able to rest until each of these people - her people - were safe and free.

16

Giddon had spent too long debating. The message had been very clear.

He just didn't want to leave the safety of his room to deliver it. He'd survived a long time by being a coward.

But as he heard the horns of Mara's boat in the distant channel, he decided it was time he took his own advice and stop hiding. Giddon packed up the few tools and the bottle of herb paste he would need to replicate the message. He knew Sy would require proof, not just a reclusive man's word.

Taking a shallow breath, Giddon cracked the door of his single room and sneaked into the shadows of the columns beyond.

The rows of broad stone columns bordered the arena thickly and helped him transition from the cramped closeness of his home to the idea of being visible and in the open. He jumped from one to the next, skittish as a catten in a lightning storm, willing his path to the palace to stay empty.

The corridor leading to the maze was much worse than the columns, and traveling the maze itself nearly shattered his resolve. Giddon puffed his way through as fast as he could, his heart beating in his throat. He flinched violently away from each of the tasting tendrils and bit his lips against tiny screams.

Kashar's knight was waiting just where he was supposed to be, and Sy was in his room like Giddon had prayed.

Giddon collapsed on the empty bed next to Sy's, breathing much more heavily than he would like. It wasn't all from fear, either. Giddon's tiny home afforded him little reason for exercise. He held up a finger and tried not to notice that Sy was hiding a smile.

"Mara has left the palace," Giddon finally managed. "She sails to Rurok today."

Sy nodded, scowling. "I heard. Now, I'm of even less use here, waiting around for Graeme to return."

"No!" Giddon snapped, interrupting Sy's impatience with his own. His message was more important. "No! You listen."

He spread his tools before him on the bed, carefully unwrapping a fleshy bitebud he'd clipped that morning from one of his own plants. The duplication spell wasn't difficult, but Grand and Mara preferred to complicate everything with these confounded plants. They were cursed creations, and he only kept them to spy on their messages.

The razored edges of the flower gleamed as Giddon used a set of finger-sized tongs to spread them apart. When the flower was laid open on the bed, resembling red flesh laid bare of a bone, he began to spread the spelled paste on the petals.

Gradually, blurred letters began to form on the pulp of the flower, like water-stained smudges.

"I can't read it," Sy said, leaning close. Giddon rolled his eyes. Certainly, the letters were all reversed, but this wasn't difficult. He sighed, resisting breathing in the boy's scent too much. It would break his concentration.

"This is Mara's message. It was sent to the EstenSands, so it must be to Zorander. This part says she travels to Rurok after a traitor."

"Kashar?"

Giddon nodded. "She sent him there herself. I believe she set him up."

"Then I have to go warn them!" Sy began to rise.

"No!" Giddon yelled, his patience running out. "Look! Look here!" His pudgy finger jabbed at the next part. The petals were forming their mirrored letters in reverse order as well, like time running backward. "Here, she tells him his soldiers are waiting. And here. The SoulShifter's time. She senses the strength of your magic, Sy. And Coren's. She and Grand can feel it even through my cloaking spell."

"What does this one say?" Sy's voice was sharp with fear as he pointed to a *W* coming into focus on the final leaf.

"Weshen," Giddon affirmed. "It rises this moon and falls next."

"Falls!" Sy cursed and jumped into motion. He had thrown half his belongings into his pack before Giddon could find the cork for his bottle of paste.

"The King will attack Weshen this moon," he murmured, though it was obvious that Sy had put all the letters together.

"If Coren returns before I do, tell her this, please. And thank you for finding me."

Giddon nodded, and Sy was out the door, gone without a trace in less than five minutes.

Giddon sprawled back onto the bed in the empty room, still breathing too heavily to return home.

Sy clutched the arm of the silent, ever-waiting knight outside his door. With his pack on his shoulders and his boots laced tightly, he felt the panic begin to dissipate and harden into diamond-clear resolve.

"Hire me the fastest coach you know of, please. I ride to EvenFall today." He would get his chance to kill Zorander Graeme, and he would do it while saving his people.

It was time for Sy to stop waiting and wishing, and take action to change his world. This prospect thrilled his instincts, and despite what awaited him after the journey, Sy was ready. He'd trained for this his entire life, and his people needed him.

The knight led him to the edge of the maze at a brisk run. In the city, he turned Sy down a narrow, damp alley. Sy handed over every coin Coren had insisted she leave with him. The knight looked at it doubtfully, and Sy added a dagger from his pack. It wasn't one of his best, but it had a jeweled handle.

"Please. I need to get to EvenFall. The King…" He bit back the words, not wanting to give the knight extra information that might compromise the plan, or the knight himself if anyone in the palace questioned him.

The man nodded, and pointed Sy further down the alley, to a tiny stall attached to a barn. They were just at the edge of the city limits, nearly where he and Coren and Kashar had entered StarsHelm several days ago.

Sy hopped into the rented coach and slammed the door. The knight had already vanished, and Sy was alone, save the driver.

With any luck, he could be in EvenFall before the King even returned to the palace for his troops, and he could be through the passage and helping fortify Weshen City before Graeme made it through the forests of Riata. Surely it took some time to move an army.

They would have a week to prepare, maybe more if Graeme hadn't quite been expecting this opportunity or order to move.

Sy sunk into the cushion, his brain running through lists of tasks that would need doing when he arrived. The summer had nearly ended, so hopefully the men would be in Weshen again, fortifying the city. They had many open spaces for archers and traps set into the ground for foot soldiers to fall into, or for his own men to hide in.

Sy wondered if the mountain passage still held, or if the magic's return had weakened its defense. He shuddered, trying to erase the sensation of reading those backward letters foretelling his country's downfall, from a flower that looked like rotten flesh.

As the wheels of the coach jostled over the road, Sy himself was restless. He staggered his too-quick breathing with fervent prayers to the Magi to keep his people safe, and to make Ashemon willing to hear his story.

Night cloaked the coach's windows more than its flimsy curtains, and the driver pulled to the side of the road to let the animals rest. Sy's thoughts refused to stop churning, and instead turned to Nik.

He added a prayer to his rotation that wherever Nik was, he was safe and approaching happiness. Nik's heart held so much sadness, Sy knew. So many scars. But his smile had been easy during those few days in EvenFall. Nik could heal if given the chance.

Sy regretted that he hadn't been able to give Nik that chance.

Not yet.

Stretching his legs as far as possible in the cramped coach, Sy promised himself that when he saw Nik again, he wouldn't let go of what they'd shared so easily. He would try his hardest to show Nik joy and give him the time he needed to heal.

The NeverCross Mountains raged all around Nik as he climbed. Higher and higher, into the void of the blue-white sky. His breathing was shallower here, but the view more than made up for it.

Empty of people.

Empty of magic.

Clear of anything that could hurt him on the inside. Of course, he could easily slip on the ice and tumble to his death, but that sort of danger he could mostly control. The stuff in his chest and his mind, not so much.

Nik's emotions had never been his own to control. He'd always only had enough strength to react to the ugliness around him.

Perhaps this was why he preferred to create beautiful things with his shifting when he had the chance.

The slavers wanted his shifting to be a weapon. But the world had plenty of weapons.

When he was alone, Nik made flowers and sand castles and tapestries of woven water and foam.

He hiked up a trail that was barely wide enough for his feet, following the tracks of a small animal. Nik had eaten all the food he'd brought in the first day, except a sack of dried, leathery meat he was portioning out. But he could survive. These last weeks with Resh and Sy and Coren were the anomaly in his life, the exception to the constant hunger, fear, and pain.

Up here, the only thing Nik had to fear was himself.

He couldn't remember the last time he'd been alone. Perhaps never, since he'd always been on the run when he'd left places. When he left Sulit, when he escaped the first slavers near StarsHelm.

Nik breathed in the mountain air, relishing how it tightened his lungs and nipped his lips and nostrils. The heavy fur cloak and wool hood he'd taken from Sy's room made the journey more than tolerable. But he missed Sy. More than he'd expected, for someone he'd kissed twice and barely knew.

He felt as though he knew Sy better than he should, though. Perhaps because he knew Coren, Resh, and now Ashemon. People were a mix of the people they spent time with. When he'd been with the slavers, he'd felt himself growing less sensitive to the violence. Cruel.

He missed MistCall, too, and he wondered if she'd gotten his message. She'd never returned it. He doubted the magic had failed. It was more likely she was unable to use her magic. Perhaps she had been captured by the Brujok. So many of the southern Sulit had been. The rebellion against the Brujok had never gone well.

Turning a bend in the path, he saw the animal he'd been stalking - a young ice rabbit, its fur as white-gray as the snow-swept rock around it. He shifted the ground up right around it, molding a tiny cage of ice before it could flex a muscle. Miniature spears of ice shot defensively from the ruff along its back as he drew the cage to him along the ground, but he dissolved their sharp points instantly.

The animal's blood was rushing fast in its veins. He could feel the sources. Nik palmed a dagger from his belt and slit the ice rabbit's throat, preferring a quick, clean death to any SourceShifting that might cause it pain.

He withdrew a fire-making kit he'd taken from Sy's room, content to let his magic rest rather than try to master the tedious task of whipping the sources into a frenzy, hoping for enough energy to create a fire. It rarely worked and used too much energy.

The meat was bland and charred, but Nik ate every scrap, scraping the fur clean and hanging it from his pack to dry. It would make a good replacement when the fur in his boots rubbed through. He planned to be on the mountain as long as he needed to heal enough. He couldn't be a danger to those around him. He couldn't destroy an innocent life because his wounds were still too thickly scarred for him to function.

When the stars blinked into the sky overhead, Nik finally admitted to himself that he might never heal enough.

The boat they had rented was far too small. It was barely large enough for one person, much less two, and Coren felt flushed with Resh's proximity. Every time she glanced up, or anywhere it seemed, she was met by his searching black eyes.

She was supposed to be coming up with a plan for rescuing the Wesh prisoners inexplicably held in the belly of Mara's boat, or at least telling Resh what she'd seen, but her focus fixated on the bead of sweat currently making its way down his neck and past his collarbone.

StarsHelm was the farthest north she'd ever been. She drew a mental map in her mind, trying to ignore his bare forearms. It wasn't nearly as warm as Weshen Isle, but here on the lake, the sun reflected hot off the water's surface. Resh grasped both oars and began to row again, pulling them cleanly through the water.

The droplet slid past his prayer beads and disappeared into the shadow of his partly-open shirt. She blinked up, right into his heavy gaze.

"You've barely said a word to me since we launched," Resh said, adjusting his legs so they stretched into her space. He lifted the edge of his shirt to wipe his temple, exposing his trim waist.

Coren slid her eyes to the side, afraid to respond. His very nearness threw her off balance. She needed to tell him what she'd seen on the royal boat, but the hateful words refused to leave her lips. As though by not speaking them, they weren't real.

"I don't know what to think of you," she said instead, surprised at the honesty that slipped from her mouth. Her very world had been out of balance lately. It was no wonder her thoughts kept slipping beyond the edges of permission in her mind.

He laughed, the sound low and repressed under the intensity of the sun. "What does that mean?"

"Why did you come with me?" This was not an answer, and she knew it. But she didn't have an answer to his question.

"You asked me to come. And when a girl I'm interested in asks me to come, I do."

She narrowed her eyes at him. "What does that mean?"

He only smiled, offering her as much answer as she'd given him.

"Why are you interested in me, anyway?" she asked.

He tilted his head. "I find new reasons every time we talk." His black shirt was damp, collecting a sheen like moonlight on water.

Coren pulled a water skin from her bag and offered it to him. He drained it without a word, then refilled it from the lake. Upturning it over his head, Resh poured the water over his hair, one hand scrubbing away the sweat from his face and neck.

Again, Coren felt dizzily off balance in a way she never had with Sy, even before they decided they were better as friends.

Before Resh could resume rowing, Coren grabbed the oars from his reach and pulled hard at the water. She grunted at the strength it took to use both, wishing her shifter magic were not so depleted from the Vespa flight and fighting the weeds and shifting through a wooden boat, for the Magi's sake. She needed to tell him what was on that boat.

"I would kill for some lemondrine tonic," she said instead, tugging the oars toward her chest again. Her thin shirt stuck to her skin, which was slick with sweat.

Resh grinned. He reached into his bag, producing a palm-sized flask. "I picked this up in EvenFall. It's not quite the same, but it might help."

She opened the flask and sniffed. Lemondrine and salt...and something else.

"Lemondrine liquor." His eyes flashed in a dare. "Try it."

She tipped the flask to her lips, and the sweetness burned down her throat. She held back a cough, squeezing her eyes shut. Something in her began to warm and expand in the presence of the concentrated tonic. It was a different heat than the prickling sun on her skin.

"It's good," she murmured, glancing up to find he'd discarded his soaked shirt and grasped the oars again.

Coren sighed as she struggled to look everywhere but Resh's flexing muscles as he rowed them closer and closer to Sulit. She'd be relieved to spread her wings and leave this unnerving tension behind.

Part of her wished there *was* no battle, though, no drama in their shared past. She yearned to be just a girl, alone in a boat with a handsome boy. Before this summer, kisses were meant for claiming, and she'd wanted none of it. She'd never wanted another person like this, but by the Magi, she wanted him now.

Conscience slapped at her desire. She had no right to imagine kisses when so many people were about to die.

"I need to tell you what happened with Mara's boat," she said, hoping to distract herself from the beads of sweat slipping down his smooth skin. "There are Weshen slaves on it. In the hold. They're in cages."

"Slaves for the Brujok?" Resh suggested, shaking his head in disagreement of his own statement. "No. Witches have never kept slaves."

"They used to search for Weshen twins." Coren remembered Kashar's story of his father. "But these weren't pairs of twins. Just random."

"Soldiers?"

She considered. "No weapons or armor. Even if they're expendable, I think Mara would protect them better than that. There aren't that many of us left." Thinking of how Mara and Zorander Graeme had reduced those numbers made her belly sick. The heat intensified, and Coren dug for the flask again.

A long draught burned her throat again, but the tart-sweet pushed her anxiety down a little more. Whatever Mara planned for those Wesh didn't matter.

"I'll stop her anyway," Coren muttered, tipping the flask a third time.

Resh rested the oars across his lap and leaned forward, snagging the lemondrine liquor from her fingers.

"Easy."

She grumbled to herself and slid down in the boat, resting her head on the edge and closing her eyes. Her ears monitored the scrape of wood against wood and the slosh and lap of the water. She pushed her thoughts from the mystery of the Wesh and the battle ahead and the impossible task of finding her family in such an enormous country.

Resh stayed silent as they made their way slowly across the lake. Coren found herself remembering the only other boat ride she'd taken, with Sy as they left Weshen Isle.

A Vespa had followed them, but it hadn't really attacked. Looking back, she wondered if maybe it was the same one, and had been following her all this time, offering itself to a shifter who knew nothing of its power.

"When Sy and I left Weshen Isle, there was a Vespa then, too." She recounted the story to Resh.

"And the one you dissipated on the plains," he reminded her.

"Maybe it was trying to merge with me. Not kill me."

He shrugged. "It's possible."

There was no way to be certain, so Coren pushed this idea away as well.

"So, when you shift, you're completely Vespa now?"

She nodded, and Resh made a disappointed sort of sound.

"What?"

He shrugged, a half-smile tugging at his lips. "I really like those wings."

She studied him, obviously missing something in his words but hesitant to ask. Although, as powerful as she felt in her full Vespa form, Coren admitted she preferred seeing her own face. There was something unsettling about seeing the vertical pupils in her eyes and the hard shell of a beak instead of her own pink lips.

Could she blend herself partially, as she had before?

The creature in her mind stirred, stretching itself wider in her head. *Now we fly?* Its voice murmured in her head.

No, she cautioned it. *Just wings.*

Just as she could shift her appearance younger, she should be able to shift part of her appearance into a Vespa. She closed her eyes and imagined herself as she'd been the first time she shifted. Human body, Vespa wings and claws.

She was more aware of her sources now, the separation between Weshen and Vespa. It was as if they had distinct colors and scents, the way flowers were discernible by their petals and perfume. She picked at the Vespa sources held deep in her bones, searching for those that felt like gray silk and smelled of sharp, cold air.

A weight grew on her back, and she heard a sharp intake of breath from Resh.

Coren reached a hand around her back and felt feathers. She opened her eyes and grinned at Resh.

246

His expression paled, though, and she felt her bones stretching and lightening against her instruction. Her nose and mouth melted together, and her vision intensified until she could see the individual fibers woven to make his pants.

A satisfied coo rumbled in her mind, and she sighed. Evidently, the Vespa wasn't interested in sharing its wings without the rest.

"Save your strength," Resh murmured, his gaze firmly on the water as he rowed.

Coren would have glared if she had eyebrows. Instead, she turned her Vespa eyes downward and concentrated on a single leg, golden and taloned now. Skinny, with leathery skin.

She tried to remember her own golden-tanned leg. Slim, with smooth skin and muscled from running the plains of Weshen Isle. She blinked her bird eyes closed and attempted to hold the vision of her skin clearly in her mind.

Coren opened her eyes and stretched a leg before her.

It was an odd mix of Vespa and girl, with golden skin that was still too leathery, and silvery nails that were too long to fit into any shoes. But perhaps it could be improved with practice.

Or perhaps it was simply a flaw that she could shift a little at a time - a glitch in her power. This thought troubled her. Since she acquired her shift in stages, perhaps the power was incomplete.

The Vespa form slipped away completely then, her strength sputtering. The eastern shore of the lake was close enough to see now, and the Queen's boat was already docked, bobbing empty in the water.

"They'll reach Rurok first," she grumbled.

"But we'll be there. Even if we aren't first, we're going to help them. We'll find your family."

She nodded, focusing her attention on the shore.

I7

Zorander Graeme had kept few secrets after succeeding to the throne of Riata and taking Mara for his wife.

But this one he'd managed to save all to himself. He alone had harnessed the power of the Weshen shifters to travel as fast as the wind and as high as the clouds. Of course, the Alchemists in his employ had known, and the Wesh who had donated their magic. But none of them were alive to tell the secret. Zorander was safe in his chariot in the clouds.

The chariot resembled a tiny coach, with space for one person to sit and two levers that adjusted direction and speed. The slim framework was carved from Weshen bones, weightless magic still contained in their very sources. The leather that enclosed the sides and top was stitched from the rarest of hides - the now-extinct Draken.

Zorander regretted this part. He hadn't known the Draken were so rare when he ordered their skin.

All over Riata, men and women wore fragments of bone and hide around their necks and woven into their belts and shoes and weapons. Talismans. Superstitions, some scoffed.

But the King's Alchemists knew better. Sulit spells bound the magic eternally into these bones and hides and joined the sources into a vehicle. Zorander could steer himself up and into the clouds, across the skies as fast as any bird, and faster than any misthorse the palace had bred yet.

It was one of his greatest accomplishments, he thought, and not a living soul knew of it.

He sped toward the NeverCross Mountains, knowing Mara would have his troops waiting when he arrived, even though the journey would take him less than two days. One-half of the time it would take by coach and one-fifth of the journey's time on foot.

Zorander wasn't truly flying, of course, but this was the closest he would ever come.

In these silent moments above the clouds, he allowed himself to think of the girl he'd foolishly thought could become his queen. The one whose glorious Vespa form would have borne him into the heavens if he'd only had the courage to claim her.

The one who wore light blue armor so she would blend with the sky, and cared more for becoming a commander than becoming his bride.

The one he had betrayed by looking the other way when Mara scented her power, like an animal scenting a threat to her den.

He had been so young then. Foolish in so many ways.

True, he barely looked older now. But his heart was that of an old, old man, with many heavy stones of sorrow tucked in its beating folds.

The afternoon wore into evening, and night arrived with its blanket of stars just above him. Zorander ate and drank as the chariot flew, saving his strength for the battle to end all battles.

All his adult life he had sought the SoulShifter, and now the time was here. The magic was returning to Weshen. He'd vowed to create Riata as a nation of power and peace, once.

His creation had been sullied by his own wishes, his debts, and the choices he made in haste and ignorance.

But now. Now, with the help of the SoulShifter, Zorander could choose differently, pay his debts, and act instead of wish. With the magic of the SoulShifter, Zorander Graeme could rule not just Riata and Weshen, but Sulit. Umbren. All the lands in the WestenSands and EstenSands, and as far as he could sail on the Prustian Sea.

He could create power and peace everywhere like he'd dreamed of as a boy.

Of course, flying through the silent skies made peace sound possible. Zorander understood the hypocrisy of what he traveled to do. The world had shown him, year after year, that peace was impossible without power, and power was impossible to retain without occasional warfare.

Weshen would not give up its power easily. The people would fight, just as they had two and three generations ago. And many would die, but not Zorander.

He was immune to death as long as his brothers followed.

And they always followed. He thought again of something Lumien had whispered in his ear, just before the seven spirits vanished.

You know we follow your blood, little brother. The palace holds us because your blood holds us. But beware the blood that is shared as well as the blood which is spilled.

Zorander, for all the world, had no idea what Lumien meant. This was nothing new, as Lumien was the most diabolical of his brothers and spoke even the simplest sentiments in riddles.

From much experience, Zorander knew that if his life was in danger, the seven would appear to his would-be murderer and offer them a choice: kill the King and inherit his curse, or bow before the eight of them. Graeme's blood came with their whispers, and so far, none had chosen that fate. All had bowed, and all had died.

This was another of Zorander's close-kept secrets, kept between himself and his Queen only.

The mixed blessing and curse of blood magic was very familiar to the Mara, of course. It was the stuff of Riatan power and Umbren nightmares.

Trapped inside Mara's half-moon blades was the blood, and thus the blood magic, of his mother and his father, Riata's Silver Sovereign. There were surely other powers there, and though Zorander was content to fight battles himself, he enjoyed the bolster of his wife's power, thrusting him to greater heights than he ever dreamed on his own.

Together they were stronger, using each passing cycle to expand their grip on the world around them.

Ashemon gathered his men around him, barely able to concentrate on their concerned faces. Instead, he stared sideways at the cliffs of Weshen Isle and the sea beyond. The men waited for his words. They all knew how much Tagsha's death had stopped him from moving forward.

But summer was ending. Time moved forward, regardless of whether man followed.

The much-loved guard had been given a proper Weshen funeral at dawn, sent to drift on the MagiSea atop a burning raft covered in headily-scented flowers. The sharp scent of the smoke floated in the seabreeze for days.

Ashemon had found no tears to fall, not the moment he learned of Tagsha's death, and not since. Instead, he found hollow sorrow and a growing rage to fill the void. Rage against the unfairness of the Magi.

Their beloved gods had taken their magic to protect them. Accepted their sacrifice.

Yet in the complex course of reclaiming that same magic, the gods had taken the people he cared for most in the entire land.

Ashemon had been a fool to let Reshra and that boy try to wake the magic; he would never admit that Weshen needed shifting to survive. If anything, shifting was a curse. Perhaps the sacrifice had been the real blessing.

If the Weshen people had never had magic to begin with, the Restless King would have never begun hunting and collecting them. He would have left Weshen alone, moving his reign first into easier, more accessible lands like the EstenSands.

Instead, the myth of the SoulShifter had tempted Zorander Graeme into madness. As a king of hundreds of thousands of people, Graeme had power over nearly everything in his life. The only part of life he couldn't hope to control was the end. But with the SoulShifter magic...

Someone near him cleared his throat, and Ashemon blinked, remembering he was not alone with his thoughts. Dawngulls wheeled overhead, their cries pulling the sun further into the sky.

He held up a hand, acknowledging his men. "Men of Weshen. Considering the recent activity, I believe Weshen City will soon be vulnerable to attack from the NeverCross Mountain passage."

Already he needed to stop and let them mutter to themselves. Many had not thought of this yet, although a few were nodding their heads. They saw the links of the chain and knew what it would pull from the depths.

"Our mountain passage was once protected by our magic, sacrificed from our blood into the hands of the Mirror Magi. But since this same magic is potent again in the blood of some of our citizens, I can only guess the passage will soon open to our enemies. The Magi do not increase and decrease our magic. They balance it. I tell you now, the summer games are over. We have a city to fortify. Gather your belongings and sail for Weshen City today."

"What of the women, sir?"

Ashemon nodded. He'd thought this through. The women were ill-equipped to fight. Hiding them would be best. "They are safe here on the island, as they have always been. However, let us ride four to a boat instead of two, and leave them a means to escape. If the city is attacked, we will hold it with our lives. Go quickly now, and speak with the Magi at every step."

Ashemon himself was in the first boat to leave, and he did not take his own advice.

Instead, he rode alone to the city, his boat crunching onto the private shore beneath the mansion. He knew the house would be empty of Resh and the Wesh boy, but he still stopped and stared into both his sons' rooms before retiring to his own.

How had his life grown so dim? It felt as though no sun would shine on his face until he died, and the funeral fire alone would warm his bones.

Syashin.

Reshra.

Tagsha.

Each of the people he had spent a lifetime watching, and shaping, and loving.

Each gone.

And his city would soon be under siege. He had been just a boy in his last battle, but he remembered. It had been decades since Weshen had suffered any true attack, but Ashemon felt the battle brewing. He could smell the tang of iron and blood on the air.

The Restless King wouldn't stay away long now.

Ashemon rang for a servant, sitting heavily at his carved wooden desk. "Bring me the commanders and teachers. Round the servants and the students. I want every living soul in this hall by sundown." He didn't understand the shifting or how it might be a weapon, but he did know how to wield a bow sword, a longknife. A dagger. Even a simple sword. He would arm every person in Weshen City with as many weapons as they could carry.

The servant nodded, his eyes round as the hole in the General's heart.

Ashemon gathered all the weapons from his personal armory. They were the most precious, and many had never been used. But ceremonial swords and gold and gems would be of no use to a dead city.

As the commanders arrived, he sent them into the other buildings to gather weapons, leathers, food, and drink. They would build a stronghold here in the General's mansion for the weak, the old, and the very young.

When the rest of his men began to arrive from Weshen Isle, he spread them through every circle of Weshen, hoping to fortify the city with the illusion of numbers, if not the real advantage.

The fastest runners he placed in the outer circles and close to the mountain passage. They could alert the others of any movement from the passage, the cliffs, or the sea. The best archers he stationed in the towers above the market. They had the highest vantage point except for the mansion itself. The strongest combat fighters he left to the residences, as a final, hopeful defense before the mansion and its rooms of young Weshen boys.

They gathered the boats on his private beach, hidden behind the mansion. Ashemon didn't want to admit it, but it was possible that at the end, fleeing may the only hope left for some.

His people were well-trained, strong, fed, and the fiercest men he knew how to mold.

But they were still so few, and the Restless King had all of Riata at his disposal.

Finally, Ashemon agreed that the handful of the Paladins who had learned Reshra's shifting should scatter themselves, one or two in each circle of the city. They hoped to be hidden weapons, ready to surprise the Riatan army.

And then they waited, practicing their assigned jobs and rationing their food to maintain strength.

Ashemon didn't know how long they would wait, but he doubted it would be long.

The Restless King was coming, and Ashemon didn't need magic or messengers to feel his fate barreling toward him through the Riatan forest and beneath the NeverCross Mountains.

StarSeer crested the hill first, gaining the initial glimpse into the valley between the forest and the cliffs of Rurok.

The trees could no longer hide her treachery, and she steeled herself for Maren's huffing figure to join her. The old woman did not disappoint. She was too weak to truly hurt StarSeer, but even still, the ground opened between them, levitating StarSeer on a newly-made and highly unstable promontory.

"Rurok?" Maren spat at her. "You've brought us straight into the middle of danger!"

StarSeer balanced on her toes a second too long for comfort before crouching onto the bit of earth. She saw the twins come to stand behind Maren, watching and listening closely. They made no move to help her, even if they had been able.

StarSeer fixed her eyes on Maren. "I am sorry to do this. But the second you left your island, you put them in danger. Have you not heard the whole world searches for shifters? Riata wants the strongest, but Sulit needs that doubled. Twins. And with the blood these two have, surely none will be stronger."

"What blood do we have, Maren?" the boy asked, still watching as StarSeer adjusted her balance on the crumbling dirt.

Maren didn't answer him. Instead, she stepped back, her feet finding the forest again. StarSeer would have to crawl and jump somehow if she wanted to leave the cliff Maren had made.

"Weren't we in danger on Weshen Isle?" the girl asked.

"Yes," Maren said. "General Ashemon holds a grudge against your family."

"But why?" the boy pushed, and StarSeer was intrigued to see him take a step away from the woods. Toward her instead.

Maren's sharp eyes weighed that step carefully, her gaze flicking between the boy and girl. "Your parents were not powerful shifters. But your grandmother was. Ashemon fears the magic more than the King, and he is a fool!"

"Did you know our grandmother?" the girl asked StarSeer.

She blinked at the girl, surprised. "No. I have lived in Sulit my whole life. You are the first Weshen I've met."

"Then how do you know who we are? How do you know our blood?"

"Child, your family's blood has pulsed through the Mother's veins for many years. The stories say your people helped us restore the Heart of Sulit once. Now it is dry and weak, and requires your help again."

"Weshen has nothing to do with your Mother," Maren said. "Our gods work for balance. Light and dark. Warm and Cool. Girl and Boy. Your Mother offers only chaos."

"The Mother does not offer chaos!" StarSeer stumbled on her patch of earth with the force of her shout. She bent lower, clutching the grass to its roots. "But our world is not diametric. There is more to its patterning than two by two. Sometimes four, or six. Sometimes eight. The Mother can balance better than simply looking at her reflection."

Maren choked a bit in her rage, and StarSeer wondered if she'd gone too far. Certainly, the Mirror Magi were valuable to the Mother. They did help the Weshen, and the Weshen did help them. The Mother would need every one of her children if she wanted to adjust all that was tilting away in the world.

259

"Maren, bring her back," Penna commanded suddenly, her child's voice ringing through the trees. "Weshen may need our help later, but Sulit needs our help now."

"We have little else to do," Kosh added, as though they were simply looking for an afternoon activity.

StarSeer managed not to smile at this idea, and Maren seemed surprised enough by the twins that she shifted the ground together. StarSeer hopped over the crumbled earth and back to the safety of the forest's edge.

"My Sulit sisters wait in that valley. Gathering. Rurok is at the far side, also waiting and gathering. Nothing has worked, save full rebellion against the Brujok. But I bring hope. *You* bring hope. We must try."

"What is your plan? Tell us everything," Maren threatened.

StarSeer nodded, even knowing Maren had no way to enforce such a threat. "I've sent a message to the southern Sulit gathered in the valley. These twins could fulfill our prophecy. If the Mother accepts them, the Brujok will accept them. The Brujok are not so different from us in that way. They only want a better Sulit. They work with Riata to gain that, but they are misled. Riata uses them."

"Riata uses all," Maren agreed. "How does your prophecy work? What happens when the Mother accepts them?"

"I wish I knew. The prophecy is much older than any of us. The nuances have been lost. But you know of the evil that rose like the sea to place Zorander Graeme on the throne and his brothers in the spirit world. That evil must be staunched. That evil is the source of our world's imbalance."

"I thought the King was the source," Penna said, her voice small but strong. StarSeer smiled at her.

"The King is a pawn. Unfortunately, we do not know who moves him yet. Some say it is Mara, but in my visions, I have seen more."

"More?" Kosh tilted his head.

"Like stairs leading down into a dungeon. Each supports the other. Each blacker than the next. We can see the velvet dark at the bottom, but we do not know how deep it goes."

With this, StarSeer gestured toward the valley. A tendril of smoke rose from a section of trees, and she smelled the heady sweetness of her witch sisters' protective spellcasting. "They wait for us."

Penna smiled, thrilling the heart and hope of the witch who thought she had lost both long ago, and they began to descend the hillside.

18

Coren helped Resh tug their boat onto the black sand of the Sulit coast. She was restless and weary all at once, and the trees beyond were full of restless shadows.

"We should camp here tonight," she suggested.

He nodded. "I don't want to enter those woods at night. We have quite a journey to Rurok still, so we might as well sleep."

She hid a yawn behind her hand. They had no tent or cave to shelter them, so they turned the boat upside down and climbed beneath it, bracing one side up slightly with a forked branch.

"Is this okay?" Resh asked, his voice echoing beneath the bent wood. She was facing the bottom of the boat and his body was curled behind hers, his back to the lake. Coren murmured her assent, not trusting her voice. Her body was too warm without the night breeze to cool it, and Resh's chest was hot at her back.

He was careful not to press against her, and she was

reminded more of how Sy had protected her from the Vespa in a similar boat. She smiled into the darkness. It was interesting to see Resh being careful with her. He was changing, and she was the reason.

She allowed herself to be lulled to sleep by the idea that he might also be worth changing for.

Sometime in the night, though, the nightmares began. They were even more terrifying on the banks of Sulit than in a silent palace room, and she woke to a palm pressed over her mouth, muffling her scream.

"Shh!" Resh breathed in her ear. "You're dreaming. Wake up!"

When she stopped writhing next to him, his fingers slipped to the side, locking on her jaw instead. He turned her face to his. Moonlight streamed in through the sliver of night beyond his shoulders.

"What was it?" he asked, his eyes pools of darkness. "And don't say nothing. You were nearly screaming, and it was about a curse."

Coren began to shake as the images from the dream sharpened in her mind. Before, she'd willed herself to forget. But Resh's fingertips soft against her throat told her that wasn't an option tonight.

"Seven figures - princes, I think. They seem like spirits. They come to me night after night. Ever since I entered the palace." She knew she wasn't making sense, but the dreams didn't either.

"What do they want?"

"My blood," she whispered. "They have some of it, but they want it all. The curse that keeps them locked in spirit form can only be broken with my blood. They laugh when I run."

"Seven princes," Resh repeated, leaning his head back thoughtfully.

Coren shivered, feeling how his fingers had begun to explore, as though the answer to the riddle might be on the skin of her shoulders and arms.

"Riata once had eight princes. Now it has none, and one King."

"What do you mean by that?" she asked. The numbers did sound familiar, but she'd never paid attention to Riata, other than to hate it and its ruler indiscriminately.

"Zorander Graeme was never meant to be King. His father was the Silver Sovereign. He had eight sons, and Zorander was the last. He should have never gained the throne."

"But they all died, didn't they?"

"Yes. Different ways, different ages. But each year brought the news of death until Zorander was the only one left. He ascended to the throne just around our age and married Lady Mara."

"But spirits don't walk the earth. They don't enter people's dreams."

Resh brought his face back down to hers, and his hand slipped around her ribs, pressing her back close to his chest. "They might if the world is unbalanced. We aren't the only country whose religion teaches balance in all things. Riatans believe in the sanctity of the FatherSun and his children. If Graeme had a hand in his brothers' death, or his father's, a curse might not be such a fairytale."

"There was something else," she said, the thought slipping like a snake through a crack in the door. "They told me that if I break the curse, I can claim the kingdom of Riata."

Resh startled, clutching her even closer. She heard the uptick in the beats of his heart, and though her body thrilled at his nearness, she distrusted the shallow breaths he drew.

"I want nothing to do with Riata, other than to see it fall," she said. Testing.

"It doesn't need to fall. It only needs a better leader."

Coren puzzled over his answer as she closed her eyes and tried to sleep again. She wasn't certain what Riata needed. Certainly, there were many good people in its grasp. But she'd never agreed with Kashar and Sy that a different leader would be any better.

She still believed, more than anything, that power led to corruption.

The heart beat steadily in its crystal box, seeming to gain strength with each contraction. In and out, it pumped the air and the invisible blood.

It was no longer alone, and the one it longed for was here, in the forests of Sulit.

It had been so long, but the heart would never forget.

The witch guarding the heart was startled from her sleep again by the chirrup of a starbird. It was close. Much closer than the delicate creatures usually came.

"Here for dinner?" the witch cackled, reaching a bony finger out and holding it still as a dead branch.

The starbird flitted and jumped along the forest floor. It lighted on top of the box, one two-toed foot scratching softly on the surface.

The heart shuddered, and the bird sang. It tilted its white, downy head at the witch, then swiveled back the other way. She didn't move, and eventually the bird hopped up onto her finger.

The witch's black tongue darted from between her lips as she clapped her other hand atop the bird, capturing it and snapping its neck between her fingers at once.

The witch withdrew a dagger carved with ancient symbols from the folds of her mossy gown. She pierced the bird's heart, the blade poking clean through the tiny creature. Blood dripped from its white feathers, gathering in a puddle on the crystal above the heart.

The sources of the box began to dissolve beneath the blood, cracking apart to let its red sustenance drip slowly onto the beating mass.

But then something happened that the witch, for all her dozens of years, hundreds of days, had never seen.

The heart continued beating, pulsing with life.

But the blood that was meant to nourish it slid right down its side. Nothing absorbed. Not a drop was taken, and still the heart beat on.

"The one is here," the witch muttered to herself. Her excitement pushed through her malaise like spring buds through earth. "The one I've been waiting for. It's been so very, very long."

Resh had barely slept after Coren's dream. As the early morning sun stole over the beach, he watched the tiny black crystals of sand sparkle. He couldn't stop thinking of what she'd said about the seven brothers and the curse.

They were in Sulit, where spirits were real, and curses matter-of-fact.

Could it be coincidence that the dream had found her stronger than ever here? She moved in her sleep, twisting onto her back, and he slid his eyes along the curve of her throat. Greedy fingers wrapped themselves in the brown and gold waves of her hair as it streamed over the pillow of her pack.

He debated leaning down to brush his lips against hers, but something in him resisted. Coren had never been like the other girls who found their way into his arms. If he wanted her to stay, he couldn't slip into old habits.

Moving again, she opened her eyes, blinking up at him. Her pupils were too dilated against the brightening sun, and her lips screwed into an adorable grimace. Resh bit at his own lips to discourage them again from touching hers.

"Did you dream again?" He pushed himself backward out of their makeshift shelter, brushing the sand from his side.

She shook her head and stretched. Her back arched, pressing her breasts out, and Resh nearly groaned aloud. This sort of restraint was unrealistic, really. And he knew there was likely another night of such torture before they would reach Rurok.

Which was where the real torture would begin.

Witches, he thought, the word like a curse in his mind.

They pushed the boat higher on the beach and attempted to blend it with some driftwood, but it was pointless.

"Well, I guess we can always fly back across," she said, sliding Resh a grin that made his stomach flip. He attributed it to the idea of flying, though.

"Absolutely not. I'd rather kiss a witch."

She laughed, and the sound loosened his joints. He could walk for miles for a sound like that. They shouldered their packs and ate as they walked the shoreline. Mara's boat loomed before them, and Resh wished they could pause long enough to search it.

What secrets would a royal Riatan boat hold?

Planks extended from its side onto the beach, making it evident the Queen was traveling by coach to Rurok. The wheel tracks in the sand were followed and trampled by dozens of pairs of footprints.

"Wesh," Coren muttered, pointing at them.

Resh tamped his anger down. These people could have been saved. Some of them, at least. If only Ashemon had listened to his sons. Their numbers game had always been set up to lose. Even the hunts couldn't produce children at the rate of a few raids on StarsHelm. They trudged along in silence after that.

By the end of the day, they had descended the side of NewMoon Falls. The towers of Rurok were distant but clear, spiraling up from the beach and into the nearby mountains. It didn't look like one building so much as

269

hundreds of tall, slim buildings placed too close together to distinguish.

"What do you think the Lord of Witches is like?" Coren asked as they moved into the shelter of a rocky outcropping for the night.

"I've heard little of him, but it's certainly suspicious. Witches have no need for men."

"None at all?" Coren seemed surprised, and Resh laughed.

"Not for children, anyway. I've heard most of them turn to each other for companionship. All the witches I've met have been liars, though, so it's entirely possible I don't know a single thing about them."

"I think I would have been happy on Weshen Isle without any men," she said, flapping a cloak in the wind and flattening it on the ground.

"Perhaps because you've never had a man show you just what we're good for," Resh said, a grin spreading across his lips as he joined her on the fur.

"War-mongering. Hunting. Withholding. Running. Betraying," she listed. "Those are the things the men in my life have been good for."

"And Sy?" he challenged.

She smiled, casting her eyes down. "Sy's different."

Resh gritted his teeth against a harsh statement. Yes, he knew very well how different his brother was. He thought of his conversation with Nik about love. It seemed Coren needed none of that. She admired Sy for his noble ideals, yet she didn't seem to believe in love.

She didn't seem to believe in lust, either, although her body responded to his every time they were close. She only clamped down on their heat, refusing to acknowledge it.

As they settled on the fur for the night, Resh was irritable enough to begin testing her. She lay next to him on her side, facing the sea. Her hair spread between them, the only part of her touching him. He reached his fingers into the waves, separating the strands a few at a time. She grew still at the touch, her spine stiffening.

But Resh continued to comb the tangles from her hair, gently working his fingers to her scalp, which he massaged until her breathing slowed and her body curved, supple in its relaxation. His hands slid to her neck, and her breathing quickened. Resh smiled to himself. His fingers slipped up and down the column of her neck, tracing its curve from her jaw to her shoulders. He kneaded the muscles there, then in toward her spine and lower along her back.

Soft noises escaped her lips, something more than a sigh and less than a moan. Resh's body awakened, and he moved closer to her. Her skin was hot even through her clothing.

He pressed gently back on her shoulder, urging her to turn toward him. She held her position, though, facing the water until she drifted to sleep.

But again in the night she turned into him, clutching wildly at his shirt as a nightmare gripped her sleeping mind. Resh woke to her body pressed full against his and her nails scraping at his arms. Her eyes were squeezed tight against the darkness, and her lips moved with inaudible words.

Resh shook her shoulders gently, but she didn't wake. "Coren! You're dreaming again!"

271

Still, she didn't wake, only gripped him tighter, whimpering. Her face pressed to the bare skin at the opening of his shirt, her lips soft above his heart, and Resh groaned. Why couldn't this happen when she was awake? Then she was kissing him, a diagonal slice of fire along his chest and up his neck and at the corner of his mouth.

He was lost. He answered the kiss, her ferocity pulling the same from him.

And still, her eyes remained shut.

She broke away, her chest rising and falling rapidly, and rolled onto her back. Resh nearly laughed aloud. The girl was *still* asleep.

Perhaps he had made it into her dreams this time, chasing away the seven brothers' curse with his touch. Resh grinned. He liked that thought. Resh tugged her closer until she lay in the crook of his arm, her side pressed to his chest. She slept unmoving the rest of the night.

When she woke the next morning and focused on his face above hers, she flushed deeply and prettily. Resh grinned.

"Sweet dreams?" he murmured, and her eyes widened. She sat up so suddenly they almost cracked noses.

"We should go," she said, hurrying to smooth her top and shake the dirt from the cloak they'd slept on. She refused to meet his eyes again until the towers of Rurok were upon them.

19

The NeverCross Mountains swung into view as the sun rose before Zorander.

Keeping high enough above the stonetrees that he would remain invisible to the men on the ground, he surveyed his troops. Dozens of battalions, each containing fifty soldiers, and each led by the Wesh commanders he and Mara had been preparing just for today. He knew Kashar kept their powers at low levels. He guessed why.

But Kashar had been useful over the years, his obsession with rescuing the slaves only growing Zorander's ranks that much more.

Now that the time to attack Weshen was upon them, he planned to fight shifters with shifters. Each of them had a significant reason to fight. A certain person's life worth fighting for. Zorander wasn't worried about their loyalty.

He landed his chariot in a sparse clearing several minutes' walk from the troops and composed himself.

He strode into camp from the side, appearing to come from examining a separate battalion. They'd never knew he had only just arrived. And if he wanted, he could leave and they would never know that, either.

But Zorander would never miss the opportunity to search Weshen for himself. The NeverCross Mountains had kept him from this city long enough.

"Do you lack anything?" he asked the first General he came upon.

"All ready, King Graeme." The man bowed deeply. "We've just heard word that the passage is indeed clear of all traps, magical or otherwise."

Graeme nodded. After hearing about the shifters Grand had sensed in the palace maze, Graeme knew the passage's magical barrier would crumble. The barrier had taunted him all these years. The Weshen people gave their magic back to their gods - becoming more vulnerable than ever. Leaving the magic easy to find but impossible to gather. Zorander could gather a person, or steal bone and blood. He could not gather invisible matter from rocks and air.

But now, the magic had returned, waking again in their bodies. They would be weak and untrained. The timing was perfection.

"It's very narrow, though," his General said, interrupting his spooling thoughts. "We can only go through a few at a time, and no misthorses will fit, I've heard. It will take the day."

Graeme shrugged. "Misthorses do not win battles, and what is one day when we've waited so many years? Send word to the other Generals that the shifters go in first. They can widen the passage for the rest of us, and we can gather on the other side before our charge."

He strolled between the battalions, having a similar conversation again and again. Gradually, the numbers on the northern side of the mountains began to dwindle as the men filtered through the passage. It was dark by the time Graeme himself went through with the last of his soldiers.

Emerging in the forest, he stepped between the lines of waiting soldiers and viewed Weshen City for the first time.

All he could see from here was the massive wall and an iron gate. Both looked run-down and easy to breach.

He turned to the waiting ranks of soldiers.

"Gentlemen, no speech needed. Do your jobs, and Weshen City's magic is ours. Bounteous reward awaits all who do their part and make it back to StarsHelm alive. Go!"

With that, the shifters tore the gate apart, and men began to swarm the entrance.

"Block the passage," Graeme said to one General. "None of our men leave until the battle is done. Send men to find the other entrances. I'm certain there will be one near the water and likely one from the mountains. Go."

He stretched in the morning light, enjoying the feeling of finally, after such patience, getting what he had always wanted: Weshen and shifter magic as the center jewel in his crown, and the promise of the SoulShifter to set himself free.

Every country and city he visited eventually gave up their pride and accepted their place in Riata's union.

Each group's talents had been pooled and stockpiled in StarsHelm, ready to help those in need.

Riata was the greatest nation in all the land, and it was because Zorander had brought together each country and shown them how to best serve the others. It was like a grand symphony of instruments, with each country adding to the harmony.

Except Weshen. They had refused his offers of peace, claiming he was a tyrant. Claiming he was nothing more than a war lord bent on aggrandizing his wealth.

Zorander did recognize that his was an enforced peace, but it was peace all the same. He was helping the world become exactly what the gods intended. Some struggle was to be expected.

It had been only three short mornings of waiting in Weshen City, once the men had all landed on the mainland. Ashemon was drinking a second cup of bitter tea when a shout echoed through his open window. A man was speeding up through the circles of Weshen City.

"The passage! They come! The Riatan army is here!" he shouted as he raced through each section, nodding to Ashemon as he caught his breath before the mansion, and began to race down the other side of the city. More shouts rippled away after his, like a stone splashing into a riverbed, washing the water higher and higher on the banks.

Ashemon stepped from the gates of his home and stared down the hillside at the rings of Weshen. The city had been built for defense, but his heart stuttered as he saw the vast Riatan army begin to trickle from the slit in the mountain. The passage's magic had failed them, as he suspected. Like ants fleeing a flooded burrow, more and more and more soldiers piled up beyond the city gates.

He had prepared for this moment his whole life, and in a way, he was satisfied he'd been right.

He'd been wrong about so many other things, but at least he could be proud of his preparation for the King's attack. His men would not be taken unaware. His women would not be trapped, defenseless. He didn't know how many Weshen would survive the day, but at least they were ready to give the King the best fight they could muster.

In the very darkest corner of his heart, though, Ashemon was thankful his sons were not here. He missed them, and he had many regrets about the summer. But he was grateful their blood would not be spilled here in their city.

As selfish pride strengthened the image of his sons prospering in EvenFall, Ashemon made peace with the knowledge that he might die today.

His lack of faith in the Mirror Magi should be shameful, but as he watched the black and cream and crimson form a tidal wave of assault on his city, he doubted. None of his men would spontaneously gain powerful shifter magic and drive away the King's army. None would be aided by MagiCreatures fighting alongside them, like the stories of old.

They were great warriors, but their numbers were far too few.

The Riatan army began to form ranks, single leaders stepping before each block of soldiers. Ashemon held a glass to his eye to better examine their methods, and what he saw pulled such wind from his lungs that his knees buckled, and he had to drop the glass to steady himself on the wall behind him.

Magic. *Shifter* magic.

The Restless King had stolen the magic from Ashemon's people and was using it against them.

He called for a messenger. "They have talismans. Magic. Tell the men!" He fixed the glass back to his eye, praying he had been mistaken. But he hadn't. Each group of Riatan soldiers wielded iron weapons and wood, but each leader had dozens of talismans, strapped to each sword and bow.

Graeme's soldiers were using the very talismans his people had painstakingly gathered from MagiCreatures throughout their land and beyond, then sold to merchants in EvenFall as souvenirs and for symbolic protection. He'd heard the rumors of the King's Alchemists - that they could take items of superstition and bind them with magic using Sulit spells.

He'd discounted it. But the King's men below wielded weapons that cut deep into the earth, separating rock and wood more easily than possible.

Then Ashemon saw something that made him wish his people had *not* come here to fight. They would have been better sailing for Sulit in their boats than bearing witness to what came next.

With each battalion General walked a brown-haired, tanned-skin figure, undoubtedly of Weshen descent.

It was a numbing and humbling treachery. His countrymen fought against their own people, who were pulling apart the very ground with their hands, ripping stone from stone as they broke apart the wall surrounding the city.

The Wesh prisoners Ashemon had refused to spend lives to help were finally home, and they were destroying the city.

Graeme's army was through the outer wall, and they had begun to tear through the animal pastures. The Wesh ripped apart every fence or gate or wall they encountered, cutting through men before their blades touched. The Riatan soldiers killed the rest and set fire to the buildings, burning Weshen City from the outside in.

Ashemon was in the eye of the storm, and it was closing in on him faster than he'd dreamed possible.

Gone was the vanity that said his men were ready for such a fight. Gone was the selfish desire for his sons to live. Gone was the pride in his ability to lead.

Ashemon Havenash dropped the glass and picked up his weapons.

With a roar, he commanded the men guarding the mansion to abandon such foolishness and rush the hillside below. Holding the city was a false hope.

Killing as many Riatan soldiers as possible was the only thought left in the General's raging mind.

He slashed through the ranks of soldiers, fiercer than any MagiCreature. He didn't need their magic. He hurled his daggers into the hearts of the false shifters. He wasn't afraid of them. He cut the talismans from the necks and hilts of the army's leaders. He had no faith in their cobbled magic.

Ashemon was a force, and he was bent on ruination.

His men rallied behind him, and they began to use their advantages like they'd been trained. They had the high ground. They knew the hidden traps and weapons stockpiles. They were well-fed and rested and bent on protecting the only home they had left.

The ripples in the waters of battle began to roll backward, sucking the bloodied and frenzied men into a center vortex of swinging weapons.

And Ashemon suddenly found himself in the center. In the eye of that storm. In the quiet, still spot of battle where two men glance at each other, then really look. When two men realize the other is the one they have hated since they had a word for hate.

Zorander Graeme stood before Ashemon Havenash, and he smiled. Haughty. Proud. Hateful. The Restless King lifted his sword, and Ashemon rushed, nicking the King just under the arm, where his armor was incomplete.

The King blinked down at the bright blood spilling onto the Weshen grass.

He looked surprised. Ashemon didn't spare the time to grin back. He darted around the King and lunged again, but something blew him back.

Golden light filled the eye of the storm, like fog rolling in from the ocean at dusk. Only it wasn't dusk, and they weren't at water's edge.

And fog did not have faces.

So, this is the great General of Weshen.

The voice was too smooth for a battle-strong man, and Graeme's lips had never moved. Ashemon stumbled backward, struggling to grip his sword. His head swiveled left and right and left again, uncertain what he was seeing.

"These are my brothers," the King said. His voice held the roughness Ashemon expected, but it was youthful. He glanced back at the King, realizing the man's face was nearly unlined. His jaw was strong. His skin was firm.

The Restless King should be a very old man by now. Yet he looked young enough to be Ashemon's brother. Younger, even.

"My brothers are part of the reason I am alive, though I am the reason they are dead."

"Dead?" Ashemon echoed the word despite himself. The faces swirled closer in the golden mist, and he realized that while they did indeed stare at him and move, their bodies were incandescent. He could nearly see the battle continuing behind them. Through them.

Dead, dead, dead. Seven times dead. Little Zorander killed us all, and he'll kill you too. Unless...

"Unless what?" Ashemon asked, his brain spinning from the idea that he was speaking to spirits. "Magic. Sulit spells!" he cried.

Not magic. Not Sulit.

"My brothers protect me wherever I go." Graeme's breathing had calmed, and Ashemon saw him raise his sword, the tip lazy in the air.

He cursed to himself. Smoke and spells, that was all. He lunged at the King, but the light seemed to block

281

him. It was like trying to wade through mud and churning water.

Kill him, inherit us. That's the nature of the curse. Keep your life, lose your sanity.

"I will not bargain with illusions!" The words had barely left Ashemon's lips when he was thrown to the ground, the breath squashed from his lungs by a massive weight. Pinned by light and air. His brain struggled to make sense of it and failed.

"I swear to you, General Havenash, these men are no illusion. They are my curse and my blessing. Their deaths gave me the throne, and my life gives them the power to remain. If my life is taken by another, my curse is also taken by another. The magic is as simple as your Magi's love of balance." Graeme stalked toward Ashemon, dragging the tip from his belly to his neck, scraping the metal chest plate hard enough to shave away a curl of iron.

Ashemon gasped, thrashing against the illogical smoke holding him down. "This is nothing like the Mirror Magi's balance. I care nothing for your spells. You and I were born without magic. Let us fight that way, and one of us will die that way."

The weight suddenly dissipated, and Ashemon leaped to his feet, grasping a blade in each hand.

Graeme stepped back, assessing him with fresher eyes. "You are a brave man. I am sorry Mara's blades are not here to soak in your blood. Your power of will and fierce nature would strengthen them."

"I'm also sorry your Queen is not here. I would kill her as well," Ashemon said and lunged for the King.

282

"Do you accept the curse?" Zorander asked again. He would almost consider letting Ashemon kill him, just to see another man suffer at the hands of his brothers. Of course, he wouldn't be able to see the torture. He would be dead.

"There is no curse," Ashemon sneered, parrying with him. "Only whatever magic you have scraped and stolen for your illusions."

They were well-matched, but Zorander's brothers blew their influence across the General's blows, sending them just an inch too left or right each time. They had no intention of letting Zorander sacrifice himself. Their fun was too great, and the curse could never be broken by a man who didn't believe in it.

Ashemon miscalculated a step, and stumbled, giving Zorander the final opportunity he needed. The General's eyes grew round with the wonder of mortal pain as the King's blade entered between the front and back plates of his armor, slipping between his ribs to pierce his heart.

He sank heavily to one knee in a mockery of salute to a King he would have never accepted. Blood leaked down the silver edge of the sword. Zorander did regret the missed opportunity to soak the talisman Mara kept in this fresh blood magic, but he knew she would use her blades well in Sulit.

One non-shifter Weshen was of no consequence against the potential blood of so many witches.

Ashemon tilted toward the ground, and the King stepped forward, holding a friendly hand against his shoulder to keep him upright. From a distance, they could have been King and Knight, performing the induction ceremony.

"You have failed," Zorander whispered to his conquest, bending lower to drive the blade deeper. "You have failed your country, and your people, and yourself. But you may concern your dying moments with the comfort that your death is no accident of fate. This event, all the truths of today, and all the twisted tomorrows - they were planned by all the gods. You and I play in their arena, our lives and deaths their afternoon amusement. Riatans have the FatherSun, Sulit have the Mother. And you Weshen have the grinning twins. We are all family, and killing each other is what family does best. Fathers kill with harsh training; mothers kill with coddling. And siblings kill with jealousy."

Zorander knew Ashemon couldn't answer him. The blood was bubbling up his throat and leaking out his lips. But his eyes showed that he understood. That perhaps he didn't agree, but he was too far gone to reason out why. The sword slipped from its gruesome sheath as the man fell to the ground, dead before he hit the dirt.

Zorander straightened. Several men nearby had stopped to watch, entranced by the sight of their King fighting. He nodded to them and strode away, allowing the crowd to part before him naturally.

There were very few Weshen men still fighting. Those remaining were alive because of dumb luck, in a few cases, but mostly because they protected themselves with shifter magic.

"Stop!" the King roared. He wanted what magic Weshen had left to offer.

His men drew back from their tiny battles, and the melee quieted. The soldiers gradually began to step into their memorized ranks, filling the spaces left by dead comrades without a blink or a word.

His Generals and the Wesh slaves they commanded began to round up the living Weshen. Anyone identified as a shifter was placed in irons. Others were slit from top to bottom, or pierced through the neck, as per preference of each General.

The blood of the country Zorander had hunted for a lifetime ran freely on its own soil, none of it any use.

"Send a party to the water. Check the mansion. Put out what fires you can."

He made no mention of looting, and he ignored the grumbles his men made after he passed.

Zorander cared nothing for the desires of his men. They had food enough and weapons enough in StarsHelm. What good were a poor country's trinkets? The real treasure was not here. Instead, the paltry substitute plodded behind his Generals, chains clanking.

As they passed, Zorander scanned the remnants of a powerful people before him. Tag-rag Paladins and bleeding boys.

None of these had the power he sought.

None of these could possibly be the SoulShifter.

He roared a curse as the short line of prisoners descended the hillside, his voice echoing down the smoking circles of Weshen City. His thoughts were a swarm of his brothers, and of Mara, and Aram, and all the holdings of Riata.

And suddenly, inexplicably, Zorander Graeme felt old. His bones felt brittle with despair, his skin dry and leathery. His muscles felt as withered as an uprooted tree, left to decay in the forest while the seasons changed around it.

If he didn't find the SoulShifter soon, the Sulit spells protecting him would fade, and he would be left alone, torn piece by excruciating piece by Lumien, Braddon, Brys, Owin, Anyon, Saith, and Derec.

20

For days, Nik felt his feet turning him south and east on the mountain trails.

He tried each morning to adjust his course, but every night only brought Weshen City nearer. He couldn't live with putting more innocents in danger, even if they asked him.

He had promised himself not to return until he'd healed, but something in the odd iron scent of the air kept calling him back.

He knew Resh had gone on to EvenFall. Had watched him from high above the passage. He also had seen the boats from Weshen Isle one day, tiny dots on the water. The men returned from their summer dalliances, presumably leaving the women and young children on the island.

From high on the side of the NeverCross Mountains, it seemed to Nik like life had continued, closing around the hole of his absence like withdrawing his hand from water. This was good. This was what he had prayed for, in many ways. But the air told him a different story. Its sources held secrets he couldn't understand yet.

The overpowering chill of the mountain dulled every scent except an ever-present metallic tang. An iron fragrance that could be blood or weapons.

Weshen City could be in trouble, and if they were, Nik was obligated to help them.

This was his reasoning as he finally allowed his feet to choose the path east. A few mornings later, he found himself once more high above the Weshen passage's entrance, just beyond the stonetrees near EvenFall.

He sat on a flat rock high on the cliff and ate cold meat from an earlier kill. His belly growled in want, and his jaw ached with the toughness of the food, but Nik paid his body no attention. Instead, he focused on the sources around him, testing to see if he was alone.

He didn't like being alone nearly as much as he'd once imagined. Nik had found something he needed in Sy, and Coren, and Resh. He'd found friends, and something close to family. Leaving them didn't feel like liberation, but exile.

Even here, though, in the peaks of the NeverCross, he sensed he wasn't exactly alone. Something was following him.

When the mountain winds howled around him, he felt a creeping presence at his back. Each time he turned to look, the surrounding cliffs were barren and still.

Just last night, he'd heard the slightest echo of weight tamping the snow down, but he'd never seen footprints larger than the animals he killed to survive.

Sitting so near to the passage, Nik sensed none of that. His nose was tuned to the iron in the air instead, and he felt the presence of men - so many, and moving. He scanned the forest far below him.

If there was an army coming to attack Weshen City, he would bring this mountain down on their skulls.

He would rain rocks and stonetrees until his strength gave out, and he slid off the mountain himself.

But when he saw the soldiers, they were not walking through the trees. They were *exiting* the passage. The same passage that should have killed any of them without Weshen blood.

They were walking away from Weshen City, carrying the cream and black and crimson flag of Riata. It flipped in the breeze far below him, a beacon of Riatan success.

Nik tried to stand and stumbled, his knees buckling with guilt. The returning shifter magic had opened the passage, and the Restless King's army had swarmed through to Weshen.

Nik's fear of hurting the Weshen had paralyzed him to inaction, and it was this inaction that made him too late. The paradox took Nik's breath and bones from him. He slumped, helpless, against the ice and rock of the mountain face.

He tried to force himself to watch the neat lines of soldiers, to gather a righteous rage, but his eyes squeezed shut. He knew that if he watched them, sensed the wasted Weshen blood on their weapons, he might slaughter the entirety of their ranks. He didn't want to hurt these men, either. Most were only following orders of a much more powerful man.

Instead, Nik allowed the cold to freeze the tears solid on his lashes, and he drifted into the darkness of his own tiny world.

This was where he would stay. Alone and safe from harming others.

The next morning was reluctant to break, and the sun pushed its straggling rays onto a gray-cast mountain. Eyes nearly welded shut with icy tears, Nik debated whether he should ever move again, or if he would be better letting the mountain claim him. The world was silent around him, the snow muffling his movements.

Then he heard the noise that must have woken him. A faint, echoing roar far below. An exhausted, furious roar, with more of a human catch to its end.

He drew the sources of water and salt from his eyes, grimacing as they ripped at his lashes. He gathered his pack and stood stiffly, rubbing his thighs to encourage the blood flow.

Nik began to climb further down the mountain. There was no reason for him to chase a wounded creature, but neither was there a reason for him to stay away. Sometime in the night's locked darkness, Nik had left behind all claim on his life and his choice in living it.

The Magi could decide if he lived or died in each moment.

He would never be slave to a man again, but perhaps he should be servant to a god.

Nik peered down into the forest, still high enough to be safe. A Grizzlin was there, pacing the exit of the passage. Its nose was to the ground, and it snuffled against the tracks the army had left.

Nik remained hidden, watching the strange animal with an intense curiosity. It appeared to be tracking something, but without the strength to chase down its prey. The animal was obviously exhausted. It ambled again in a circle, moaning a growl to the wind before collapsing its rear haunches. Another quieter roar lifted into the air.

It was a mournful sound, Nik realized. It drew him toward the creature, much further down the cliff than was smart.

He'd never seen many MagiCreatures. He knew them by sight because of pictures, but the slavers had kept him well-protected from anything stronger than themselves.

Then, as Nik watched from the safety of the rocks, the animal's great form began to shrink and shift into a form that was seared in Nik's memory, but which twisted and terrorized his dreams.

Sy. Nik felt his jaw slacken as he stared.

The same form that entered Nik's mind each night, bringing him the sweetest of dreams and the most heart-wrenching of nightmares, as his imagination admitted how deep in he was.

Somehow, like an odd answer to a prayer to the Magi, Sy slumped on the ground below Nik, too exhausted and heartbroken to even notice he was being watched.

Forgetting his vow not to use his shifter powers, Nik smoothed the rock face and skidded down the mountain to where Sy lay.

His eyes fluttered open. They didn't focus on Nik before slipping closed again. Sy's head lolled to the side. His breathing was steady, though, and Nik didn't smell any of the tang of blood that had drawn him from the mountain top in the first place.

For that, he was grateful, but as he bent to tug at Sy's body, he felt no great spark of magic.

Prodding at Sy's sources, Nik felt the dregs of power. Sy had nearly used everything in his body to get here. If he used any more, he risked something the slavers called the *fourth shift*, when the blood itself seeped through the skin, completing an act of devastating magic but killing the shifter.

Sy needed rest, and this was no safe place to sleep.

Nik hooked his arms under Sy's, bending his elbow joint beneath Sy's shoulders. Shifting the ground beneath them into a slight roll, Nik pulled Sy into the cool darkness of the mountain passage.

The tunnel was nothing like what Nik remembered.

The walls were farther apart, widened and shifted away. He felt the disturbance in the sources. Shifters had done this, but not with finesse. The floor was hard and caked with the footprints of hundreds of men, splashes of sloshing water, and dripping blood.

Nik felt none of the pressure against his temples or the queasiness in his stomach that the passage had brought him last time. The Weshen passage had been cleared of all its magical barrier.

And when the barrier had fallen, Nik had no doubt the Restless King had been waiting to force his way into Weshen.

This must have been what the Grizzlin - what Sy - had smelled. As Nik pulled at Sy's muscles and bones, he struggled not to break. Here in his arms was the very

292

person he wasn't ready to see, and this was the news he most didn't want to affirm.

Yet it was Sy. He was here, in Nik's arms. His beautiful body was drained, but it was whole.

He would be broken inside after he woke and remembered.

But so was Nik.

Perhaps the Magi had arranged this after all, pulling Nik away from Resh just in time to be with Sy when he was needed.

Nik hadn't been close enough to look at Weshen City in many days, but he already knew what waited on the other side of this passage. There were too many booted, bloodied prints leaving the passage. Too much trampled grass on the road back to EvenFall.

Nik was thankful, at least, that Sy slept through all the hours it took to drag him through the passage and up into the mansion. Sy didn't open his eyes to see the bodies of his friends and countrymen, caked with blood and dirt. He didn't sniff the air that still held smoke and stench from burning buildings and flesh. He didn't taste the dry mouth of loss.

Miraculously, the mansion stood, mostly untouched.

One end was smoking and blackened with fire, but the side Nik knew - the side where Sy's room had been - stood quiet and too-normal.

Nik used one last bit of his shifter strength to slant the stairs into a ramp, hauling Sy's unresponsive bulk up and up until they reached the bed that both had slept in separately, but never together.

Nik didn't stop to examine why it was so important to him that Sy sleep in the comfort of his boyhood bed. He just made it happen. He pulled Sy onto the bed and removed his boots. Tucking them both under the covers, Nik leaned his head against Sy's chest, listening to the steady thud of his heart.

And he slipped into a dark sleep, filled with black fire and golden smoke, where nothing was as it should be.

Many hours later, when the room was nearly black inside and out, Nik awoke to Sy coughing.

Sy sat, blinking around himself in the night. "Where…"

Nik moved slowly. Cautiously. It occurred to him that Sy might not appreciate being brought here. That he might not want Nik in his bed. That he might wish he were in pursuit of the King this very moment instead of several hours in the wrong direction.

"Nik," he breathed, a choked noise coming from his throat as he slumped down into the pillows, turning his face away. Nik's breath came ragged and labored too, as he struggled to find a word that wouldn't break Sy any further.

"The city…" he began. Sy held up a hand without looking, as though to push the words and thoughts away. As it fell, his fingers brushed Nik's chest, curling into a fist of fabric. He pressed his knuckles into Nik, the pain sharpening Nik's breathing. Then the hand flattened, hot and large on Nik's chest.

Sy moved on the bed, not quite rolling, but somehow pulling Nik closer and slightly beneath his body. His arm curved around Nik's shoulders, drawing him deeper. Nik swallowed, his throat dry with need - need for more and need for less.

He was terrified to hurt Sy, but he knew that hurt was everywhere. Once the sun rose, there would be no denying the pain scattered all over Weshen City.

"Make me forget," Sy whispered then. "I want to pretend my city is only sleeping, and the stars smile on us."

Nik choked on his desire, knowing the deadly danger in such a request.

It wasn't the first time he'd been asked to do such a thing, and he'd vowed never again to be the potion that made the real world drift away. He wasn't strong enough to resist such a pull himself, and he didn't want to slip away into dreams and ignore reality until it cut him open and bled him dry.

But this was Sy, he reminded himself.

Sy would never treat him like that.

Nik skimmed a hand up Sy's arm, squeezing at the corded muscle there, massaging the tension from his shoulder. The arm loosened and fell to the side, inviting Nik closer. Sy's neck stretched back as he turned his face to the ceiling again. His head sunk into the pillow, and Nik pushed his lips to the sweaty-sweet skin, resting them in the hollow of Sy's collarbone.

His tongue slipped between his lips, and Sy moaned, the sound reminding Nik for just a second of the Grizzlin's agony. He stopped. This wasn't what Sy needed. But the next noise from Sy's lips was more growl, and Nik felt strong hands grip his arms, pulling him above Sy in the bed.

The sheets twisted so he was pinned, held aloft like a toy. In the darkness, he could barely see the outline of Sy's teeth, and the glint of his eyes.

The sensation panicked him, and he squirmed in Sy's grasp, twisting away and struggling desperately to free his legs. He flopped onto the other side of the bed, breathing hard for all the wrong reasons. It was too close to memory. Too close to nightmare here in the darkness.

"What is it?" Sy asked, his voice very careful. Measured.

Nik felt his heart rip open just a bit. He was poisonous. There was too much cruelty sliding around in his memory to be anyone's drug of forgetting. "I..."

"You can't," Sy finished for him, already rising from the bed. "It's okay." He walked out of the room and into the adjacent bathroom. The lock clicked over on the door.

Nik bolted out of the bed, shaky hands raking his hair back. They tangled in his matted curls, and he realized they both needed a bath. And food.

The things they each wanted to forget would never leave them. But Nik had found his way out of such darkness before. Taking care of the body was taking care of the mind, and that much, he *could* do for Sy. He raced down the steps, spreading his shifter power far to find the kitchen. Not a living soul stirred anywhere in the mansion, but the kitchen held plenty of food.

Enough to feed a battalion, Nik realized with a grimace. Ashemon had been ready for the King. It just hadn't been enough.

He pushed these thoughts away and filled a tray with all the same foods he'd watched Sy eat during their stay in EvenFall: cured meats and tart cheeses. Dark, seeded bread. Deep red chokecherry wine and a crock of yogurt with dried berries.

When he clattered into the room, Sy had just stepped from the bathroom. A towel wrapped his trim waist, and Nik nearly dropped the tray. He managed to slide it onto the bed, his eyes darting around the room in a pointless effort not to stare at Sy's bare chest.

"So...Grizzlin," he blurted, feeling his cheeks heat.

Sy nodded, running his fingers through his wet hair to lift it. "It found me. On the way to StarsHelm."

Nik nodded, uncertain what to ask. Obviously, Coren and Sy hadn't been successful in killing the King. Unless the battle here in the city had been retaliation. But he doubted StarsHelm could have regrouped so fast.

"Kashar told us a true creature shift was complete. That Coren's was only partial." Sy sat on the bed and took a handful of bread and meat. He was still in the towel, and Nik's eyes magnetized to the muscular thigh that was revealed.

"I should bathe too," he managed, his voice sounding strangled in his head.

Sy only nodded, eyes downcast. Nik rushed to scrub the dirt of traveling from his skin and rinse the tangles from his curls. Dripping cold water on the tile of the floor, he hesitated, one hand on his dirty clothes and one on the towel.

He hated putting dirty clothes back on. But the towel might send a message one of them wasn't ready to answer.

Nik feared it might be himself.

He picked up the pants. His nose wrinkled. They were *really* dirty.

Cursing, Nik wrapped the towel around his waist and burst through the door. He was certain his eyes were wild, but Sy only sat on the bed, drinking deeply from a mug of wine.

Sy was wearing pants.

Nik cursed again. "My pack. It's downstairs."

Sy shrugged. "I have plenty of clothes. Through that door."

"I've already stolen most of what will fit," Nik answered, fighting a flush. Sy laughed once, and the sound chipped away some of the tension. Sy stood and opened the closet door, gesturing for Nik to enter.

He began pulling pants and shirts down from their shelves, shaking them out. Nik tried to measure their lengths and widths while keeping one fist on the towel. Sy held a soft shirt up to Nik's chest, and his fingers brushed the skin of Nik's arms. They stayed, tips resting against his taut muscle. Then they curled around Nik's bicep, and Nik sighed, this time leaning into the gentle touch.

Standing, face to face, he felt even. Equal. Steady.

He raised his eyes to meet Sy's storm-dark blue ones, and the spark they'd enjoyed in EvenFall kindled and roared between them again. Sy dropped the shirt to the floor, his hand slipping to Nik's back, tugging him gently closer in something just more than a hug.

Nik leaned into the touch, letting Sy lead. As long as the lead allowed a little slack, he was willing. Sy gripped his shoulder blades, cupping their sharp wings with both hands as his lips lowered to meet Nik's.

Somehow, they had both grown hesitant and gentle and careful.

"I don't want to be your medicine," Nik murmured, feeling emboldened with Sy's fingers skimming down his back, coming to rest at his hips, just above the scratch of the towel.

"I don't need medicine. I need a friend," Sy returned, his lips hot on the shell of Nik's ear.

"I don't want to be that, either," Nik said, a grin spreading across his lips.

Sy pulled his face back enough to look Nik in the eyes. "Yes, you do. You just want more than that, too."

And he let himself fall backward into the furs and leathers, toppling Nik with him. Nik marveled that Sy had already learned to let Nik have the freedom to move closer or farther away, and realizing this made Nik suddenly ravenous to prove Sy right.

He *did* want more. He wanted to be everything Sy might want and need. And he wanted it now, not after he had healed.

They were both broken. They would heal together. Heal each other.

Nik kissed Sy as hard as he dared, searing his thoughts and desire into Sy's lips and skin. Their whole world became each other, as though passion swallowed them whole, and every touch was new.

Sy watched Nik sleeping in the pale morning light. At some point, they had moved back to the bed, the exhaustion of too little sleep calming their hands and slowing their breath.

Nik was beautiful on the pillows before him, lips parted in soft breath and a tangle of curls surrounding a face that looked more at peace than Sy knew Nik had ever been. Sunlight dappled the worn wooden floor from the balcony windows. Sy wanted so much to stay and ignore the horrors beyond this serene bedroom, but he had never been that sort of person.

Sy knew what he had to do.

Nik still needed to heal from something, and Sy was only going deeper into battle. He reached into the pack Nik must have carried through the passage and all the way up the hill. Rummaging in the bottom of a deep pocket, he found the note Nik had left him through Resh.

Turning it over, he scrawled an answer to Nik's words.

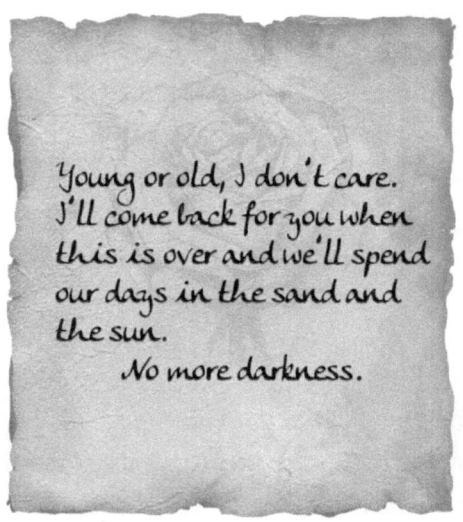

Young or old, I don't care. I'll come back for you when this is over and we'll spend our days in the sand and the sun.
No more darkness.

He also left a map of the city and circled the secluded beach where he guessed Ashemon would have had boats waiting. He hoped Nik would go to the island. That's where the Weshen men would have retreated if any were still alive. That's where the women and young children should be waiting. They would need a protector. A teacher.

Sy wished he could go too, but he would not repeat his father's mistakes.

He would not hide in Weshen while Zorander Graeme walked the world free.

Leaving the mansion was like walking into a nightmare. There were bodies everywhere, left to bleed and rot in the late-summer sun. Animals roamed free of their fences, bleating and searching for blades of green in the scorched grass. Failed, masterless weapons glinted in the sun, so many that Sy could almost believe he looked at the twinkling ocean if he squinted.

How easy it would be to give in to grief. It seemed there was nothing left here to fight for, so it would be simple enough to abandon the fight. It would be easy to slip back into bed with Nik, then find a new home where they could live, alone but together.

Sy forced himself to keep walking, away from the mansion and desperate thoughts like these. Halfway down the hill, he found his father.

He dropped to his knees next to Ashemon, ashamed that no sobs wracked his chest. But Sy had said his goodbyes to Ashemon once. He would have taken his father back one day. He would have saved him had he been here in time.

But looking at the dead sources that no longer held Ashemon's soul did not tug tears from Sy's eyes.

Instead, it kindled a fire in his chest, and that fire began to spread, searching for nourishment. All around him he found familiar faces, now distorted in death. Running away might be easy, but it would never make him happy.

The fire of revenge raged, feeding his magic until he felt he could race all the way to StarsHelm in his Grizzlin form.

He wouldn't, though. He would practice his magic, not strain it. He'd arrived here so weak that he couldn't have saved anyone, even if they'd still been here. That mistake must turn into a lesson.

As Sy walked through the streets, he added weapons to his pack, knowing he could sell the blades in EvenFall for coin. He also stopped to pick a sack full of lemondrines. His power had been so depleted on arrival, but he hoped to build his stamina on the journey back to StarsHelm.

If the Restless King had been here, and Sy knew in his gut that the man had, then he would be returning home, ready to celebrate.

Sy would find him at his most vulnerable, glutted with success, and he would strike him down.

Coren was once stronger than him, but she had rejected the magic's price, and it had left her. Now, Sy was possibly the only Weshen shifter with a creature form. It was his duty to hunt and kill the Restless King.

Born to be a Paladin, blessed to be a Grizzlin: Syashin Havenash was ready to kill Zorander Graeme.

And when the deed was done, perhaps he could be just Sy again. He could return to Nik on the island, and they could grow young together as the years passed.

21

The Lord of Witches slouched on his throne, impatient for the day to begin. He had not slept in three nights for the excitement. He had not slept since Strike delivered the news that Grand was coming, and she was bringing presents.

Lord loved presents.

Especially when they promised to be so, so bloody as this one.

"Is Mara close yet?" He knew he could rise and walk to the window, but he preferred to watch the young witch scamper to peer beyond the castle walls.

"No sign of her carriages yet, My Lord."

He sighed.

"You should sleep," Strike said, entering the room with a dynamic stride. He liked that about her. Her energy and strength. It meant he could be lazier. Lord could be plenty strong when he wanted. He was a man on the throne of witches, after all. But he rarely wanted the trouble.

"And she's bringing the shifters?" Lord asked. He'd asked this many times since the message had been delivered.

Strike merely nodded, unfazed by his obsessive repetition. "Have you been practicing your shifting?" she asked.

He shrugged. "It takes so much energy."

"My Lord, you must be ready," she chided.

Lord thought of a good retort, but he was too bored to engage her. He slumped further in his seat. His crown caught on one of the ornate carvings at his back and slipped to the side. He righted it with a single finger, sighing.

Another witch burst into the door, tripping over herself in an effort to hurry but not run.

"My Lord," she gasped. "The Sulit are in the Listening Forest! Just beyond the walls!"

Lord watched her, glaring. He waited until she had gained her breath, but only because her huffing speech annoyed him.

"How many?"

"Perhaps a thousand. The trees can be difficult to understand, My Lord."

His eyes rolled back into his skull. "Then don't rely on them. Really, Strike. Can't we send proper scouts?" Lord had never understood the witches' practices of listening to the trees and the rivers and the pebbles. It seemed so primitive.

And he had no use for their Mother, either. Or any of the gods he'd come across in his young life.

He was self-taught and stronger than any shifter he'd met; no Mirror Magi had a hand in that. No Sulit Mother had put him on a throne meant for females.

Lord summoned the strength to rise. His fingers tugged the sources of his chair seat to a tilt, sliding him gracefully out and up. He sauntered to the window and gazed down at the forest. His eyes fluttered closed as he spread his senses, searching for the sources beyond the castle walls.

He searched the black-barked trees for Sulit witches, feeling the sparkling tang of their blood, like bubbled chokecherry wine. Sweet and fizzy. He counted, skipping ahead a dozen at a time. This was too easy. Why did they trust trees?

This was why the Sulit and the Brujok, despite their ambitions and resolve, would never be permitted to follow him when he turned his attention on Riata.

The Brujok thought to discard *him* once he helped rid them of Graeme's hold. He almost laughed aloud, forgetting they still watched him.

After this battle, Sulit would unite under him. Mara would open the doors of Riata and no one would ever discard him again, unless they wished a slow and excruciating death.

"Fourteen hundred," he announced. As he moved to step away from the window, he caught another type of source, tucked deep in the forest.

"And three shifters. An old woman. Young *twins*." He swiveled and fixed Strike in his gaze, gratified to see her terror before she tucked it away. "Bring them to me, or die trying."

Strike and the other witch flew from the room in a blur of robes, and Lord began to pace, his apathy forgotten.

Someone had unearthed the twin prophecy again. Some fool southern witch was bringing these unfortunate shifters into a deadly mix, like adding an explosive ingredient to an incendiary potion.

It was a thorn in his boot, every step a reminder of all that had been lost, and all that could be lost again.

Last time a witch had brought Weshen twins into Sulit, they had both died trying to prove the prophecy true. Lord assumed that meant it was false, but Strike had cautioned him that only the most powerful would be able to bring balance to the world.

This had not soothed his anxiety, and she bore a scar along her spine to prove it.

Lord knew balance between two opposing forces was the religion of Weshen, but it was hardly the same in Sulit or Riata. Each country had its own teachings about the repercussions of imbalance and the method to restore the world. These contradictions kept the battles coming and the world in its current and constant state of chaos.

Lord did not subscribe to any of the balance theories. He believed the world's natural state *was* chaos, and that balance was a false idea created by people.

None of that mattered in the face of zealots, however.

These twins were a threat to his plan, and they must be brought before him, examined, and executed if need be.

Maren fought the Brujok who grasped her arms, but between the vines securing her wrists and the witch's nails, she couldn't break free. She was nearly thrown into a cold, oddly masculine throne room, her old knees banging hard on the dark marble.

Steps approached her, but the witch kept Maren's face pressed tight to the stone. All she saw was the heel of a perfectly clean leather boot.

"An old Weshen shifter. Come to play with the Sulit?"

Maren smiled grimly to herself. "So it's true. A man on a throne before a country of women." She twisted her face just enough to witness the flash of disgust on the witch's face. Her smile grew, but she hid it before anyone could see.

The boots before her kicked out, connecting with her stomach. Maren let slip a guttural noise, and she heard Penna's muffled shriek somewhere behind her. Fingers dug into her scalp and yanked her head back by her braid.

The witch held her face still as the man turned to gaze down at her.

Maren gasped, despite herself.

Her brain sparked, working and struggling to make sense of the figure before her. A spirit, surely. A trick of the witches. It just wasn't possible for this person to be alive.

"What is wrong with her?" the young man asked, his eyes darting to the witch. He began to pace, impatience in each click of his heel against the marble.

"I don't know, My Lord," the witch answered, peering down into Maren's eyes. Maren blinked away from her gaze, focusing instead on the young man before her.

"You look like your father," she whispered.

The Lord of Witches stopped moving. His back was to her, draped in a velvet cloak the color of trees at night. It swished and floated just above the floor as he turned in a slow circle to face her. "What did you say?"

"You look just like your father, *Iyesh*."

The name rolled from her throat and landed in the room like a bolt of lightning. The witch's grasp faltered, and Maren scooted out of reach. The twins behind her stopped struggling in the grips of two other witches, transfixed by the name of their dead brother.

"You don't remember me, but I'm Maren. I lived on the island with you. We all thought you dead."

The young Lord was slack-jawed before her, and she guessed it was a rare look for him. It only served to remind her of the child he'd been last time she saw him.

"Stormcloud chickens..." His voice was barely a breath, and he seemed to have forgotten himself for a moment as he remembered her and a snippet of his childhood.

"These twins are your brother and sister. Penna. Kosh. Your family."

The cloak rippled and twisted around him as he swirled away from her, banging both fists on the seat of the twisted throne. "I have no family. You're mistaken - I'm not who you think!"

But the shout was full of denial and desperation, and Maren had no doubt she had guessed his secret. But *why* was it a secret?

Surely, he remembered more than her chickens.

Had the witches forced him here? Or had he won the crown?

The witch who had captured her recovered enough to clamp a hand over Maren's mouth. When Jyesh paced away toward the window, the witch leaned close to Maren's ear. "If you tell him another word, I will slit your throat here and toss those children from the balcony. Prophecy or no, we can't have Lord start thinking he has shifter family. No one cares for him now except the Brujok. *We* are his family now. We took him when no one else would. Keep your mouth shut, and your blood stays in your veins."

Maren obeyed, but she promised herself it was only temporary.

"My Lord, this woman is obviously under duress. You simply look like one of her poor Weshen relatives." The witch's voice was soothing, and Jyesh's shoulders began to retreat from their defensive positions. From her bound position on the floor, Maren watched while the witch approached her Lord, whispering words under her breath. She tucked a gnarled hand into her robe and withdrew a crumble of herbs.

Jyesh didn't even notice the trickle of herbs across his throne as the witch stepped behind him.

His eyes grew dim before them as the spell began to work.

A memory charm. But not even as perfect as the one the Weshen used on their boys when they were taken from the island to train in the city.

Maren's head pulsed with the ache of her still-bleeding gash and the exhaustion she knew was coming for her. She needed to stay awake for the twins. Needed to figure a way out of this mess.

"Take them away." The Lord of Witches rose from his throne, fully recovered and evidently under the witches' control once more. Strength straightened his spine, and cruelty pulled his jaw tight. "Put them all in the fourth tower."

"Yes, Lord," the witch answered, bowing to him. Maren caught the slightest hint of a triumphant smile on her face.

The three witches dragged their prisoners from the room, and Maren's last glimpse of the Lord of Witches was a tall, cold man, staring at nothing. Her heart cracked at what the little boy had grown into - had been *made* into.

Kosh stumbled along next to her, and Penna on the other side. Their eyes were wide, but not with innocence. Their small mouths mirrored each other's in slits of determination.

Maren didn't understand the Brujok's game.

She was just an island woman, unlearned in politics and battle. But if Kosh and Penna were in danger, she would fight for their safety with every shred of magic and muscle left in her tired body.

It wouldn't be enough, though. As they spiraled up and around the towers of Rurok, Maren prayed to the Magi to send her help.

Kosh and Penna, hearing her mumblings, added their whispered pleas, and together they begged the gods to send them a tomorrow.

"Can you sense them, like Nik does?" Resh asked Coren as they ducked into the woods just beyond the towers of Rurok.

Coren bit at her lips, working to send her senses through the trees and stone, farther than the limits of everyday sight and hearing. She wasn't nearly as strong or as practiced as Nik seemed to be, but she *did* find masses of people.

It was like identifying the source of a noise in a black-dark room, or a smell on the passing breeze.

"There are many in the towers, but also in the woods beyond the towers." She knew this wasn't helpful, but thankfully, Resh didn't comment. Surely, the people she sensed in the woods would be southern Sulit, come to fight their northern sisters.

The towers would be full of Brujok and the Wesh Mara had brought.

She said, "Let's try to slip around the towers and get into the woods where the southern Sulit might be. Maren brought the twins to the south, so it's possible some of the witches gathered here would know of her. They might even be our allies."

A lump rose in her throat as she tried to swallow a curse. Not against Maren, exactly. The old woman had been trying to help Penna and Kosh escape a possible banishment. She'd had no way of knowing how dangerous Sulit had grown.

None of them could have predicted that all their enemies would begin gathering in the very place she sought safety.

"There will be many guards." Resh scanned the towers before them. "And can't the Brujok sense us, maybe even right now? Surely they also have those magical detection spells here." During their journey, Resh had wrung every bit of information from her about StarsHelm and their time there.

Coren saw the lust in his eyes when she spoke, and it wasn't always for her.

She nodded. "Guards or not, what choice do we have?"

Resh suggested they dart across the strip of black sand between the forest and the lake, keeping close to the water. "The noise of the falls should cover our movement, at least."

Coren glanced back at the NewMoon Falls towering behind them. The roar of water pounded in her chest. Taking a deep breath, she tightened the straps of her pack and sprinted for an outcropping of large boulders, Resh directly beside her. They paused to catch their breath, then repeated the process, dodging behind rocks as they wove toward the shore.

Anyone watching from one of the tower windows high above them would certainly see them. Coren imagined they would look like tiny insects fleeing the spots of sun.

"How many towers are there?" Resh breathed, kinking his neck to stare up at the castle. The spray from the falls misted their faces with cool water, and he cursed appreciatively, running a hand through his dark hair. His eyes caught her watching, and though Coren was sweaty and hot from running and nearly sick with anxiety about her family, she had the sudden urge to crush his lips down on hers.

His mouth parted in a half-smile as his eyes flicked down to her mouth, and Coren raged at herself, biting her bottom lip back behind her teeth. Of course he would read her thoughts as plainly as if she had acted on them.

"It's the excitement," he whispered, crouching lower behind the rock. "Just like the hunts."

"What?" She glared at him.

"The thrill of the hunts is tied to excitement. Racing heartbeats from running, but also desire. The knowledge that you might get caught, and the anxiety that you don't know exactly what that means, and the anticipation of finding out."

"You really do take everything to the bedroom," she said, turning away. But his gaze was too intense, and the corner of her mouth tugged up a little.

"And I'm right. Because I'm a master at reading people. I can read you so easily, Coren. You think you're so well-hidden behind that mask of independence and that shell you've gathered like a wall from your hurts. But you can't survive without love."

"I don't need your love."

"I'm not talking about me," he answered, and his voice was so much quieter that she turned her face back to him. "The love of your family and your friends. Maybe one day of a man. But you're excited now because you think your family is here somewhere. You want them to be here, even though it's dangerous, because then at least you'll all be together. Your anticipation at seeing them is so high it's flushing your cheeks and sparkling your eyes. You've never looked so beautiful."

She heard the rightness in everything he said, like fitting a perfectly-shaped stone into the last empty slot in a wall. Her understanding of why they were here and why she was excited about it, rather than simply terrified. It made sense.

She hated that Resh had been the one to point it out to her. What else could he read in her poorly-hidden glances?

"We should go." His eyes were on the horizon. "I see movement."

She peeked around the rocks. A trio of Brujok guards had descended onto the beach. Coren couldn't tell if they were dressed in Mara's colors or simply wore mostly black.

"You stay here," she whispered. "My magic is what they sense. I'll draw them away."

Resh nodded, though the grimace on his face told her he wanted no part of such a plan. He made no move to stop her, and she was pleased with his trust in her power.

Coren slipped her pack from her shoulders and dropped it in the sand.

"Come out, come out, little Weshen shifter!" One of the witches twirled her fingers, and the scattered weeds on the beach stood up at attention. They tugged their roots from the sand and tumbled toward her, forming a braid of plants. Coren remembered this trick from the maze.

"We have lots of your people here today. Wouldn't you like to watch them die? Front seats?"

Coren felt a growly yell forming in the base of her throat, but Resh grasped her waist. "Be careful," he pleaded. His other hand came to rest on her cheek, turning her toward him. Before she could twist away, he brushed his lips gently against hers. The touch was too soft and too quick, and his eyes challenged her.

He let her go. "Be sure to come back so I can do that properly."

Coren raised a brow at him. Her tongue darted out to taste the spot he had kissed, and he cursed, sliding helplessly down the rock. She grinned, then sprinted from their hiding place.

The witches were ready for her, but she was ready for them, as well.

The sand was too soft beneath her feet, and she quickly gave up on running around the vines. She closed her eyes and jumped into the air, screaming to the Vespa inside.

And now we fly!

Her wings snapped open, and she reveled in the shriek of one of the witches. They didn't know all of her secrets, after all.

She let the power of the Vespa course through her, shifting every bone and turning her skin to feathers, her fingers to golden claws.

Opening her beaked mouth in a scream of warning, she circled high above the three Brujok. One of them gathered the weeds tighter, making her rope longer and thicker. It hurled itself into the air like a snakka striking from a dark hole, but Coren dodged the vine. Another vine swirled toward her from the sand below, snapping off a single feather.

Coren spiraled higher, and she felt the spirit of the Vespa guiding her in her ascent.

Now we fly, and now we kill!

She startled at the change in thoughts, feeling her claws tighten as though they were digging farther out of her skin. A luminescent drop of poison formed on each point.

Now we kill!

The voice was insistent. Coren felt both powerful and powerless as the Vespa urged her higher in the sky, then down and down and down, hurtling like a bolt of lightning toward the main witch.

Coren felt the impact of her wings on the witch's body, bursting it beneath her like breaking the surface of the ocean. She fought to stay conscious and in her Vespa form as the witch's blood sprayed like foam and her organs plopped out like fish thrown from the sea.

Coren shuddered and closed her eyes against the gruesome image, her skinny bird-legs staggering back across the sand. She flapped her wings, and droplets of blackish-red blood flew from her feathers. She smelled the blood and sensed its source. It was sparkling darkness, like the night sky filled with stars.

She finally managed to push herself back into the air, but her falter had cost her.

A vine of green leaves and brown roots wrapped its way around her leg, spreading up her skin like webbing. It tugged her sideways, and her wings jerked out of rhythm. Another vine grew from the side of the first, binding her legs together more quickly than she could react.

Coren was falling, her wings no match for the vines that twisted down into the sand below.

She beat desperately at the air, searching for the sources of the vines to tear them apart. But she was growing weaker. A third vine snaked up her belly, ripping out the soft down there as it squeezed the breath from her.

Coren screamed again, at the Vespa inside her as much as the witches. She needed to stop fighting the air around her, but her wings flapped and flopped, beyond her rational control.

The vines pulled her closer to the beach. She was going to land hard. She had to break her fall, and she couldn't do that with the flight instincts of the Vespa coursing through her body.

Now we walk! She began the chant, yelling it in her mind.

The Vespa was reluctant to subside, but Coren mastered it barely a second before her own feet hit the sand. She landed in an awkward, leg-locked crouch, but now she had enough magic to rip at the sources of the spelled vines.

The two remaining witches circled her, muttering spells. One glanced in rage at the remains of her fellow witch and tossed a trembling handful of orange sand at Coren.

The grains burned like fire as they touched her skin, and Coren dropped to her knees in pain.

"Little Weshen girl, you will die for what you did to our comrade," the witch hissed.

The vines she had torn apart scattered lifeless and brown, but the witches worked together. One raised a dozen more vines, and the other threw handful after handful of the burning sand at her, until Coren choked on pain and her eyes rolled back in her head.

Her body slumped onto the ground, and she sensed the vines all around her, like a cage too small for breath.

Her final fight was staying alert enough to hear their plans.

"She needs the lemondrine. She's of no use like this."

"We must secure her first."

"Then we will take her to Lord. He's been waiting for such power."

Resh watched the witches drag Coren toward the towers. Every fiber in his body seethed to follow and rescue her, but he knew he would only be overpowered and useless. Coren hadn't been strong enough to fight three at once, so certainly he wouldn't be.

He didn't think they meant to kill her. Even after she'd performed the death spiral on one, they had refrained.

He needed a new plan. He took note of which tower they approached, and as his eyes tracked its height, he found a wide window spanning the top floor, like half the wall had been removed. A figure stood watching, too far to make out. Resh wondered if there truly was a man on the throne here, and what he might be like.

He wondered what Sy would have done if he'd been here, but he knew the answer. He'd have used his magic and followed Coren anywhere. Resh gritted his teeth.

First, survival. Then rescue. But one day, he promised himself, he would find and claim his Weshen heritage.

Resh's senses picked up a change on the beach around him. He might not have the same sensing abilities as Coren or Nik, but he hadn't trained as a Paladin for years to be outsmarted by a sneaking witch.

He heard her raspy breath and smelled the iron tang of her finger blades long before she crept around the rock.

Their eyes connected as she scanned the two packs on the ground, and he casually readied a blade in each hand.

"A little Weshen lord?" She smiled, her lips pressing together to hide a blackened tongue. Her fingertips clicked together in rhythm, the blades like untrimmed nails.

Resh shrugged. "I'm no-one important."

The witch laughed, her head rolling back onto her shoulders. "Yes, I know. None of the Weshen filth are important to the Brujok. But you are important to that one." She pointed a pale finger to the open, empty beach.

Reflexively, Resh glanced toward where Coren had been captured, and it was a mistake.

The fingertip blades slashed out at him, marking the soft skin of his cheek and down his neck. The torn skin began to tingle immediately, and Resh fought to stay standing as the poison swirled through his blood, racing toward his heart.

He knew this poison. He'd trained with it many excruciating days.

Only a few seconds remained before his body would be paralyzed.

He allowed his shoulders to slump against the rock. As the witch chuckled and advanced, he let his head droop and loll over his chest. She took another step, and he lunged toward her, burying both blades in her chest.

She shrieked and gurgled, her mouth filling instantly with blood as he twisted the knives through her lungs. Her hands clutched at his forearms, their tiny blades piercing his skin in a final attack.

They slid down the rock together, and Resh was vindicated that even though he would soon lose control of his body and be vulnerable, she would soon die.

With his last thought, he yanked the blades from her skin and sheathed them, gore and all. He heaved himself behind the rock and curled beside his pack, his fingers hunting for the antidote he'd bought in EvenFall.

But the poison reached his hands before he found it, and his fingers curled into themselves, locking into impotent fists.

His arms and legs did the same until Resh was balled like an infant, and just as helpless.

His eyes burned with exposure as he focused all his energy on breathing. His lungs retained just enough control to keep him alive and conscious, which was the point of the poison.

The witches liked their prey alive.

And soon enough, a shadow fell over his still form, and hands grasped his stiff arms beneath the shoulder. All he could do was watch the falls grow smaller as he was dragged across the sand and into a waiting, wheeled cart.

"So many treasures washed up on the beach today," a voice cackled from beyond his line of vision. "Lord will be pleased."

22

Mara stepped delicately into the center of Tower Four, avoiding the stains of blood. Grand followed her close behind, and Aram directly third.

Grand gazed up to the ceiling of the hollow tower, counting dozens of cages suspended by thick chains from the ceiling. They hung from different heights, so the prisoners could not see each other. Each chain ran the height of the tower and looped into a massive pulley system, allowing the prisoners to be lowered and raised at will.

It was the opposite of a dungeon, and Grand had always loved its effect on the prisoners. Even if they could have escaped their spelled bars, nothing waited for them on the other side but open air and a killing drop. Hearing the echoes of others' cries on the rounded walls broke even the best of them.

She breathed in the sources around her, feeling for what magic might be awaiting her Queen's disposal.

"Kashar is here," she said, surprise widening her eyes at the Knight's familiar non-magical signature.

Mara shrugged. "I assumed Lord would place him here to wait for us."

Grand did not question her Queen further, though she wondered just what role Kashar might be playing in Mara's game. Even he hadn't been dense enough to believe he'd been sent to Rurok to barter a peace treaty.

Then she sensed something that made her toes curl and her lips stretch in a luxurious grin. Another familiar source swung high above them. The shifter girl from the maze. The scent of Vespa was thick in the air, swirled with the lemondrine and salt of a Weshen Isle childhood.

Grand turned her smile on Mara, but she tucked it away immediately at the woman's sour expression.

"It stinks like shifters in here," Mara said, covering her nose with her sleeve. "I'm going to my rooms. Bring me Kashar."

She stalked from the tower, heading to the floor in the first tower that the Brujok kept prepared for her visits. It was in the same tower that Lord inhabited, and was as richly-appointed as the Lord of Witches' rooms.

Grand thought that interesting, but she kept it to herself. She didn't want a man on the throne of Sulit, but neither did she want Mara.

Perhaps one day the two would slit each other's throats, and the Brujok could happily mop up the blood.

Grand located Kashar's name in the log book and found the correct number. She unwound the chain from its hook and activated the pulley. There was little magic in the Rurok prisons, making it easier to track the magic of the prisoners.

The iron cage lowered, shrieking through each stiff link. The noise bounced unpleasantly off the rounded walls and echoed through each swaying cell. Grand chuckled at the shouts and curses that were added to the screech.

"Have you made any new friends?" she asked Kashar as his face finally lowered to her level. He glowered at her, leaning against the opposite side of the bars. She unlocked his cage and walked away, leaving him to struggle with the latch. As he followed her into the hall leading to the next tower, she pulled a long, narrow box from her cloak.

"Queen Mara waits for your company. Try to escape, and I'll bind you with bitebud ropes." She slid open the edges of the box to show him the plant. It rubbed two petals together in warning, the serrations sharpening against each other.

"I have no reason to run from my Queen," Kashar answered.

"Liar." Grand didn't bother to look back. She knew he was following.

They entered the largest of Mara's rooms. Though it was the same size as Lord's throne room, the furnishings were as different as day. Aram lounged on a plush black sofa next to a fire as tall as a man. The floor was solid white stone, rough to the touch. Curtains of Riata's colors - black and crimson and cream velvet - draped the opposite wall of windows. They were tied back to showcase the NewMoon Falls framed in the distance.

Grand bowed to Mara, then Aram, and wandered to the view. She could also see the valley below from here, with its gathering troops. It appeared that the battle was imminent. Grand itched to be spellcasting amid her Brujok sisters, but she held her tongue.

There were other things at work here, and much more was at stake for her sisters in this room than out of it.

"You have been our Prodigal Knight for many years now." Mara circled Kashar. His eyes tracked her around the room, but he moved no other muscle. "And yet, still. I wonder where your true allegiance lies."

"I am pledged to StarsHelm. To your Grace and your husband."

Mara nodded, a smile slipping across her face. "But it has not always been so. You were born in Riata, yet you once fled it for a different country. For the love of a woman."

"Weshen do not believe in love anymore, your Grace."

Mara paused her pacing and glanced at Aram. "I've heard such strange things. But I don't believe them. Not any more than I believe that Weshen has been without magic all these years."

"Of course, the Wesh your Grace possesses were never deprived of their shifting," Kashar cautioned.

"Of course. Yet there have been banishments. Changes to the passage beneath the NeverCross Mountains. Tales of girls who fly and boys who roar."

Grand examined Kashar carefully as Mara spread her secrets wide for him to gaze on. His jaw tightened, but that was all.

"I wasn't certain you were even capable of true loyalty, my Knight. Until this summer, that is. Until I smelled her in my maze, with your scent all over her tracks. You have interesting friends, Prodigal Knight, including that woman who creates creatures in the Riatan woods. But it's your family I find most intriguing."

"I have no family."

Mara raised a brow. Grand bit back a chuckle. She loved it when they tried to lie.

"Perhaps you once thought so. But blood never lies."

Kashar remained silent, but Grand could smell the sour sweat dripping down his back. Mara crossed the room to Aram and bent low, murmuring in her brother's ear. He grinned and rose, exiting the room.

"I delivered your message to the Lord of Witches, my Queen. I was repaid with a bed of swinging iron. Now you come to question my loyalty?" Kashar barely controlled his voice.

Grand watched her Queen, waiting for the killing blow, the flash of curved blades. But Mara simply smiled and turned to the door, watching its blank face expectantly. Soon, it opened again, and Aram held it wide for the strutting form of the Lord of Witches.

"Lord, my servant claims to have delivered my message. But I think perhaps he is lying."

"I received him," the Lord said, striding to the fire and turning his back to the Queen. "He did not interest me, so I thought to hold him until you arrived to collect him."

"Did you even look at him?" Mara said, laughter tugging at her question.

Lord turned his face just enough to glare at her. But his profile was enough to send a shock through Kashar's posture, pulling him even straighter than before.

The movement pulled Lord further around, and Grand nearly twisted her neck swiveling her eyes between the two men.

One was young, and one was old, but side by side, they were like two ditches lining the same road.

"Jyesh." Kashar croaked the word before his knees buckled, and his frame sank to the floor. His body fell heavily back onto his heels as he gazed up at the Lord of Witches.

"Yes, my Prodigal Knight. Here is your son, alive and turned traitor to his country just as you once did."

Grand couldn't help the cackle of glee that escaped her lips as the shock worked its way across both men's faces. Mara sank gracefully onto the sofa, Aram smirking by her side, and luxuriated in the sated smile of a well-fed catten.

"Return him to his cell," the Queen said.

StarSeer blinked her eyes open, trying to recall just what had happened.

She was alone in the Listening Forest, flat on her back in the valley below Rurok. Daylight filtered weakly through the black branches and rose-tinged leaves above her. She rubbed her pulsing temples, gazing into the trees. It took several seconds for her eyes to focus on them.

"Help me see," she whispered to their branches, slipping her fingers against the bark of the nearest trunk.

The vision took her mind quickly, and her heart moaned as the trees helped her remember that she had not come to this forest alone.

Maren, Penna, Kosh.

Gone.

The trees showed her their view of the spectacle. She watched behind her closed eyes as they showed her a pair of Brujok. None of them had sensed the witches coming. They had bound Maren instantly and beaten her with barely a flick of a spell. Dragged the three Weshen away toward Rurok as she swooned helplessly in the dirt.

The fact that the Brujok had left her here mostly unharmed must be significant, but she wasn't yet certain in what way.

The battle begins, the trees whispered, bringing her focus to why they were in the valley before Rurok in the first place. Their unison was urgent. *Sulit dies. The Mother grows weak.*

"How do I help the Mother?" StarSeer choked. The Brujok were slaughtering their own people in the name of power.

The natural world had been broken apart, its order upturned by a man on the throne and witches vying for things they should not want.

The battle begins, the trees repeated. *Join your sisters, or the towers of Rurok will fall.*

StarSeer struggled to her feet, the blood flowing too quickly to her brain. She leaned against a trunk, nearly embracing it.

She was no warrior. No trained fighter.

The battle begins. Join your sisters now. The splintered voices in her brain were like dead leaves crunching beneath her feet.

Heaving a breath, StarSeer gathered her courage and stumbled through the trees in a weaving run. The branches parted for her, bending like soft arms to catch her when she would have fallen.

As she drew nearer to the bottom of the valley, the noise grew in muted shouts and cracking branches. The trees around her groaned their hatred of being forced into a fight, their roots caught in spells to destroy the witches they loved.

She tripped over a fallen witch, her stomach heaving as the ground slipped and slid away from the body, dropping it gently into a new trench before the dirt tumbled back to cover her fallen sister. The Mother was trying to reclaim her power straight from the fallen ones' bones.

StarSeer had heard of such desperation by their goddess in ages past, but no-one alive had seen it.

The Mother grows weak. Join your sisters.

StarSeer pushed past the empty ground where the witch had disappeared.

Clearing a stand of trees, she found herself at the edge of the battle. Spells shot through the air, lighting it with a hazy rainbow of colors and a symphony of trilling song. For a long moment, StarSeer could only stand in awe of her sisters' beautiful power.

"The Brujok are weak!" a nearby witch shouted. "They fall before us like autumn leaves!"

Triumphant shouts reached her from all directions as each spell seemed to shoot straight to the heart of a

Brujok. StarSeer was sick at how quickly their enemy fell. The Mother was not absorbing their bodies, though.

Where they fell, they stayed, unmoving. She frowned. Surely, the Mother would want all her children's power.

A witch barely an arm's length away screamed and writhed to the ground, falling limp in a matter of seconds. StarSeer dropped next to her, but she was already gone. Until this moment, StarSeer had wanted nothing but revenge on the Brujok. Desperately.

Revenge for her mother, killed in the first rebellion. For her partner, who had loved her so fiercely and gently for three years before disappearing forever into the towers of Rurok.

But now that these witches fell before and beside her and all around her, their souls swept aside in the fire and water of Sulit spells, StarSeer knew her desires were wrong. Witch against witch gained nothing but darkness.

The Mother grows weak, the trees urged, shaking their leaves at her from all angles.

"Stop!" she screamed into the fray, but no-one even looked at her. The spells still broke through the branches, twisting the trees apart in their haste to kill.

"Stop! Sulit are not murderers!"

A witch pushed her to the side, swiping at a streak of blood on her face. "If you won't help, then leave it to the rest of us! Save the wounded!"

"The Mother grows weak!" she screamed, running sideways through her sisters. None paused to listen to her.

Someone near her shrieked in a horrible sort of raging joy. "The front line is broken! The towers are open to attack!"

A shout of victory broke over the tired Sulit as they saw the evidence of progress. Dozens of fallen bodies lay before them. The clearing smoke of spent spells revealed an open field between the forest and the towers.

Against all they had reasonably believed, the southern Sulit had beaten the first wave of Brujok witches. StarSeer trembled for the significance of such a thing. The trees behind her took the silence as a chance to drop their wounded branches and torn leaves, and her dress fluttered in the whoosh of falling limbs.

It did not seem like a victory.

Though many of the Sulit had cheered the change, something in the energy of the forest silenced them now. The trees began to whisper again, but they no longer spoke a language StarSeer understood. She glanced at her sisters, left and right. Their expressions were fearful as they heard the same incomprehensible mutterings.

The Listening Forest had turned away from them.

Their connection to the Mother was in grave danger, and StarSeer knew each of them felt it in the tightening of their muscles and the hollowing of their hearts. Why hadn't the Mother drawn the Brujok bodies into herself? Had their transgressions been too many? Were their souls now banished from the great well of power within their land?

These thoughts seemed mirrored on the faces of her sisters, all of whom gathered near, waiting to see what would happen. Surely, there were more Brujok than these hidden in Rurok.

Surely, the Lord of Witches watched them from somewhere.

Then the trees' whispers above them changed, growing harsh and scolding. The broken bodies before them quivered, and a slight shimmer of magic shot the air through with diamond-pale energy.

StarSeer burst forward, sprinting to a fallen Brujok. Her knees hit the ground hard, and her hand reached to grasp the black robes. Her fingers closed instead on a ragged brown tunic. The form beneath her was suddenly too small to be a grown witch.

"It's a child," she whispered, choking on the words. "A child!" she shrieked.

Sulit witches began to creep fearfully from the trees then, joining her on the still ground. All around them, the dead Brujok were transforming. *Shifting.* Every single body before them was a Wesh shifter, and most were barely grown.

A sob broke from StarSeer's throat, and the trees whispered, breaking back into the Sulit language.

The Mother grows weak. The balance tilts. Sulit dies.

All around StarSeer, her Sulit sisters wailed and despaired at the trickery that had forced their hands to spill innocent blood. Somehow, the Wesh had been made to shift their appearance, then bound into that shape. StarSeer felt the remnants of such a binding spell. Saw its markings on the cheeks and wrists and scarred skin of each child she turned to.

The trees whispered their warning over and over, before fading into a devastating silence, isolating themselves from the Sulit.

StarSeer and her sisters mourned, but they understood they had no-one to blame except themselves. In using their magic to murder, they had forsaken the Mother's teachings as much as the Brujok.

Sy had barely slept the whole journey back to StarsHelm. His thoughts had swirled like a rip tide, pulling him under the surface of his mission to wrestle with anguish over leaving Nik and despair over losing untold numbers of Weshen.

He had been too late, and he would never forgive himself for it.

His mission to kill the Restless King had suddenly shifted from a necessary step in rebuilding his world to an act of pure hatred and revenge. The man had stolen the life from Sy's country, and he must not be allowed to live.

Sy had practiced shifting into and out of his Grizzlin form a dozen times a day, and he'd drunk nothing but lemondrine water since leaving EvenFall. His blood pulsed with more energy than he could contain. He traveled light and fast.

It felt like a lifetime had passed, but it had been mere days since he'd left the bloodied circles of Weshen City.

As Sy charged through the quiet evening streets of StarsHelm, hopelessness filtered back in. What if the King wasn't here? What if he was, but he was too well-protected for Sy to even reach?

Sy swerved into the maze and fought his way through the tendrils. Wielding a short blade in each fist, he hacked at the magic-tasting vines. The arena loomed to his side, and somehow he found the exit to the hall of doors where Giddon lived.

The round man opened the door reluctantly.

"You shouldn't be here," he said. Sadness pulled his voice to a low moan.

"I'm here to kill Graeme. He slaughtered my people." Even in his head, the words sounded foreign and bland. Sy had pushed his emotions so far down, saving them for the grim battle ahead. His training had taught him what he needed.

"You should be in Sulit."

"Coren!" Sy said, advancing so quickly that Giddon gave a little cry and sank into a chair, eyes wide.

"All of them. Coren, your brother, Kashar, Queen Mara, Graeme. They're all in Sulit!" Giddon's voice was barely a squeak. "But there are new Weshen here. Graeme's men brought them."

"Prisoners." Sy cursed, and his fist slammed the wall. A hopeful part of him pushed above the ash of his heart, though, ready to grow. If there were survivors, they could rebuild. They'd done it before.

"Only the ones with magic. So few... But Kashar isn't here to protect them..."

It took everything in Sy's control not to roar at the man. It wasn't his fault. But by the Magi, if the King's Alchemists hurt one more of his countrymen, he would tear Riata to shreds.

"Go to Sulit," Giddon urged. "Go tonight."

"Can you help them?" Sy knew Giddon had powers he feared to use. "Will you?"

Giddon trembled. "I will try."

Sy nodded. This was better than he had expected from the reclusive spellmaster. The rest would have to wait. Regardless of what else might befall his country or his men, Riata died this moon.

"How long?" Lord asked, twisting to face Mara. Ice filled his veins, slowing the blood and making his limbs stiff and awkward. Grand had needed to bind Kashar with ropes of bitebuds to remove him from the room, and the man's screams still echoed down the hall.

"I have known him as long as I have known you, and I have known you together for longer than that."

"What does that even mean?" Lord swirled to her, flicking his wrist at the sources of the fire. They jumped a foot higher, then another. Aram narrowed his eyes.

"You are Jyesh Ashaden, son of Kashar and Sorenta. When I decided to make you Lord of Witches, I decided you would be a better ruler without that foolish man's influence."

"You made me forget my family," Lord said. His voice sounded hollow in his head, or maybe it was his head that was hollow. "Just like the Weshen tried to make all their sons forget their families."

Queen Mara laughed, her breath hissing from her throat. "Yes. The irony is gorgeous. You were banished from your family for trying to stay with your family. The Weshen balance."

"That was never what the Mirror Magi meant by balance," Lord said, rolling his given name around in his mouth. *Jyesh*. He had never quite forgotten its syllables, but they had been used so seldom as to become memory rather than identity.

Who was Jyesh Ashaden? Did he still exist, or was the Lord of Witches a separate person, formed from the same sources but inescapably altered?

"I want to see him again."

"No."

Lord snapped his face up, the surprise of denial pulling his rage to the surface. He bit at his words, though. This was no Brujok servant. This was Queen Mara of Riata, and he owed her much.

Grand opened the door again. She was alone. "My Queen, the battle progresses as planned."

"Wonderful."

Mara rose fluidly from the sofa and approached the window. She turned slightly and tilted her chin to Lord. Her slim fingers beckoned him forward.

"Come see my strategy. See the bodies, there?"

"Fallen Brujok." Lord didn't care about such a thing, though he was surprised the southern Sulit had done so well.

"Look more closely. Close your eyes and look."

Lord regarded her with something just short of fear. He knew Queen Mara was capable of horrific things, but he'd never seen her so proud as when Kashar had been pulled screaming from the room, yanked from the son he had long believed dead.

Several seconds passed. Lord watched Mara, and Mara watched the fields below.

Sighing, Lord closed his eyes in a curious obedience. He stretched his senses beyond the walls of the tower, bypassing the crowds of Brujok waiting just out of sight. He found the dead bodies between the rebellion and his army, and he began to sift through the mess of sources.

His lips twisted in confusion. These were not Brujok.

"Wesh?" His eyes flew open, and his hands were bound before he could strike out at his Queen. "You dare to murder Wesh children on Sulit soil?"

"And what do you care for Wesh children?"

Lord seethed at her, unable to form the words. He shouldn't care anything for them. He'd ignored everything about Weshen for over a decade now, ever since his people had betrayed him.

But these children had not been part of that. Their deaths here would destroy the most beautiful parts of Sulit.

"Why?" he managed.

"To break them." Mara smiled, gesturing to the witches gathered far below. "To break the Mother's hold on the Sulit, so the witches can rise to their full glory."

Lord glanced to Grand, who had been growing more satisfied with each word.

"No southern Sulit will join you," he sneered at the two women.

"They don't need to join us," Grand answered. She turned to Mara. "Is it time?"

"Yes."

And before Lord could react, Grand hit him with a barrage of spells. Her bitebuds snaked from her pockets and sliced at his skin, binding him with pain and paralysis. She withdrew a handful of silvery dust from a pouch at her belt and blew him a kiss. The powder streamed into his eyes, stinging them shut like saltwater, and he felt the potion slowing the blood in his veins until he could no longer move or speak or breathe.

Lord began to slip into blackness, unaware of anything except a rocking motion, like the boat that had carried him from his mother's clutching, impotent arms so many years ago, across the MagiSea, and into the mouth of the Hungry River.

He thought he'd survived the banishment, but only now did he realize he'd been dead for quite some time.

23

Coren had been thrashing against the bars of her cage for what felt like hours, and still it held firm.

The thin figure in the other cage remained slumped against his bars, unconscious and huddled deep in his fine velvet robes. She couldn't see his face, but she'd been told who he was. Queen Mara had given Coren *both* of his names.

She wasn't certain she believed it.

She wasn't certain she *wanted* to believe it.

The last time one of her family members had resurrected from the dead, there had not been a happy reunion.

Their two cages were alone in the sky, high above the battlefield. All the open space only served to press in on her and remind her how insignificant and helpless she saw, despite her vast power.

Coren scanned the battlefield below again, but all it did was serve to re-open the horror of realizing all the

Wesh she had vowed to help were strewn dead on the grass. She'd been as tricked as the southern Sulit, hope soaring when the first line of Brujok fell, only to have it crushed beneath despair as the spells wore away and revealed the bodies of so many dead shifters.

Her tears had come, and her rage had come, and still she was nothing but a girl who couldn't shift into a bird, in a cage. The bars and everything else around her were spelled to resist her shifter magic.

The slight breeze swung her cage from its pole and chain, like a body on gallows. She was high enough to catch level glimpses of Mara, watching the battle from the sweeping tower windows. The Queen watched her, too, as if waiting for something. Or perhaps she was waiting for the Lord of Witches to wake and realize how he'd been betrayed.

If someone had told Coren this morning that she would be beaten by two Brujok and captured, locked in a cage and swung like a martyr hundreds of feet above a battlefield, and forced to watch as unsuspecting southern Sulit slaughtered what they believed to be Brujok witches, would she have simply decided to stay on the beach in Resh's arms?

Coren knew she should still feel despair, or rage, or something. She should wonder what had become of Resh, or her father, or the twins, or Sy. But all she felt was empty. And the only wonder was the boy swinging at her side.

"Jyesh!" she called again, her voice sharp against the wind. The shape of the name was odd in her mouth. No answer. "Lord of Witches!" No movement.

The spellcasting began again below, a fresh wave of Brujok advancing on the Sulit. Coren had no idea if these were indeed Brujok, or more of Mara's tricks. The Sulit hesitated, and it was a mistake.

Sulit witches fell in flashes of light and fire and smoke and screams. Vines shot up from the earth and strangled them and broke their wrists and ankles, crumpling them to the earth. The ground itself opened in deep fissures, swallowing the thrashing witches whole. Even the trees seemed to be weeping for the fallen, their pink leaves floating to the ground in great clumps.

Coren was numb. What could she possibly do to help?

Resh would probably tell her to pray. She began to mutter a supplication, but all it did was call forth his intense eyes and full lips. If he had been captured on the beach, it would be her fault. She had asked him to come with her. She'd been a coward.

Coren was afraid she would always be a coward.

Iron clanked beside her, and she swiveled her head to the boy. He blinked his eyes open, grimacing against the sun.

"Strike!" he yelled like a child searching for his mother, squeezing his eyes against the brightness around him. "Strike, where are you?"

"Your Brujok are not here to answer you," Coren answered him.

He tilted his head toward her voice, but his fingers scrubbed at his eyes like a tired child's. "Who's there?"

"Corentine," she pronounced slowly, as though he should know. Though why she wasn't sure. She certainly didn't recognize his shrill, spoiled voice. She could see now that his face resembled Kashar's, though much younger, and Coren's heart began to beat a little faster.

"Sister." His voice was a gravelly whisper now, and something in it drew the ire she'd searched for all these hours above the horror of pointless battle. She pulled herself to standing, grasping the bars of her cage. They only hung a few feet apart. She looked down at the crumpled form, trying to reconcile this with the image of her eight-year-old brother on the Weshen beach, dissipating a man to save himself from leaving his family.

The helpless, pain-twisted image she had carried in her mind so long, locked away from tarnish.

"Somewhere, deep inside your heart, you were once my brother. But I'm not certain I can ever call you that again. The things you've allowed to happen to our people..." Vaguely, she gestured below them.

He raised his lashes finally, his eyes locking onto hers. "I had no part in this. I knew nothing of Mara's plan until today."

"No, not this single battle. A lifetime of battles. Surely you knew of those. The Wesh locked in StarsHelm. The slavers' torturous ways. The families forced to live apart and in fear of the King." Her voice grew with each atrocity until she was shrieking at him.

"Family?" He spit the word. "Family has never helped me. The Brujok are my family now."

Coren cursed at him. "The Brujok care nothing for you. By the Magi, you're locked in a cage!"

"I have always been locked in a cage," he murmured. "Just never one this small."

"You could have escaped. You could have returned to us at any time. Yet you chose to remain here in your

346

towers. Your only cage was your mind!" Coren thought he was too much like Kashar.

He shook his head, and she shook her cage. It swayed and bumped into his, jarring his face up to hers. "What would you have me do?" he cried.

"You're the Lord of Witches! You were once the most powerful Weshen, and you were only eight! What *can* you do?"

"My magic is dead."

"Liar!" Coren glanced to the tower behind her again and noticed that Mara was no longer standing in the window.

His eyes narrowed on hers, mirrors of her amber and gold eyes, and steeped in just as much rage. "You're right. I am powerful. But why should I save you? You did nothing to help me! Why should I help the southern Sulit or the Weshen? None of them care for me!"

"Your Brujok and your Queen don't care for you, either."

"Don't you think I know that?" He stood, hauling himself to face her. He had grown taller than her, and the look on his face was harsh. Coren saw the ruler in him - the learned ferocity it must take to rule Brujok. "Sister, I have spent more years of my life with witches than with Weshen. They are cruel and manipulative, but so were the Generals of Weshen."

Coren didn't argue. She had felt the same about Sy's family for as long as she could remember. But Sy would be different. Resh could be, too, she believed. If either of them made it through these battles alive, that is.

"The General's First Son is not the same. He's noble, and he's in StarsHelm right now, waiting for the Restless

King to return so he can kill him and bring Riata to its knees."

Jyesh evaluated her, pursing his lips. "But Queen Mara will simply take the throne of Riata."

"Then help me get out of here, and we can kill her as well. She's the one who put you in this cage."

"I know. She also locked me in that tower. A most impotent Lord of Witches."

Coren studied her brother for a long moment. He had grown hard and unfeeling, but was he so different from her? She'd had the twins to protect, but they'd also helped her remember the good in the world. Jyesh had fought to protect himself, to survive. But ultimately, he'd grown up surrounded by cruelty.

"Jyesh," she whispered. "You've been dead for so long. Everyone believed that little boy perished in the sea. Maybe he did, and you can't go back to the innocence of before your banishment. But you still have family. I am your twin. Let me be half of your soul again, like the Magi created us."

He gazed down at the battlefield, where it was nearly impossible to tell southern Sulit from Brujok anymore. Dozens of dead littered the ground, and hundreds lined up on both sides to meet their same fate. The air was thick with opalescent smoke.

"Our little brother and sister are here. Kashar, too. And the old woman. I have them all locked away in Tower Four."

The words were quiet and simple, but they acted like a blow to Coren. She stumbled back, slipping to her knees in the cage as it swung hard on its chain. Her stomach heaved with the motion. Her chest felt as though it had cracked open, and her heart was beating in the cold, open air. Exposed and raw.

"I need them, Jyesh," she whispered.

"Lots of people think they need them. The twin prophecy is believed by many."

"I care nothing for prophecy and power! Help me free them, and we can be a family again! We can be whole!"

"What shall we do? Buy a house on the lake and live with Kashar like farmers? The world is not so simple, sister. I'd have thought you to be smarter than such a notion."

Coren flushed. He was so broken. Surely there were things he wanted still, even though he had no more trust for his family or his country.

"Are you not powerful enough, then?" She laced the question with disappointment and sadness. She let him see that he was no longer the brother she had longed for. Coren hated the act, but she'd seen how people responded to Resh. She hoped she'd learned enough from him to pull something alive from her dead brother.

"I have plenty of power."

Coren bit back a smile, turning her face to the tower behind them. It was still empty. Where was Mara?

"I sense it," she agreed. "But it's dead. Atrophied."

"No. The Brujok only believe me to be weak. I could overpower them any moment I wish."

"The Brujok are done with you, Jyesh. You've been cast aside. Again!" She stirred his anger further. He allowed it, tensing his shoulders and standing straighter. "You don't have to be a pawn any longer, a false Lord of Witches. You're my brother, Jyesh, son of Sorenta and

Kashar, grandson of Lorental. You have more magic in your veins than all the people left in Weshen. By the Magi, use it!"

The speech worked its own magic, and Coren let herself smile as Jyesh let a growl build inside his belly, corralling its power until it burst from him like thunder across the sky.

The bars around them shook and splintered as he broke their spells, shifting them though it should have been impossible. Coren felt the change in their sources, just as she'd done with the vines in StarsHelm. He remade them into something new, allegiant to him.

Coren flushed with a snap of power as her shifting was freed. As the cage in the sky disintegrated around them, she shrieked to her Vespa.

Now we fly!

Now we kill! It returned.

Her wings powered from her back. She had never shifted so fast, and it left her dizzy with strength. She swooped and clutched at Jyesh's robes as he tumbled from his cage. Her claws circled his waist, holding him close as she spiraled higher.

"Down!" screamed Jyesh.

Coren spiraled down, reining in the force of her wings. When they were mere feet from the ground, she dropped him. He rolled and shot to his feet, surveying the battle before them. Witches had paused their spellcasting to gape at her Vespa form and the delivery of their Lord.

Several near him bowed deeply, murmuring his title.

"I am no longer your Lord!" he shouted. "Call me Jyesh, of Weshen!" He threw his arms wide, and the earth fissured before him, separating many of the warring witches. Coren flapped higher, watching for the crackle of spells. Spotting a Brujok advancing on a southern Sulit, she crashed her body into them, knocking the Brujok away without real injury.

She didn't want to kill, despite the insistent voice in her mind.

Coren and Jyesh repeated their actions, pulling the witches from their fights as best they could. She landed on the bloodied grass and shifted her body back, keeping her wings at the ready. "Your battle is a false one!" she yelled to the dirty, blood-stained women before her. "Your strife has been manufactured, and the ends you seek are not your own!"

Jeering broke out among the Brujok, and Coren squared herself at them. "Your Lord of Witches is nothing but a pawn for Queen Mara, and if you follow either of them, you are no follower of Sulit!"

"And you're no witch, so leave us to our fight!" someone screamed. A thick vine rose and coiled before Coren, threatening to wrap her tightly.

"Cease this nonsense."

The voice was soft, but it carried like a siren call into each of their brains, drawing every pair of eyes to the figures approaching from the towers.

Queen Mara glided through the battlefield, as regal as if she strode through a hall of admirers in expensive finery. Her robes were the ebony and crimson of Riata, the dull red of dried blood and silky black, and they floated just above the gore in the grass.

Aram followed just behind her, his bulk strange in this sea of women. His face was hard, and he flipped blades through the fingers of both hands, staring down any witch who did not bow her head before Mara's presence.

Coren moved to rush the Queen as she stepped delicately over a dead Wesh, but Mara simply flicked her wrist, and Coren fell to her knees, paralysis binding her mouth and muscles like invisible rope.

"I am not your Queen," she began, turning to look at each group of witches, no matter their allegiance. Many nodded and sneered at her words. She held her hand for their silence. "But I want to be. Too long have you warred against each other. Too long have you placed a Lord above you, when no witch needs parry with any man. Women of Sulit, I came to you as a tiny child, and you took me in. I have risen to the rulership of Riata through my own means."

"Like marrying a man!" a witch cried from the dense crowd.

Mara nodded. "It is true I married a man, but now, he does my bidding. His family name may carry the crown, but now his family is dead, and I remain. Witches, it matters not whether your allegiance is to the southern covens or the towers of Rurok. Come to me now, as I once came to you. Be my children, as I was once your child. Allow me to be your mother, as you have none left."

A beat of silence washed over the Listening Forest and the valley and the towers. Even the falls beyond seemed to dull their rushing waters.

"The Mother lives!" The single voice of dissent rose from the ranks of the southern Sulit. Immediately, others joined it.

Coren was close enough to see the corner of control slip from Mara's face before the Queen shrieked and released a devastating spell. The trees cracked and bent their branches down like spears and bars, pinning the southern witches where they stood. Several cried out as sticks pierced their limbs and torsos, and others yelled in fury as they scrambled to rip apart the wooden bars with their spells.

But none were as strong as Queen Mara.

Coren watched in despair as life after life was taken, the souls of the witches snapped free of their bodies like wildflowers gathered by the handful. Tears slipped down her cheeks, salting her lips. She stared helplessly across the field of dead at her twin, who was free of any spell from Mara. Why didn't he help them now? Her soul reached for his, begging him to be the child she loved again.

Pleading with him to help her save the good in their world.

But he made no move to help. Mara reached a hand to Jyesh, and he stepped toward her without expression, as though magnetized by her presence.

All around them, Coren watched as the souls of witches and Weshen floated like plucked petals in the summer breeze. Their pale colors were beautiful to watch, but wrenching to feel.

Aram stepped toward her then, filling her vision, bending down to look in her eyes. His own eyes were like tunnels, and the deeper she followed them, the faster she realized his soul was gone, too. She felt shock course through her body as that realization turned into wonder: she was *looking* at souls.

She was seeing the impossible, right now, right before her.

Aram spun away from her, nearly tackling his sister in his haste. He tugged her casting arms down and yanked her to face Coren. He hadn't made a single sound, but somehow, Coren knew that Mara had heard his discovery.

The smile that spread across the Queen's face broke Coren's heart wide and poured it full of an acidic fear.

"Welcome back, SoulShifter," Mara said, dropping her hold on everything but Coren. The souls vanished all at once as darkness descended in Coren's vision.

Mara's energy lit the room as she paced, waiting for the girl to wake.

The SoulShifter, Grand repeated to herself, watching the still form in equal parts amazement and greed. Such power, such potential. But she'd already proved to be an unwilling pawn. Nothing like her malleable brother.

Lord had incredible potential, but he had never advanced past the first level of the Weshen shifting. Coren seemed less powerful, but she had mastered her creature form, and now showed signs of an awakening ability to see souls. That was the precursor ability to shifting souls - the power Mara had sought her entire adult life.

The power the Restless King had destroyed a nation to find.

354

Once Mara and Grand had found Coren in the StarsHelm maze and smelled the blood connection to the Lord of Witches and Kashar, they wondered if being twins would cause their levels of power to equalize each other's. Feed off each other's.

They had hoped that reuniting Lord with his father and sister would break his magic open. The arrival of the younger twins and the old woman had seemed a further bonus in their experiment, but Lord had cared nothing for them.

He had much less connection to them, after all. They had not even been born when he was banished.

The girl stirred, breaking into Grand's musings.

"Jyesh…"

"He is not here, Coren," Mara said, bending over her. "I don't have you bound right now, but be assured I can do so in an instant. You are powerful, but I am more so."

Coren blinked up at the Queen, hatred firming her face.

"I want my family."

"Which ones?" Queen Mara's smile was that of a bargainer. "I hold your father, Kashar, in a cell in the fourth tower. I have your siblings, the young twins, and the old woman. I have your brother, who has barely acknowledged your existence since learning of it. I even have someone who isn't family, but fights like a Weshen Paladin."

"Resh," Coren whispered.

"I'm amazed a single Weshen girl has attracted so many admirers. I'd always imagined you were a solitary people. Love. Family. Magic. Denial of all those powerful pieces has been a part of Weshen culture as long as I can remember."

"Then you must have never been there. You can't believe what outsiders might say."

An odd expression passed over the Queen's face, and Grand studied her. There were secrets still that Mara was keeping close. Closer even than Grand had access to. But then, so were the witches hiding plans.

"What do you know of SoulShifting?" Mara asked, wandering toward the fire.

"It's a myth. We've never known one."

Mara shook her head. "Not since the Shift, as your people call it. But it's not a myth. Tell me, what color were the Sulit souls?"

Coren startled, raising herself to a sitting position on the sofa. "Like flowers. All colors," she murmured.

Grand sucked in a breath. It *was* true.

"What do *you* know of SoulShifting?" Coren asked the Queen.

Mara was silent for a long moment, staring into the fire. "Only that it is the final power I need to claim."

"You will never claim it from me. I don't even know how to access it, and I would never do so for you."

"Not even to save one of your own?" Grand stepped forward, ignoring Mara's glare. "You came so far to save your family. Would you truly end their lives in a refusal of such a request?"

Coren narrowed her eyes. "If I were the SoulShifter, I wouldn't need to worry about life and death."

Mara swirled toward her, soft laughter spilling from her crimson lips. "Precisely, my child. Precisely."

"But I'm not. Seeing souls is not the same as shifting them."

"It could be the first step," Grand insisted. "Let me bring one of them here," she asked her Queen. She was certain she could force more of the girl's power with the life of one of their prisoners. Mara only waved her fingers, dismissing the idea. She crossed the room and leaned into Aram's ear, whispering something no-one else could hear.

Grand stiffened. She didn't enjoy her job nearly as much when Aram was involved.

"Fetch me the twins," Mara said, turning to Grand. "And ready a message for Zorander."

24

Coren stood and began to cautiously walk the room.

She didn't trust the Queen or her brother not to harm her, but she had too much nervous energy to sit and wait for her family to be delivered. Aram tracked her movements with his hollow holes of eyes, but Mara gazed out the window.

Coren studied them in quick glances. They looked nothing alike, but they did seem to have the sort of wordless communication she'd once shared with Jyesh, and which Kosh and Penna delighted in.

Why did Aram seem to exist only to do Mara's bidding? Why hadn't he made a life of his own?

And if Mara had indeed come to Sulit as a young girl, where had Aram been then? There were many unanswered questions surrounding the Riatan Queen, and something about her drew Coren in. She saw the woman's evil, yet she sensed there was once more to her than retribution and cruelty.

It wasn't found anywhere in the sway of her slim hips or the slant of her eyes. It certainly wasn't in the harsh flick of her magic.

And despite what she'd seen on the battlefield, Coren had no window into the swirl of the Queen's soul. Whatever power had manifested earlier was gone now.

The door to the tower opened, interrupting Coren's puzzling. The Brujok witch had returned.

The sight of Penna and Kosh padding behind her wrenched a sob from Coren's throat, and she hurled herself at the twins. Mara allowed the reunion, and Coren squeezed them as close to her as she could. She ran her fingers over their small faces and bodies, searching for injury. She found none.

They were dirty, and their bellies growled, but they were whole. They were *here*.

Coren was muttering a prayer of thanks to the Magi when Mara cleared her throat. She glanced up at the Queen, standing stiffly and pulling one child beneath each arm. One hand rested protectively on each narrow chest.

"What do you want?" she asked, knowing the Queen would want to bargain. Despite what Coren had boasted about a SoulShifter caring nothing for life and death, she would give anything to save these two souls.

Mara tilted her head and glanced back to Aram. He sauntered nearer to his sister, placing a hand on her shoulder.

Without a word, Mara held her palm flat, pushing it through the air at Coren and blasting her and the twins across the room and out the tower's wide windows into the afternoon sky.

The children shrieked and flailed as they fell, and Coren scrambled against the nothingness of air to grasp at them. She caught Kosh's tunic but missed Penna's. The girl slipped through her grasp, screaming and kicking in terror.

Instinct slammed through Coren as her Vespa form cracked through her body. Her four wings snapped across the sky, and she ducked beneath the twins, catching Penna with a broad wing. The girl clutched a handful of feathers, and Coren struggled to bear the weight and the wrenching pain.

She wrapped thick claws around Kosh's waist, praying she wouldn't scratch any of the deadly poison into his skin.

She was still falling too fast, though, unable to fly properly with one wing weighted down. She wheeled toward the tower and slammed her side against the stone wall, scrabbling at its rough surface with her free claw.

Pinning her sister to the stone with her lower wings, Coren grasped Penna's waist with her free claw just before she fell away from the tower again. One twin now clutched in each yellow-gold, poisonous claw, she flapped hard and sped toward the forest.

Past the battlefield, which had emptied of witches. Past the edge of the forest, where Mara had destroyed the trees.

Into the thickest part of the woods. Coren bent her body around the twins and crashed through the canopy, clenching her beak shut against a shriek that might give away their location. Her spine hit the ground with a thud, and the twins rolled from her grasp.

Heaving against the pain, Coren drew her wings in. So many feathers had been ripped away by sharp branches and stone and the twins' frantic clutching. She was exhausted from the adrenaline that was now ebbing from her blood.

And Penna and Kosh had huddled together several feet away, staring with enormous eyes at the creature before them.

Coren closed her eyes and summoned the strength to shift back, dropping to her hands and knees in the dirt.

"Coren!" Penna cried, crushing into her. "I was so scared!"

Kosh gripped his sisters with both arms, squeezing them together. "Maren is still in the tower," he said, looking up at Coren.

"Don't worry. I'll get her and all the other people Mara has stolen. I'm so glad you're safe," Coren said, her words cracking. She buried her face between their heads, her shoulders shaking with relief. Tears ran freely down her cheeks, wetting their hair.

The snap of a branch from behind them flung Coren into a protective stance again, and she shoved the twins behind her. One hand searched beneath her tunic for the handle of her whip, the only weapon she could use without depleting more of her magic.

A slim witch stepped hesitantly from behind a large tree. Her hair was mussed and her dress torn, but she didn't bear any identifying signs of the Brujok.

"Star!" Penna twisted free of Coren's grasp and ran to the woman. Her arms wrapped around the witch's waist, and Coren studied them.

362

"I'm so sorry," the witch said. "It's my fault these children are here."

"What do you mean?" Coren asked, her shoulders straightening as she readied herself for anything.

"I have the ability to see things. It's my gift from the Mother. Sometimes I see the future. I saw these twins, and I saw the throne of Rurok, and I knew they were meant to be here. I don't know why."

"Bringing them here nearly got them killed."

The witch's face fell, and she stared at the ground.

"Coren, it's okay. She helps us," Penna said.

"The Mother needs of their power. She will protect them because they're part of the good in the world. The balance we need."

"Gods do not protect." Coren shook her head. "They give, and they take. That is the only balance they care about."

The witch regarded Coren for several seconds, her hand idly stroking Penna's hair. Coren realized the twins had come to depend on this woman in the weeks they'd been separated.

"Can you keep them safe?" she asked, hating the necessity of the words, and their implication. The Magi knew she had no business trying to do the same. Not with the Queen after her magic.

The witch nodded. "As much as is possible in such times."

"Where can I find you?"

Before the witch could answer, Penna stumbled back to clutch at her sister's hands. "Please don't leave us!" The tears spilling from her eyes undid what was left of

Coren's resolve. She gathered the little girl in her arms, fighting her tears and losing.

"Penna, stop. It's okay," Kosh said, coming to rest a hand on his sister's arm. "Coren has to find Maren. And Jyesh."

"You know of Jyesh?" Coren asked, blinking at him and wiping her eyes.

"The Queen brought us to him. Before the battle. He rejected us, but it's not his fault. We weren't even born when he was banished."

Coren sighed, running her hand in circles across her brother's narrow back. He deserved a childhood, not this war. Not these incomprehensible demands from a brother he'd never known and a Queen he didn't serve. From witches whose future he held no stake in.

"I can keep them safe. Our people need them." Star stepped toward Coren. "The Mother has always taught that twins from Weshen would be our people's salvation. That their gods would help her restore the balance to the world and push the shadows back into the darkness."

"Shadow. Do your people know Shadow?" Coren asked, suddenly noting the language.

"All people know Shadow. It is the force which unbalances the world. It can never be beaten."

"I'll find a way to beat it," Coren said, her voice hard enough that Star didn't comment on her ignorance.

Coren knew nothing of Shadow, other than its links with Umbren and blood magic, and the idea that it could be buried underground or shifted into fragments for some time. But she didn't care - if it threatened those she loved, she would find a way.

She bent down and placed one hand on each of the twins' cheeks. "I will come back for you, I promise. I'll send someone to you here in the forest. Maren, or Kashar. I need to find my friends. And I don't trust Jyesh with you. Our brother is the Lord of Witches," she said to Star. The woman's eyes grew wide.

"How?"

"We thought him dead. But the Sulit saved him, and the Brujok and Mara led him to the throne. They used him. Groomed him from a boy to be their pawn."

Star blinked, her lips parting. "I had no idea. How could I have missed such a trick in my dreams?" She began to mutter to herself, and Coren turned back to the twins.

"Please be safe," she choked out, though she knew it was an impossible promise for a child to make. For anyone to make.

There was every chance that when she left them and flew back to that tower to rescue her family, she would never return to these children. But now, she realized that staying with her siblings would only put them in more danger.

Coren was finally starting to understand Sy's obsession with killing the King. Killing Mara would protect everyone she loved. Running would only attract the animal instincts of the Queen.

She embraced Penna and Kosh once more, then stepped into a shaft of sunlight allowed by a break in the canopy. Star handed her a large leaf with a map scratched into its flesh.

"You may find us here."

Coren thanked her, then shifted only her wings from her back. She didn't want the twins' last glimpse of her to be a Vespa, but herself, powerful the way they would one day become.

The three of them watched her as she pushed off the ground and shot into the air. Coren swiped at her cheeks as she flew higher than needed, cooling the heat of her grief in the clouds. Her skin shifted to feathers and her tears dried as her trembling cheeks and lips hardened into a beak.

She shrieked into the empty sky, pressing away the fear of leaving her siblings again - hopefully she was right in trusting StarSeer. The twins trusted her though, as had Maren, and Coren reminded herself there were so many, many reasons to keep Penna and Kosh away from Rurok just now.

Queen Mara would be waiting, and she still had to find Maren, Kashar, Resh, and Jyesh.

She would figure a way out of this.

Resh felt like death.

Or what he imagined death might feel like.

That cursed witch had poisoned him and brought him Magi knows where, and he was starving, and by all that was doubled and balanced, the floor beneath him was *swaying.*

Resh hauled himself to a sitting position, groaning at the stiffness in every muscle. As his eyes adjusted to the semi-darkness, he discovered he was locked inside one of a dozen or so metal cages, all swinging from fat-linked chains in the innards of a gutted tower.

He began to swear, slowly and ceaselessly, as he heaved himself to standing. He squinted around the tower.

Most of the cages appeared empty, except for the one directly across from him.

In that one hunched a rumpled, glowering boy around his age. His robes were filthy but obviously finely-made. Resh narrowed his eyes. There were only so many men alive in Rurok, and he had an ugly suspicion that this just might be a toppled Lord of Witches.

"Hey, so how do we get out of here?" Resh called across to the boy. There was no movement of answer, as though the boy hadn't even heard. "Hello!"

Nothing.

Resh lapsed back into muttering obscenities as he systematically checked each of the bars circling the edges of his swinging prison. He dug a coin from his pocket and flipped it into the darkness. It took a good three seconds to hit the stone floor at the bottom. Nope. Too high to jump, even if he figured out the bars.

He lunged forward, throwing his weight in a single direction, then lunged backward. Again and again, until his cage swung like a pendulum, knocking edges with the boy's cage before clanging into the wall.

That got a reaction.

The boy threw his hands wide on instinct as if to cast a spell. Nothing happened.

"Bound magic?" Resh called, shaking his head to clear it of the horrible ringing. Finally, the boy turned his eyes on his prison mate.

Resh felt his brows hike. This kid looked Weshen, with skin the color of wet sand, hair like dug earth, and eyes like the sea at sunset. Eyes like Coren's, Resh realized. Blue sea shot with gold.

"Who are you?" Resh asked as they swayed closer again, the cages close enough for them to grasp arms. They didn't.

The kid shrugged, hanging his head again.

"Look, I'm figuring a way out of here, and I'd love some company. What's your name?"

"They once called me Lord of Witches." The words were almost too quiet for Resh to hear, but they were unmistakable all the same. Resh whistled under his breath.

"Did the southern Sulit win the battle, then? Did they imprison you?"

At this, the boy leaned his head against the bar and choked out a bitter laugh. "Sulit would never win against Brujok. I was put here by Queen Mara. Just as you were, and all the others she has tricked."

"I wasn't tricked. I came here knowing all witches are liars. They captured me on the beach. I came here with a girl, though. Perhaps you've seen her. Corentine." He spoke the name softly, emphasizing the syllables to see his reaction. He wasn't disappointed. The other prisoner sat forward, staring into Resh's eyes as their cages passed each other again.

"Why were you traveling with her? Are you a servant?"

Resh was surprised into laughter and a rash answer. "Hardly. I am the Second Son of Weshen."

The boy raised his brows. "A General's son." He smiled, and the sight of it made Resh very uneasy. "And what will you do when you escape?"

"Find Coren. Find the King. Kill him if my brother hasn't already."

"The King is not your enemy. He is moved by a power greater than his own. A pawn."

"He's done plenty to qualify as an enemy, regardless the motivation. Actions make a person, even if they're carried out under orders."

"Then I am your enemy as well."

Resh decided this young man was skilled in playing games. He might be a worthy opponent, now that he had slipped out of self-pity. "Perhaps. But if you are against the crown of Riata now, then we may as well be friends."

The boy shook his head. "I don't have friends. I don't have family, either. I am alone, as a Lord must be."

"Do you have another name? Lord is simply a title, and one that seems to have been taken from you."

The boy swept his glare across Resh. "I am not required to give you the power of knowing my name."

Resh grinned. "Witch superstition, right? Never tell someone your full name. Well, Weshen don't believe in such tales. I am Reshra Havenash, Second Son of General Ashemon Havenash of Weshen." He threw his arms wide. "So, tell me, what power do you now possess over me?"

"That remains to be seen."

"Will you escape this tower with me, former Lord of Witches, now enemy of the crown of Riata?" Resh asked, his voice slanting toward a taunt.

The boy studied Resh long enough that he gave up and started checking his cage again. Palming a blade, he began to work at the screws that held the door to its frame. The metal was slippery and seemed to accept his blade like water, unaffected by his scratching.

"The iron is spelled. It blocks all other spells." The boy closed his eyes and leaned back against the bars.

"Aren't you supposed to be a powerful spellmaster?" There was no answer. "Then again, if the Brujok could trap you, perhaps you were just a pawn as well, completing their orders until they were finished with you."

The Lord of Witches was up and pressing his face to the bars instantly. "I used much of my power escaping a similar cage earlier today. But I have more power than any of those miserable Brujok, and mine isn't all spellcasting."

"Then prove it. Escape their prison."

Rage quivered the boy's features, and Resh felt the air around them swirl with energy, like the city before a storm sweeping in from the beach. Before his eyes, the boy shrank and slimmed until he was a tiny child, and he slipped easily through the bars. Stretching his form back, he leaped nimbly to the next cage down, clutching its empty, swaying form. Resh leaned over as far as he could see, watching the figure hop from cage to cage until reaching the bottom.

"Sulit spells are not as prepared for my level of shifter power!" the boy called from the floor. Resh couldn't see

370

what was happening, but his cage began to lower, its chain feeding through a pulley at the ceiling and down the wall. As he approached the floor, he wondered where all the Brujok were.

Even with such an advanced prison, surely there were guards about. It shouldn't be this easy to escape.

Resh's cage clanked to the floor. The boy was nowhere to be seen, and Resh cursed the luck. How would he get out of this blasted cell? He hated his lack of magic even more.

But several seconds later, the boy entered the room again, a young witch in tow.

"Open it," he hissed, twisting his fingers. She started to shake her head, then shrieked as blood rose from beneath her skin, misting the air.

Resh's stomach heaved. This was what Sy described Coren doing to a Vespa, and her brother once doing to a man. The feeling of an inevitable truth crept up on him again. He didn't want the Lord of Witches to be a Weshen shifter. He didn't want this cruel-eyed boy to have anything in common with Coren.

"Open it!"

The witch sobbed through the blood in the air and nodded. The boy released her, and she stepped to Resh's cage. Pulling out a carved stone key, she began chanting quietly. Her face was near his and full of fear.

"Thank you," Resh whispered, the words slipping out despite his instincts. He knew witches were nothing but liars. He'd killed more than a few in his missions and while training. But this girl was barely his age, and there was an odd innocence in her eyes despite her Brujok markings.

She didn't respond, but as she clicked the key in its lock, the door of the cage began to melt into itself, the metal slinking away enough that he could squeeze through.

As soon as Resh's feet touched the stone floor of the tower, the girl screamed, her body contorting. Blood sprang into the air in a cloud of droplets, bursting her skin and shattering her bones into tiny fragments that hovered around them.

The Lord of Witches laughed, and Resh felt sick.

Resh understood then how power such as Coren's could become something very different - not beautiful and sensual like her Vespa form, but sinuous and evil like this twisted boy.

"Why is a Weshen the Lord of Witches?" Resh asked, uncertain if he wanted the answer.

The Lord glanced back, a vicious grin on his face. "Let's find my sister, and I'll let her explain everything."

The Restless King steered his chariot of Weshen bone and Draken hide through the fog above the thunder of NewMoon Falls. As it flew, he imagined the bridge he hoped to build between his kingdom and Sulit.

The thought of crossing such a structure with his masses of troops, ready to sink their fingers into the rich magic of the Sulit soil gave him a thrill few things could anymore.

Sulit would be his. Mara had promised him the witch country, just as soon as Weshen was destroyed, and now he had completed her mission. He'd even skewered the arrogant General himself.

His brothers had been pleased to keep their quarry, and Zorander had been pleased to keep his life. Now Mara had sent word that the SoulShifter had indeed awoken, and his chest puffed in anticipation of ridding himself of his tormentors.

Zorander's brothers would not be in this world much longer.

He coasted his chariot through the wide windows of Mara's rooms in the tower. She stood by the fire, Aram nearby as always. Her favorite guard was missing, though, and otherwise the room was empty and still.

"We have been anxiously waiting for you, my King," she said, giving him a smile that reminded him of the night they had first met.

Like the night he earned the throne of Riata, a challenge from Mara waited for him here in Rurok.

The King stepped from the chariot and tugged his tunic straight, fluffing his robes. He stepped to the fire and warmed his hands, chasing away the chill of the falls.

"Weshen is dead," he murmured, though he knew that she knew.

She took a deep, luxurious breath. "Yes. My King has done well. Our beautiful noose tightens."

"I gathered what magic I could at the palace for us, but your message stated it was all for naught."

"Nothing in this game is for naught, my love. But it is true that you do not hold the SoulShifter in StarsHelm's prisons."

"Is it your young Lord, then?" His question brought a smirk to Aram's lips, and Zorander scowled at the man and his cursed privileged position. He had resented Mara's brother since he'd first laid eyes on him, but she could not be persuaded to stray from his side.

Where there should have been two on the throne of Riata, instead there were three.

"The Lord of Witches is strong, but he did not develop the power as I expected. However, he had a valuable secret all these years, locked inside the cave of his mind. A sister. A *twin*," she added, and Zorander's heart sped up, thumping in his ears like a misthorse.

He knew the lore of the Weshen twins. Two such powerful shifters could make all the difference in his fight for power.

Or they could tear his kingdom to pieces.

"Where is she?"

"I thought to tell you one other thing before giving you that information." Mara's voice twisted into something hard and fanged, and Zorander took an instinctive step back.

He had seen this look on her face once before, and suddenly he didn't want to know any more about what she'd found.

But Aram sidled up next to him, a broad hand clapping his shoulder. Mara circled to his other side.

"Imagine my surprise when I found a Weshen shifter who had attained her creature form, sneaking into our palace first, and flying through the forest here. But not just any creature, Zorander. A *Vespa*."

The pause was heavy with meaning, and Zorander felt the desperation of a young man in love creeping back into his soul, as strong today as it had been that other day, decades ago.

"It turns out that I'm not the true Queen of Riata after all." Mara gave a bitter little laugh, and Zorander struggled to stay standing.

"I have no idea..."

"Oh, yes, you do," she hissed. "Perhaps you didn't know then, but you are not a stupid man. I am not the true Queen because I have never produced a viable heir to the throne. It wouldn't be a problem or an annoyance at all, except for the tiny fact that someone else bore your heir."

"Lorental," he whispered, his eyes filling with stinging tears that had never fallen.

"Somehow, that creature bore another creature, and that one still another, begetting Weshen babies like the disgusting animals they are. And now..." Mara turned away, her movements tightly controlled. "Now, my King, your granddaughter is here. You will meet her tonight, this very night, under a full, gorgeous Sulit moon."

Zorander Graeme opened his mouth, then shut it again. What could he possibly say? He'd known Lorental had a child, a daughter. For FatherSun's sake, the girl had been half grown when Mara murdered her mother.

But *his* child?

No. *That* he had never guessed.

His heart both cracked open to meet the child, and congealed cold at the omission that could have changed everything.

For years, even after he'd assumed the throne, Lorental had wavered between inviting him to bed and snubbing his every attempt.

But she had eventually stopped crossing his path, and as the years passed he'd seen her less and less. Once she'd become a well-respected Commander in his army, she had essentially barred him from her life. He'd mourned the loss, but Riata had needed him.

Mara had wanted him, insatiably.

And eventually, he'd nearly managed to forget Lorental. Until the Separation. Until the night Mara's guards and his knights had caught her fleeing his decree that all Weshen must remain in the palace.

Like a coward, he'd turned away as the executioner sliced open the throat of the only woman he'd truly loved.

Mara was watching him now, her eyes lowered into hoods of aggressive lust. But her desire wasn't for him. Her eyes were fixated just above his, on the silver and black-diamond crown circling his head.

He understood the reasons, even more now, but never had Zorander realized how deep Mara's resentment had grown, and how dark her plans for revenge. "You always hated her."

"Always," his wife agreed, and her calm terrified him.

"Is this why you hated Weshen so much? Why you were so insistent on its ruin?"

Mara flushed. "Is their insolence in denying Riata not enough?" she snapped.

Zorander studied her. It wasn't like the Queen to lose her temper. She saw his expression and smoothed her own. "We are not through discussing this, but rest assured I have uses for Lorental's granddaughter. *Your* granddaughter. She will not be killed unless she proves unable to provide what I need."

Zorander ignored her veiled threat and sank onto the sofa, his mind reeling with all he had just learned.

Lorental had borne him an heir when his wife had been unable to do the same.

By Riata's archaic laws, *Lorental* was the true Queen. Her descendants would have claim to his throne. And now her - their - granddaughter possessed not only the Vespa form he'd loved so much, but the SoulShifter power he'd hunted his entire life.

Zorander couldn't believe the luck the FatherSun had granted him, after a lifetime of turning wishes into curses. He had a kingdom, and now he had a family again. More, he could use this new family to finally rid himself of the remnants of his old family. The SoulShifter could use her power to put his brothers to rest, and he would finally be free to live.

Zorander glanced up to Mara, a question forming on his upturned lips.

"Go upstairs. I'll send her to you."

He stood, joyous anticipation spreading through his heart, even as he tried to ignore the smirk on Aram's mute lips, and the foreboding feeling festering in his chest.

25

Dipping below the clouds, Coren swooped toward the tower and flapped through the great windows, her lower wings trailing on the white stone floor.

She shifted in a split second, landing in a crouch before a grinning Mara. The Queen was not surprised she had returned.

"Your shift's power is beautiful to behold. Or it would be, if I didn't have a personal aversion to such creatures. Now, you asked what I wanted. The better question is what will you give me?"

"I swear I have nothing to give you. The SoulShifter power is not mine to control." Coren was stalling, and Mara humored her. Aram stared without expression, and the cursed Brujok guard cackled to herself.

Mara gestured to the forest beyond the window. "You think you've saved your siblings, but I *want* those children free to wander the Sulit forest, just as I once was. Free to learn to cast spells and speak to trees, but also free to know they will never again see one of their own kind. Just like Jyesh, I want them to feel the hope that someone will come for them, cursed with the realization that in the end, no-one ever did."

"I *will* find them again."

Mara shrugged. "If you do, I will slit their throats and claim their blood magic. Witches have eyes and ears in every living thing. Their training is too important, and my heart simply won't allow you to meddle."

"They won't be trained to do anything for you!" Coren snapped. "You've stolen one of my siblings. You will not have the others!"

The Queen only clicked her tongue in disappointment and raised her eyebrows at Aram, who grinned.

Coren struggled to untangle the knots of problems Mara had laid before her. She needed to find Jyesh and convince him to leave Mara and Sulit, to come away with her and heal. She needed to figure out where Resh and Kashar and Maren were being held.

But only blank, panicked thoughts swirled in her mind until the door of the tower room banged open.

Another Brujok stumbled in. Blood dripped from a gash on her forehead, but she hadn't taken a second to wipe it away. "The Knight!" she cried. She stepped further into the room, and Coren felt her heart jerk to a stop. The witch was dragging a limp form behind her, but it wasn't Kashar.

"Maren!" she cried, stumbling to her knees before the broken body.

Maren struggled to open her eyes. "Twins?" she rasped.

"They're safe. Maren, what happened?" Coren raked the old woman's hair from her clouded eyes. There was so much blood caked around her jaw and neck.

"She shifted the floor from under me," the witch admitted. "But her power is weak. She's old."

Maren huffed, but it quickly turned to a blood-spattering cough.

"What of the Knight?" Mara asked, turning on the witch. The Brujok shrunk from the Queen.

"He escaped."

The woman was gone before her words had echoed around the room, her body flying from the open window. Coren heard the fading shriek, and then several seconds later, a crunch of bone meeting ground.

"Grand!" the Queen yelled, her eyes flashing. "The others!"

The other witch sprinted from the room without a word.

Coren turned to Mara to ask who else the Queen worried about, but she felt a tug on her hand. She looked down at Maren, who winked once, the hint of a smile at her crimson-flecked lips. "Neshra's waiting."

Her eyelids slid closed, and Coren tipped her head to the woman's unmoving chest, clenching her teeth against a sob. Maren's mention of the man she'd loved as a girl ripped into Coren, and all she could think was that somehow, it was a message to Coren not to give up on the promise of love. In Coren's mind, the words twisted into the mandate that she must prevent the rulers of Riata from ruining any more lives.

A brush of silken air slid across her cheek like a caress, and Coren knew it was Maren's soul leaving its physical shell. It was just like she'd once felt her cousin Tellen's soul, and today had seen all those of the dying Wesh and Sulit.

She had no idea how to shift a soul, but like the other shifter abilities, this one must be mirrored as well. Perhaps seeing the souls was one half, and shifting them the other.

Coren hoped she could learn the power before Mara figured out how to take it from her, or awaken it in Jyesh

Rising from Maren's body, Coren began to recite the traditional burial prayers to the Mirror Magi, her lips continuing to move as she watched Mara and her brother. What would they do now? What could she do?

The door banged open again before any of them could decide, and Grand marched in, an air of triumph preceding her movements. Behind her were a trio of tall Brujok escorting two young men. Coren's heart gave a leap when she saw the last two of her family and friends accounted for.

The Brujok pushed Jyesh to the front, where he stood stiffly next to the Queen. His robes were filthy and torn, but his face had a light in it Coren hadn't seen here in Rurok. A pride that laced her final memory of Jyesh, sailing away on the MagiSea with nothing in his belly or his boat to help him survive.

He stood a little too close to Mara for Coren's comfort.

The Brujok parted, and Resh stumbled as one of them pushed him forward. His hands were bound before him, and his face wore a look of pure rage. Coren's heart nearly tripped over itself in its haste to decide between relief that he was alive, and fear that he might not be for long, and aggravation that here was one more person she had to figure out how to save.

"I've thought of you a bit, too," Resh said, his smirk telling her that each of those thoughts had been all too plain on her face. "Don't trust your brother, though."

Before Coren could ask what he meant, Mara wiggled her fingers at both boys, and they stumbled backward, each clawing at lips that had suddenly melted together. "Jyesh and this Weshen boy do not need to be part of our discussion. Aram, manage them."

Aram dragged each boy to the sofa, shoving them down and pinning them easily. A blade flashed at each of their throats, and they grew still. Mara blocked Coren from pushing past her.

"We have things to discuss, Weshen girl."

"What did you do to them?" Coren couldn't keep her eyes off the boys. They were breathing, at least.

"A simple spell to seal their lips. Useful for disobedient children. Though I never had any of my own to try with."

"You'd make a horrible mother." The statement slipped out, and Coren bit her lips shut too, knowing she needed time with this woman. Information. Not a fight, not yet.

"I was never granted the chance. Would you like to know why?"

Coren stared at Mara. This was not the conversation she had imagined having with the Queen. She thought they were going to discuss her shifter powers. But Mara began to pace gently, a few steps to the side and back.

"My chance at motherhood was stolen from me by a cruel, horrible woman. A woman so evil the world began to breathe again the day she left it. This woman, dear Corentine, was your grandmother."

"My grand-" but Coren felt the spark of magic over her lips, and the terrifying sensation of her lips sealing forever. Her fingers stuttered over the smooth mass that was once her two lips.

"*My* story. Mine. Your grandmother was once a Weshen living in the palace. A Weshen whore bent on having my husband for her own. *She* stole him; *she* stole his blood. *She* stole my right as Queen!" Mara's voice screeched higher and louder with each iteration, and Coren began to feel sick.

Resh had told her once that her own grandmother was the reason for the Sacrifice. That something Lorental had done had made the Restless King turn against the Weshen people with the sort of violence that destroys entire countries.

She'd never believed him, but now she was afraid she'd need to start.

"Yes, your blood holds the trace of her magic. She was a Vespa shifter, too. And powerful. Oh, she was powerful," Mara laughed, a hint of hysteria creeping into her voice. "Nothing compared to my magic, of course, though she certainly tried. But as it turns out, when she died she left me one final curse, one blessing. One more move to make in this game. I may not be the true Queen of Riata, but you are still mine to control!"

Coren gasped as the spell was ripped from her mouth. Even with the ability to speak bestowed on her again, she had no idea what to say.

Then Mara removed the spell from Jyesh as well, and he spluttered, shooting to his feet.

"That means *I* am the heir to Riata's throne as well! The King's blood runs in *my* veins, just as it does in hers!"

Mara watched his excitement with boredom, and Coren realized again that although Jyesh should have turned against Mara by now, he still believed she might help him. He couldn't see that whatever use Mara might have in mind for them, it was not to welcome them as members of the royal family.

"I am the older twin. I have no desire for your crown or your kingdom, and I reject it on behalf of my brother as well," she called, cutting over Jyesh's continued ramblings. "Give me my brother and my friend, and I will disappear. You will never need to worry about one of us threatening your kingdom."

Jyesh began shrieking obscenities to the contrary, and Coren caught Resh's narrowed eyes. She gulped at the desires that flashed in his midnight eyes, the silent words that somehow burrowed into her brain.

Resh wanted the King dead, and the Queen. He wanted Coren on the throne, and himself beside her. He wanted Jyesh to disappear.

Coren felt dizzy with the implications of Resh's plain ambition, and her brother's desperate railings. Did none of them want to dissolve Riata? Did none of them want peace?

"Don't you want to meet your grandfather?" Mara interrupted.

Coren blinked, her mind failing to accommodate a single other request.

Besides, she hadn't been raised to think this was an important thing. Weshen families were split, women from men, and she wasn't supposed to know or care who her grandfather was.

But all this fell away with the knowledge that her grandfather was the very man she and Sy had traveled miles to find and plotted dozens of ways to kill. The man she knew Resh would risk his life to murder, even knowing he would be no match for the old King.

The blood flowing in her body this very minute was partially from the man she had hated most, her entire life. A man whose blood made her a Riatan princess, not a Weshen outcast.

All of these images and more flashed through Coren's mind, and she found herself nodding.

Yes, of course.

She would *very much* like to meet her grandfather and ask him what in the name of the Mirror Magi had he been thinking when he allowed her grandmother's death and her people's destruction.

She would also very much like to dissipate him limb from limb.

"He's waiting for you upstairs, in the throne room."

Mara's simple answer dropped Coren's bravado and jaw to the floor. "Now?"

"Of course. I asked him to drop in. He was on his way from Weshen. Actually, no. He was on his way from StarsHelm, where he placed a dozen or so Weshen men in the prisons. The only survivors, I hear."

Resh bolted from his seat, hands raised to claw at Mara, but Aram delivered a crushing blow to his skull. Resh crumpled where he was, and Coren reeled, trying to process what Mara had said.

"Weshen…"

"Yes, it's gone. Good riddance. Filthy people. No better than the animals you hunt."

Coren felt her Vespa struggling to slip to the surface, screaming in her head to kill and kill and kill. But there was an odd, invisible barrier just above and beneath her skin - something preventing her from shifting.

"I bound your shifting." Mara examined Coren, then flicked her eyes to Resh, splayed motionless on the floor. "Handsome boy. A good lust for power. Useless without magic, though."

Coren heard the threat. She turned to Jyesh, who hadn't shown a single muscle of reaction at the news of Weshen's destruction.

"Did you know? Do you even have any compassion left for your people?"

His eyes hardened, and her stomach flipped. She saw he'd never forgiven, even if he'd been spelled to forget. Weshen had banished him; there would never again be loyalty there.

Coren attempted to gather her thoughts, mentally shutting down what she couldn't change right now.

She pushed down her rage and grief for her people, her mad desire for revenge, and her sorrowful confusion on finding a brother who wanted nothing to do with his people. She locked away all her pride and scheming, and she focused on how she could save her own tiny, vital group.

Once they were safe, she could return here and deal with Zorander Graeme.

"I want my friend. And I want my brother. Unharmed," Coren said. She had come to Rurok to find the twins, and she'd done that. "And we'll leave. Just let

387

us leave. You can have your kingdom." It was only a partial lie. She wanted to disappear more than ever now. Find a quiet place in the forest, hunt what food they'd need. She wanted to heal, and to love, and to live. Not to kill.

"Don't you understand, yet?" Mara asked, a kind smile resting on her full lips. It wasn't a kindness born from love, however, but the kindness one bestows on suffering, ignorant animals. Something like the kindness of slicing the throat of a rockrabbit caught in a painful trap. "I don't want you to leave. I can be reasonable with your requests, but you have something I want."

"I don't have the SoulShifter power. I can't give you what you want," Coren repeated, cursing. She was no bargainer. No politician or warrior. "I just want my brother back."

"And you have Jyesh - you always have, even when you were too selfish to sense him. He is part of your blood. But his soul is mine and has been for too many years. The bond is not going to break. You must join me, then join *with* him, to truly save him."

Coren shook her head, not understanding. Mara sighed, as though she thought Coren nearly too stupid to bother with.

"The Sulit cling to a twin prophecy, that a set of twins that will rise against the evil in the world and create balance between all the peoples and all the gods. Jyesh is powerful enough to be one of those twins, but he cannot rise without your help."

"But *you* are the evil in the world," Coren whispered. "I will never join you."

"No," Mara bit out, the kind smile faltering. Her stature seemed to grow before Coren's eyes as her anger flickered hotter than the fire behind them. "No, I am not the evil in the world. I was once an innocent flower, just like yourself. But the most beautiful flowers also hide dangerous poisons. Once my heart was opened to the realization of what had been done to me, that betrayal turned me into what you see now. I'm a powerful woman, Corentine. Perhaps the most powerful in all of Sulit and Riata now."

"Yet you want my power, too," Coren said. All the King and Queen ever did with Weshen was take their power. "What can a SoulShifter do for you, even if I could learn that power? Do you only want to live forever?"

Mara smiled gently. "I may be old, but I don't want the Magi to give my life back, child. I want them to *take* the lives of those who hurt me." The gentle curve of her lips sharpened like a blade, and Coren shivered.

The woman was mad. She wanted the SoulShifter power to kill, not to heal, and she would twist Coren and Jyesh into twin blades of vengeance to get what she wanted.

There must be a way out of this trap. Coren knew she could figure it out if only her attention weren't so divided.

"If I agree to let you teach me what you've taught Jyesh, can I at least take Resh to the beach, where his boat waits? If he's of no use without magic, then let me trade a bit of mine for his life. Please." She saw Jyesh watching her with a curious expression, and she flushed, uncertain whether he approved of her proposal.

Mara seemed to consider. She shrugged. "You may fly him to safety, but if you don't return immediately, I'll simply have my Brujok hunt him down again."

Coren began to breathe easier. Another knot unraveled before her. The binding beneath her skin released as Mara unwove her spell. Once Resh was safe, there would only be Jyesh. She knew she needed more time to convince him to leave.

She spread her wings and tugged Resh to his feet. He was groggy and barely awake as she pulled him to the window ledge. The colder air blowing through the window revived him, and he turned fearful eyes to her. His face paled to a greenish hue.

"I can't, Coren."

"You have to. Hold on tight, and don't look down."

Unable to fully lift Resh, she wrapped her arms around his chest tightly and leaned over the edge. Their combined weight tumbled them backward out the tower window. Resh's face mashed against her neck to hide his eyes from the fall, and his arms gripped her so hard she lost her breath. Coren flapped hard, desperate to carry the weight of a fully-grown man. The muscles across her back and down each wing screamed as she wheeled over the tops of Rurok's towers and toward the beach.

"I won't drop you," she gritted out, praying it was true. Her wings faltered, and they dropped several feet too quickly, just before she skidded to a stop in the sand near their boat. Her knees gave out and Coren rolled to the ground with Resh beside her.

He curled to the side just in time to vomit in the sand. Coren bit back a grin and tossed him a skin of water from one of their packs.

"Wait for me here," she said. And she shot into the air before he could say a single word. She didn't allow herself to look back, knowing if she did, she might hesitate in what she needed to do now.

Landing back in the tower, she shifted away her wings and faced Mara and Jyesh. She couldn't hope to beat Mara, especially not with Aram watching by the fire and Jyesh still such an unknown.

But perhaps she could convince Jyesh yet.

Before the Queen could slip a single word of spell back around her body, Coren grasped Jyesh in her SourceShifting power, spreading his arms wide and lifting a sheer layer of skin and a mist of blood into the air.

"You are no longer the Lord of Witches, but neither are you in line for the throne of Riata. We are Weshen, and we have a country to rebuild." Her words were steel and blade, and Jyesh's eyes were wide with pain and surprise. "You will abandon your search for power you do not deserve."

Mara chuckled. "He will never bow to such a request. But perhaps it would be interesting to see how he fares in the wild again." A shiver crept along Coren's shoulders as she noted the language comparing them again to animals. "Take him, too. But again, you must return immediately, or my Brujok will feast on Weshen blood tonight."

Coren gritted her teeth as she used nearly all her strength to make a second trip across the sky, dropping Jyesh next to the boat with Resh. Shifting back to her own blessed body, she snaked her whip down her waist and flicked it at Jyesh, warning him not to move.

Resh pushed up from the sand, still unsteady on his feet. "How did you-"

Coren cut his words short with a kiss. She meant it to be brief and chaste, but Resh pressed her close, holding her against the rocks. His hands were firm and demanding on her waist. He dragged one hand up her ribs and cupped her head with long fingers, tilting her neck to deepen the kiss. His lips raked heat along her jaw and down her throat, and Coren forgot to breathe.

Coren felt a surge of power deep in her core, tied to her shifter magic but not like anything she'd felt before.

"I told you to meet me here so I could do this properly," he murmured, raising his lashes. His eyes were like the deepest part of a moonless night. "Just think what I'll give you when we reach the palace."

"I want you to go without me," she whispered, stepping away somehow. "Take my brother and find Sy. I have to return to Mara."

"No. No!" Resh grabbed at her, as though he might shake the word into her mind. She wrenched her arm away, glancing at Jyesh.

"If you harm Resh, I will deliver you to the Brujok myself," she threatened her brother. "Go, both of you."

Before they could protest, Coren tossed her whip to Resh. She snapped her wings into existence and rose into the night air, shooting across the sky to the towers of Rurok one last time.

26

Sy's boat crunched into the black sand of the Sulit beaches, just north enough of the falls to avoid being sucked over.

He didn't bother to look for cover in the forest or rocky outcroppings of the shore. Instead, he dropped his pack in the boat and strode down the center of the sandy, moonlit beach, straight for the towers of Rurok.

Swigging lemondrine every few steps, Sy goaded his magic to surge ever higher. Giddon had warned him it was temporary, but Sy cared nothing for the future past this night.

He was only staying long enough to find and kill Zorander Graeme.

Using his senses the way he'd seen Nik do, Sy stretched himself to find any living witches. Two waited ahead, close to the base of the nearest tower. He readied his shifting, resolving to save the Grizzlin for the King.

But there were plenty of other weapons at his disposal.

The Brujok stepped from the shadows of the tower, their robes seeming to cling to the darkness rather than absorbing the silvery moonlight on the beach.

"My business is with Riata's rulers," he called. "Not with witches."

He heard a light cackle. "Yet here you are on the witches' beach."

"Has the King arrived?" he pressed.

"We have no king. Only a foolish little Lord."

"I seek Zorander Graeme!" Sy's scant patience had evaporated at her attempt to play. He rose a towering wall of sand from his right, blocking the trees from sight. Calling another farther down the beach, he trapped the witches close to him.

"Silly Weshen," one of them snickered to the other.

Vines twisted and grew from the sand beneath his feet, and Sy dropped one of the walls to tear at them. Their spells were strong, but so was he. He tore apart their sources, shredding them back into the sand. Before the witches could try again, he drew a blade and hurled it at one.

Sy didn't stop to examine just why the thunk of his blade entering her chest was so satisfying in the budding night. He only rushed the second witch, who was now enraged and using much more power.

He tore at the vines of her magic, wondering why the Brujok continued to resort to such an attack when he and Coren had such little trouble evading it. Again, he managed to best the guard, his second blade slicing into her throat. It had been only a few minutes and relatively quiet, so Sy hoped grimly that he wouldn't come across any more.

He approached the tower, searching for any hint of magic or non-magic people. Giddon had warned him that the Queen would be here too, and she was the strongest spellcaster of them all, even the native witches.

The tower seemed mostly empty, and he moved to the next one. Grinning, he realized the base of the second tower was empty, but several rooms in the upper floors were not.

Swirls of energy and magic drew him in, and though he searched meticulously for more guards, it seemed the tower waited like an open invitation. He began to climb the twisting stairs, checking floor after floor for the people he most wanted to embrace, and those he most wanted to kill.

As Sy stalked up the endless stairs of the tower, he wondered what the King would look like. He'd heard the rumors of his unnatural youth and his odd silver hair.

The first room he checked was warm and inviting, with a fire burning bright and a luxurious sofa before it. It was empty, though, and Sy passed it by without more than a cursory glance.

He reached the last stair. The top of the tower rose in a hollow point above him, and only one door remained.

Instead of risking a creaky hinge or the trap of guards just inside the frame, Sy stretched his senses. One person waited inside for him. Only one person, but a different, larger energy swirled inside the room as well. Sy gritted his teeth. It could only be the brothers Coren had warned him of.

The seven older Graeme princes, each felled before their chance at the crown. Until only Zorander was left: the boy who was never meant to be King.

Sy cared nothing for spirits or curses tonight. His mind was filled to the brim with the spirits of his dead countrymen, and his life had felt cursed already since the day his father banished him from his own people for daring to bring them salvation. Sy snorted, realizing his musings were stalling the mission.

He began to shift apart the sources of the heavy iron and wood door. A slit before his eye revealed a darkened throne room with an empty throne. Unlit candles hung from the ceiling, circled above the dais. An unmoving figure stood at the window, in a shaft of moonlight from slightly-parted curtains. Sy shifted more of the door, slipping through without a sound.

The figure turned, his face illuminated by the round moon. The Restless King stood before Sy, tall and much too young to be so old. He should be decades past Ashemon, yet he looked barely thirty.

He nodded to Sy. "I know why you're here, son of Weshen."

"I am not only a son of Weshen. I am its new General, as I'm sure you know the position opened recently."

Graeme did not admit the kill, but Sy knew he faced not only his people's tormentor but his father's murderer. He could scent the blood of his family on the man's hands.

"You don't want to kill me, boy. You could never handle all the darkness that follows me. It will follow whoever takes the life from my body, forever, until all my debt is paid. The dead never rest."

"Darkness means nothing when the light has already been extinguished, and I don't rest much, either." Sy advanced another step. He didn't want to talk. He wanted to fight. Kill.

The energy he'd felt from the stairwell surged in the room, and a golden glow began to form behind Graeme. Vague shapes of men ranked behind the King, and quiet laughter echoed the curved walls, creeping into Sy's ears and kneading at his stomach.

He didn't care if these ghosts were somehow real, or simply magical illusions.

Nothing would stop him from the dream of a tomorrow without Zorander Graeme in it.

With a roar of satisfaction, Sy shifted into his Grizzlin form, his bones cracking and expanding, his muscles bulking huge beneath the golden-brown fur. His back claws dug into the slick marble of the throne room floor as he shoved ahead, lunging for the King.

The man's eyes flew wide with surprise, but he made no sound as Sy's front claws sunk deep into his chest, piercing and ripping at the skin, spilling the royal blood and slicking the floor with crimson.

Sy roared again, but his body was thrown backward. He landed hard on his spine and twisted, struggling to right his powerful form. Golden figures surrounded him, pinning him with trails of fog and transparent fingers. He struggled against them, but a different magic was at work here.

The King gurgled and coughed, struggling to his side to lean against the wall.

"My brothers will have your life," he wheezed, "and your death."

A smooth voice chuckled above Sy, pausing his wild thrashing. "Young Weshen, be still. Hear our terms. I am

Lumien, seventh son of the Silver Sovereign. I would have made a great ruler. Even greater than my little brother. But I was cut down the way you mean to do with Zorander. You use clean, shifter magic, and so your kill *would* be clean. Except I was killed with a bargain."

Sy heaved, wrenching a limb from one of the brothers. He didn't want to listen to their stories. He wanted to kill the King.

He roared again and nearly escaped their hold completely before they regained it.

"Patience, little Grizzlin. This bargain allowed Zorander to take our lives, but it also allows us to take his. Slowly, one single day at a time, we consume him. And if you kill him - if you take that life in one stroke - you will deprive us of *so much* pleasure."

Sy felt his shifter power draining, as though the spirits were siphoning energy from him. He tried to roar again, but it came out human. His form was shrinking, his fur receding and forming his metaled leather gear again.

"Yes, we feed off the magic in our host. Zorander has spent a lifetime building his magic to sustain us. It takes a lot to feed seven princes. Do you have enough to sustain our feast, silly First Son?"

Sy yelled again, kicking out at the face of the one speaking. His foot connected the way it might with water. Ripples pulsed through the face, but as Sy's foot fell, the golden light simply filled the form again. It was angry now, though, and Sy felt his arms and legs being wrenched tighter, as though they were being pulled from his torso.

"I don't think you have what we need. You simply aren't powerful enough."

398

The door of the room banged open. "I have power to spare!"

Sy's heart surged with hope and despair, twisted together in the knowledge of Coren come to help him. How she'd found him, he didn't know. But she couldn't take on this curse any more than he could.

"Zorander Graeme, you have done your evil. Your soul will be judged by whatever gods might grasp it, but your time here is done." She spun to the brothers, shifting only her four wings into being.

Her power focused and concentrated in those feathers as she beat at their golden fog, sending it tumbling and dissipating into the corners of the room, just like she'd once done with Shadow.

Sy marveled at her. She had never looked so beautiful, with her hair streaming and her eyes glinting with a slight bird-like slant. Blue sky and golden sun glinted in her eyes. But it wasn't the beauty that made her desirable. It was the power. Sy swore to himself, suddenly very glad his brother was not here to see her like this.

Even Graeme stared at her, transfixed.

She turned to the King, surveying his wounds.

Before she could move, though, he held out a hand, palm up, as though to offer her something. Sy glimpsed the glint of a black diamond resting in his hand.

"I never believed it until now," the King managed.

"Me, either," Coren returned, but her voice wasn't kind. "For once, Mara told the truth."

Sy struggled to his feet, intent on finishing his mission.

"Sy, no." Coren shifted a section of the marble floor over his boots, trapping him momentarily.

"Coren!" Her name came out like a growl, but she didn't flinch.

"He's family," she whispered, stepping toward the bleeding man. The King dropped his ring into her hand, closing her fingers around the black diamond, and curling his hand over hers.

"He's a murderer!" Sy burst out before her words could even sink in. The marble slid from his feet, and he stepped closer.

She spun to face him. "He's my grandfather. He's done terrible things, but he's paying his debts." She gestured to the golden swirls that had begun to gather themselves along the back wall again. "Sy, killing a killer is nothing noble. It's a false balance."

"Weshen is gone. Slaughtered. My father, the men. The boys. All dead."

She stumbled back a step, her head shaking side to side. "I know."

"The Restless King ordered every death, Coren. He was *there*."

She glanced at the man on the floor, her face a battlefield of opposing desires. His face was pale, and his robes soaked with fresh blood, but his eyes still tracked between the two of them.

The King wouldn't die from the wounds Sy had given him already.

He needed to finish what he'd begun, whether Coren agreed or not.

Without a single extra movement to warn her, Sy drew a blade from his thigh and leaped across the few feet, shoving Coren to her knees as he passed. The blade plunged into Graeme's heart without a sound, until the iron scraped against the marble as it exited his back.

The King's lips parted, but no final words came. Instead, only crimson blood dribbled down his chin as his eyes clouded and grew glassy with death.

Coren screamed, scrambling toward him, her eyes fixated on the air just above his body. She glanced back to the golden mist, which was advancing now like a tidal wave of sucking currents and foam. "No," she whispered. "No!"

But the brothers descended on the body of their youngest sibling, pooling around it and mixing the blood with their light. Laughter and faint screaming echoed around the room, as though carried from far away on an invisible breeze.

"Get back!" The command rang out from the door, and Sy turned to see Queen Mara, followed by her brother. Mara's face was livid as she strode toward the body of her husband.

Her fingers flicked at the golden forms, sending them careening into the shadows and beyond the windows into the night sky.

Mara surveyed the dead King with disgust before turning to Coren and Sy. She held one palm out before each of them, and Sy felt his body straighten and stiffen in paralysis. Coren gasped as the same happened to her.

"I do love a fool," Queen Mara cooed, her laughter creeping up Sy's spine and locking around his neck like fingers. "You belong to the darkness now, Weshen. And *you*..." she turned her grin on Coren. "How noble of you to try and protect your scum family again. You should have taken your mother's initiative and thrown yourself

401

into the depths of the ocean. Your family has done nothing but ruin the Weshen people for generations. But now this struggle is nearly at an end. I have no husband, but I have a throne and a country to expand. You two have done nothing but provide me with a reason for revenge and an easy path to the SoulShifter."

Her laughter began again, and she let them drop. Her magical hold fell from their limbs as they hit the marble, and Sy heard Coren moan. Heavy footsteps stopped between them, and Aram approached, holding a gleaming sword to each of their throats.

Queen Mara stepped toward her husband. Reaching behind her, between her robe and dress, she withdrew two curved blades.

They glistened in the full moon's light.

"The Kitsuun blades!" Sy spilled the words without thinking. Resh had searched for those blades for years, though Sy had believed them a myth.

Mara smiled at him, then bent to the King's body. She drew the first blade across his neck, opening the artery there. His blood spilled from the new wound, still warm enough to steam in the night air. She doused the blade, soaking its length. As she held it up to the light, Sy heard Coren gasp.

The blood didn't run down the handle, but soaked into the polished metal, disappearing like it was fabric. Mara did the same with the other blade, soaking them again and again until no more blood ran from the King's body.

As Sy watched, transfixed by the Queen's secrets unfolding, he noticed a slight movement from his right. Coren had somehow managed to overcome the Queen's spell and draw a blade of her own when Aram was distracted by Mara's blood-letting. She hurled herself into Aram's legs, toppling the great man to the marble and hacking her knife into his thigh. His blades clattered from his hands, and his eyes were wide with surprise and pain.

Coren was on him in a second, working with all her strength to shift his skin and bone and blood.

His body separated, then shifted back, like water when a knife is withdrawn. His mouth opened in a silent scream of pain as she dissipated him again, but the effects lasted only a few seconds before his body slipped back to its natural state.

Mara screamed as though her own body was dissolving. She scrambled to sheath her blades as Coren struggled again and again to dissipate Aram.

Sy lunged for the Queen, but she shrieked and threw her arms wide in a burst of spellcasting. Sy went tumbling onto his back, and Coren's head hit the stone wall with a thunk that turned Sy's stomach inside out.

Before he could rise, Mara was before him, brandishing the Kitsun blades.

"I can't kill *you*, or I will inherit the curse of Zorander's brothers. But I can find everyone you love, Weshen. I know your brother travels the beaches before Rurok even now, searching for this girl. I know all about your beautiful Wesh boy, and what stalked him silently through the mountains. I know exactly where Corentine's twin siblings are traveling to right now. I can smell their budding magic for miles, and I know just what the Brujok ache to do with their blood. Choose your weapons wisely, First Son of Weshen."

403

She stood before him, regal and terrible in her bloodied robes and her jaw held tight and proud.

Sy wanted to gut her.

More than anything. More even than the King's death, which he had won in a hollow victory.

But the stakes now were too high. Queen Mara stood before him, a vision of darkness and power, brandishing the twin blades over her brother's still form.

She held everything he needed to survive in the palm of her hand.

"I know you thought killing the King would bring peace. Don't take your mistake so hard. I've been playing my game longer than you've been alive."

Her voice was haggard with exhaustion, but still, her words fell heavy on Sy's heart.

The King had been nothing. All along, it had always been Mara.

He knew what he had to do. Across the room, Coren began to stir, but before she could open her eyes, Sy shifted into his Grizzlin form and roared toward the Queen.

She made no move to protect herself.

The blades did everything.

The metal pierced Sy's fur and deflated his shifter form like a sail with no wind. He fell to the marble, writhing in an agony he'd never experienced.

His last view was of Mara, impossibly gathering the bulky form of Aram in her arms, and jumping out the tower window.

Coren staggered to her feet and felt along the wall as she made her way to Sy.

His body was still, and though he had shifted back to normal, tufts of golden-brown fur littered the floor around him, as though Mara's blades had shaved away some of his magic.

The golden light of the seven princes danced in the corners, toying with the edges of the heavy curtains, but it did not approach.

Coren glanced at the body of the Restless King. Drained of blood and all the things that made a man, the husk now seemed tiny and ancient. The shredded, blood-spattered robes had stiffened, and his eyes had clouded over.

She knelt next to Sy. He was breathing, and a moan escaped his lips.

"What have I done?" he whispered.

"Our enemy lies dead. Another rose in his place, but you completed the mission we began so many weeks ago. The Restless King is dead, Sy." Coren tried to sound warm and proud, although it seemed their dangers were even greater than before.

She didn't mourn the King, though he had been family. He was still the source of all she had hated for years. But the knowledge that Mara had controlled many of his actions, and that he had once loved her grandmother enough to create a child, all made Coren doubt that she could celebrate tonight as a victory.

"So, you've claimed the title of General?" she asked, wondering what Resh would think.

"General of a country that no longer exists," Sy said, heaving himself to a sitting position. His voice was bitter, and spoke of a grief Coren knew would never leave him.

"There are Weshen in StarsHelm. And Mara didn't mention the women. They may have survived. We will rebuild. We have before."

Sy gripped the rough stone wall and hauled himself up. He glanced again at the King, then back to Coren, studying them together.

"All this time, no-one ever knew he had an heir."

"I don't think my mother knew. I think Lorental kept it a secret from everyone."

"He watched her die," Sy said, disgust in his voice. Coren remembered Kashar's story, and her heart ached for the hurt this man had caused and endured.

"It was all Mara. She was behind it all. But if she tries to return to StarsHelm, we can fight."

Coren faced Sy and opened her palm. Still clenched inside was Zorander Graeme's ring, the symbol of Riatan rulership.

"I want nothing to do with that throne, but I will keep her from it with every breath I have," she declared.

"Then we better beat her there," Sy agreed, a faint smile crossing his lips. "Do you have a way home?"

"If I know your brother, yes." She allowed the flush to creep up her neck as she met Sy's eyes. Resh would be waiting for her. He wouldn't have listened to her orders to leave without her.

Supporting each other and trailed by a light golden shadow, Coren and Sy made their way down a seemingly endless stair and out the door onto the black sand beach.

27

StarSeer heard the man crashing through the forest. She knew he was likely trying to be quiet, but no man is ever as silent as a witch.

He smelled like the twins. Somewhat, anyway.

Non-magical, but the same blood.

She bent close to them. "Stay here. I need to find him before he comes upon us and is surprised into attack." They nodded, accepting her simple explanation. Surely, he wouldn't attack his own children, but perhaps he didn't know…

And Weshen men didn't trust Sulit witches, as a rule.

StarSeer sensed a Brujok as well, tracking him through the forest. That one wouldn't stop. They never did. StarSeer gathered her strength and began to weave a spell from the sap of the branches around her, creating a box of invisibility they could slide into and wait out the Brujok guard.

The spell took several minutes too long and sapped nearly all her strength, but she managed to tug the twins inside it just as the man stepped into view.

"Stop!" she said, holding up a hand. "I am Sulit and no threat to you."

"All witches are a threat today." His face was bloodied and his bare arms were scratched deeply. He didn't appear to have a weapon, and she sensed no magic in him.

"If you give me one minute, I will show you the children you seek."

His eyes narrowed. "I seek no children. I seek a way home."

"Home is with your family," StarSeer said, casting her eyes to the ground. The man startled, his posture growing less defensive.

"I found Maren and two young twins on the shores of the Shedreck River. I have brought them unwittingly into the heart of a battle, but you can help me save them now. They are there, beyond the branches. But a Brujok follows you. We must hurry."

StarSeer saw him wavering. He didn't trust witches, and she suspected he had good reason not to.

"Kosh and Penna?" he whispered, finally.

She nodded and started for the area her spell enclosed. "Show your faces!" she whispered to the twins. Two small heads popped out from behind a trunk, and she heard a choked cry from the man. He rushed to them, and they skittered behind the tree again.

"My children," he managed, holding hands out to each of them. The boy tilted his head, scrutinizing the man, but the girl smiled gently and slipped her fingers into his.

StarSeer wove the entrance of their hiding spot closed just seconds before the Brujok glided before them. She

408

held her breath as the fierce witch stared right through her, then moved away, deeper into the forest.

It seemed like an eternity before StarSeer could find her heartbeat and breath again.

"We must hide these children," she said, turning to the man. "Many more Brujok will come for them."

"Thank you," he said, tears slipping down both cheeks. "I am Kashar, once of Weshen and Riata. Neither is home to me now."

"Home is with your family," StarSeer repeated. "We must hide deep in the forest until the rebellion is over. I know the way to a safe place, and Coren has a map to find us later."

She took Penna's other hand, then Kosh's, and led them into the heart of the Sulit forest. Kashar followed her obediently, and she cast silence spells around them as they walked deeper into the Listening Forest.

All around them, lacy, pink leaves fell like soft caresses. A gift from the trees. Then, just beyond reasonable hearing, StarSeer imagined she sensed the trees beginning to whisper to her again. Tears filled her eyes - the Mother would heal.

Sulit would heal, and these twins were the key.

Later that night, when they stopped for rest, StarSeer smiled at the twins' anxious faces, pushing away her nerves.

They had begged her several times to find Coren, to track their sister in her dreams. "I'll try, but my visions don't work like that." Unfortunately, her magic didn't work on call.

Their father placed a hand on each of their shoulders, hugging them close. StarSeer had been hesitant to travel with a man, but so far, he had been honorable and protected the children unfailingly. He'd listened to her every instruction with trust, and his presence now put her at ease.

StarSeer sat on the cool ground inside the protective compass she'd spelled earlier. Her fingers drifted over the dirt and leaves. She closed her eyes and tried to picture their sister, giving in to the trance that would leave her completely vulnerable.

It might take several tries, but a shifter as strong as Coren was certain to appear in her visions eventually.

StarSeer let her mind roam the land, coasting over the Listening Forest and the towers of Rurok. She tracked her vision across SunMelt Lake, following the trail of shifter magic right to the edges of StarsHelm. Its power was doubly strong, even triple, as Coren traveled with her brother, the former Lord of Witches, and her friend, the new General of Weshen.

The witch smiled.

It was true, then, what the trees whispered.

Zorander Graeme had died in the towers of Rurok. Queen Mara and Lord Aram had vanished from the witches' tracking. The throne of StarsHelm waited for its new master - a girl who took the form of a Vespa and was rumored to see souls.

Perhaps one day she would even wield the power of the SoulShifter, and be able to grant new life. Of course, the other possibility was there as well. The SoulShifter could grant death instead of life.

This thought seemed to swirl and twist at StarSeer's mind, asking her to check her visions more closely. Mara would surely find a way to heal her power and her brother. She might even turn to the dark kingdom of Umbren for such a task.

And there. StarSeer saw it, and her head fell back and back, hitting the ground beneath her.

Somewhere in the forest, Mara shifted and vibrated the earth, crumbling and cracking it to the core. She searched for the power that could help her heal and defeat both pairs of Weshen twins.

StarSeer's body shuddered as her mind watched something crawl from the depths of the ground.

Even as Coren and her friends hurried to claim the throne, Shadow rose and followed, ready to claim them.

StarSeer opened her eyes. "Your sister lives," she said to the twins. Her eyes rose to Kashar's. "But none of us will live for long if Mara offers her power to Shadow. We must hurry."

The boat was crowded, but none of them complained, Resh least of all.

This had been the worst day of his life, but now that he sat thigh to thigh with Coren in the front of the boat, heading to StarsHelm, he allowed himself to feel a glimmer of hope.

Sy at the back of the boat, silent and pale. Jyesh slumped in the middle, thankfully dozing. Resh didn't know if Coren suspected him of drugging her brother, but it had been worth it. The Lord of Witches had a mouth Resh would rather not listen to.

Coren watched Jyesh, her eyes slipping over and over his ripped robes. Resh leaned in to whisper in Coren's ear. "How can you trust him?" In truth, he wanted to *beg* her not to trust Jyesh, but it was her brother.

She shook her head without a word.

Resh wasn't certain if this meant she didn't trust him or didn't know. "All he knows is cruelty."

Coren fixed Resh in her eyes, and he saw her fears. The set of her jaw told him of her determination, though. She wouldn't give up on her brother. Not again. "He'll heal. I know he will. He has to."

Resh refrained from asking her how, and instead he watched the moonlight glint off the Riatan ring still clutched in her palm. The black diamond both absorbed the night around it and reflected the stars above.

Resh wanted to touch it, to slide his fingers over the symbol of power. He wanted her to slip it on her slim fingers and admire the kingdom she now held in her palm.

A princess of StarsHelm, one day a Queen of Riata. A Weshen shifter, perhaps even the SoulShifter.

Resh thrilled at the mere thought of these titles. He tried not to be jealous of her power, or desirous of her simply *for* that power like Nik had warned.

Could he really continue to separate the two? Coren wasn't just a girl to him.

She'd ceased being that the day she found her wings, and he found her lips. She wasn't just a source of beauty and passion and compassion for him to desire, and she wasn't just a means to fuel his lust for power.

She was both, and she was much more.

A twisting and tightening had begun in Resh's chest, like two sources shifting together. Though he wasn't certain if it was what Nik and Sy felt, he knew it was something he never wanted to stop feeling.

Coren glanced at him and caught him staring at the ring. She tucked it into the folds of her tunic, hiding it from view. Resh noted the gesture. He would need to work hard to convince her he didn't want her power.

By the Magi, he would need to work hard to convince himself of the same.

What would be so wrong with him helping her rule a chaotic country?

"Nik will go the women's island, won't he?" Coren picked at the specks of blood dotted the backs of her hands and her forearms, then she cupped a handful of lake water to wash with. The red only smeared into the droplets, coating her skin pink in the moonlight.

Sy closed his eyes against the question. "I think he will. He doesn't like to be alone. I hope they can help each other until we return." Sy was so covered in the King's blood that it would be pointless to wash until he could strip away all his clothing and soak in a tub. Even Jyesh had ugly wounds from witch nails and iron.

Only Resh was relatively clean of blood. He'd been knocked unconscious during all the important bits. He sighed at the indignity.

"What happens when we get to the palace?" Sy asked, glancing behind him at the towers of Rurok. His voice was dull.

They had all expected to feel triumph at their victory, but instead it seemed their losses were great and their gains so little.

For now, at least, there was no sign of the golden glow that had followed Sy out of the tower and onto the beach. Resh knew his brother carried some sort of curse, but he had no idea why, or what that would mean. He knew it was somehow related to the nightmares Coren had been having, but he didn't understand that either.

"We find Graeme's advisers and dissolve the kingdom," Coren answered after several seconds. "Then we can take the Wesh slaves and go home."

Resh barked out a short laugh, and she turned to him with fire in her eyes. "That will never work. If we dissolve Riata, thousands will be without a safe home. How could you do that when it's the very cruelty we've been fighting?"

"I can't take the throne of Riata," she returned. "And neither can he." She gestured to Jyesh, whose head still rested on the edge of the boat. "He needs to heal, and StarsHelm is not the place for that. We need to take him back to Weshen."

"Weshen is gone," Sy answered. He stared out at the dark water. "Even if we bring the Wesh with us, there's nowhere for them to go."

"Then we rebuild," Coren said. "I'll make a home for my brothers and sister to live. I know where they're going in Sulit now. We *will* be a family again." Her voice was soft yet unyielding.

Resh shook his head at her stubbornness. He had no doubt she would accomplish all these things.

But there was more to the world than the small scope of her plans. Resh knew Coren would never make a good leader on her own. She would need help, and he feared who in StarsHelm might offer their advice to a new Queen.

He stroked his fingers along her arm. She shivered, though the night was not cool. He leaned closer. "If Riata needs a ruler, even for a short time, who else would you have it be?"

Her eyes flashed. "Sy."

Resh glared. Always Sy. "He has already claimed himself General of Weshen, though he says the city is gone."

"I can't rule Riata, Coren," Sy agreed. "You and Jyesh are the heirs. It's the only way to keep Mara from reclaiming the throne, or some other adviser. You have to assert your blood rights, and convince the King's advisers that Mara has no claim as Queen. It must be you."

Resh saw the fear in her eyes. She truly didn't want to rule. He slipped his fingers between hers, tugging her hand into his lap.

"We'll all be there for you," he said. "Sy and I have been trained to lead since we were children. We can help you find the balance."

Finally, she nodded, but she didn't meet his eyes. "Only until we can find peace for all the people Zorander Graeme hurt. You're right. They deserve a safe home, too."

The boat rocked gently forward, and neither Resh nor Sy pointed out that nothing was going to be this simple. Coren thought to rule for a few months, retrieve her siblings from Sulit, and hunt rockrabbits on the plains the rest of her years.

Sy met Resh's eyes over her ducked head, and they both nodded.

Resh would be there for Coren when Sy was rebuilding Weshen or learning to deal with the limitations of his strange new curse. Sy would be there for her when Resh couldn't fight Jyesh's flexing of power and shifter magic.

Together, the brothers would help Coren sort the mess her grandparents had made.

As the boat glided through the moonlit water, Resh dreamed that one day, a renewed Weshen could work with a cleansed Riata and a healed Sulit. The three countries could be partners, united against whatever common enemy returned to rip them apart.

Nik stared out at the MagiSea, frozen in a cycle of never-ending fear. Each day since Sy had left, Nik had ventured a little farther from the safe, sweet-smelling room in the mansion of Weshen City.

Each day, he had discovered fresh horrors that sent him scuttling back to the mansion, where he lit every torch and candle he could find, burning them all night long.

Today, he had finally reached the beach Sy marked for him on the map. There were no bodies here, no bloated remains of Weshen men. Only boats, moored to a narrow dock and bobbing silently in the waves.

Nik didn't know if he dared untie one.

Sailing to the women's island would take him into the night. He didn't want to be anywhere but Sy's bedroom when darkness fell. Whatever had followed him in the mountains lived in the darkness here, too. He was certain of it.

Nik watched the boats until the sun sank too low on the horizon, then he sprinted up the steep stairs to the back of the mansion. Curling into his nest of blankets and clothing on Sy's bed, Nik watched the room, examining every shadow and flicker of candlelight until his eyes finally drooped shut.

Even in sleep, though, he didn't rest.

His dreams were filled with Sy and Resh and Coren, but also with the faces of the dead men beyond the mansion, and the one young man who had killed something vital inside Nik.

The next morning, Nik rose with a renewed sense of desperate determination.

He couldn't hide here any longer. He was utterly alone, and that thing would eventually find him. If he couldn't find Sy and his friends, he would at least find if the Weshen women lived. He thought of Lorenya. She would be kind to him, he hoped.

He packed quickly, just a few items of clothing and weapons he'd come to trust. A stale loaf of bread and the last wheel of cheese. Several water skins.

And the note Sy had left him, worn as smooth as leather from Nik's fingers.

He hurried down the stairs and out the back door and down the outside stairs and onto the dock. Rushing made him anxious, but moving slowly made him panic.

He untied a boat and hopped in, water sloshing over the side at his clumsiness. His oar bit into the water, and Nik focused his shifting on the waves before him. He shot away from the dock and the mansion, across the glittering MagiSea.

The hours and the sun on the sea dragged the energy from him until he was reduced to floating, praying his boat would wash ashore before nightfall. For once, the Magi decided to grant his wishes.

Stepping onto the beach of Weshen Isle, Nik realized he had no idea what to tell the women if indeed they allowed him to stay.

A child ran past, swiveling his head to look at Nik, then skidding to a stop and running back the way he'd come. Soon another child approached with the first, and then another, until Nik was surrounded by small boys and girls.

They tugged him onward until he found himself at the edges of the women's village.

Female faces peered at him from yards and windows and paths. He didn't see a single grown man, and that brought his memory careening back to the bodies still rotting in the circles of Weshen City.

Nik faltered, considering racing back to his boat, or even shifting a wall of sand between himself and the searching eyes. How could he ever tell them what had happened across the sea?

Then a voice called out, and Nik heard his name for the first time in so many silent days. He searched the growing crowds and found Lorenya, the confident girl he'd first met on the plains of this island.

The first woman here who had found her shifter magic.

"Nik, why are you here?" she called, hurrying toward him.

"The city…" But the words would not come.

Lorenya put a gentle hand on his arm, and he calmed beneath her touch. "What is it?"

"The passage has fallen. Weshen City is gone." He choked on the final word, and the women and children around him pressed closer, then fanned away, whispers and cries and shouts spreading through the village like ripples across a pond.

Nik slumped forward into Lorenya's opened arms, taking what comfort she offered. "Come with me," she whispered. She led him to a house that had only two rooms, one for eating and one for sleeping, and she pressed him into a bed that was surely her own. She pulled a cover to his chin, as though he were a sick child. Nik realized that in a way, that's exactly what he was.

"You'll be safe here, as long as you want to be."

"And then?" he asked, noting the implied ending.

"When you're ready to fight again, you'll lead us back. We can rebuild because we have before. Nothing can truly end us if we're not ready to be ended. Our city may be gone, but Weshen lives here."

Her palm came to rest on his chest, the gentle weight above his heart soothing his anxiety. Her other hand rested on her own chest, linking their hearts in a symbol of home. Resh felt the burden he carried ease enough to relax into the pillow, and his eyes slipped closed.

419

Lorenya lowered herself to the floor beside the mattress, never taking her fingers from his skin, and she began to hum.

The song was one he'd never heard, but somehow its gentle notes reminded him of Sy.

Finally, Nik slept, and he dreamed nothing of shadows or darkness following him. He dreamed only of the people he loved, and a home, and sand, and stars.

ACKNOWLEDGEMENTS

IF YOU'RE STILL here by this point, then you are a true reader, and I want to thank YOU!

I love to write, and you love to read, so let's be friends! Seriously.

It's hard to write the middle books. Things aren't as shiny and new, and the end is still so far away. But there are a ton of people who helped wrangle this dreaded "sophomore" tome into production, and I'm so grateful for my team.

My ever-supportive parents and my beautiful family and friends still win the favorite fans of all time award. They give me motivation, an ear to talk off, and babysitting to follow this dream of storytelling, and all of those things are priceless.

I hope my children look back at our busy "summers off" and remember my lessons that if you have a dream worth following, you work when you can. I'm sorry I didn't swim much with you, but in my defense, that water was cold!

David, thank you for allowing me to support our local Panera at least once a week this summer. And as for the surprise new coffee maker? That's why I married you.

If you're looking for a great developmental editor, I wholly suggest Mary Rosenblum of New Writers Interface. Unless she's reading my next story, and then you can't have her! Gold, I tell you.

Likewise goes immeasurable gratitude to my favorite beta reader slash legal advisor, Cecily. She has a few other titles, but those are also a secret.

Can I say Deranged Doctor Design covers are amazing? You saw it. You bought it. Amazing, right? I'm looking forward to sharing many more of their covers with you. If you have the ebook version of this story, please check out the hardback and paperback for more gorgeous design work from DDD and Eight Little Pages. This series has such a rockstar wardrobe.

I can't possibly name all the fantastic people I've met and worked with on social media and my wonderful Stargazer Reading Group. Special shoutouts to the AAYAA and For Love or Money groups. Y'all are amazing, and worth everything a girl has in this life.

Should I say something cheesy again? Of course. I'm a Libra – silly and sentimental, all in balance.

Keep your sights in the stars, and stay out of the shadows. You've been welcomed and warned.

Hey, reader. Hilary here!

I hope you enjoyed the magical world of
**Twist of Truth and Tomorrow:
SoulShifter, Book Two**
as much as I do.
To find out the real story behind Zorander
and Mara, get the novella
**Rise of Restless and Ruined:
A SoulShifter Prequel**

FREE only for my
Stargazer Reading Group.

Visit me at

HILARYTHOMPSONAUTHOR.COM

to join and claim your free copy!

Hilary used to be such a practical girl. Then she let the stories out, and claimed the titles of stargazer, daydreamer, and believer in all things magical.

Fairy tales, myths from all cultures, and the wonderful "what if" are the foundation of her stories. Villains, heroes, and sidekicks clamor for equal attention. Happily-ever-afters, too (of course), but be warned that the road will twist and turn and seem to dead-end before the magic of a sweet romance leads back into the sunlight.

When she's not writing, Hilary teaches Creative Writing, Literature, and College Writing, drinks too much coffee, and reads as much as her eyes can handle. She plays superheroes and dress up games and reads books in bed with her independent, willful children, and plays at homesteading and world traveling with her soulmate of a husband. She tends to ignore laundry and dirty dishes.